Hector Berlioz and the Development of French Music Criticism

Studies in Musicology, No. 97

George J. Buelow, Series Editor

Professor of Music
Indiana University

Other Titles in This Series

Hector Berlioz and the Development of French Music Criticism

by
Kerry Murphy

U·M·I Research Press
Ann Arbor / London

Produced and distributed by
UMI Research Press
an imprint of
University Microfilms Inc.
Ann Arbor, Michigan 48106

Library of Congress Cataloging in Publication Data

Murphy, Kerry.
  Hector Berlioz and the development of French
music criticism.

  (Studies in musicology ; no. 97)
  Bibliography: p.
  Includes index.
  1. Musical criticism—France.   2. Berlioz,
Hector, 1803-1869.   I. Title.   II. Series.
ML3880.M85   1988   780'944   87-30227
ISBN 0-8357-1821-2 (alk. paper)

British Library CIP data is available.

Contents

Appendixes

Preface

The need for "criticism" in musicology is an issue that has been raised by musicologists Joseph Kerman and Leo Treitler—most recently in Kerman's provocative book *Musicology*.[1] Kerman sees the critical activity as that of "studying the meaning and value of art-works," that is, examining the work of art as an aesthetic object. He holds that the most solid basis for criticism is history.

In *Musicology* Kerman comments briefly on the critical writings of E. T. A. Hoffmann. He does not discuss the work of other nineteenth-century or early twentieth-century critics such as Hector Berlioz, Robert Schumann, Hugo Wolf, Claude Debussy or G. B. Shaw. Yet the work of these critics makes it necessary to moderate Kerman's general lament about music's impoverished body of criticism in comparison to that of the other arts.

Carl Dahlhaus stresses the need to understand aesthetic concepts historically: "It is the business of explicit criticism . . . to formulate ever anew and incessantly the historical context into which musical works and their interpretations fit."[2] If one agrees with Dahlhaus that criticism needs to be historically conscious and interpret "changes in a repertory" and in the "structure of a tradition,"[3] then this body of nineteenth- and twentieth-century criticism is surely of great importance to the musicologist.

Very little work has been done on the history of music criticism. Such work could provide not only information on changing repertoires, performance practice, concert life, and so on, but also provide an historical insight into aesthetic concepts and their continually evolving meanings. If history is taken as the main basis for criticism, and I believe it should be, criticism must also examine its own history.

This book aims to establish the ground for further study of Berlioz's criticism. It could be argued that Berlioz wrote not criticism but music journalism. "Journalism" is perhaps a more appropriate label for some of Berlioz's writings, such as his swift overnight reviews of *opéra-comique*. However, the majority accomplish more than "the sorting out of successes and failures."[4] I shall not make any distinction between journalism and criticism in his writings. Such a distinction would be both pedantic and messy.

Biographical information given in the notes has come from a variety of sources, mainly the *Dictionnaire des littérateurs, Grand dictionnaire encyclopédique Larousse, Grand Larousse encyclopédique, New Grove Dictionary of Music and Musicians, Grand dictionnaire universel du XIXe siècle,* and *Larousse du XXe siècle.*

All translations, unless otherwise stated, are my own. I would like to thank H. Robert Cohen for his kind permission to use his translations of Berlioz's criticisms of opera. I would also like to thank the editors of *Musicology Australia* and the *Revue Internationale de Musique Française* for permission to include material originally published in their journals.[5]

It gives me pleasure to acknowledge the generous assistance I have had in preparing this book. First of all I would like to thank the library staff at the Bibliothèque Nationale, *Salle de Musique* and *Salle des Périodiques*—in particular the kind interest and help of M. J. Watelot. The staff of the music library at the University of Melbourne have also given friendly help and encouragement and I am very grateful for the assistance given to me by their chief librarian Margaret Greene. The faculty of music of the University of Melbourne have been extremely generous, in particular in granting me the funds to return to Paris to check my sources in 1983. Meredith Moon, ex-staff of the faculty has always been a source of inspiration and given continual help and encouragement. Staff of the University of Melbourne Computer Centre have also been extraordinarily helpful and patient with me, in particular Jeff MacDonell and Ailsa Mackenzie without whose help I would never have managed to master the University word-processing system, let alone the problems associated with a text using two languages. I am also very grateful to the University of Melbourne for awarding me a postgraduate scholarship for four years, enabling me to do the bulk of the research necessary for this book, and awarding me a three month "writing-up grant" on completion of my study.

Staff at the Percy Grainger Museum in Melbourne have provided invaluable support; the curator, Kay Dreyfus, has given me unfailing help and encouragement for many years and I owe her a great deal of thanks.

Other individuals I would like to thank for their friendly advice are nineteenth-century specialists Peter Bloom and Elizabeth Bartlett. François Lesure was an invaluable help and support to me during my stay in Paris, both regarding library resources and research methodology. Berliozian Hugh Macdonald has also been unstintingly generous with help and advice, and I am particularly grateful to both these scholars for their assistance.

Finally, I must say how lucky I am to have such a wonderful family and husband: their support, in so many ways has been exceptional and it is no exaggeration to say that without them this book would never have been completed.

Abbreviations

For complete references, please see the Bibliography.

Reference Works

NG   *New Grove Dictionary of Music and Musicians*

NBE   *New Berlioz Edition*

Periodicals to Which Berlioz Contributed

GM   *Gazette Musicale de Paris*

JD   *Journal des Débats Politiques et Littéraires*

Le Rén.   *Le Rénovateur*

RGM   *Revue et Gazette Musicale de Paris*

Berlioz's Writings

ATC   *A travers chants*

CG 1   *Correspondance générale,* vol. 1, ed. P. Citron

CG 2   *Correspondance générale,* vol. 2, ed. F. Robert

CG 3   *Correspondance générale,* vol. 3, ed. P. Citron

CG 4   *Correspondance générale,* vol. 4, ed. P. Citron, Y. Gérard, and H. Macdonald

Corr. inéd.   *Correspondance inédite,* ed. D. Bernard

Mém.   *Mémoires,* 2 vols., ed. Pierre Citron

Mem.	*The Memoirs of Hector Berlioz,* trans. and ed. David Cairns
MM	*Les Musiciens et la musique*
SO	*Soirées d'orchestre,* ed. Léon Guichard
SW	*Briefe an die Fürstin Carolyne Sayn-Wittgenstein*
VM	*Voyage musical en Allemagne et en Italie*

Introduction

Overview of the Literature

Research concerning Berlioz has been dominated by three major events; first the publication of Jacques Barzun's monumental *Berlioz and the Romantic Century*, second the foundation of the *New Berlioz Edition* (*NBE*) under the general editorship of Hugh Macdonald, and third the publication of Berlioz's *Correspondance générale* under the general editorship of Pierre Citron.[1] For anyone working on Berlioz's literary works the new editions of his *Les Soirées de l'orchestre* (1852), *Les Grotesques de la musique* (1859), and *A travers chants* (1862) are also significant.[2]

Not much has been written on Berlioz as a writer. As part of the Berlioz Festival of 1980, a colloquium on Berlioz's literary and critical works was held at the University of Grenoble.[3] In addition a paper on Berlioz's music criticism was given by Katherine Kolb Reeve at an international conference, *Music in Paris in the 1830s,* held at Smith College, Massachusetts, U.S.A., 1982.[4] Kolb Reeve has also contributed an excellent chapter on Berlioz as writer to Scribner's *European Writers,* volume 6.[5]

Two North American dissertations have been written specifically on Berlioz's music criticism. These are H. Robert Cohen's *Berlioz on the Opera (1829–1849): A Study in Music Criticism* and Katherine Kolb Reeve's *The Poetics of the Orchestra in the Writings of Hector Berlioz.*[6] H. Robert Cohen's dissertation questions whether there is any central unifying aesthetic in Berlioz's criticism and argues that there is a system in Berlioz's criticism of opera during the period 1829–49, a system that centered on "dramatic appropriateness," whereby a work's merit lay in its fidelity to its dramatic implications. Katherine Kolb Reeve's dissertation is particularly rewarding for its literary background and its positioning of Berlioz's ideas in reference to nineteenth-century literary figures, most notably Victor Hugo. Although she draws on Berlioz's entire critical output, she concentrates largely on his articles on Beethoven as being those most relevant to her study of the "poetics" of the orchestra.

Two other relevant North American dissertations in related areas are Dorothy Hagan's *French Musical Criticism between the Revolutions (1830–1848)* and Peter A. Bloom's *François-Joseph Fétis and the "Revue Musicale" (1827–1835).*[7]

Apart from those reviews published in the volumes *Voyage musical en Allemagne et en Italie* (1844), *A travers chants, Les Soirées de l'orchestre, Les Grotesques de la musique,* and a posthumous publication *Les Musiciens et la musique* (1903) edited by André Hallays, there is a recent selection of Berlioz's criticism made by Gérard Condé, *Hector Berlioz: Cauchemars et passions.* Unfortunately Condé alters the text at times; to quote him: "What should one do if Berlioz makes an error in a date (given of course that he does not draw any conclusions from it) . . . rectify it, as the author would have done himself?"[8] This is indeed what Condé has done; also he forms single articles from a number of reviews that are concerned with the same issues. It is obviously not intended as a scholarly edition, yet it serves the purpose well of making known to the general public a large number of articles by Berlioz.

Most of Berlioz's articles however still lie hidden in the numerous newspapers and journals in which they were first published. This situation is in the process of being rectified. For some years now a team of researchers from the Université Laval, the University of British Columbia, and the Paris Conservatoire, under the dual direction of H. Robert Cohen and Yves Gérard, have been working on a publication of Berlioz's reviews. The aim of the project is to make the complete Berlioz criticism available to the public as soon as possible. To this end, little editing is being done; the aim is simply to reproduce a facsimile edition of the articles themselves. Eventually a two-volume critical apparatus and a computerized index will also be published. Workers in the team are being scrupulous in their attempts to track down every article written by Berlioz.[9] A bibliography of Berlioz's criticism also appears as part of D. Kern Holoman's thematic catalogue, published as volume twenty-four of the *New Berlioz Edition.*[10]

This book is divided into two parts. In the first part I study Berlioz's activity as a critic within the general context of music criticism at the time. I discuss the music criticism of a number of critics contemporary with Berlioz in political as well as literary papers in order to convey some idea of the scope and limitations of the music reviewer at the time. A subdivision has been made here of "music critics with a social conscience" where I give a brief examination of the music criticism of Joseph Mainzer (1801–55) and of the criticism in several Saint-Simonian publications, in particular *Le Globe.* I am less concerned with the influence of Saint-Simon on the general music critic, which has been examined by other scholars,[11] than with the music criticism of the already converted Saint-Simonian.

I have given a brief summary of the journals to which Berlioz contributed and examined his relationship to each and the motivations behind his own criticism. Criticism of the day involved a degree of corruption. Malpractices will be discussed separately and also in relation to Berlioz's own criticism. The question of whether Berlioz's role as a composer compromised his role as a critic arises here also. This part of the book concludes with the identification and analysis of some unsigned articles by Berlioz.

Thus, the first half of this book is basically an examination of the machinations of the musical press in early nineteenth-century Paris, in which context I try to place Berlioz's criticism. The second half of the book looks more directly at Berlioz's actual criticism and specifically at his criticism of his contemporary composers. The majority of Berlioz's reviews of this period are of the Opéra, Opéra-Comique, and instrumental concerts, mainly the Conservatoire concerts. This reflects not so much Berlioz's tastes but those of the Parisian public and of the editors of the various journals to which he contributed. These reviews form the basis of the study of Berlioz's views about his contemporaries. The Opéra, Opéra-Comique, and Conservatoire concert series were also important social institutions and I have examined them separately. The Théâtre Italien, the other important concert venue at the time, is not included here, mainly because Berlioz reviewed Italian opera relatively infrequently.

Berlioz is bold, self-assured, and opinionated from his first article, and his prose style consistently shows remarkable fluency and ease. The book covers the consolidation of Berlioz's position as a professional critic, from his first letters to the editor of 1823 to full-time criticism written concurrently for numerous papers from 1834 onward. I have chosen to stop at 1837. This is the year that Berlioz edited the *Revue et Gazette Musicale,* which is an indication of the extent to which he had become established as a journalist and critic. I have also drawn on Berlioz's references to criticism in his *Mémoires* and correspondence, which naturally spans a longer period than from 1823 to 1837.

Berlioz is now justly recognized as a great composer. His criticism provides a fascinating counterpoint to his music, to which his reflections, judgments, admirations, and dislikes refer continually. This is not to say that Berlioz continually talks about his music, for the reference is implicit rather than stated. His criticism provides not only an insight into the musical life of his time but also into the creative life of a composer. We are fortunate indeed that he was so articulate, well-read, and possessed such literary skills. His despairs, passions, and ecstasies are portrayed with an enthusiasm and eloquence that make reading his criticism never boring, always stimulating, and invariably provocative.

Historical Background

Berlioz's career as a critic began during the Restoration (1815–30) and was consolidated during the reign of Louis-Philippe (1830–48).

The Revolution of 1830 amounted to little more than a change of dynasty from the Bourbon to the Orléans line. Immediately before 1830, of a population of 29 million, only 90,000 were eligible to vote. After 1830, with the franchise law of 1831, 174,000 were eligible—hardly a significant increase.[12] The number of people who could read and write was just beginning to outstrip the number totally illiterate when Louis-Philippe's reign was approaching its end.[13]

The newspapers during the Restoration were fairly expensive and could be bought only on a quarterly subscription basis. The subscription figures were not high[14] and did not increase much during Louis-Philippe's reign.[15]

However, the number of people who followed the press was larger than the subscription figures, since both provincial and Parisian libraries and reading rooms often ordered one copy of a paper which was then circulated amongst its members and sometimes even read aloud to those unable to read. This happened most frequently with "left-wing" papers. A police report of 1830 stated that one copy of *Le Constitutionnel* might have as many as a hundred readers, whereas one copy of *La Quotidienne* would have at most a family of readers.[16] Although politically the 1830 rebellion was fairly ineffectual, it did have an effect on public life, which became more "materialistic and immediate. The spectacular amateurs like Chateaubriand . . . gave way to a race of professional politicians like Duchâtel and Guizot."[17] We see a similar rise of the professional artist in the concert world. During the Restoration the concert life of Paris was relatively quiet, but this changed after 1830 when, to quote William Weber, "the salons of the upper-middle class and the Orléanist nobility suddenly leapt into prominence, and the dynamism they generated made Paris the musical capital of Europe for two decades."[18] Legitimists—that is, supporters of the Bourbon monarchy—and their families tended to stay away from concerts during the 1830s, though a certain number continued to frequent the Théâtre Italien. During the Restoration this was thought to be a safe place to take a "well brought-up" young girl who, it was assumed, would not understand the words.[19]

The weakening of aristocratic influence and dominance during the reign of Louis-Philippe (something which had been happening since the Revolution) and the consequent lessening of amateur sponsorship gave free reign to the development of middle-class commercialism in Paris. Musical life became competitive and music was seen as a saleable commodity available to a general public. This period also saw the consolidation of the printing press and publishing industry, and a consequent outpouring of books, sheet music, and periodicals. The emergence of music criticism was a sign of the number of people now participating in an active concert life.

The phrase "burgeoning middle class" is used so often in reference to this period that it has become a cliché. However, the term "middle class" has to be treated with caution, as William Weber has pointed out in his excellent article "The Muddle of the Middle Classes."[20] According to Weber the middle-class public that became so prominent in concert life during the reign of Louis-Philippe was in fact a select upper-middle class, a group of people who for some considerable time before 1830 had been taking part in a similar life-style to that of the aristocracy and now were merging with them to form a new "upper" class. Weber makes two clarifications in reference to the repeated use of the adjective "rising" in discussion of the "middle class" in this period. He stresses first that the "middle class" did not suddenly rise during the 1830s but had been rising since the Renaissance, and second that the word "rising" should be understood in the context of the descent of the aristocracy.

The term "middle class" or "bourgeoisie" was a generic term used to refer to an enormous number of diverse groups that included industrialists, financiers, merchants, tax-farmers, lawyers, civil servants and so on, and generally all wealthy nontitled families. Such groups had widely differing interests, though, to quote Weber, they did begin to take on

> a set of roles and styles seen most clearly in family life, leisure pursuits, and professional organization. The burgeoning book and magazine trade, which preached the virtues of these trends, made the sense of a middle-class way of life a powerful force in the manners and morals of the time.[21]

However, Weber pleads with us not to "personify it as a middle-class spirit." The overlapping interests and activities of, for instance, aristocrats and artisans makes such labels unwise. In my subsequent use of the term "middle class" I would like Weber's clarifications to be borne in mind.

The concert life of the 1830s centered around the Opéra, Théâtre Italien, Opéra-Comique, Conservatoire concerts, and numerous private concerts given in salons of the day. Jeffrey Cooper in his book *The Rise of Instrumental Music and Concert Series in Paris 1828–1871* states that instrumental music was presented at more than a hundred series of concerts or seances over the period 1828–71, including programs by orchestras, chamber ensembles, soloists, composers, teachers, amateur societies, and groups associated with educational institutions.[22] There were for example orchestral concerts performed by the Concerts Valentino (1837–41), Institution des Jeunes Aveugles (sporadically from 1836), Société de l'Athénée Musicale (1829–44) and chamber-music series organized by Pierre Baillot (?1820–36) and Théophile Tilmant (1833–?38).[23] The private salons which had previously featured exclusively amateurs now often had the attraction of a professional virtuoso. Music performed at these salon concerts was varied; it could include popular romances, piano arrangements of current opera highlights, operatic arias, and virtuosic instrumental pieces for piano and violin. Several of the professional musicians of the day also held private concerts where chamber music was performed.

Artists often gave benefit concerts either for themselves or for friends. These marked the beginning of the public concerts. The Conservatoire concerts or Société des Concerts formed, in terms of management and performing practice, the first strictly professional series in Paris. Ironically, however, only a select elite was able to attend the concerts.

Popular music of the day centered around the *romance,* a tuneful strophic song with simple piano accompaniment.[24] Its popularity was enhanced both by the proliferation of newly available sheet music and the arrival of the upright piano as a stalwart member of the middle-class household. There were a number of cheap orchestral concerts, for instance, café concerts, promenade concerts, summer outdoor concerts and the Musard concerts. An English woman visiting Paris in 1835 described a popular indoor concert conducted by Philippe Musard in the following terms:

> At half-past seven o'clock, you lounge into a fine, large, well-lighted room, which is rapidly filled with company: a full and good orchestra give you during a couple of hours some of the best and most popular music of the season; and then you lounge out again, in time to dress for a party, or eat ices at Tortoni's, or soberly to go home for a domestic tea-drinking and early rest. For this concert you pay a franc.[25]

J. M. Bailbé, through an exhaustive examination of secondary novelists of the day, demonstrates the important role played by music in the leisure activity of the middle classes and in the literary imagination of the day. Bailbé argues that many of the *romanciers* he studied were knowledgeable dilettantes, quite discerning in their musical judgments, and able to give reasons for their appreciations.[26] Some attempt must be made to define the word "dilettante" since it is constantly used in all the literature of the day, including Berlioz's criticism.

Henri Girard states in his book *Emile Deschamps: Dilettante,* "The *dilettante,* from the Restoration up until the end of the Second Empire, was the man of the world, the passionate lover of Italian music."[27] The Parisian Théâtre Italien was most popular during the Restoration, when Rossini's operas dominated the musical scene. During the reign of Louis-Philippe, Rossini's supremacy was severely challenged by Meyerbeer, and the word "dilettante" began to be used in reference to devotees of Meyerbeer and Halévy and also occasionally to designate enthusiastic followers of the professional virtuosi, such as Liszt and Paganini. One critic in 1830 even claimed that there were two camps of dilettantes, *le mouvement* (Beethoven, Mozart, Weber) and *la résistance* (Rossini).[28] It would appear that though the term was originally used only in reference to the Théâtre Italien it came to be used for an enthusiastic follower of whatever was fashionable in music. It also came to be used to refer to other arts.[29]

The term "dilettante" was most frequently used during the July monarchy for followers of opera, and it necessarily implied a certain fanaticism.[30] Evidently, however, the dilettante's knowledge of music was quite extensive. He was probably, after all, the most avid follower of the music critic. As Vincent Duckles says in an article on the historiography of nineteenth-century music: "The influence of the dilettante was, on the whole, a salutary one in the development of the discipline."[31]

Sometimes the word "dilettante" is used as a synonym for "amateur." Cecilia Hopkins Porter in an article on the Lower Rhine Music Festivals talks of a "dilettante singing society" and of the "enduring dilettantism" of the eighteenth century.[32] The use of the term in early nineteenth-century France, with its connotation of enthusiasm, its original association with Italian music, and lingering association with opera in general, counts against its being taken as merely synonymous with "amateur." The word is defined in *Trésor de la langue française* as "someone who finds pleasure in something."[33] Some confusion could arise here over the two meanings of "amateur" in French, one the opposite of professional and the other referring to someone who takes pleasure in something. The second meaning is obviously much closer to the original meaning of dilettante than the first.

The French use of the term dilettante did begin to take on derogatory connotations; it implied a superficiality and a following of music for the sake of fashion. In a review of a Conservatoire concert in 1836 Berlioz actually played on the ambiguity of the word amateur by distinguishing it from dilettante. In describing the audience's reaction to the close of the concert season, Berlioz tells of the amateur who waits around mournfully for the re-opening of the series, and the dilettante who goes happily off to other more popular concerts. The dilettante attended the concerts because they were fashionable; the amateur, out of love for the music performed.[34] This anticipates the twentieth-century use of the term dilettante which is frequently pejorative.

Berlioz did not find writing music criticism particularly congenial, yet his activity as a critic became an essential part of his life. Many people at the time appreciated his criticism more than his music. The role of critic was a difficult one to maintain with integrity. I shall trace the difficulties and rewards encountered by Berlioz in his tightrope walk between diplomacy and honesty.

Part One

The Role of the Music Critic in the Early Nineteenth-Century Press

1

Survey of the Music Criticism in Contemporary Journals and Newspapers

During the first part of the Restoration, musical press in Paris was sparse. The newspapers did have a theatrical-musical coverage, and the post of reviewer was a sought-after job because of its small perquisites of free admission and the like. This position was not reserved for someone with the necessary knowledge, but was open to all, the prerequisites if any being a lively writing style and a turn of wit. Lucien de Rubempré, that fashionable journalist in Balzac's *Illusions perdues*, remains the most vivid, if cynical, portrayal of the fundamental decadence of the theater critic of the time.

It was some time before any critical distinction was made between dramatic and operatic theater; both were seen as belonging to the domain of the literary critic. The most striking consequence of this lack of differentiation was that criticism of opera was mainly a criticism of the libretto only. It was against this in particular that Castil-Blaze, the first self-consciously styled "music" critic of the time, was rebelling.[1] François Castil-Blaze, or "xxx" as he first signed his name, was most renowned for his arrangements and adaptations of other people's works, which he undertook with the aim of making them accessible to the general Parisian public. His most infamous arrangement was *Robin des bois,* based on Weber's *Der Freischütz.*[2] Castil-Blaze took over the post of music critic for the *Journal des Débats* from two literary critics, Geoffroy (1800–1814)[3] and Duviquet (1814–20),[4] and in his first article categorically announced his departure from his predecessors: "This chronicle will be devoted exclusively to music. The musical aspects of both new and old operas will be examined and analyzed with care, according to the accepted principles."[5] He broadened the scope of the review to include regular coverage of areas other than opera such as instrumental music and religious vocal music, areas which in general required a more technical musical knowledge. Castil-Blaze also wrote on theoretical issues such as the "literary music critic."[6] Despite his background, Castil-Blaze's musical analysis in these early reviews is fairly rudimentary. He tends to be descriptive rather than analytical and uses a number of vague, emotive adjectives which add little to the readers' knowledge of the work. To give a short example from a review of a concerto of Viotti:

> In the new concerto of M. Viotti, the *tuttis* are very vigorous, the first movement is brilliant, with the sweeping style that is characteristic of this illustrious violinist's approach. The *adagio* is delicious, but the rondo does not have enough nobility.[7]

Later in his life Castil-Blaze's articles became less descriptive with sometimes quite detailed and extended examination of the music.

These early articles did not set a standard for exemplary criticism, but they did set a precedent in music criticism at that time. The fact that Castil-Blaze wrote for an important political newspaper was significant also, since it meant that he was reaching a fairly substantial audience and establishing new expectations of what areas should be the concern of the music critic.

The other major contributor to the development of a distinct music criticism was François-Joseph Fétis.[8] Fétis became influential at a later date than Castil-Blaze, and it was in 1827 that he founded (and ran almost single-handedly for the next five years) his *Revue Musicale*. Before the founding of the *Revue Musicale*, no other music journal had existed for more than a two-year period in France, with the exception of the *Correspondance des Amateurs Musiciens*.[9] By the end of the 1830s two other music journals were also established; *Le Ménestrel* (1833) edited by Antoine Meissonnier and Jacques-Léopold Heugel, and *La France Musicale* (1837) edited by Marie and Léon Escudier.

Fétis's reviews were scholarly and serious. In writing for a presumably informed and limited audience he was obliged to make few concessions to the musically uneducated public. He covered a broad spectrum of areas with an emphasis on researched historical articles on music. Reviews of current concerts were included, but were by no means the most important section of the magazine. During the 1830s Fétis began writing articles for political newspapers as well, usually on serious musical issues rather than reviews of concerts. Detailed analysis of Fétis as a critic can be found in Peter A. Bloom's unpublished dissertation on Fétis and the *Revue Musicale*.

Thus, it was during the second half of the Restoration that music criticism as a separate discipline began in the Paris newspapers and that the first serious music journal was established. As said in the introduction, the late 1820s saw the expansion of orchestral concerts and the consolidation of a purely instrumental musical genre, which demanded a new critical response and played an important role in expanding the scope of the music review. By the reign of Louis-Philippe most newspapers had at least an occasional separate music review. The lists of free *Entrées* for theaters conserved at the Archives nationales in Paris show an interesting change between 1831 and 1836.[10] The 1831 list comprises composers, performers, police, doctors, and professors at the Conservatoire, with a few critics such as Fétis. The 1836 list has the same basic outline, but with the major difference that a large number of journalists are now included, whose names are listed quite formally alongside the names of the newspapers they represented.[11] Not very many critics signed their articles during the late Restoration or the early years of Louis-Philippe. They either left their reviews unsigned, or initialled, or else signed with a pseudonym (see appendix C). But by 1835 many specialized critics, Berlioz included, started signing their names in full.

Music criticism in Paris in the 1830s was not of a very high standard, yet some interesting work was being done that should not be totally ignored. In order to place Berlioz's criticism in its contemporary context, I have looked at music criticism in a number of journals and newspapers of the time, most of them from the period of 1834 to 1836, the years in which Berlioz started his full-time occupation as a critic. However, he did not work in a professional capacity for any of these publications.

Before starting this summary of the press, it is necessary to give some explanation of terms. Music criticism in newspapers and journals appeared under various headings, such as: "Chronique musicale," "Bulletin musical," "Spectacles de Paris," "Chronique de Paris," "Revue musicale," "Critique musicale," and "Feuilleton musical." The first four of these headings referred basically to the same thing, an overview of the week's musical and sometimes also theatrical events. The last three headings are usually used interchangeably to refer to music criticism in general. That is, under these headings, one might find a theoretical essay on music, a review of a recent concert, or an historical article on a particular composer. Originally, the term "Feuilleton" referred specifically to a review of a performance of the previous night. Jules Janin cutely defined it as "a little cry of joy that the spectacle of the day tears from us."[12] Given that it was only in the mid 1830s that articles on music other than reviews of performances of opera and *opéra-comique* began to appear regularly, the title "Feuilleton musical" did on the whole retain its original definition. However, it also came to be used to refer to any sort of article on music. In his *Mémoires* Berlioz does make a distinction, saying that a *critic* only writes when he has something to say and the *feuilletoniste* writes about things that he is obliged to write about.[13] But in practice, as Ursula Eckart-Bäcker remarks, Berlioz's labeling himself a *feuilletoniste* could have signified any of the following: music critic, music journalist, and writer on music. All of these terms were more or less synonymous.[14] The plain heading of "Feuilleton," as distinct from "Feuilleton musical," in the political newspapers usually referred to a column devoted to the arts in some form or another—literature, drama, music—that contrasted with the political content of the rest of the paper.

In this brief survey the political newspapers consulted were: *Le Constitutionnel, Journal de Paris, La Mode, Le Moniteur Universel, Le National, La Presse* (founded in 1836), *La Quotidienne, Le Siècle* (founded in

1836), and *Le Temps*.[15] *La Quotidienne* and *La Mode* were Legitimist; *Le Constitutionnel, Le Moniteur Universel, Journal de Paris, La Presse,* and *Le Siècle* were supporters of Louis-Philippe, though the last two were more nominal than active political supporters. *Le Temps,* which had been formed by Jacques Coste in 1829 to combat the retrograde tendencies of Charles X's government, was in the process of becoming a mini-encyclopedia (*journal encyclopédique*) during the mid-1830s. It claimed to be independent of political allegiance but tended generally to support the government. *Le National* was Republican during this period.

Many of the newspapers of the time often changed political allegiance over the course of the century, so it must be stressed that my comments on their political leanings refer to the period from 1834 to 1836 only. Three literary journals were also consulted: the *Revue de Paris, Revue des Deux Mondes,* and *L'Artiste.*

Music criticism in these newspapers and journals was still dominated by critics with preponderantly literary rather than musical backgrounds. However, there was generally not just one critic employed, but several different people. There was also a small group of "serious" critics—Mainzer, Desnoyers, Castil-Blaze, Blaze de Bury, d'Ortigue, and Fétis—whose work stands out from the rest. For the sake of convenience I shall refer consistently to this group as "the serious critics," in order to differentiate them from their less serious colleagues. The qualification of "serious" is of course only comparative. Jules Janin is an example of a less serious music critic.[16] A spirited, witty writer, Janin is reputed to have "said something bad about everything he had said something good about."[17] He wrote frequently on music.

In his column the one critic often covered *théâtres*—including opera, *opéra-comique, variétés,* and vaudeville—and the occasional book review.[18] Some papers and journals had a chronicle of the week's (or month's) events, including musical events, which appeared alongside extended articles or reviews of music. Such chronicles often included the other areas mentioned above, as well as gossip about well-known singers, actors, and actresses. The *Revue de Paris* and *Revue des Deux Mondes* had brief "Chronique" sections, though in neither case was it a regular feature. In the *Revue des Deux Mondes* it was the editor Buloz who wrote the "Chronique," which was entitled "Chronique de la quinzaine" and covered recent political events and literature as well as music.[19]

The literary journals the *Revue de Paris* and *Revue des Deux Mondes* had some serious articles on music, and several historical essays, such as Castil-Blaze's articles on Lully for the *Revue de Paris* (1835),[20] and Blaze de Bury's *Poètes et musiciens de l'Allemagne* series in the *Revue des Deux Mondes* (1836). However, articles on music were sparse in both journals and not every issue would have something on music. The same was true of the feuilleton in *Le Siècle,* largely written by Louis Viardot and Louis Desnoyers.[21] Though it had interesting articles on a variety of areas from time to time, including the occasional Conservatoire concert, the number of articles was very limited. The three newspapers with the best music criticism—in terms of the areas covered and the quality of the writing—were *Le Temps*, *Le National*, and *L'Artiste*. According to Eugène Hatin, after 1830 *Le Temps*

> announced that it would "dedicate itself to the profession of true principles, to the progress of ideas, to the maintenance of order and liberty, independently of the men and parties that triumph or fall. To collect progressive ideas, bring them to maturity, and develop them, such will be its task and the spirit of its polemic."[22]

An ambitious program, and one perhaps not altogether feasible at the time, since the paper, needing to capture the middle-class reading public to survive, had, to some extent, to gear itself to that market.

In its music reviews *Le Temps* included general articles on music and also encompassed a broad range of musical genres—opera, orchestral music, including Berlioz's concerts and the Conservatoire concerts, chamber music, and, given the least coverage of all, *opéra-comique*. *Le Temps* had a large collection of people contributing to its music criticism, including Loève-Veimars,[23] Adolphe Guéroult,[24] Fétis, and d'Ortigue. To an extent writers took charge of specific areas. Loève-Veimars, for instance, wrote on the Théâtre Italien, d'Ortigue on the Conservatoire concerts, and Fétis wrote more general articles with such titles as "Philosophie de la musique."[25] Chamber music was irregularly reviewed. Most of the important musical events were covered; for instance there were articles on the German opera performed at the Théâtre Ventadour in 1834 and on music performed at the Gymnase Musical. Fétis and d'Ortigue were the only two critics to have any musical training. Although the other critics had a literary formation, their criticism was always enthusiastic and concerned and, while on occasion revealing the need for greater musical knowledge, showed a fair musical understanding.

Le National had two critics. One who signed himself "X" (Hippolyte Rolle [?], see appendix C) reviewed *opéra-comique* and other lighter works; the other, Louis Desnoyers from 1832 to July 1836 and Joseph Mainzer from July 1836, reviewed opera and wrote general, speculative articles on music. Mainzer's reviews were broader in scope; for instance, he regularly reviewed the Conservatoire concerts. Both he and Desnoyers clearly spent a great deal of time on their articles, taking them seriously and even at times with a pedagogical zeal.

It is interesting that of the papers covered in this survey the two with the best criticism, *Le Temps* and *Le National*, were politically the least conservative. The frequency and length—Desnoyers' articles for *Le National* often extended over nine columns at the bottom of three pages—of music reviews in both papers suggest enlightened editors. Both newspapers also had people on their staff who had been involved in, or were sympathetic to, the Saint-Simonian movement.

The important role assigned to music by the Saint-Simonians had perhaps influenced the papers' attitude towards music criticism. In both papers there was more than one critic, and individual writers were allowed to cover their own areas of interest and expertise.

L'Artiste was a literary journal founded in 1831. It had a number of excellent critics writing for it, such as Gustave Planche and Théophile Gautier. Its best criticism was in the areas of literature and fine arts, and though Fétis wrote the occasional article for it, most of the music reviews were unsigned or written by literary critics. The striking feature of the music criticism was its abundance and scope; all the Conservatoire concerts were reviewed, as were the occasional chamber music concert and all major operas and *opéras-comiques*. *L'Artiste* and *Le Temps* were the only two newspapers in this survey to cover the Conservatoire concerts regularly, but the standard of criticism was not particularly high. At times it was aggressively antianalytical and often written in a rhetorical and florid fashion. A striking feature was the tone of religiosity and awe the critics adopted whenever they discussed Beethoven. As was almost always the case with the literary music critics, intense scorn was expressed for Scribe's libretti.

Some of the criticism in these newspapers is harsh in its criticism of works that were generally popular. Louis Desnoyers, for instance, wrote several highly critical articles on Meyerbeer's *Les Huguenots* (1836). François Buloz defended his own condemnation of Halévy's *La Juive* with the self-righteous remark:

> If you find that I am being severe towards a conscientious and talented man, I would reply that for an honest and pure critic only good or bad works exist, and that it is our duty to cultivate the former and prune them so that they blossom in the sun, and to pull out the latter without pity.[26]

Such discussion of the critic's role was quite common. Often writers talked of various styles of criticism, the three main ones being termed the analytical, the impressionistic, and the *admiratif*.

The analytical or more scholarly style of criticism was usually seen by the average music critic as stemming from Fétis and considered dry, pedantic, and unsuited to a newspaper or literary journal. In discussing the possibility of using this style a critic for *Le Temps* wrote:

> God keep me from embarking upon the analysis of a symphony, unless I copy the *Revue Musicale*, and say, as it does, *that the return in the principal key is prepared by a perfect cadence on F sharp, the dominant of the key of B natural*: a language that marvelously suits the specialized readers of the *Revue*, but not an ignoramus like me, and that does not suit the non-specialized audience of *Le Temps* any better.[27]

Despite this claim, Fétis did not in fact use very much analytical terminology in his newspaper articles. As can be seen from the example given by the *Le Temps* critic, what was commonly termed analytical was basically a descriptive style that made use of musical terminology.

The impressionistic style, the obverse of the analytical, involved discussing music purely in terms of the writer's emotional responses and taking it as a stimulus for poetic reverie. It attempted to present the impression that the work made on the critic and also to recreate an impression of the work's power for the reader. Albert Tsugawa describes the impressionistic critic as follows: "He emphasizes and verbally gestures; in rich evocative language, layer on layer, he pieces together various impressions until a pattern is formed. Into this pattern may go . . . anything that conceivably might evoke in the reader the response that approaches in quality his response to the work of art."[28] The chief danger of such criticism was, of course, that the work of art itself became irrelevant and lost in the cloud of impressionistic prose describing it. The impressionistic style was widespread during the early nineteenth century; it is often this style that is referred to when people talk about "romantic" criticism. It had its master in E. T. A. Hoffmann in Germany in the first decades of the century and moved to France a little later. The following statement about Beethoven by a critic for *L'Artiste* is a brief example of the impressionistic style: "In fact, do not all Beethoven's works evoke in you that infinite sadness, and that exaltation of the soul that feels the need to unite with God!"[29]

L'Artiste specialized in this antianalytical style and saw such an approach to music as a superior one; witness the following doting comment on the audience at a Conservatoire concert: "A public that doesn't attempt afterwards to analyze an overture or a symphony, that spontaneously understands the composer's thoughts."[30] This approach to music criticism was typical of the literary critic with the dilettante's knowledge of music. Even Blaze de Bury,[31] one of the finest literary music critics of the time, whom Arthur Pougin called an "impassioned dilettante who took the trouble to reflect before saying what he thought,"[32] felt that the best critic was not one who analyzed but one who "felt." Blaze de Bury summed this up in his maxim, "To judge is to understand, to understand is to feel."[33] The following quotation from a review of the overture to *Der Freischütz* gives a brief example of Blaze de Bury's style: "Listen to the veiled sounds of the horns, this mysterious beginning so profoundly imprinted with that virile forest-life whose tableau is about to unfold before you."[34]

Not all the literary music critics had the same approach to criticism, however. One notable exception was Gustave Planche, whose approach could be classified as classical, certainly in comparison to Blaze de Bury's approach. René Wellek says of Planche's classicism, "He is not a classicist in the sense of idolizing the seventeenth century or defending the rules. He is rather a fiercely independent upholder of 'good sense.'"[35] Planche advocated "disinterested" criticism which would always retain control over its feelings.[36]

In the body of his criticism Louis Desnoyers frequently harangued against what he called the "style admiratif" or the "prostitution d'éloge." This referred basically to the critic's indiscriminate use of adjectives such as "admirable," "sublime," "magnifique"—words used to such an extent as to rob them of any real meaning. In an article on the language used by music critics, Catherine Portevin comments that critics, to avoid naming what it is that music refers to, often make global judgments in the exclamative mode.[37] Desnoyers's plea for rational, not delirious, enthusiasm was perfectly justified, as the average music review of the day was filled with strings of such adjectives often accompanied by equally long strings of exclamation marks. Berlioz occasionally used the "style admiratif" as it is described here, but in moderation;[38] and he also at times complained of its indiscriminate use by other critics. Berlioz wrote in this style mainly in responding to the works of three specific composers: Beethoven, Gluck, and Weber. In these instances the "style admiratif" refers not just to the use of certain adjectives but to a whole mode of eulogy.

Several general preoccupations can be gleaned from the work of the small number of "serious" critics discussed in this survey. The most predominant preoccupation was an interest in and concern for the role of music criticism and the critic's mission or goal. All these critics felt they had some responsibility to guide the public taste; they aimed at providing more than a merely diverting account of a spectacle.

Castil-Blaze was very aware that his musical "expertise" equipped him to make judgments on a composer's technique. He continually flaunted the extent of his knowledge and delighted in finding passages in a work that he felt came from the work of another composer. This practice was probably allied to his own work as an arranger and adapter of other people's music, as also was his continual, vain challenge to the public to identify which sections in one of his arrangements were by a certain composer (for instance Weber) and which were Castil-Blaze's imitation of that composer. Throughout his criticism Castil-Blaze spent considerable energy in both directly and indirectly defending his own compositions and arrangements. This was perhaps the unconscious goal behind his criticism. His conscious goal as a critic seems to have been the enlightenment of the public and artists about the "true" nature of musical composition, which could only be perceived by someone with the necessary training. He certainly did not have any coherent aesthetic of the "true" nature of music. His musical training had not made him a great composer, so perhaps he felt that criticism was an area where his background gave him some authority and stressed the importance of compositional knowledge for this reason.

The critic's role was much more clearly perceived by Mainzer, Desnoyers, and d'Ortigue, who wrote at length on the subject.[39] All three saw the critic's role as an ethical one, that of intelligently and correctly guiding the public taste.

Mainzer's belief in the critic's pedagogical role interplayed with his desire to propagate choral singing amongst the working classes.[40] Since he believed that the critic did have the power to influence the public, he naturally attempted to use his column as a means of promoting the idea of singing for the people. This did not mean writing only about his own efforts, but also about any concerts in Paris or the provinces that had been mounted by some group or other of singers. Mainzer obviously saw his personal mission as being to promote singing for the people wherever possible. Papers such as *Le National* and the *Revue des Deux Mondes* gave him free rein to do just that. I shall be returning to Mainzer in the next chapter.

Desnoyers perceived the critic's goal in more general terms. He felt that the critic's aim should be to "instruct" and "enlighten"—a simple aim, but one which he felt had been completely neglected by his contemporary critics. Desnoyers saw his colleagues' criticism of performances as bound by limited time and space and as lapsing into mere description consisting of banal and meaningless clichés. He gives the following as an example: "Nothing could equal the beauty of this spectacle. . . . The finale produces an effect that is impossible to describe . . . [and] the magnificence of the *mise-en-scène* does homage to the talented director."[41] He does not suggest that extra time and space be allotted to the critic, which is odd since he must have been aware of the advantages of both these factors. Instead he claimed that for music criticism to achieve its mission of forming and guiding the public taste, it had to be more analytical and precise, so as to examine *why* certain effects were produced. Desnoyers' own carefully considered and researched criticism certainly attempted to achieve this aim to the best of his ability, and it is a pity that he did not have a more developed musical formation and broader musical interests.

Of the three men, d'Ortigue was the most involved with the question of the critic's mission.[42] He was concerned with the critic's perception and understanding of the ethical content of music and the way in which that content, if present, was to be conveyed to the public.

D'Ortigue was a friend and follower of Lamennais,[43] with whom he worked during 1830 on devising a theory of the arts in which Platonic precepts were intermingled with new ideals of social progress.[44] Art was seen as expressive of the natural world and as an educative tool in the moral upbringing of the people.[45] D'Ortigue puzzled over the possibility of music criticism being based on an immutable law of beauty, which would govern all good compositions. Although he concluded that such a law did exist, his conclusions on its critical application remain vague and confused.[46] This law was supposedly aligned with nature and in contact both with the infinite (God) and humanity (the people) and the critic was to use it as a criterion with which to assess the value of a composition. No concrete indications of how this assessment might be achieved were given, as it was assumed to be an intuitive process. D'Ortigue's continual concern for the moral implications of music and music criticism possibly shows the influence of the Saint-Simonians as well as that of Lamennais.

J. M. Bailbé, in his book *Le Roman et la musique sous la monarchie de juillet*, mentions many instances of the popularity of Beethoven's music in the works of nineteenth-century French *romanciers*. The following extract from

Balzac's short story *Gambara* (1837) gives a good example of the manner in which Beethoven's music was described at the time:

> In opening Beethoven's *Symphony in C Minor* a musical man is soon transported into a fantasy world on the golden wings of the theme in G natural, repeated in E by the horns. He sees all of nature alternately lit up by sprays of light, darkened by clouds of melancholy, and brightened by heavenly songs.[47]

The literary music critics during the 1830s were enamored of Beethoven. Blaze de Bury compared a Beethoven symphony with Shakespeare's *Hamlet,* Goethe's *Faust* and *Werther,* and Chateaubriand's *René*—all works that, for Blaze de Bury, expressed the troubles, melancholy, despairs, and hopes of modern man.[48] As orchestral and instrumental music were not, as already mentioned, always regularly reviewed by critics, d'Ortigue reviews are rewarding for their continual espousal of the Conservatoire concerts. He said in his introduction to the *Balcon de l'Opéra,* for example, that one Conservatoire concert was worth more than three months of performances at the Théâtre Italien.[49] Both d'Ortigue and Mainzer spread their reviews of orchestral music over a number of newspapers. This might have been because editors asked them specifically to review these concerts, though it also might have been that they themselves insisted upon which areas they would review.

D'Ortigue felt that instrumental music was by its very nature more open to contemplation and likely to propel one into the realms of the infinite. This view was a commonplace of early nineteenth-century German writings on music, in particular the writings of E. T. A. Hoffmann. As Carl Dahlhaus remarks, the reversal of opinion on absolute music in the early nineteenth century was drastic. He quotes an article from the *Allgemeine Musicalische Zeitung* of 1801 which describes the "pure" music of C. P. E. Bach as being "all the purer the less it is dragged down into the region of vulgar meaning by words (which are always laden with connotations)" and comments that "the very same absolute music that was 'mechanical' in 1750 now reveals the 'poetic.'"[50]

In an enthusiastic and somewhat confused outburst, d'Ortigue proclaimed that instrumental music was life in microcosm:

> Instrumental music unites the diverse inspirations that have presided over different periods of art, religious inspiration, dramatic inspiration, lyrical inspiration; at the same time it absorbs sacred and operatic music; it encapsulates traditions, launches into the past; it mixes Catholic art with the art of emancipation, faith with science; it is social and individual; it is alternately meditative, contemplative, mystic, sublime, picturesque and colorful, impassioned and shameless.[51]

In his reviews of instrumental music d'Ortigue always attempted an analysis in which he professed that he aimed not so much at understanding the relationship between the sounds and sensations, as at following what he felt to be the composer's "idea" through the different instrumental combinations and contrasts.[52] Given d'Ortigue's interest in Plato it was probably the Platonic concept of "idea" that he had in mind here.

D'Ortigue also wrote at length on the Théâtre Italien and the influence of Rossini. In places he suggests real appreciation of Rossini, in particular *Guillaume Tell,* but he also constantly remarks on what he saw as the fundamental superficiality of Rossini's music, which he felt could lead only to decadence. In d'Ortigue's opinion, Rossini's music had carried superficial and brilliant qualities to their highest degree and, when performed by the world's greatest singers (as was almost always the case), it was attractive even to someone convinced of its immorality.[53] Other critics, for instance Desnoyers, were more favorable towards the Théâtre Italien. Desnoyers later published a book, *De l'Opéra en 1847,* which is a defense of Rossini.[54] In general during this period the Théâtre Italien was less popular but more highly esteemed than the Opéra. As J. M. Bailbé remarks: "From the Opéra to the Italiens one has the impression of having gone up a rung in the area of real understanding and musical intelligence."[55]

Of all the critics mentioned, the only one to remain consistently supportive of and encouraging to Berlioz as both composer and critic was d'Ortigue. While Fétis, Castil-Blaze, and Mainzer supported Berlioz at various stages they all eventually turned against him. Peter A. Bloom demonstrates that Fétis had good reason for doing so as Berlioz had himself unjustly attacked Fétis.[56] Desnoyers and Mainzer both made virulent attacks on Berlioz. Although they did criticize his music, their attacks, surprising in their vehemence, were directed more at his criticism and personality.

Desnoyers's attack forms part of his book, *De l'Opéra en 1847.* He attacks Berlioz's use of language: "amongst other instrumental discoveries, M. Berlioz has thus invented a charming rhetorical instrument, that one could call a continuous stream of pun," his enthusiasms, and what he saw as Berlioz's self-preoccupation in his reviews.[57] Desnoyers's tone is petty and he makes some grave errors, such as mistaking all of Castil-Blaze's reviews in the *Journal des Débats* of the 1820s for reviews by Berlioz.

Mainzer devoted the whole first issue of a journal he founded, the *Chronique Musicale de Paris,* to an attack on Berlioz.[58] Given that this was the only issue of the journal ever to appear, one cannot help wondering whether Mainzer created it solely to have a venue in which to attack Berlioz. For the most part Mainzer's attack is ill-founded. He misinterprets Berlioz's views on Grétry, Choron, and the Mozart *Requiem,* to name just a few items. Mainzer shows himself to be intensely jealous of Berlioz's position of critic for the *Journal des Débats* and dwells at length on the perniciousness of having someone with Berlioz's opinions working for such an important paper. Mainzer mentions one interesting point however, which is his knowledge of Berlioz's self-borrowings in reviews of the same concerts for different papers. Although Mainzer exaggerated the scope of the self-borrowings, the fundamental point was valid and rarely commented on by the critics of the time. Peter A. Bloom observes that Fétis also used self-borrowings; his articles for *Le National* were "almost but not exactly the same as those that appeared simultaneously in his own *Revue Musicale*."[59] Berlioz was aware of having offended Mainzer: "I dread an article [on the *Requiem*] in *Le National* from that gross Mainzer, because I did not use his workers' choir; he was very cross and will not miss the opportunity to take his revenge."[60] The harshness of the revenge is rather surprising.

D'Ortigue's loyalty to Berlioz as a composer was not undiscriminating. He could for instance question certain aspects of the *Te Deum* that worried him,[61] and indeed they fundamentally disagreed about the role of expression in church music. However, d'Ortigue's criticism appears to have been influenced quite extensively by Berlioz. There is early evidence of Berlioz's influence in d'Ortigue's article on Berlioz for the *Revue de Paris* in 1832, which is composed almost entirely from notes written by Berlioz.[62] This sort of occurrence was quite common. Berlioz was for instance continually writing little advertisements for his forthcoming concerts, or notices about his concerts outside France, and sending them to newspapers and journals. Other composers engaged in similar practices; Meyerbeer had perfected the art of self-advertisement, though usually his secretary wrote the notices. In later articles, however, d'Ortigue expresses ideas, such as his opinion of the "Dies Irae" from the Mozart *Requiem* and of *Fidelio,* that are uncannily similar to those of Berlioz.[63] And in an article about the Opéra-Comique he quotes at length an unidentified opinion on the changes that needed to be made to the Opéra-Comique. Although he qualifies his quotation simply with "this is what has been said, and well said," the nature of the comments unambiguously points to Berlioz.[64]

D'Ortigue was involved all his life in bringing about reforms in church music in Paris and was particularly interested in the restitution of Gregorian chant. He wrote extensively on church music (both articles and books) and on the music of Beethoven and Berlioz. He clearly was a figure of major importance in the musical life at the time.[65]

Although Fétis, Mainzer, and Castil-Blaze all, to an extent, wrote or arranged music, Berlioz was the only critic during the 1830s who was really an active composer as well as critic. Desnoyers and Blaze de Bury were basically literary critics interested in music, and I would agree with H. Robert Cohen's classification of Fétis and d'Ortigue as critic-historians.[66] In conclusion, though most papers and journals at this time (1834–36) did not have regular and informed criticism, there was nevertheless a move towards achieving it and, certainly amongst a small group of critics, an awareness and interest in the present and future role of the music critic.

2

Music Critics with a Social Conscience

For some music critics of the 1830s, social issues were a vital concern. Ralph P. Locke's *Music, Musicians, and the Saint-Simonians* studies the Saint-Simonians' use of music and the movement's influence on contemporary musicians. Its influence on music criticism, in particular that of Fétis and d'Ortigue, has aroused some interest.[1] The music criticism examined in this section however is that written by converted Saint-Simonians. This shall be followed by a brief discussion of the work of a music critic with a social conscience, Joseph Mainzer, already mentioned in the previous chapter, who worked in Paris in the 1830s. Mainzer is interesting on two counts, for his own music criticism and for the music criticism that his singing classes provoked.

The effects of the Industrial Revolution really only became apparent in France during the July Monarchy, when rural craftsmen thrown out of work by the introduction of machinery left the provinces for Paris only to encounter high unemployment and appalling living conditions. The uprising of 1830 had renewed revolutionary consciousness. The startling poverty of the working classes forced itself upon the consciousness of the rest of society. One of the groups most sensitive to their plight was the literati—the "social romantics," George Sand, Victor Hugo, Alfred de Vigny, and Lamartine, to name the most well known. The novels of George Sand in particular typify the new social and political commitment of the novelist; as one of her contemporaries said "the world she lived in never received a wound from which her heart did not bleed."[2]

The literary critic Sainte-Beuve wrote in *Le Globe* October 1830: "People and poets are going to walk together, from now on art is the common ground, in the arena with everyone, side by side with tireless humanity."[3] One of the features of the new cheap press introduced in 1836 by Emile de Girardin was the *roman feuilleton* or serialized novel. The first great success in this genre was Eugène Sue's *Les Mystères de Paris* which, with its subject matter of the "working classes," had an enormously enthusiastic following amongst the newly emerging literate working class.

The terms "the people" and "the working classes," it should be stressed, became widespread only during the July Monarchy, when there was a change of terminology from "the mob" and "the populace" to "the people," and a change from talking of crime and the criminal classes to poverty and the laboring and working classes.[4]

During the first half of the nineteenth century, France was in a state of political experimentation. After the revolution the old social systems were lost, as was the authority of the church. Political idealists were suddenly free to propose new systems, and many did, the two most important ideologies being those put forward by Saint-Simon and Charles Fourier (later labeled utopian socialists by Marx). Not concerned with changing class structures, Saint-Simon and Fourier were mainly interested in harmonizing class divisions. In both systems, the arts and in particular music played an important role. It was the theories of Saint-Simon that had the strongest influence on music criticism and both directly and indirectly influenced many of the artists, musicians, and writers of the 1830s. The movement also produced some music criticism of its own which, though not of a very high standard, forms an interesting element in the overall pattern of music criticism of the time.

Henri, Comte de Saint-Simon (1760–1825) called for the construction of a new society which, with science and industry as its twin pillars, would have as two of its principal aims the abolition of all privileges of birth and the universal fraternity of mankind. This social reorganization would be based on industrial co-operation, managerial efficiency, and the development of a technocratic elite. Saint-Simon envisaged a society in which industry owners and workers would work harmoniously together, with the workers having faith in the managers' judgments and decisions, and in which stability, not equality, was the object.[5]

A book written by Saint-Simon in 1825, *Nouveau Christianisme*, contained two important developments: first, Saint-Simonism was described in terms of a religious movement with its own structure and hierarchy, and second, the artist assumed an important role within the organization of society. Both these aspects became increasingly important to followers of the movement, and by 1830, after the death of Saint-Simon himself, Saint-Simonism was spoken of by many as a religion, with artists as its prophets.[6]

The leading manifesto of the Saint-Simonian conception of the artist's role is written by Emile Barrault and entitled *Aux artistes: Du passé et de l'avenir des beaux-arts*.[7] Barrault elaborated upon the Saint-Simonian conception of history as consisting of two distinct types of period, an organic one and a critical one. In the former, the artist was integral to society, and his work was directed towards the moral improvement and uplifting of society, all of society being unified by a single set of values. The most dramatic example of an organic period was the Middle Ages, with the Gothic cathedral the central "art-work." On the other hand, in a critical period, for instance the Roman Empire, the artist was isolated and concerned with the self rather than society.

Barrault's article, which contains his famous catchphrase, "the fine arts are the cult and the artist is the priest," is an appeal to artists to come and take their place as leaders of humanity.[8] He described the artist as a unique being possessed of special spiritual privileges, with an intuitive understanding of social problems and of God and an ability to convey this understanding to humanity at large by means of his direct appeal to the emotions.

Enfantin, the leader of the movement after the death of Saint-Simon, also wrote on the role of the artist.[9] He defined the artist as "the man who always leads others back to social unity. Social sympathy, or in other words, the *Love* of God, alone dictates to him his acts and his words."[10] Of all the arts, music was cited by Barrault as the most powerful as it was the only language common to all men. Music symbolized the harmonious society and it soared above the rational and intellectual spheres, uniting men on a purely emotional level. Barrault, as spokesman for the Saint-Simonian movement, was asking the artist to become a leader of society under the guidance of the movement; as one writer ironically put it, the arts were being requisitioned as the best publicity agent.[11]

One of the most puzzling questions about this rather confused conception of the artist's role in society is what exactly was meant by the word "artist." From Barrault's article one has the impression that the artist is not in any way someone with a technical skill, with a craft. His power seems rather to be a disembodied emotional gift.[12] More significantly, after espousing his belief in the great role to which the artist is destined, Barrault cries, "And we too, we are artists!" where the "we" presumably refers to himself and the other leaders of the Saint-Simonian movement.[13] His final appeal to the artist reads: "Come, come then to us, all those whose heart knows how to love, and whose brows can be inflamed by noble hope! Let us join our efforts to lead humanity towards this future."[14]

This concept of what constitutes an artist is obviously very special; it appears to be defined more by the attitude to society than by any particular skill. As Paul Bénichou astutely asks, was the artist to become a priest or vice-versa? Another Saint-Simonian tract quoted men such as Moses, Jesus, and Luther as poets alongside such prophets as Rabelais, Molière, Byron, Napoléon, and others.[15] Ralph P. Locke points out that behind the rhetoric of Barrault's essay (and it was after all a recruitment call), "one can begin to see that the artist is still being called, not to discover ideas, but to spread them, not to lead humanity, but to 'join efforts' with those who are already leading it in a chosen direction. . . . [I]n his eagerness to persuade artists, he [Barrault] placed the emphasis where it suited his purpose, on the centrality of the artist's role, even to the point of proclaiming . . . that the artist was now the priest."[16] This was not something that the rest of the movement's leaders would have fully agreed with. Indeed the Saint-Simonian Eugène Rodrigues clearly placed the artist subordinate to the priest: "The *artist* . . . is the *word* [*verbe*] of the PRIEST."[17]

This confusion over what constituted an artist might explain why artists did not join the Saint-Simonian movement in large numbers. Nevertheless, quite a number of artists were interested in the theories of Saint-Simon during the 1830s: Vigny, Sainte-Beuve, Sand, Heine, Liszt, Nourrit, Léon Halévy, Hiller, Mendelssohn, Félicien David, and even Berlioz. The composer Félicien David was the only one to commit himself whole-heartedly to the movement.[18]

Liszt's involvement with the movement is intriguing, and has been examined by Thérèse Marix-Spire and more recently by Ralph P. Locke.[19] Though himself fêted by society, Liszt was very aware of the subordinate role society accorded artists in general and found the notion of the artist as "priest" and leader very appealing. He wrote a series of controversial articles on the role of the artist-musician in society. These articles showed great concern for the way in which art seemed to be heading.[20] Ralph P. Locke's article on Liszt and Saint-Simonism explains that although Liszt disassociated himself vigorously from the movement during the 1830s, 1840s, and 1850s, at the end of his life he admitted the influence Saint-Simon had had on him.[21] This influence (alongside the influence of Lamennais) is apparent in Liszt's life if one looks at the way he abandoned his virtuosic career for a life of serious composition of orchestral and piano music,[22] his deep concern for innovations in church music, his general philanthropic attitude, and his habit of giving free piano lessons, benefit concerts, and the like.[23]

Berlioz's brief involvement with Saint-Simonism has also been charted by Ralph P. Locke.[24] Locke states that despite the fact that Berlioz's name does not figure in any of the Saint-Simonian archives,[25] he displayed an interest in the movement which extended beyond the famous letter he wrote to the Saint-Simonian Charles Duveyrier.[26] The letter, written in 1831, is full of hot-blooded enthusiasm for the social side of the movement, though Berlioz always retained his skepticism for religion of any genre. Locke instances several areas which he felt could be interpreted as demonstrating Berlioz's sympathy for the cause, such as his continued friendship with the Saint-Simonian Tajan-Rogé,[27] the scenario in his proposed oratorio *Le Dernier Jour du monde,* and his lifelong dream of an "Utopie fraternelle." Locke concludes that Berlioz realized that "Utopie fraternelle" was only a dream, but a sublime dream, and one that he could never forget.

Whatever the direct influence the Saint-Simonians had on Berlioz, he did share some of their concerns and frequently wrote scathingly about the low standard of musical life in Paris and the maltreatment of the artist. To give an example:

The *Adagio* in *A flat* serving as a foil to the *quadrille* of *la brise du matin!* This is indecent and could only happen with a nation as frivolous as ours, where the dignity of art and that of the artist are entirely unrecognized. This monstrosity could only appear normal to those good bourgeois who are *amused* by everything and willingly consent to listen for a minute to Beethoven during the intervals of a galop and a waltz because they have *heard it said* that he was a *very good* German musician.[28]

He appeared however to have felt some ambivalence about the power of the artist. On the one hand he could applaud Liszt's aim to bring music to the people, saying, "Less than ever before is it the time to hold oneself aloof, since there is a job to be done, and the materials are there."[29] On the other hand, in a review he denigrated the Saint-Simonian ambiance at the tenor Nourrit's funeral, saying, "All this jumble of theater, theology, republicanism, and love of absolute domination seems to me to be prodigiously absurd."[30] Perhaps it was only the Saint-Simonian rhetoric to which Berlioz objected, for he continues his description of Nourrit's funeral: "This is touching however and is very upsetting for those who have intimately known this unfortunate man."[31]

The early 1830s was probably the period in his life when Berlioz was most sympathetic towards any "socialist" ideas.[32] His accounts to his family of the July uprising are enthusiastic to the point of being rather manic, talking of the "magic revolution" and the "sublime people!" Berlioz felt guilty that he had not been more actively involved in the uprising:

> This idea, that so many brave people paid with their blood for winning our liberties while I am one of the many who did nothing, does not leave me a moment's rest. It is another torture.[33]

He was filled with naïve optimism for the future of the country, in particular for the arts:

> Fortunately we are approaching the emancipation of the theater, this revolution is designed to free the arts; I will succeed ten times earlier than I would have without it.[34]

This view was not shared by the political leaders of the July uprising, but suggesting as it does the influence of Saint-Simonism, points to Berlioz's awareness of the movement. Also, at a slightly later date, he expressed admiration for Lamennais whom he had met at d'Ortigue's house: "Lamennais; genius consumes him, eats him up, burns in him!! What a devil of a man! He made me vibrate with admiration."[35]

For a short period, then, Berlioz was quite emotionally involved with the concept of a political and artistic regeneration of society. His correspondence of 1831 showed an interest in the workers' uprisings in both Lyons and Bristol. His enthusiasm apparently frightened his mother, for in a letter to her Berlioz denied political involvement of any kind, saying that such subjects only bored him.[36] By 1832, he was expressing skepticism about the productiveness of such uprisings[37] and for the rest of his life he was to describe himself as apolitical, as for instance in this extract: "You know perhaps that I write the music feuilleton for *Le*

Rénovateur, a legitimist newspaper. I want to have it sent to you. . . . As I am not at all serious about politics, you can imagine that the color of the newspaper means absolutely nothing to me. I never touch on anything that is outside my domain."[38] Pierre Citron postulates, correctly I think, that Berlioz's apoliticism was largely the result of distaste for the way the political uprisings developed.[39] Certainly the July 1848 revolution evoked only disgust in Berlioz: "Paris . . . [is] a *club* of madmen and idiots, shouting, gesticulating, conspiring, writing, without knowing what they yell, what they scribble, whom they menace, and what they demand."[40] He despaired for the future of art:

> With things in such a state, to dream of peaceful intelligent work, of the quest for the beautiful in literature and the arts, is like wanting to play a game of billiards on a ship broken by a storm from the Antarctic pole, the moment when a leak in the hold is announced and an insurrection of sailors between decks.[41]

Numerous publications were put out by the Saint-Simonians, such as *Le Producteur, L'Organisateur,* and *Prédications,* and all were basically propagandist.[42] In October 1830 the Saint-Simonians bought and took over *Le Globe* as a "house" journal to propagate their ideas, retaining editorial control until April 1832.[43] It is interesting to look at the type of music criticism written for the paper during this time—the criticism, that is, written by converts to the movement, not just by people like d'Ortigue who were attracted to certain of its ideas.

Most of the music criticism for *Le Globe* appears to have been written by the one person, who unfortunately did not sign or initial his articles. However, towards the end of 1831 and early in 1832 there are a few different critics writing, and in 1832 some reviews are signed by Adolphe Guéroult.[44] The tone and subject matter of Guéroult's signed reviews suggest he was also the author of a number of the earlier unsigned articles, particularly on the Théâtre Italien.[45]

Not all the criticism in *Le Globe* shows the influence of the paper's politics. In fact at the beginning there are some reviews of the Opéra-Comique that could have come from any of the daily political papers. Those reviews that were written with a Saint-Simonian slant are propagandist. Although these writers predictably disapproved of certain areas—such as the Opéra Balls and the vaudeville that depicted only the felicity of peasant life, excluding the misery—on the whole they shared the subject choice of the average newspaper critic in reviewing almost exclusively operatic music. This is not very unusual for the time but does also reflect the fact that vocal music was favored by the Saint-Simonians for being more able to convey an ideological message.[46]

The bulk of the *Le Globe* criticism makes compelling reading. The serious, earnest tone of the critic, at times sentimental, at times dramatically rhetorical, glows with a keen fervor and sincerity. Not wanting in any way to be part of the frivolous society he so despised, his prose is even self-consciously serious. In one review he hastens to justify the use of some gentle sarcasm saying that perhaps, at times, such means are the only way to attract the attention of a facile public.[47]

A recurring image in the criticism is that of the artist versus the audience. The white-gloved members of the dilettante audience snigger behind lorgnettes and gossip coldly about the artists in between applause. The audience is egotistical, hard-hearted, superficial, incapable of understanding or aiding the artist in any way. The artist is to some extent a plaything, treated as a source of amusement and no more. The critic for *Le Globe* aims to change the audience, shake it from its egotism, "refind its heart from inside the suffocating, icy envelope that grips it," and also to alert the artists to the more dignified and dynamic role that they could fill in society.[48] The considerable discussion of the malaises of contemporary society that this aim requires at times seems pertinent and enlivens the review, and at other times seems quite gratuitous.

I shall first give some examples of the former. In a review of a concert by a child prodigy, eight-year-old guitarist Jules Regondi, the critic argues very sensitively about the humiliations of displaying children before the public. He talks of the need for a new society where all children, whatever their birth, will be educated and will be allowed neither to perish from hunger nor to have their talent exhausted before a room full of "idlers."[49] In a review of Weber's *Oberon* the critic discusses with pathos the suffering in Weber's last years and how nobody in society was prepared to help him (Berlioz was to say much the same thing at a later date).[50] And, as a final example, in a review with the provocative title "The Bishops and the Opéra" the critic (this time signed Cavel) argues that a recent government subsidy which gave more money to the head of the Opéra than to the Church was an indication that people were now more interested in opera than religion. This leads him to stress the awesome position of leadership that artists could assume and the need for more worthy sentiments to be expressed in opera.[51]

It is disappointing that much of the criticism in *Le Globe* appears not to have been written from within a theoretical framework, but rather to have had theory applied to it as a structure superimposed at various points. The critic has to keep reminding himself to bear in mind the ideological expectations of the journal. Highly rhetorical language abruptly appears, often making for a disconcerting change of literary style.

A review in 1831 of *Robert le diable* is a striking example of this. Three-quarters of the review consists of a straightforward description of libretto and music, both of which the author finds admirable but with a few reservations. In the middle of the description of the third act he suddenly self-consciously breaks the narrative:

I was up to here in my account, and I was getting carried away by the taste and emotions of this beautiful world full of feathers, flowers, and precious stones, taking pleasure in recreating just as I had felt them, the strange beauties of this great drama where all the prestiges of art are assembled; but just then a horrible piece of news was circulated. The workers of Lyons in full revolt, the cannon sweeping the squares and streets; finally, the mutilated people, master of the town, hanging this new type of slogan from the public monuments:

> Live working
> Or die fighting.

I was no longer in the mood for either Robert, or Mademoiselle Taglioni, or the prodigious décor of Ciceri. The people emaciated, starving, in pain; the people ignorant, sickly and coarse.[52]

The review of *Robert le diable* is completely abandoned. The author continues by asking who will come to the aid of the workers of Lyons. He answers the question himself, with a flamboyant appeal to artists:

O artists! brilliant, exalted troupe; you who possess the genius for all seductions and know how to enrapture jaded souls with the spectacle of your marvelous creations; you who make your life one of charming away troubles and multiplying the joys of the century's fortunate ones, will you never unite to move them, to stir them into love for the suffering masses?[53]

It is not clear whether the writer is proposing that the artists should go to the aid of the workers in Lyons, or merely appealing to artists in general to direct the attention of the bourgeoisie to the plight of the masses.[54] It is as though the writer has introduced the situation of the workers at Lyons simply to talk about the social role of the artist.

The critic completes his review of *Robert le diable* the following week with an extremely long, minutely descriptive, and enthusiastic article on all aspects of the opera. This time he closes with a short two-paragraph homily beginning, "This opera proves to us that music, dance, stage design, in a word, all the arts for which the Académie Royale is the focus, are getting better day by day, even when their complete absence of social inspiration imprisons them in a narrow, cold realm."[55] He concludes somewhat ambiguously that he is very pleased at the progress made at the Opéra, because artists are about to be called upon to fulfil a great mission; this, he claims, is why he mingles with them (does he mean goes to the Opéra?) in order to show them how to fulfil that mission.

A review of a concert of Paganini turns into a plaint on the "maux du siècle," followed by a recruitment call:

Here come leaders of nations, men strong of head, heart, and arms, who will classify you according to your capacity, love you like fathers, fill you with social inspiration, command glory for you! See the numerous artists grouping around you in chorus to share deliciously with you, in the voice of the pontiffs of the future, exciting the people to their peaceful, creative work in science and in industry.[56]

There is a patronizing tone in this call coupled with a curious naïveté about the creative artist. Ralph P. Locke comments that the Saint-Simonians gave few details about the kind of music they wished composers to write.[57] The criticism in *Le Globe* reinforces this and suggests also that their critics had little background musical knowledge and certainly not much idea about the aims and desires of the creative artist.

Another common trait in these reviews is an unease fed by guilt at taking pleasure in enjoying music that was being enjoyed at the same time by a large audience of so-called "idlers" ("oisifs"). The reviewer feels impelled to make some statement about the rest of the audience and also to demonstrate that he is not just mindlessly enjoying the music, but is at the same time continually aware of the larger social issues. To an extent this was also one of the points being made in the review of *Robert le diable,* and it occurs as well in reviews of Rossini's music. In an amusing review of *Tancrède,* for instance, the critic starts his review by talking of the two different worlds that exist: one of the woman leaving the Opéra wrapped in her coat or cashmere shawl, passing unnoticed a man dead from hunger, and one of a man such as he who is troubled by such things. He asks sententiously:

> Is it my fault if, apropos *Tancrède,* with the memory of this charming composition full of freshness, tenderness, and chivalrous exaltation, such somber thoughts come back to me? Is it my fault if with the cries of those that die of hunger, that fall petrified, stiff with cold, I disturb the complacency of those who swoon with enthusiasm at the harmonious accents of a music that is not the pathetic expression of such deplorable miseries?[58]

Having shown his moral depth, the critic then launches safely into a very enthusiastic review of the opera: "Oh! how I love this *Tancrède.*"[59] The review is not allowed to finish however without a closing lesson, which starts with the critic expressing his guilt at having so enjoyed the opera, especially in a world where the arts are reserved to only a few, and concludes, "I am almost ashamed to give in to the pleasure of letting myself be rocked by these delicious cadences."[60] He appeals to the public always to remember the voice of the "suffering class," even when plunged in the midst of some self-indulgent entertainment, and also to look out for occasions where the "masses" are singing. Once again this demonstration of social awareness on the part of the critic appears quite gratuitous and not linked in any real way with his review of the opera.

Neither Emile Barrault nor Enfantin was a follower of Italian opera; indeed both were strong supporters of the Austro-German tradition.[61] On the other hand, the Saint-Simonian Olinde Rodrigues suggested that for composers of the Saint-Simonian cause a combination of the musical techniques of Rossini and Beethoven would be ideal.[62] It is more Rodrigues's approach that the critic in *Le*

Globe follows, although it is not necessarily Beethoven that he balances with Rossini but rather what he terms the "German school of composition." He feels that basically the sad, "somber, and tender" music of the German school responded more to the suffering and melancholy disposition of the man of the time, but that the ideal would be a combination of German science, unity, and sensibility with Italian inexhaustible variety, gaiety, and facility.[63] However, it seems likely that our *Globe* critic secretly enjoyed Italian opera more than German. The very words he uses to describe the shortcomings of German music, "oddities," "monotony," "too obvious display of workmanship," suggest that these features may in fact dominate for him. Nevertheless he enthusiastically throws down the gauntlet to future composers to try their hand at combining the two schools, in writing music aimed at the betterment of society.[64] A short article on the instrumental music of Ferdinand Hiller gives another example of this appeal to the two schools.[65] As Ralph P. Locke states, Hiller was obviously seen by the Saint-Simonians as a potential recruit for the cause because it was rare that any nonvocal music was reviewed for *Le Globe*.[66]

The evidence of a preference for Italian music and in particular the music of Rossini becomes more pronounced towards the end of the paper's days. Adolphe Guéroult, for instance, writes as an unabashed Rossini devotee. One isolated review of a Conservatoire concert in 1832, signed "C. N.," also expresses great enthusiasm for Beethoven, but rather than suggesting a fusion of Beethoven with Rossini the writer just wishes that Beethoven could be performed by ten thousand players with armies of choirs so that everyone, not just the small Conservatoire concert audience, could appreciate his greatness.[67]

The focus of these reviews is hard to define. They appear to be aimed at the artists more than *Le Globe*'s reading audience which would presumably have largely consisted of those already interested, or involved, in Saint-Simonism.

The main aim of the articles is perhaps the demonstration of the critic's "good faith," his understanding of the important role to be assumed by the artist. It is unfortunate that the critics of *Le Globe* did not have a greater knowledge of music, but the reviews are nevertheless interesting, and unusual for the time.

Several other journals had criticism of a Saint-Simonian bent. One example is the *Revue Encyclopédique,* which from 1831 until 1835 was edited by two dissident Saint-Simonians, Hippolyte Carnot and Pierre Leroux. The criticism for the *Revue Encyclopédique* was not as propagandist as criticism for *Le Globe,* but it did make some practical demands. For instance it agitated for music for the people, for reforms in church music, and for things such as a larger hall and more easily obtainable seats for the Conservatoire concerts.[68] However, the music criticism for this paper also suffered from a lack of musical expertise. It is revealing that when discussing the moral influence of music on the proletariat, one of the paper's literary critics, Hippolyte Fortoul, uses Meyerbeer's *Robert le diable* as an example:

The idealistic and intimate score of *Robert le diable*, has also been properly understood and just as clearly judged by him [the proletariat] as by the dilettantes. Should you invite him often to such emotions, he will return home more serious, happier, more thoughtful, and more moral.[69]

Even if the example had been a work as "uplifting" as Beethoven's *Fidelio*, Fortoul's remarks would have been equally naïve.

The extent to which the vocabulary of the Saint-Simonian movement infiltrated contemporary music criticism has been interestingly analyzed in Dorothy Hagan's dissertation *French Musical Criticism between the Revolutions*. Hagan talks of Heine's rebellion against the Saint-Simonian influence and his desire for a strong separation of art, politics, and religion. She also quotes a review by Blaze de Bury where, agreeing with Heine, he expostulates: "According to the extravagant theories now current, [a musical composition] has no value or meaning unless it teaches a lesson or enunciates a dogma. . . . One of these days will see Plato's dialogues set to music."[70] Théophile Gautier in his preface to *Mademoiselle de Maupin* satirizes the utilitarian line taken by many literary critics:

What good is this book? In what way can it be applied to the moralization and the well-being of the most numerous and poorest class? What? Not a word of the needs of the society, nothing civilizing or progressive? . . . Society suffers, it is prey to a great internal rending apart (translate: no one wants to subscribe to useful newspapers). It is up to the poet to look at the cause of this sickness and cure it. He will find the means to do so in sympathizing heart and soul with humanity (philanthropic poets!—this would be something rare and charming).[71]

To have exerted a pervasive influence on music criticism the Saint-Simonian movement did not need great music critics. Its influence is evident in the criticism of people, such as d'Ortigue, who were not participating members, but whose search for a moral music criticism can be linked to Saint-Simonian concepts.[72] Perhaps Desnoyers was cognizant of the movement's ideas on art; his criticism at times suggests that he was, as does also the criticism of Fétis. Joseph Mainzer would certainly have been familiar with the movement's aims.

Joseph Mainzer was forced into political exile from Germany in 1833 and moved to Brussels and then Paris. In Paris, Mainzer gained his livelihood by his activity as a critic, writing for a large number of journals, some only occasionally: *La Balance, Revue Musicale, Revue des Deux Mondes*, and some on a more regular basis: *Le National, Revue et Gazette Musicale* and *La France Musicale*. Mainzer's reputation during his Paris *séjour* however came mainly from the series of free evening singing classes he set up to teach the working man. These classes drew such numbers that they attracted the attention of the police of Louis-Philippe, under the suspicion that no such large gathering of workers could be innocent. Mainzer's classes were extremely popular and indeed became quite an attraction in Paris for visitors and intrigued locals.

Critics—by critics I am referring to a random survey of reviews of Mainzer's classes in the daily press—and literati, such as George Sand, referred to the composition of Mainzer's choir as the "working class," the "real people." Reference is frequently made to muscular arms and working clothes. It is therefore surprising to find, in a review by Charles Merruau in *Le Temps* 1837, a list of the composition of the choir, most of whose professions, he remarks, are those that demand "the most highly developed intelligence, and in some way or another touch on the arts." He lists printers, engravers, silversmiths, sculptors, book-binders, metal founders, joiners, and even a few students.[73] If we add to this list our attendant critics, and an interested audience of composers, artists, literati (Meyerbeer, Berlioz, Liszt, Lamartine, Hugo, George Sand, Vigny all attended from time to time), and foreign visitors to Paris, quite a different picture builds up of the composition of the classes.

The literate artisan class was the one most interested in bettering its condition economically, socially, and politically. At the end of 1830, three newspapers were published specifically for this new audience—*Journal des Ouvriers, L'Artisan,* and *Le Peuple.* So it is not surprising that this group formed the basis of Mainzer's choirs. They were later to form the basis of the *Orphéon* movement too. What is apparent from the reviews of Mainzer's concerts is that the majority of critics and literati had a fixed vision of the working classes which they superimposed on the reality of the situation. They enjoyed presenting an emotional picture of men whose coarse exteriors concealed noble simple hearts which needed only to be stimulated by the double enchantment of uplifting texts and music to become transfigured; art was alien to them and hence a revelation. The critics wanted to perceive the choir as composed of the lumpen proletariat, and not of skilled tradesmen, many of whom were engaged in highly artistic activities already.

The sentimentalizing of the working classes evident in these reviews is very much part of the trend in popular literature of the day, of which the novels of Sue are but the best-known example. The following quotation signed F. Liszt but generally acknowledged as being by Marie d'Agoult is very representative:

> While the elegant world hurries each evening to the dazzling halls of our lyric theaters, in the depths of a suburb, in the glimmer of several ancient lamps hung on four naked walls, gather, once a week, men coarsely clothed, with muscular arms, with intelligent eyes, listening with a childlike submission to the teaching of a professor who devoutly dedicates himself to a noble and saintly task; that of the musical education of the people.[74]

Of course just because these critics were sentimental does not mean that they lacked any genuine feeling and concern for the disadvantaged; in a sense they were just making use of a rhetorical mode which had been established as the appropriate way to talk about the working classes. One does suspect however that the critic is simply reveling in his own patronage, which is why many of the reviews are unsatisfactory; they say little about what actually happens in the classes, and more about the critic's self-conscious response to the concept of the "working class."

Mainzer himself was obviously firmly convinced of the moral value of his classes, even referring to them as a "school of moralization."[75] He said that singing softened the rigors of poverty and consoled those who suffered, but more than that he felt that music (vocal music with texts) could change the "lax" morals of the worker, and make him go home after work instead of drinking in the bar. In social terms "singing" could make men more contented with their lot both in the home and in society. Mainzer's view of the social role of art fits into what Ralph P. Locke has labeled the "'democratic' or 'recreational' view [that] sees in art a wholesome leisure-time activity for all the active, productive members of society, even the most humble."[76]

Although most of the criticism of Mainzer's classes tells us more about the critics than the classes, this in itself is interesting as it shows to what extent prevailing notions of the working class infiltrated the criticism of the day. The most striking thing about these notions is just how middle class they were. Obviously the critics's idea of moral improvement was the adoption of middle class values. The fact that, on the whole, they did not pass any sort of judgment on the standard of music performed, or the standard of the singing, was a reflection of the way they viewed the working class. In ethical terms Mainzer and his critics did not question that the morality they advocated was perhaps not as congenial to "subordinate groups" as it was to their own way of life.

Mainzer's own criticism shows an interesting mixture of conservative and progressive tendencies. Perhaps it could be classified as being politically adventurous and aesthetically conservative—not, of course, an uncommon combination.

He used a large amount of his criticism as a venue for propaganda for his theories on music education. Many of these articles were drawn from his book *Singschule* (1833) and are used again in English translation in *Singing for the Million* (1841). Mainzer clearly was hoping for some sort of official position in singing instruction in Paris and these articles certainly would have put his name and theories before the public eye. Also, he felt a kind of missionary fervor for his work; he was after all not charging for his classes and given his theories on music's social and moral force, his criticism takes on a political significance. If carried through to their logical conclusion his theories could only be interpreted as propaganda for a better society.

In certain aspects Mainzer's criticism shows similar idealistic trends to other criticism of the time, for instance, that of Berlioz. Mainzer points despairingly to the materialism of the century to which music too had fallen prey.

As a devoted follower of Rousseau, Mainzer was convinced of the fundamental superiority of vocal music to instrumental music. His most repeated complaint is the lack of vocal music performed at concerts, as he said: "Without vocal music, all repertoire is monotonous. . . . If instrumental music is not supported by poetry it is vague and difficult to understand. . . . [I]nstrumental music has only second place in the musical domain."[77] Also, of course, as with the Saint-Simonians, Mainzer saw music with texts as a superior means of education. He even felt that vibrations of the human voice had a unique capacity that other instruments lacked for evoking sympathetic vibrations in the listener.

Mainzer's reviews of concerts other than those traditionally reviewed present a picture of Parisian musical life that is not generally covered by the daily press. *Le National* (where he wrote most frequently) was obviously sympathetic to his views and allowed him fairly broad scope. Some of the areas he covered for them were the musical education of the blind, national music, outdoor music, the prohibition of instrumental music in churches, and so on.

Of these areas one of the most interesting is his criticism of concerts at the Institution des Jeunes Aveugles.[78] These reviews contain a clear social message.[79]

I shall examine them in a little detail. First of all Mainzer praises the Institution for giving the students an opportunity to learn music and have training as musicians, and hence the possibility of a role in society outside the traditional one of beggar. He says that he was prepared to be indulgent about the quality of execution of the young musicians but was instead astounded by the precision and assurance of their ensemble work and their profound musical sensitivity. He regrets, predictably, that the concert was all instrumental—no vocal numbers. In the course of his reviews of the Institution concerts Mainzer makes some quite specific complaints.

First, he wonders whether orchestral work (ensemble work) is the best training for blind musicians, suggesting that instead more emphasis should be placed on preparing them for jobs for which it has been shown that they are ideally suited, such as organists, music teachers, or solo performers.[80] He hints that although the orchestral concert was an impressive display of what they could do, ultimately it was not as orchestral players that they would be able to find jobs.

Second, he complains about the actual physical condition of the building of the Institution which he said was cramped, dingy, unhealthy, and very damp. The implication seems to be that its inhabitants could not see to complain. What is the point, he asks, of giving the blind an education if at the same time you are destroying their health for the rest of their lives? Mainzer repeats these complaints in his various reviews of the concerts; he is clearly very concerned with making a social comment, and obviously hopes that something might come of his complaints.

Mainzer would have agreed with G. B. Shaw's maxim that the critic's main aim was to agitate for reforms. Apart from his active propaganda for his singing classes, he makes some quite specific demands about reforms in the Parisian musical life. The majority of these reforms concern the teaching of vocal music.

Mainzer's criticism is thus prescriptive on both a practical and on a more theoretical level. On a practical level, he made specific complaints about Parisian musical life and suggested changes that could be made. On a more theoretical level, underlying all his criticism is the supposition that society can be changed for the better through the medium of vocal music. Although clearly influenced by current socialist theories, Mainzer was apparently not directly involved in a political movement. His vocabulary is not permeated to any great degree by the jargon of utopian socialism. Rousseau, if anyone, is the greatest influence on his criticism.

Even if Mainzer's theories must finally be seen as a by-product of bourgeois idealism they were nevertheless based on passionate personal moral conviction. Just as the writers of social romanticism, for instance Lamartine and Hugo, did not really enunciate a method to put at the service of their idealism,[81] Mainzer and the reviewers of his classes did not express any consistent theories or even any real opinion on the social problems of the working class. But the fact remains that whether patronizing, sentimental, superficial, or reflective and perceptive, whether sincere or merely following a fashion, their criticism existed, it was read by the public, and along with the literature of the social romantics and popular serial novels helped prepare the spirit of the 1848 revolution.

3

Berlioz's Position as a Critic

Berlioz's Relationship to the Journals and Newspapers to Which He Contributed

Berlioz's articles written during the Restoration number only fourteen and none of them are signed in full. The major journals to which he contributed during this time, *Le Corsaire, Le Correspondant,* and the *Berliner Allgemeine Musikalische Zeitung,* were not principally political journals and were relatively unharassed by government press regulations. Berlioz's articles for each journal were obviously controlled to an extent by the editor's interests and desires, though in each case the style and mode of expression used in the articles remained recognizable as Berlioz's own.

Berlioz's first step into journalism was certainly not timorous. His articles for *Le Corsaire* are highly opinionated and flamboyant.[1] The only pointer to the author's youth—he was twenty years old—is perhaps the arrogance of some of the statements. For instance, his claim in the 1824 article to know all Gluck from memory, though undoubtedly true, has a swaggering ring, a tone absent from later reviews.

Le Corsaire (Journal de la littérature, des arts, des moeurs et des modes) ran from 1822 to 1852 and during that time underwent many transformations. At the time Berlioz was contributing to it, it was a gossipy, satirical paper which claimed to be stimulating debate with provocative articles on issues such as "romanticism," the vogue for Italian things, and dilettantism. Both the tone and subject matter of Berlioz's three "Polémiques" for the *Corsaire* are very much in keeping with the tenor of the journal; they are informal, sarcastically witty, and lively.

The central concerns of the articles are on the one hand attacking the Théâtre Italien, Italian vocal technique, the monopoly of Rossini, and ignorance of the dilettante, and on the other promoting, in particular, the ill-appreciated merits of Gluck, and, in passing, Méhul, Sacchini, Salieri (*Les Danaïdes*), and Spontini (*La Vestale*). These and similar issues are discussed in Berlioz's correspondence of this time where he talks, for instance, of the "virus" of dilettantism.[2] All three *Corsaire* "Polémiques" take the form of letters to the editor, so presumably they were instigated by Berlioz himself. All discuss issues Berlioz felt very strongly about. As Pierre Citron comments, apropos an amusing letter from Berlioz to Edouard Rocher in which he chastises Rocher for lying about attending Salieri's *Les Danaïdes,* Berlioz was so fanatical about music at this time that his friends did not dare admit not having been to hear an opera that he had recommended to them.[3] The 1825 *Corsaire* "Polémique" ends with a scathing condemnation of Castil-Blaze, in particular for his review of Gluck's *Armide,* but also indirectly for everything Castil-Blaze stood for, both as a critic and as a composer-arranger. Obviously Castil-Blaze's column had been regularly followed by Berlioz, and in the light of his future collaboration with the *Journal des Débats* one could hypothesize a nascent interest in the position as critic held there by Castil-Blaze. On the other hand, since Castil-Blaze's column was the only semiregular music criticism at this time, it is not surprising that Berlioz followed it with interest.

Berlioz does not appear to have written any articles during the years 1826 to 1828, except for an impressive letter he wrote to three papers in 1828, in which he defended himself against criticism for giving a concert comprising only his own music.[4] The years 1826 to 1828 must have been very traumatic ones for Berlioz, with the family frictions over his choice of career, and his desire to prove as soon as possible that he could make a career for himself with his music—a depressingly difficult task then and, indeed, one that would remain so for most of his life.

In a letter to his friend Humbert Ferrand in June 1829 Berlioz claims he is besieged by requests for articles.[5] Although to say "besieged" is probably an exaggeration, if he were being solicited for articles it is odd that this should have taken place as late as 1829, so long after the *Corsaire* "Polémiques." But it is possible that the requests spanned a period of some length. In a letter to his mother in May 1829 Berlioz states as a "fait accompli" that he was the Paris correspondent for the *Berliner Allgemeine Musikalische Zeitung.*[6] The editor of the *Berliner Allgemeine Musikalische Zeitung,* Adolf Marx, was in Paris in 1829 and had perhaps approached Berlioz about the job. This was presumably early in the year, for his first review appears in February. Why Marx approached Berlioz is not known. They might have met by chance—possible enough in Paris in music circles—or Berlioz himself might have offered his services. In the above letter to his mother Berlioz makes it clear that it is not the pay, which was extremely low, that interests him about the job, but the opportunity to become known in Prussia. Later in the same letter he claims that no one knows he is writing for the *Berliner Allgemeine Musikalische Zeitung,* so it is puzzling how he planned to become well known, though presumably most of the people connected with the running of the journal would have known the name of their Paris correspondent. Marx thought highly of Berlioz's music[7] and later in the year published a long analysis of the score of *Huit scènes de Faust*, so perhaps this was the kind of recognition for which Berlioz was hoping.[8]

Berlioz's lively *Corsaire* articles had probably gained him quite a reputation and this seems the most likely reason for Marx's invitation. Berlioz's articles for the *Berliner Allgemeine Musikalische Zeitung* are written in the same lively and witty manner as the articles for *Le Corsaire*. The subject matter had obviously been solicited, because for one thing all the reviews are of actual performances and are not articles on musical issues, and for another they are all reviews of performances of *opéra-comique* and opera. In his reviews of the *opéras-comiques* Berlioz sets his precedent of witty diversions, ineffectually screening his scorn for the lighter manifestations of the genre.

It was in 1829 that Berlioz also began writing for *Le Correspondant*. In a letter to Ferrand written towards the end of 1828 Berlioz asked him if he knew a certain M. d'Eckstein sufficiently well to write a letter of recommendation to him on Berlioz's behalf.[9] He had learned that Eckstein was on the editorial staff of *Le Correspondant* and wanted to know if it would be possible to be given the job of music critic for the paper. Early in 1829 Berlioz had an interview with Carné, the journal's editor, and his first article appeared on 21 April 1829.[10] In the same letter to his mother in which he mentions the *Berliner Allgemeine Musikalische Zeitung* articles Berlioz also talks of his collaboration with *Le Correspondant*, but phrases it so that it looks as if the journal approached him for the articles, rather than the other way around: "The editor asked me via two of his journalists to take charge of the music articles, treated on a grand scale. . . . These gentlemen have paid me all sorts of compliments about this; they write to me every week asking for the second article I have promised them and made them wait a long time for."[11] Such distortion of the truth eloquently testifies to Berlioz's desperate attempts to justify his choice of career in his parents' eyes.

Le Correspondant began 10 March 1829 and in 1831 was replaced by the *Revue Européenne*. Started by Lamennais in the period between his ultramontan- ism and future progressiveness, *Le Correspondant* was the organ of the "Association for the Defense of the Catholic Religion" and had royalist tendencies.[12] Literary and philosophical issues not connected with religion were also discussed in the journal; as Berlioz remarked to Ferrand: "The arts will have a distinguished place there."[13] Berlioz's first article for the journal is appro- priately on the subject of religious music, "Considérations sur la musique religieuse." He was probably asked to write on such a topic, but the subject was also one that genuinely interested him. Three principal issues are raised in the article: first the similarities between religious and dramatic music; second, Berlioz's dislike of dramatically unmotivated academic fugues in religious music; and third, the lack of venues and performers for religious music. All three issues are constantly raised throughout the course of Berlioz's career as a critic and were to become highly relevant to Berlioz's own "religious" music.

His second article for *Le Correspondant* had apparently been another attack on the Théâtre Italien. In a letter to Ferrand, Berlioz tells how the article was considered too harsh, and that he was requested to write something on a different subject. He ironically concluded, "So the Prostitute finds lovers even amongst religious people."[14] No doubt the royalist members of *Le Correspondant* staff would have included many fervent supporters of the Théâtre Italien.

Berlioz's next three articles for *Le Correspondant* consisted of a biographical discussion of Beethoven and his music. These articles mark the beginning of Berlioz's passion for Beethoven's music, which he had heard for the first time at the end of 1827, and he had attended every possible performance since. His correspondence of the time continually refers to the power of Beethoven's music; a letter to his sister Nanci even relates an 1829 performance of Beethoven's last quartets in a very similar fashion to its later discussion in *Le Correspondant* article, 6 October 1829.[15]

An interesting aspect of these *Correspondant* articles on Beethoven is Berlioz's emphasis on "suffering" in relation to great art; in Berlioz's opinion, Beethoven becomes really great only after he has suffered, and he, Berlioz, is one of the few to understand the Beethoven late quartets, because he too has suffered and can therefore empathize with them. Berlioz's letters of 1829 to 1830 talk incessantly of his suffering, "this *capacity for suffering* which is killing me,"[16] and he saw it as distinguishing him from ordinary men. The anguish he suffered was intimately connected with music, since music was the one means of delivering him from his very singular states of emotional agony:

> There is in me a violent *expansionary force,* I see this immense horizon, this sun, and I suffer so much, so much, that if I did not contain myself, I would cry out, I would roll on the ground. I have found only one means of completely satisfying my *overpowering emotion,* that is music.[17]

Berlioz's single article for *Le Correspondant* in 1830, his first article under the new monarch, continues the romantic slant of his articles on Beethoven from 1829. This article, "Aperçu sur la musique classique et romantique," is the only article in which Berlioz talks enthusiastically of "romanticism."[18] Appropriately for 1830, he defines a romantic as a renegade, a "rule-breaker"; romanticism is free inspiration, where classicism is the adherence to strict scholastic rules; a classicist is forbidden to research effects that have not been already anticipated by the rules. In his previous articles Berlioz had already gleefully noted instances where he felt that Beethoven had courageously broken rules, and in the 1830 article Gluck is portrayed as the great "romantic" in the same way that E. T. A.

Hoffmann portrayed *Don Giovanni* as one of the great "romantic" operas. Berlioz states that Gluck's mode of composition was dictated by passion and changed only according to the dramatic demands of the text, and he clearly felt that the path taken by Gluck and Beethoven was the one to follow. Thus, in this article he is implicitly describing himself as a romantic—a romantic in the sense of someone governed by the rules of "passion" rather than pre-ordained scholastic rules. Since Berlioz rarely discusses romanticism, especially in opposition to classicism, it is significant that 1830, the year of Hugo's *Hernani,* Stendhal's *Le Rouge et le noir,* and Berlioz's own *Symphonie fantastique,* is the date for his brief exposé on romanticism.[19]

In conclusion these early articles give few signs of the author's youth or inexperience. The *Corsaire* articles are somewhat immature, perhaps, in their humor and tendency to unqualified condemnation, and in Berlioz's not very subtle attack on Castil-Blaze. The pervasive mood of the articles is also one of youthful enthusiasm and vigor—Berlioz as "young romantic" or *Jeune France.* However, as already noted, many of the issues that were to become central to Berlioz's criticism throughout his life are formulated in these early reviews. He was a confident and assured writer from the very beginning of his career.

Berlioz finally gained the *Prix de Rome* in 1830 and spent the following year largely in Italy. The articles he wrote on his return to Paris for the *Revue Européenne* and *L'Europe Littéraire* are, not surprisingly, concerned with his time in Italy and the *Concours* for the *Prix de Rome.* In 1832 he wrote an article entitled "Lettre d'un enthousiaste sur l'état de la musique en Italie" for the *Revue Européenne.* The article had perhaps been requested; as Berlioz remarked in a letter to his mother: "I have just had a friendly letter from *De Carné,* one of the founders of *Le Correspondant* whose talents my father greatly admires; he has written asking me to scribble something on the current state of music in Italy."[20] Berlioz's article condemns, virtually point by point, every possible aspect of musical activity in Italy.

During the first half of the nineteenth century many writers wrote and often published accounts of their travels abroad, particularly in Italy, in the form of letters to a friend. Berlioz also found this form convenient, and many of his travels are described through letters such as the lengthy series of letters from Germany and Russia that form a portion of his *Mémoires.* The letters are informative and chatty, and written in a narrative style that Berlioz used with great skill. He never retracted his opinions on the low standard of music in Italy, even though he was criticized for them. His article for the *Revue Européenne* was the first of many on the subject; the second was published the following year for the journal *L'Europe Littéraire: Journal de la littérature nationale et étrangère.* *L'Europe Littéraire* was a spectacular journal with luxurious presentation and had numerous well-known literary figures such as Hugo, Heine, Balzac, and de Vigny working for it. Unfortunately, though not surprisingly, given the generous payments it made to contributors (Berlioz for instance was paid fifty centimes the line), it collapsed for financial reasons after only a few months.[21]

The journal was founded by Victor Bohain (1805–56) and Alphonse Royer (1803–75). Berlioz knew Bohain, who directed the Théâtre des Nouveautés when Berlioz had a brief singing job there during the late 1820s.[22] "Journal d'un enthousiaste," his article on Italy for the journal, is again a fast-moving, entertaining narrative, in which Berlioz conveys, rather self-consciously, his melancholy at the cultural desolation of Rome. The concept of "souffrance" is brought up once again; this time Berlioz expounds on how he must necessarily suffer more than the average man because of his unusually high degree of "sensitivity" (which seems to have been a fairly common complaint amongst artists at this period).

Berlioz's other two articles for the *L'Europe Littéraire* are fairly bitter expositions on the *Concours* for the *Prix de Rome* and recount his personal humiliations from the previous years and the farcical nature of the whole examination. All three articles for *L'Europe Littéraire* are written in a very fluid and vivid narrative style. Berlioz presumably thought highly of them himself since they are all reproduced almost word for word in the *Mémoires*.

In 1833 Berlioz began writing for *Le Rénovateur*. Although he wrote only five articles that year, over the next two years, 1834 and 1835, he regularly wrote an article a week, contributing seventy-nine articles by the time *Le Rénovateur* closed down in December 1835 in order to fuse with the ultra-legitimist *La Quotidienne* in 1836. In 1834 Berlioz started his permanent position with the *Gazette Musicale,* a position he kept for twenty-six years until 1859, and in 1835 he started writing for the *Journal des Débats,* a position he kept twenty-eight years until six years before his death in 1869.[23] So, though his contributions to *Le Rénovateur* began at an earlier date, 1834 is the year that marks the beginning of Berlioz's full-time activity as a critic.

To each of these papers Berlioz had a different relationship and it is best to proceed by examining each in turn.

Le Rénovateur, founded in 1832, was a legitimist daily which was quite frequently censored for its views on the monarchy. In May 1833 it amalgamated with the *Courrier de l'Europe* and changed its name to *Le Rénovateur, Courrier de l'Europe.* Berlioz's friends Ferrand and d'Ortigue also worked sporadically for the paper. For *Le Rénovateur* Berlioz mainly reviewed performances, though he occasionally wrote more general articles and book reviews.[24] He reviewed all the Conservatoire concerts, the premières of new works (though sometimes it is difficult to tell whether he was at the first performance or not), including new operas and *opéras-comiques,* ballets, a vast assortment of minor concerts by visiting artists and local artists, singers' débuts (often at the Théâtre Italien), Musard's concerts, music performed in churches, and works performed at the Théâtre Ventadour.[25] In 1835 he reviewed twelve *opéras-comiques,* more than in any other year. The overall number of *opéras-comiques* reviewed by Berlioz during this whole period is astounding, given his basic lack of enthusiasm for the genre. Examined as a whole, however, his criticism for *Le Rénovateur* covers basically all the major areas of musical activity in Paris at the time, and the works he reviewed catered to the interests of a large range of people. Presumably the readership of a paper like *Le Rénovateur* would have been very varied, and Berlioz was no doubt requested to cover as many areas as possible.

Berlioz claims in a letter to Ferrand that it is in *Le Rénovateur* that he least conceals his "true opinions": "I still keep *Le Rénovateur* where I only half restrain my bad temper over all these little pleasantries."[26] Certainly his reviews of *opéra-comique* for *Le Rénovateur* are fairly caustic. Berlioz does nothing to disguise, and if anything he exaggerates, his boredom with such music. It is in *Le Rénovateur,* too, that Berlioz complains the most bitterly about the musical taste of Parisians, singers who ornamented their parts, and the poor standard of choirs and orchestras. While in 1834 he blamed the public for the low standard of music in Paris, by 1835 he had begun rather to blame the directors of theaters for presenting poor music to a public which was perhaps capable of appreciating better things. Throughout the course of his articles for *Le Rénovateur* Berlioz also posits the existence of a small group, to which he felt he belonged, an elite, a "musical aristocracy" which in contrast to the general public had an elevated understanding of music.

The lively and witty tone that distinguishes Berlioz's *Le Corsaire* articles is continued in a large number of the *Le Rénovateur* articles, particularly in his reviews of works or events that he felt to be unimportant. There are even occasional reviews in which Berlioz writes on nothing except the lack of performances worthy of review or the frustration he feels at writing a feuilleton when he could be composing instead.[27] However, he takes his reviews of chamber music and orchestral concerts, in particular the Conservatoire concerts, very seriously, although as befits music criticism for a political newspaper he offers little analysis of works.

The *Gazette Musicale* was founded in 1834 by the expatriate German music publisher, Maurice Schlesinger. Schlesinger's aim in founding the magazine was two-fold: first, he wanted a venue through which he could promote his own editions; and second, he wanted to form a music journal that, with more literary articles on music and less musical analysis, appealed to a wider audience than Fétis's *Revue Musicale*. Schlesinger gathered around him an impressive editorial team composed of literary and musical figures. For instance, in January 1835 the editorial committee included, amongst others, Adam, Berlioz, Castil-Blaze, Fétis, Dumas, Halévy, Janin, Mainzer, Liszt, d'Ortigue, and Marx. In November 1835 Fétis's son, Edouard (who had been running his father's magazine since 1833 when Fétis moved to Belgium), decided he was no longer interested in continuing the *Revue Musicale*. Rather than close down altogether, Fétis senior reluctantly agreed to a merger with Schlesinger's *Gazette Musicale,* which though still commonly known as the *Gazette Musicale* then became the *Revue et Gazette Musicale.*

Fétis contributed various articles himself to the *Revue et Gazette Musicale* over the next few years, but gradually withdrew his collaboration altogether.

The *Revue et Gazette Musicale* provided a good coverage of actual events alongside serious articles on music, snippets on overseas musical events (mainly in England, Germany, and Italy), and literary fiction with a musical theme.[28] Jules Janin, for instance, specialized in *Contes fantastiques* in the style of E. T. A. Hoffmann. One of the most well-known and successful literary-musical ventures to appear was Balzac's short *nouvelle, Gambara.*[29] Berlioz himself contributed various musical *nouvelles* in the style of Balzac's *Gambara,* for instance, "Le Suicide par enthousiasme" (1834) and "Un Bénéficiaire et Rubini à Calais" (1834).[30] As a musical magazine the *Revue et Gazette Musicale* was naturally geared to a more specialized audience than was a political newspaper, and articles could be analytical without fear of not being understood. Such articles did not comprise the majority; Schlesinger's aim was that the music-lover without a scholarly musical education should still be able to find things to interest him in the *Revue et Gazette Musicale.*

In a decision that doubtless appealed to Berlioz, the *Revue et Gazette Musicale* consciously disengaged itself from the enthusiasm at the time for the Théâtre Italien and works of Rossini. Indeed a number of *Revue et Gazette Musicale* articles express very similar opinions to those of Berlioz, for instance, a distaste for the vocal ornamentation in Italian music, and attacks on the poor standard of the chorus and orchestra of the Opéra-Comique. The critic Henri Blanchard wrote articles that were even more antagonistic towards Rossini and the Théâtre Italien than those of Berlioz.[31] Berlioz took the opportunity of having a "musical audience" to write serious, extended articles on one particular work or composer. For instance, in 1834 he wrote an article in two parts on Gluck, four on *Iphigénie en Tauride,* and three on *Guillaume Tell.*[32] By January 1835 Berlioz had written seven articles exclusively on Gluck, none of which was a review of a performance. The major reviews of performances were of the Conservatoire concerts.

Berlioz was not required to review only the premières of operas. For instance, an 1835 article in the *Gazette Musicale* on *Robert le diable* is not a review of the performance, but a study of one specific quality of the opera, namely its instrumentation.[33] It would have been unlikely for such an article to appear in any political newspaper other than the *Journal des Débats* unless it had immediately followed a review of a performance. In 1836 the *Revue et Gazette Musicale* published three articles Berlioz had written in an exchange on the *Concours d'Institut* with a M. Germanicus Pic. Once again, a political paper would have been unlikely to encourage such a lengthy debate. However, Berlioz still wrote some articles to order for the *Revue et Gazette Musicale,* such as a series of biographies of Italian musicians in 1836.[34]

During the period 1834 to 1837 Berlioz also wrote a series of unsigned articles for the *Revue et Gazette Musicale,* largely on topics which he had already covered in the *Journal des Débats* and *Le Rénovateur* (see appendix B). These articles shall be discussed in chapter 5. Berlioz mentions that the *Revue et Gazette Musicale* paid him badly,[35] yet the number of articles he wrote during this period suggests that he enjoyed writing for the journal. It must have been liberating to write on subjects that really impassioned him, such as the music of Gluck. Schlesinger's high regard for Berlioz is shown by the fact that he entrusted the paper's editorship to Berlioz in 1837.[36]

No striking alteration to the *Revue et Gazette Musicale* is apparent under Berlioz's editorship in 1837; the paper continued much the same as before. During the year 1837, however, Berlioz wrote a total of thirty-seven articles for the *Revue et Gazette Musicale,* which was more than he had any previous year and more than he would in any one of the following years. The articles cover a very broad range; Berlioz wrote on the Conservatoire concerts, operas, several *opéras-comiques;* he wrote a *nécrologie* on Le Sueur, a *nouvelle* on *Benvenuto Cellini,* some general articles such as "De la musique en général," and a fairly daring open letter to Schumann. The letter is daring in that it largely consists of an open defense and explanation of Berlioz's own music. It is doubtful that he would have tried to print this letter under the editorship of Schlesinger. Yet on the whole Berlioz had no real interest in changing the content of the journal, as he had enough to cope with in his music.

Schlesinger's choice of Berlioz as his temporary successor says something of his standing as a critic by 1837. The days of the "free-lance" articles were behind him; he was now an established and respected critic and, even at this early date, the best music critic in Paris.

Berlioz's music criticism for the *Journal des Débats* was unquestionably the most significant collaboration he undertook. The *Journal des Débats* was founded in 1791 by Louis Bertin senior,[37] and along with many other papers and individuals had changed political allegiances several times during the course of the early nineteenth century. For example, it had supported Napoleon, though when Charles X came to power it claimed that Napoleon's police had forced their support.[38] During the Restoration the paper's greatest asset was the journalism of Chateaubriand, who had followers and admirers amongst both the émigrés and the bourgeois royalists. When Chateaubriand's political career ended, the *Journal des Débats* withdrew its support of Charles X's ministries and in 1830 switched its allegiances from Charles X to Louis-Philippe. Chateaubriand however remained loyal to Charles X and consequently broke his ties with the paper.

The *Journal des Débats* did not suffer badly from its mercurial changes of heart and was popular all through the first half of the nineteenth century. The Bertins, two brothers and a son, Armand, not only supported Louis-Philippe, but they, and Armand in particular, were also very friendly with the important statesmen of the day. Naturally the *Journal des Débats'* support of the monarchy meant that the paper complied with the press regulations and escaped the fines that were crippling other newspapers (see appendix A). Although the *Journal des Débats* did indeed follow a party line, the quality of its journalism was such that it was followed by many people who were not of the same political persuasion, but valued the high standard of factual reportage the paper presented.

In 1834 Bertin senior published one of Berlioz's articles, "Rubini à Calais," which had previously appeared in the *Gazette Musicale*.[39] Berlioz went to visit Bertin, ostensibly to thank him for printing the article, but also perhaps with the idea that Bertin might offer him a job, which, as it happened, he did. Berlioz was offered the reviews of concerts and *variétés musicales,* while Jules Janin still reviewed the opera and ballet and Delécluze the Théâtre Italien.[40] In February 1837 Berlioz gained the coverage of the opera and *opéra-comique (théâtres lyriques)*, though Janin still retained the ballet.[41]

In a letter to his sister Adèle in 1835 Berlioz stated that the *Journal des Débats* paid him a hundred francs an article regardless of the length.[42] A later letter to his sister Nanci in 1843 states that an article of four columns was paid fifty francs and only an article of eight to twelve columns was worth a hundred francs.[43] Perhaps the situation had changed over the years, but it seems more likely that the latter statement was the correct one, especially as the majority of Berlioz's articles are of eight to twelve columns. But in either case the pay was extremely generous.

Music critic for the *Journal des Débats* was an important position to have, not only because of the paper's prestige, but also because, with its reputation for "good" criticism, people had grown accustomed to looking to it for serious music criticism. Berlioz was very much aware of the paper's importance. As he remarked to Ferrand: "It is a very important affair for me; the effect they have on the musical world is quite striking; it is almost an event for the artists of Paris."[44] At times he even comments ironically on the public's high regard for the paper; an article entitled "Tribulations d'un critique musical" describes an eager article-seeker who exclaims to Berlioz,

> And what an article you are going to write for the *Journal des Débats*! It is so fortunate for you; don't waste such a subject in the *Gazette Musicale;* no, an important journal with eighteen thousand subscribers, there's your opportunity.[45]

The jealousy of Berlioz's fellow critics, Mainzer for instance, is also evidence of the paper's importance.

Jules Janin's exaggerated eulogy on Bertin (senior) in his book *Les Symphonies de l'hiver* no doubt had some truth behind it. Talking of Bertin, Janin says,

> He chose us; he found us; he encouraged us; he adopted us; he made us free, rich, honored, independent of all political vagaries and changes of fortune.[46]

Bertin probably rendered many services to Berlioz that are unknown,[47] but two at least are. First, Bertin tried to use his influence to get *Benvenuto Cellini* performed at the Opéra, as Berlioz says in his *Mémoires*:

> Duponchel regarded me as a kind of lunatic whose music was a conglomeration of absurdities, beyond human redemption; but in order to keep in with the *Journal des Débats* he consented to listen to a reading of the libretto of *Benvenuto*.[48]

Second, Bertin successfully arranged for the payment of the last two months of Berlioz's pension for the *Prix de Rome*,[49] and at various stages lent Berlioz money. Berlioz comments in his *Mémoires* on an occasion in 1846 when Armand Bertin advanced him a thousand francs.[50] Berlioz's respect and admiration for Bertin and all his family is well documented in his correspondence.

Berlioz's articles for the *Journal des Débats* over the period 1835 to 1837 are more often reviews of performances than articles on general musical topics, and fulfil the traditional role of the feuilleton in the political newspaper. In 1835 Berlioz reviewed almost exclusively instrumental and orchestral works, which largely consisted of the Conservatoire concerts but also of isolated performances of religious works and solo concerts. He also wrote, yet again, several articles on Gluck and his infamous trenchant article on *Zampa*, an *opéra-comique* by Hérold. The subject matter of Berlioz's *Journal des Débats* articles in 1836 remained largely the same as those of 1835. In 1837, however, on taking over the responsibility of the *théâtres lyriques,* Berlioz's *Journal des Débats* reviews began to concentrate more on the opera and *opéra-comique*. It was not only the premières of operas that he reviewed but benefit concerts (*bénéfices*) and débuts as well. Obviously he was obliged to review these works; his job now entailed coverage of specific areas.

Berlioz's articles for the *Journal des Débats* are serious in tone, perhaps not as analytical as some of the *Revue et Gazette Musicale* articles, nor as casual as *Le Rénovateur* articles. He obviously felt a responsibility to Bertin to perform well, and only very occasionally does he revert to the flippant, ironical tone of many articles for *Le Rénovateur*. This tone is not very prominent in the *Revue et Gazette Musicale* articles either, except in some of the unsigned articles, notably the 1836 articles signed "Un Vieillard stupide" (see appendix B).

Perhaps the protection of Bertin did give Berlioz the confidence to express more freely what he felt about certain works. A case in point is *Zampa,* which he reviewed mildly for the *Gazette Musicale,* leaving all his aggressive comments for the *Journal des Débats* articles. Bertin obviously had enough confidence in Berlioz's opinion to take a risk, if indeed it was a risk, in publishing the article.[51] On the other hand, Berlioz's respect for Bertin may have meant in some instances that he restrained his comments so as not to cause any trouble for his editors.

The *Journal des Débats* was the paper with which Berlioz remained the longest. Many reasons must have influenced his stay—Bertin's importance in political circles, the wide audience reached by the *Journal des Débats,* and, probably above all, the generous remuneration. The *Journal des Débats* was also one of the longest-running papers.

During 1837 Berlioz also contributed some music reviews to the *Chronique de Paris,* a political and literary Sunday newspaper.[52] His articles number only six, but as they review the month's activities, each is two to three pages in length, which was unusually long. The articles are sophisticated versions of the weekly or monthly *Chroniques* often found in the political papers at the time. Whereas such columns usually made fairly superficial comments on the week's or month's entertainment, Berlioz would pick one or two of the major events and discuss them as thoroughly as the medium would allow. He would often include polemical discussions of musical issues in his article. Berlioz's last article for the *Chronique de Paris* was written several months before the paper's closure in December 1837.

Motivation of Berlioz's Criticism

Berlioz showed an awareness of the importance of the press from his first years in Paris. Before the performance of his Mass at St. Roch on 10 July 1825, he and Humbert Ferrand had mounted a "gig" and delivered invitations to all the press.[53] He was despondent at not having the time to do the same for his concert at the Conservatoire in 1828.[54] He felt that the Théâtre Italien was the only venue that did not need to solicit reviews since the fact that it was fashionable ensured regular newspaper coverage.[55] Although he sought reviews, Berlioz did not have a very high opinion of the quality of the criticism. For instance, concerning the reviews of his Mass on 22 November 1827 he remarked:

> *Le Corsaire* and *La Pandore* raved about me, but with no details: just those banal things that they say for everyone. Castil-Blaze promised me he would attend and I am waiting for his judgment, also Fétis and *L'Observateur;* these are the only journals that I invited, the others are too concerned with politics.[56]

The scarcity of music critics at the time is highlighted by the fact that Berlioz awaits a review by Castil-Blaze, a man for whom, as the 1825 *Corsaire* article shows, he had little respect. By 1828 Berlioz no longer sought Castil-Blaze's reviews, and he comments apropos the reviews of his concert at the Salle des Menus Plaisirs in 1828,

> Castil-Blaze, not being in Paris, could not attend my concert; I have seen him since; he has however promised me that he will write about it but is in no hurry to do so; thank-goodness, I can easily do without him.[57]

Berlioz is not satisfied with Castil-Blaze's review of a later concert on 1 December 1829: "Castil-Blaze does not go into any detail; these animals only know how to talk when there is nothing to say."[58] However, had Castil-Blaze read the 1825 *Corsaire* article, his lack of interest in Berlioz would hardly be surprising.

In his *Mémoires* Berlioz describes the anger he felt in his early years in Paris at the ignorant statements made in the press by Rossinists about the music of Gluck and Spontini. He claims that this anger provoked him into attempting a written reply to the statements: "I was reading the ramblings of one of these lunatics when I was seized by the desire to answer them."[59] Berlioz's first reviews were thus aesthetically motivated; his desire was to defend "great art" against ignorant misrepresentations. His awareness of the power of the press and of the paucity of music criticism at the time, coupled with both a desire to become known and a more spontaneous need to defend his ideals, were possibly the reasons for his entering the field of criticism. Although not initially motivated by financial gain this fairly soon came to be an important consideration.

Anyone writing about Berlioz's music criticism is forced to try to understand what appear to be several puzzling contradictions. For instance, Berlioz complained bitterly about writing criticism, yet he continued to do so even when in his later years making a living was not such a problem for him. He spoke of the burden and toil of writing: "Musical composition is a natural activity for me and a pleasure, prose-writing a burden."[60] Yet his articles flow easily with an energy and liveliness that suggest enjoyment in his task. French musicologists Edmond Hippeau and Adolphe Jullien, writing at the turn of the century, both came to the conclusion that Berlioz had distorted his "true" attitude to criticism. Hippeau surmised that even if the career of critic was not always easy, writing was an easy if not agreeable task for Berlioz.[61] Jullien claimed that the motivation behind Berlioz's criticism was the desire to communicate his hatreds and enthusiasms. He also claimed that Berlioz's position in French musical circles was due entirely to his work as a journalist and to his friendship with powerful journalists.[62] However, later in the century Jacques Barzun repudiated such disbelief in Berlioz's complaints. Barzun believes that the job of critic was indeed a drudgery for Berlioz: "It would obviously have been much pleasanter for him [Berlioz] to keep his witticisms and stories for friends at his fireside."[63] Barzun is devastated at the thought of what music Berlioz might have left behind had all the time he spent on criticism been spent on composition.

Without wishing to suggest too great a compromise, I would say that the reasons for Berlioz's entry into criticism became both financial and personal—the need to defend his ideals and sustain a public image. Although he does write very easily and with obvious enjoyment, there were occasions when it clearly was drudgery, such as when doing the *opéra-comique* reviews for *Le Rénovateur*.

In fact, in his correspondence and *Mémoires*, Berlioz has discussed his mixed feelings about becoming a critic. As early as 1829 Berlioz wrote to his mother of his need for the money brought to him by his reviews: "I will really need that to bring me some money, since I waste nearly all my time in copying parts for something I am preparing."[64] In chapter 21 of the *Mémoires*, describing his first feelings about becoming a critic, Berlioz expresses his dual motivations clearly:

> I began to see the attractions of the idea. What a weapon I would have for defending the beautiful and attacking whatever seemed to me opposed to it! There was also the consideration that it would add a little to my income, which was still very meager.[65]

On the other hand, Berlioz at times spoke of his criticism as being essential to his well-being regardless of the money it brought him. In these instances he tends to use military similes, talking of criticism as a shield, or as armor, a sword, or weapon with which to fight the world:

> This self-perpetuating task poisons my life. And yet, quite apart from the income I get from it, which I cannot do without, I see no prospect of being able to give it up. To do so would leave me without weapons, exposed to all the rancour and hatred that I have incurred by it. . . . Indeed, a sole compensation that journalism offers me for all its torments is the scope it gives to my passion for the true, the great, the beautiful.[66]

Berlioz was aware of the advantages of becoming a public figure and of being associated with powerful papers. In 1837, commenting on the many papers seeking his services, he remarks that he has accepted the request to work for the *Chronique de Paris* and *Encyclopédie du XIXe siècle* "because the power that these newspapers will give me will further contribute to the lively influence of the *Débats*."[67]

Gérard Condé postulates that Berlioz's borrowing of choirs and halls for performances of his music was made possible only by his notoriety as a critic.[68] This view was held at the time also. An article in *Le Corsaire* of 1840 argues that

Berlioz was only tolerated as a composer because of his position as a critic: "But by the means of a blunderbuss called the *Journal des Débats*, M. Hector Berlioz is able to have his acrobatic operas and metallic symphonies performed; M. Hector imposes himself in the theaters, at official ceremonies, on directors, on ministers, on the director of the Beaux-arts."[69] As already mentioned, in his later years Berlioz did not really need the money he gained from his reviews for the *Journal des Débats* in order to survive. Yet he continued to write, and continued to complain. Once again, Berlioz himself sums up the situation perfectly in a letter (14 February 1861) to his son Louis:

> However I do have to persevere in writing to earn my miserable hundred francs, and to give me ammunition against so many odd-bods who would kill me if they weren't too frightened to do so. And I have a head full of projects, of works that I cannot undertake because of this slavery.[70]

Perhaps Berlioz sincerely believed that he did still need this money. John Klein, in an interesting article on Berlioz's personality, has commented on Berlioz's fear of not having enough money in these later years.[71] Still, the important point is that the need to defend himself was as strong as the financial need. Right to the end of his life Berlioz was reluctant to relinquish his powerful position on the *Débats* staff. Even a year later, in 1862, when obviously quite exhausted by the task of writing, Berlioz had to pretend to himself, as much as to his correspondent, that since it was fate that decreed his continued collaboration it was beyond his control:

> I do not want to be a domestic anymore, nor climb on the back of the wagon of fools and idiots, but on the contrary I want to be able to throw stones at them if I please. But the witches of Macbeth have not predicted anything for me. . . . [F]or a long time yet I shall praise the men and things that I hate most. God wills it![72]

In 1862 Berlioz wrote to the Princess Sayn-Wittgenstein announcing his retirement from criticism and composition: "I wanted to have nothing more to do, nothing, absolutely nothing, and I have succeeded. At any time I can say to death, that terrible release: whenever you want."[73]

This letter gives the disturbing impression of a man who wants his life to end, and yet it was another five miserable years before Berlioz died. However much it burdened him, and despite the undeniable drudgery and boredom of so much of it, criticism was an important, perhaps essential, part of Berlioz's life.

The question whether he would have composed more music had he not been a critic is a difficult one to answer. It is not just a question of Berlioz's having more time for his music, since other factors also come into play, such as a receptive intellectual environment. At various stages during his life he wrote with desperation about his lack of time to compose, for instance: "It is hard to have to admit that I *do not have the time to work* and that I am doing practically nothing of what I am best at!"[74] In 1859 the Princess Sayn-Wittgenstein was encouraging him to write another opera based on *Antony and Cleopatra*, yet Berlioz again claimed that he did not have the time.[75] Whether indeed he would have written *Les Troyens* without the intensive and intelligent encouragement of the Princess is also a difficult question.

But it was not only the burden of criticism that was hindering Berlioz's composition; a variety of other factors contributed, such as the lack of professional support. As David Cairns remarks in his introduction to the *Memoirs*: "It is heartbreaking to think of all that he might have written with a little more encouragement from the musical authorities of the day."[76] Gérard Condé suggests that Berlioz could never have made his living from his music, since it appealed to such a small audience:

> His job as a critic spared Berlioz the necessity of composing to live. Not having the facility of an Auber or the opportunism of a Meyerbeer, he would however have been incapable of it. Despite his romantic illusions about a possible popular success, he must have realized quite early that the originality of his music restricted it to a limited elite of connoisseurs or sensitive souls.[77]

Berlioz himself commented in a letter to his sister in 1854 that he could not, at times, see the point of writing music:

> One no longer says, "what do I know," like Montaigne, but, "What's the point of it?" I am obsessed by plans of vast and inventive works that I could write; I begin and then I stop: why take on such a work, I say to myself, why become enamored with such frightening enthusiasm? . . . To see it either delivered up to children or brutes, or buried alive.[78]

The *Mémoires* finish with the pathetic vision of Berlioz beginning to doubt his own "genius."[79]

It can be said then, that if Berlioz had both not been obliged to write criticism to live, and had also been born into a more encouraging environment, he would undoubtedly have written more music.[80]

In placing Berlioz's music criticism in its context, it is interesting to note that his criticism was relatively mild. For instance, Berlioz's review of Hérold's *Zampa*, which so horrified both his contemporaries and later writers, is quite mild in comparison to some of the statements made by his fellow critics on, for example, the libretti of Scribe. Another interesting aspect of seeing Berlioz's criticism in context is realizing that its idealistic and pedagogical aspect was not unique, but shared by several of his colleagues, and indeed was an important element of the intellectual climate of the day.

Berlioz's early criticism does have a fairly strong prejudice against the Théâtre Italien. This attenuated slightly with time, as Berlioz became reconciled to more of the music of Rossini and Bellini. However, in general Berlioz appreciated less, and wrote much less about the Théâtre Italien, than the majority of his contemporary music critics. Conversely, he wrote more, and in greater detail, on instrumental music and, in particular, on the music of Beethoven.

No other French music critic at the time wrote as well or as much as Berlioz. This fact is indisputable, yet it should not be taken to mean that none of his contemporaries wrote worthwhile music criticism. As outlined in chapter 1, much interesting music criticism was written by other writers, and it is important to see Berlioz's work as part of a critical community, not as an isolated phenomenon. Berlioz's enthusiasm for the Conservatoire concerts and music of Beethoven, for instance, was shared by a large number of fellow writers. Where Berlioz differed was in the amount of space he devoted to such issues and also, in most cases, in the standard of his criticism in these areas.

4

Critical Practices of the Day

What Constituted a Good Review

In order to say what constituted a good review in Parisian music criticism of the 1830s, various parameters need to be fixed. I shall examine what was "good" in terms of the criticism of the period and not in any broader historical context. However, by "good criticism," I usually mean criticism that is well-written, and in general musically informed. The musical magazines had expectations about the extent of musical knowledge required from the critic that differed from those of the newspapers and literary journals. Little technical knowledge of music was required of the average writer of feuilletons for the political newspapers, though a degree of such knowledge was desirable in articles written for the music magazines such as the *Revue et Gazette Musicale.*

Much of the music criticism at the time still consisted of reviews of opera and *opéra-comique.* This was the traditional area for review and as such entailed certain expectations and established practices. The major commitment in these reviews was to the detailed retelling of the libretto, presumably because the public wished to know the story of the work before attending. However, the libretto was sometimes available at the performance. In a letter to Deschamps, Berlioz comments, apropos his review of Niedermeyer's opera *Stradella*:

> I am thinking of what I asked you regarding the analysis of the piece; I think at the moment that it is not much use, the printed libretto will be sufficient; I had forgotten when I asked you to tell me about it that one could get hold of it at the first performance.[1]

Thus the need for retelling the libretto was not purely a practical consideration but also an integral part of the critic's artistic undertaking; he had to relate the story before he could pass critical judgments on the music. With Berlioz, for instance, judgment of the music was frequently based on whether the libretto had lent itself to musical development or not. If Berlioz had several articles about the one work, he often devoted one entire article to the libretto; if he had just the one article, he spent approximately half the review on the libretto, and often less.

This seems to have been about the average amount of space to spend on the libretto, and any more space indicated that the critic was either unable to discuss the music or was deliberately avoiding doing so (see chapter 6).

After describing the libretto the critic usually proceeded to some comments about the music. The extent of the musical coverage depended on whether the critic had access to the score, and was interested enough to want to see it. Critics who did not have access to the score usually discussed the work in general terms, commented on the merit or lack of merit in various of its scenes, and drew some general conclusions on the value of the music. Critics who did have access to the score on the whole presented a more detailed examination of the music and attempted to explain why the music did or did not succeed. Berlioz condemned the review that stated only that the music was successful, without making any attempts to explain why or in what way: "It is not enough to *enumerate* them [the real beauties], they have to be demonstrated, that is, if it is possible to demonstrate beauty."[2]

Berlioz often told his reader when he had not had access to the score, though it is in any case clear from the review itself. Frequently, of course, the critic just did not have the time to consult the score even if he wanted to, since the newspaper editors demanded that the reviews appear immediately after the première of a work. Berlioz felt that in these situations it was difficult to appreciate the score properly:

> A first hearing [is], as I have already said, completely insufficient to distinguish even the most striking points of the score. The necessity of discussing new works immediately after their first appearance, a necessity imposed as much by the practices of the press as by the interest of the theaters, is as annoying for the artists as it is for the critics.[3]

Occasionally Berlioz remarked on insights that the knowledge of the score gave to his aural perception. For instance in a review of *Les Huguenots* he pinpointed a section in the second act where a study of the score gave partial justification for an abrupt harmonic progression—the justification was only partial because Berlioz felt that the preparatory chord he found marked in the score could not be noticed aurally unless one were aquainted with the score.[4] Conversely, in another instance, this time in reference to works of Monpou, Berlioz remarked that displaced rhythms in the score were ignored in performance since singers were obliged, despite themselves, to put the rhythm where it fell naturally:

> Thus, several bits of the works that I have just cited are written with total symmetry and scholastic square-cutness, with only the strong beat of each bar being displaced. But this displacement is for the eye alone. One recognizes it in reading the score or in watching the movements of the conductor; in the listening it doesn't exist, the force of the musical feeling obliges the performers unconsciously to put the rhythmic accent back in the place that the melodic form naturally assigns it.[5]

The critic's discussion of music was usually followed by commentary on the *mise-en-scène*. Since Berlioz rarely commented at any length on the *mise-en-scène,* which he saw as accessory rather than fundamental, it is possible, given the importance of the *mise-en-scène* at this time, that his reviews of opera disappointed many of his readers. However, they had only to turn to one of the other papers for a more detailed coverage of it.

The opera review would usually finish with an assessment of the standard of performance of the principal singers in particular, and, though of lesser importance, the orchestra and chorus. Berlioz often used this section to give advice to singers on ways in which they could improve their performance.

In summary, then, a "good" review of an opera at this time entailed a quite standard way of looking at the libretto and—though not necessarily in this order—music, *mise-en-scène,* and standard of performance or interpretation. The amount of musical commentary—to call it analysis would be an exaggeration—depended on the critic's knowledge of the score and the readership to which the review was directed. This separation between the general public and specialized audience is not strict, however, for Berlioz wrote almost as many technical articles for the *Journal des Débats* as for the *Revue et Gazette Musicale.* For the most part Berlioz's reviews of opera followed the pattern outlined above.[6] Although, as mentioned earlier, some of his public may have seen his minimal commentary on the *mise-en-scène* as a limitation, this was compensated for by the extent of his commentary on the music.

No such patterns can be discerned in the reviews of music other than opera. In the large mixture of "other subjects" covered in the musical press, the concerts most consistently covered were the Conservatoire concerts. To give a brief idea of what else was reviewed, Berlioz's reviews during the 1830s also covered chamber music concerts, religious music performed in churches, and concerts given by virtuosi.

The majority of other reviews can be grouped loosely together, as all in some way dealt with instrumental music as an "independent medium." The extent of the critic's musical knowledge was more important here, since he could not pad out his review with a description of the libretto. With no recourse to the "words" of a composition, the critic had no choice but to turn to the music.[7] This was obviously fairly daunting for many critics, who, when reviewing a symphony for instance, substituted another kind of narrative consisting of a descriptive recounting of the music in terms of the poetic associations it aroused in them—the so-called "impressionistic" criticism mentioned in chapter 1. This resulted in the music review that described the effects of the music upon the listener-critic, but stopped short of examining what it was that caused them. As Carl Dahlhaus remarks about responses to Beethoven's symphonies in the 1820s: "In order to avoid having to relinquish familiar esthetics, listeners searched in Beethoven's symphonies for esoteric programs, rather than grasping them as evidence of a transition to the hegemony of instrumental music."[8] Berlioz also at times engaged in poetic reverie, though instead of using the music as a trigger for associations only loosely connected with the music itself, his reveries were closely based on the music and changed as the music changed.

In reviews of instrumental music the critic usually discussed first the music performed and then the performers' technical skills and manner of interpretation. As with the opera reviews the extent to which the critic was able to make critical comments about the music depended upon his access to and familiarity with the score. In reviews of both opera and instrumental performances, the performers' adherence to the score was an important issue for Berlioz, and he frequently rebuked artist and/or conductor for departures from the score. Departures from the score were common but rebukes for such were not, since most critics did not possess Berlioz's familiarity with scores nor were they particularly concerned with the issue. Occasionally critics would state that they had been to rehearsals and consequently felt more familiar with the music and capable of critically evaluating it. In one review Berlioz even uses the fact that he had not been to a rehearsal as a reason for not discussing the music, a symphony by Onslow.[9] This suggests that Berlioz did try to attend rehearsals although in this particular instance it also sounds suspiciously like an excuse for not discussing the music.

In the case of the Conservatoire concerts and concerts put on by virtuosi, critics also seemed to feel themselves behoven to discuss the concerts as a social phenomenon. These concerts were after all a new occurrence, which obliged the critic in some way to situate himself in relation to their novelty.

Judging from what can be gleaned from comments made in the journals and books of the day, the general feeling about critics was one of antagonism towards the sort of "pedantry" and too excessive "scholasticism" of which Fétis was seen, in my opinion often unfairly, as the major offender. A livelier writing style was preferred.

Berlioz's combination of a spirited literary style and an informed knowledge of music was unique amongst the contemporary Parisian critics. His literary gifts were in a way a bonus since his criticism is valuable in itself for its interest in the primary texts, the musical scores.

Malpractices

Music and theater critics are lamentably susceptible to bribery. The twentieth century is no exception to this, as Guy Hocquenghem states in his *Minigraphie de la presse parisienne*: "Favors are the true cement of the press."[10] The corruption of the Parisian press of the first half of the nineteenth century was notorious, even in its day. Balzac's *Illusions perdues* provides a clear picture of the journalistic ethics of the day. The picture Balzac draws, though colored by his personal bitter experience with the press, is nevertheless reasonably accurate and modeled on real people. Balzac wrote a *Monographie de la presse parisienne* which analyzes various different types of journalist under the generic title of *Gendelettre* ("comme gendarme," Balzac comments). He talks, amongst others, of *Le Jeune critique blond,* with sub-genres such as *Le Farceur, Le Négateur, Le Critique de la vieille roche,* and *Le Feuilletoniste.* Honesty is the least valued commodity in the profession. Balzac remarks apropos *Le Feuilletoniste:* "Between money in the pocket and using the most beautiful aspect of the intellect, the press didn't hesitate: it took the money and renounced the scepter of the in-depth article."[11]

Although Berlioz was not party to accepting bribes to write good reviews, it appears that he occasionally did pay money to ensure favorable reviews. It was something he deplored doing, as he wrote in a letter to Liszt in 1853:

> I will take your advice for Frankfurt if I decide to go there; I already suspected that these highway critics existed, and that it was necessary to throw a *sou* in their hat when passing before their Blunderbuss.[12]

It is unlikely that critics such as Mainzer, Desnoyers, or d'Ortigue accepted bribes either, but other critics were not so scrupulous and succumbed to the attraction of money easily gained. Emile de Girardin described a journal of the day as one

> whose financial speculation is founded on the ransom pitilessly extracted from some actor or actress who pays to prevent being called awkward, ugly, or detestable in the next day's feuilleton.[13]

Louis Gouin, Meyerbeer's secretary, commented in a letter (in clumsy French) to his master in 1833:

> Yesterday I heard [Ch. Maurice] say—speaking to Caraffa in the foyer of the Opéra—that the music of *Ali Baba* was even worse than it had been judged to be. And this morning the person that yesterday evening said this to him has probably been bribed (because he can be got cheaply). M. Charles Maurice wrote an article the direct opposite of the words that I heard come from his mouth. Only *Le Moniteur* dared say that it was booed; the fact is true and it is quite a boring work.[14]

The fact that only one newspaper mentioned that the work was whistled at shows how little credence could be given to the reviewer's report of a work's reception.

Charles Maurice was the most outrageously corrupt critic of the day.[15] He edited a journal called the *Courrier des Théâtres* which provided a daily listing of all current performances at the major theaters of the day from the Variétés to the Opéra. Maurice ran what could be best termed a protection racket, whereby artists, playwrights, actors, singers, dancers, and composers paid him for a good review, and if they neglected to pay were given a poor review or simply not mentioned at all. Maurice's articles were little more than the stringing together of a few banal phrases and hardly deserved the title of "Critique musicale."

The importance artists attached to Maurice's column is surprising and presumably lay in the large audience reached by the *Courrier*. In a sense, the journal filled a similar role to that of the present-day *Pariscope*. Anyone wanting to know what was being performed in Paris at the time would have looked for a *Courrier des Théâtres*. Although other newspapers also listed performances of the day, none were as detailed or comprehensive as the *Courrier*.

In 1856 Maurice published a book of the letters written to him during his editorship of the *Courrier*. The book contains an astonishing number of fawning, unctuous letters from famous artists.[16] A large number of the letters talk quite specifically of "protection." Donizetti for instance writes that he is putting "my *Marino Faliero . . .* under the protection of your talent."[17] The Elssler sisters, too, request his protection: "Please would you, we beg of you Monsieur, continue to protect us as you have done up until now,"[18] as does Loïsa Puget: "Please take my début as a dramatic composer under your protection."[19] Other letters consist only of exaggerated praise; Arrago writes, "I have found only one journalist who writes high-class theater criticism; and that journalist is you."[20] Although not mentioned, it is highly probable that money accompanied these letters.

Maurice was not the only music critic at the time to exact money for favorable reviews. It is reputed that Jules Janin at times operated in a similar fashion.[21] As Antoine Adam comments, "If one wants to appreciate Janin's virtue, one should read Count Apponyi's journal for these astonishing confidences of the journalist: 'I am like a kept woman, I am fashionable, I must exploit this madness; in a year, I will perhaps be worth only a hundred sous.' For the moment—1834—he was 'worth' a thousand francs the eulogy."[22] Pier Angelo Fiorentino, an Italian music critic working in Paris in 1849, was also renowned for accepting bribes; Charles Soullier in *L'Union Musicale* called him "a great music critic very familiar with the mysteries of the sound—of money."[23] But no other critic was as blatant or as unsubtle in his maneuvers as Charles Maurice and his infamous cry of "your money or your life!"[24]

In his introduction to the Garnier edition of *Illusions perdues,* Antoine Adam remarks, "Balzac understood that the essential character of his time was the all-powerfulness of money. Bookshops, theater, journalism, and belles-lettres were dominated by this new and abject tyranny."[25] Money certainly had the power to open doors that earlier in the century would have remained sealed; even the doors of the Opéra-Comique could be swung by money. Berlioz talks with a mixture of bitterness and pity of a certain rich M. Fontmichel from Provence who, because of his wealth and his desperation to have a work performed in Paris, had been cajoled into paying to have his work performed at the Opéra-Comique. M. Fontmichel was nevertheless being badly treated by the management who were demanding unreasonable sums of money for services that were by rights automatic.[26]

Meyerbeer is the name that is, and has always been, most frequently associated with favors obtained by financial influence. The suggestion that he bribed all his critics has been questioned by Heinz Becker, at greatest length in his book *Der Fall Heine- Meyerbeer,*[27] but also in other writings such as the *New Grove* entry on Meyerbeer. In *Der Fall Heine-Meyerbeer* it is Heine that Becker portrays as the corrupt one, as the insidious critic who, adept at moral blackmail, extorted money from Meyerbeer for not writing bad criticism. Becker provides convincing documentary evidence that corroborates his argument.

Heine's criticism of Meyerbeer is curious. The early criticism written before he turned so vehemently against Meyerbeer already has several ambiguous undercurrents.[28] Heine describes Meyerbeer as a timorous, anxious man, who is desperate for public approval, paranoid about failure, and continually alters his works in rehearsal and in the manuscript.[29] This image is then contrasted with an idolatrous portrayal of Meyerbeer as a "colossus," the builder of Gothic cathedrals in music, and a leader of men.[30] The two images sit oddly together. Heine raises the question of the fickle populace, which could turn against the composer, and asks rhetorically whether wreaths of flowers thrown at the head might hurt, and whether flowers thrown by dirty hands could dirty the composer also.[31] Was Heine hinting here that the people who were doing this had been *paid* to do it?

Heine takes up the subject of floral wreaths again in his later witty, explosive attack on Meyerbeer in *Lutèce.*[32] Here he ridicules Meyerbeer, saying that the weight of his floral wreaths must be now so heavy as to require the help of a little donkey to trot along beside him and share the load. This article probably did a great deal to spread the belief that Meyerbeer controlled the press. Heine very adroitly uses the orchestra as a metaphor for the press, talking of Meyerbeer's skill at "instrumentation" which he later defines as "the art of employing all sorts of men as instruments."[33]

Becker claims that impecunious music critics such as Fiorentino and Scudo persistently asked Meyerbeer for loans, the implication being that, once again, the instigators of "money transfers" between Meyerbeer and certain critics were the critics themselves. Even if this is the case, however, there is no doubt that Meyerbeer did most assiduously court the press. He was neurotically obsessed with the success of his works and concerned with every detail that could contribute to that success. He was not in Paris during the performances of *Robert le diable,* but his secretary wrote him a letter after every performance in which he gave details of the takings, standard of performance, and the public response. Meyerbeer kept up regular correspondence with innumerable journalists and subscribed to a very large number of papers. The splendid banquets he gave the press before the premières of his works were not insignificant affairs. Becker, who equates them simply with the modern press reception with refreshments, is clearly understating the case.[34]

Money was not the only means by which Meyerbeer courted his following. In his article on Meyerbeer and Fétis, Peter A. Bloom, though admitting that money did pass between the two, suggests that their friendship was more than just mutually opportunist.[35] Meyerbeer was a very powerful person and was always prepared to do favors for his friends. He was canny in the ways in which he stimulated allegiance. The tenor Duprez recounts in his *Mémoires* that when Meyerbeer asked him to sing in *Les Huguenots* he bet him that the work would not reach its eightieth performance. The wager was Meyerbeer's author's rights for twenty performances. The eightieth performance was attained and Duprez was duly paid. Duprez notes this as one of the subtle means used by Meyerbeer to stimulate the zeal of his performers.[36] Though money played an important role in the artistic world of the time, it was not always manipulated in the unsubtle manner of Charles Maurice.

Factors other than money also had undue influence over the critical fraternity. Political allegiances, for example, played a significant part in the critics' response to Louisa Bertin's opera *Esmeralda*.[37] Although it was not often that political influence infringed upon the artistic world, it is interesting to look at this particular instance, as it illustrates the malleability of the critics.

Louisa Bertin, daughter of Louis Bertin, was undoubtedly helped enormously in her career by the importance of her family. As a woman she stood very little chance of having a work performed that had the pretensions of being a serious opera. Her chances of success would have been stronger had she, like her contemporary Loïsa Puget, contented herself with writing chiefly romances.[38] Several critics even remarked in their reviews on the unsuitability of the opera genre for a female. Blaze de Bury commented:

> Besides, is it really the work of a woman to summon up orchestral tempests and to move the chorus? . . . To find the voice of tears and of the heart is a beautiful enough task to occupy the leisure time of a woman.[39]

Although her sex would have counted against her, it was also extremely difficult for anyone without the right connections to have a work performed at the Opéra—witness the extraordinary problems Berlioz had throughout his life. Berlioz commented on the acceptance of *Esmeralda* by the Opéra administration: "It is the power of the *Journal des Débats* alone that has had this work accepted by the Opéra administration."[40]

The reviews of *Esmeralda* were almost entirely governed by the relationship of the various newspapers and journals to the *Journal des Débats*. As one critic was driven to expostulate: "One doesn't go to the opera to count the friends and enemies of the *Journal des Débats*."[41] Jules Janin wrote a series of sycophantic review articles for the *Journal des Débats* that were full of unreserved and eulogistic praise.[42] This was of course to be expected, though a more objective critical response to the work would have been more astute. To look at a few of the newspapers that attacked *Esmeralda,* an article in *La Mode* (a Royalist journal) maliciously suggests that Louis Bertin (senior) had bribed the director of the Opéra in order to have his daughter's opera performed.[43] Frédéric Soulié of *La Presse* wrote twice on the opera, once before its première and once after. The first article was very satirical, mocking Victor Hugo for coming to the assistance of a poor woman who had to help her only the *Journal des Débats,* which had "opened doors, pressured the reading committees, [and] beaten time to the singers and the orchestra."[44] In his second article Soulié is obviously at a loss over how to attack the work. He finally takes as his point of departure the question of "sacrilege," claiming that the opera is sacrilegious. Soulié's comments on this question give no evidence of his having actually attended the opera. His review, used purely as a means of attacking the Bertins, attacks Louisa Bertin:

> For the glory of a duo you have insulted the church; for the honor of a recitative you have maligned the priest. . . . [M]r Hugo's verses could challenge religion, but they have been made to be sung in chorus because of their use to the Bertin dynasty. The result of all this is that . . . the *Débats* is stronger than God.[45]

The work was a resounding failure; the second performance had to be stopped because of cries of "Down with the Bertins! Down with the *Journal des Débats!*"[46] Berlioz said in a letter that *Esmeralda* was beaten by a systematic opposition, in which politics played a large part.[47] Berlioz wrote two articles on the opera for the *Revue et Gazette Musicale,* while Janin covered the work for the *Journal des Débats.*[48] Berlioz's first article, written before the première, is unsigned (see appendix B) and merely argues for an objective reception of the work. He accurately foresaw the type of response the work would produce. After the première it was suggested by many people that Berlioz, who had to some extent supervised the final composition of the opera and all the rehearsals, had himself composed the better parts of the score, in particular the Air of Quasimodo in the fourth act. Berlioz's second article on *Esmeralda* was thus very difficult. Naturally he wanted to write a good review, and he seemed sincerely to appreciate the work. He wrote to a fellow critic, Théophile de Ferrières, "There are really some remarkable things in this score, and people who are impartial will be very surprised."[49] On the other hand he did not want to write the type of sycophantic eulogy written by Janin, but wanted to be seen as distinct from the Bertin family. His article, which is one of the few to look closely at the opera as a musical composition rather than a political maneuver, achieves an impression of objectivity. Berlioz remarks on several faults in the work, which he put down largely to the author's inexperience. He also praises many qualities and individual sections, and the overall view is one of tempered praise. In a footnote Berlioz firmly denies the rumors that he helped in any way with the composition of the Air of Quasimodo.[50] The article would have pleased the Bertins without making Berlioz appear a pawn of the Bertin family. It is clear then, that for the Parisian music critic the interest of a work was often quite extrinsic to the work itself.

In 1852 Berlioz's opera *Benvenuto Cellini* suffered an ignominious failure at Covent Garden because a cabal organized by a group of Italian opera supporters disrupted the performance with whistling and shouting. Berlioz wrote to Armand Bertin, explaining what had happened and asking for his aid:

> I think, then, that the best, if you want to say something in the *Journal des Débats*, would be to announce simply that the *first performance* was last Saturday, under my direction, in the presence of the Queen, who stayed until the last note of the last chorus; that several pieces were asked for again and that the execution and the *mise-en-scène* were quite remarkable. Do me a favour by putting in these few lines.[51]

Berlioz is in fact outlining a review in which, though all the information contained would be correct, the overwhelming fact of chaotic failure is omitted. Berlioz's letter to Gemmy Brandus, editor of the *Revue et Gazette Musicale*, is almost identical.[52] The ploy of deception by omission was widely used, usually in instances where the critic wished to disguise his true feelings.[53] Other ploys were also employed to the same end. Balzac, in *Monographie de la presse parisienne,* comments on the literary critic who, out of consideration for a journal or a powerful friend, has to review a book he does not like and writes an article on, rather than about, the book.[54] This could perhaps involve a simple retelling of the plot—a tactic many music critics employed in their reviews of opera and *opéra-comique*. Berlioz's use of the technique will be discussed in the following chapter.

In his book *De l'Opéra en France* Castil-Blaze describes a method for reviewing mediocre works. He introduces his method by talking of "those occasions" when the critic is obliged to praise a mediocre work. It is obviously a fairly mundane occurrence and Castil-Blaze remarks that it would be indiscreet to want to know who engages the critic to perform the task. As Castil-Blaze remarks on his own method:

> One must at least acquit oneself with aplomb, in passing lightly over the weak spots, keeping absolutely silent about the faults, and exclaiming over the beauties, the remarkable melodic passages and the sections which could unquestionably be shown to be first rate.[55]

The literary music critic, observes Castil-Blaze, is incapable of writing one of these subtle reviews because, not having any musical knowledge, he is unable to select which sections to praise.

Berlioz frequently had to review works that he didn't like,[56] and when doing so he seems to have employed tactics similar to those of Castil-Blaze, but differed in that unlike Castil-Blaze he usually included a few mild remarks on the major faults of a work. It is often difficult to discern what Berlioz's feelings were about some works. Luckily, however, there are several instances where he states in his correspondence that he does not like a work he is reviewing, and a study of the reviews of works to which he refers in the correspondence helps gauge the sincerity of some of his other reviews. It should be stressed here that there is never any question of not knowing when Berlioz genuinely likes a work. In such reviews his appreciation could even be termed glaringly obvious. The reviews under consideration here are those of the middle ground, and the task is one of distinguishing reviews of works that Berlioz likes, but with reservations, from those reviews of disguised dislike.

One of the works that Berlioz disliked, but had to judge otherwise in his reviews, was the opera *Stradella* by Niedermeyer.[57] In a letter to his sister Nanci of 1837 Berlioz talks bitterly of the objectionable concessions he had to make in his reviews for the *Journal des Débats* of opera and *opéra-comique*:

> It is a very difficult position to keep without terrible concessions. Thus in a few days I am going to have to say *indulgent* nonsense in a credible manner about an *enormous* musical folly called *Stradella,* whose dress rehearsal I attended last night at the Opéra. . . . But I warn you not to believe anything I say about the music, for in fifteen years I have encountered nothing so *tranquilly insipid.*[58]

He reviewed the work twice, once for the *Journal des Débats* and a second time in an unsigned article for the *Revue et Gazette Musicale*. Over half the *Revue et Gazette Musicale* article and three-quarters of the *Journal des Débats* article consist of a retelling of the libretto; both detail qualities and sections appreciated by Berlioz alongside sections that he liked less. He makes numerous double-edged, if not blatantly ironical, remarks:

> In this work M. Niedermeyer has given us proof of a lot of talent, but this talent, to judge it on first impression, would have probably been used to more advantage on a subject that was not so vast and more in keeping with his tranquil nature and quiet ways.[59]

He further remarks:

> He limited himself to saying what he felt, without trying to make new conquests, nor searching "un mieux qu'on dit ennemi du bien."[60]

Though the tone of the articles here is flat and unenthusiastic, the overall impression is certainly not one of disapprobation. Berlioz has successfully masked his dislike of the work.[61]

Other critics did not seem to feel the same necessity as Berlioz to make concessions to Niedermeyer. For instance, Blaze de Bury, writing in the *Revue des Deux Mondes,* talked of Niedermeyer's "desperate timidity,"[62] and the critic for the *Revue de Paris* remarked that "the music . . . frequently lacks force, always lacks character, but is sometimes charming and vivacious."[63] In the letter on *Stradella* to his sister Berlioz stressed that apart from putting him in an awkward position with the journal there were a thousand reasons for not slating the work of someone who stood in the same position regarding the Opéra as he did himself. But in his *Mémoires* he comments that "every untrue word on behalf of an untalented friend causes me acute distress."[64] There appears to be no question of obliterating that distress by telling the truth and Berlioz accepts these reviews almost as unfortunate necessities. He did however believe that in some cases the truth was transparent. As he said:

> It costs me such violent efforts to bring myself to praise certain works that the truth comes out between the lines, as in the action of a hydraulic press the water seeps through the pores of the metal.[65]

It is rather surprising, that in a later discussion of *Stradella*—in his "Chronique musicale" for the *Chronique de Paris*—Berlioz allows himself to be quite openly dismissive of the work's lack of originality. He applauds his colleagues' reception of *Stradella,* pointing to an amelioration in the musical morals of the day.[66] By the time this review was written *Stradella* was on its way to becoming a failure. Apparently Berlioz felt obliged to support it *contre-coeur* at its première, but when it was generally accepted as a failure he was free to give his true opinion. Perhaps also he felt less obliged to the editor of the *Chronique de Paris* than to the editors of the *Journal des Débats* and *Revue et Gazette Musicale,* and correspondingly freer to express his true opinions.

To an extent, then, Berlioz made the decision to disguise his true feelings himself, as for instance when he could not bring himself to attack the vulnerable young composer on his première. But in other instances it must have been the constraints of the editor and journal for which he was writing.

There are several cases where Berlioz refused to review a work. He did not for instance want to review the premières of either *La Juive* or *I Puritani* for the *Journal des Débats,* and in a letter to Humbert Ferrand dated 1835 Berlioz states, "In spite of M. Bertin's invitation, I did not want to review *Les Puritani* or *La Juive;* I had too many bad things to say about them; I would have been accused of jealousy."[67] However, he reviewed both for *Le Rénovateur,* a week after their premières.[68] In both reviews he barely conceals his dislike. His review of *La Juive;* says very little about the music, but says that the opera itself disappeared under the weight of the choreography. Many other critics, such as Castil-Blaze and Buloz, felt the same about *La Juive,* though someone like Gautier could not praise the work enough saying that the work put Halévy "in the first rank of modern composers."[69] Berlioz's opinion of Halévy did change over the years.

Already in 1838 in his review of *Guido et Ginevra* for the *Revue et Gazette Musicale* (11 March 1838), he was less censorious. The review is hardly enthusiastic however; he gives no real analysis of the music—a task he leaves to another collaborator—and details sections that were appreciated by the audience rather than by himself. If Berlioz had thought the music worthy of detailed analysis, he would no doubt have done it himself rather than leave it to another critic. Berlioz's reviews of Halévy's *Val d'Andorre* and *La Reine de Chypre* are different, however. Of the *Val d'Andorre* (1861) Berlioz comments in a letter, "It really is good. . . . I said *what I think* in my feuilleton."[70] And in his review of *La Reine de Chypre* in 1861 one senses a real appreciation of the work.[71] He comments that Halévy's music needs time and attentive study. Perhaps he had decided that his former judgments of Halévy had been rash, for he does use an example from *La Juive* in his *Traité d'instrumentation*.

Berlioz's review of Bellini's *I Puritani* examines only the first two acts. He excuses himself saying that he was very tired after three hours and felt that to judge the third act conscientiously he would have to do so on another occasion—which needless to say he does not do. The review is very much in the mould of Castil-Blaze's method. Berlioz details little sections he likes and several pieces he doesn't like (which include the two most popular pieces). He makes numerous flippant statements such as: "Apart from the chorus who constantly kept a respectful distance from the *time* beaten by the orchestra, the execution was magnificent," and: "Bellini knows his public, and if he sometimes had the courage to lower his style and to speak a language more within the grasp of his audience, he no doubt only did it in order to *get across some beautiful things*."[72] Even a reader unaccustomed to Berlioz's irony would have been able to appreciate such statements.

In a letter to Schlesinger in 1835 Berlioz begs to be relieved of the review of an opera, *Un Caprice de femme* by Paer, saying by way of excuse that "an article counter it would not suit you."[73] In fact he eventually did review the work for *Le Rénovateur,* and in a manner more favorable than not. In 1837, while Berlioz was acting editor of the *Revue et Gazette Musicale,* Schumann sent him a large collection of piano music for review. Berlioz clearly felt unequal to this chore and not prepared to compromise himself, for he promptly asked Liszt to undertake the review, saying, "It seems to me that you are the only one who could do it thoroughly."[74] The editors of the papers undoubtedly influenced the scope of the critic quite extensively. Berlioz clearly felt he could put reviews in *Le Rénovateur* that were not serious enough to be put in the *Revue et Gazette Musicale* or *Journal des Débats,* and it is unfortunate that there are not more letters of transaction between Berlioz and his editors.

The general level of corruption in the press of the day was high, and Berlioz's veracity was affected, too, in a variety of ways; another way, not yet considered, was the manner in which his role as a composer impinged on his critical objectivity.

Effect of Berlioz's Role as a Composer

As a critic who also composed, Berlioz was possibly even more susceptible than other critics to the editor's control. His awareness of the power of the press and his desire for publicity and a good coverage for himself would have led him to see the advantages of being on good terms with editors. Berlioz frequently asked fellow critics, as well as newspaper editors, to insert small preview notices of his concerts in their criticism. When he wanted good publicity for one of his books or works, again Berlioz wrote to his colleagues. For instance, apropos of the publication of his *Traité d'instrumentation* Berlioz wrote in his correspondence, "I have therefore recourse to all my colleagues who have shown and who daily show benevolence towards me, so as to give this work all the publicity possible."[75] He reciprocated in a similar manner; for instance, when Liszt asked him to mention the Conservatoire at Geneva in one of his reviews, Berlioz devoted an entire article to it in the *Revue et Gazette Musicale* and a portion of another article in the *Journal des Débats*.[76] On another occasion, in a review that was supposed to be of the concerts of the Société Philotéchnique, Berlioz mainly discusses the merits of some poetry by his friend Ernest Legouvé that had been read as part of the concert.[77] Berlioz does mention in his *Mémoires* the exasperation he felt at the devious ways in which many artists sought to win a good notice:

> When you have the misfortune, as I have, to be both critic and creative artist, you have to suffer an endless succession of Lilliputian trivia of one sort or another, the most nauseating of all being the cringing flattery of those who have or are going to have need of you.[78]

This exasperation can at times be felt in the notice itself; for instance in a notice on a concert by Henri Herz (written in response to a sycophantic request from Herz) Berlioz comments:

> I was not able to attend the Henri Herz concert, but I knew that, in spite of the *great excitement* caused by an antimusical evening . . . Herz's hall could not hold all the listeners that the poster had attracted. I knew that the new Herz piano concerto had been a brilliant success. Everything becomes known, in spite of the efforts of certain artists to hide their triumphs from the public's knowledge.[79]

Herz would not have missed Berlioz's irony, having himself supplied the information.

Yet at times Berlioz was willing to perjure himself if a good friend demanded a favor. In a letter to the English music critic James William Davison, obviously in response to a reproach from Davison, Berlioz, apologizing for harshly reviewing a singer whom Davison supported, says, "Anyway, what does it matter, one lie more or less? Do you want me to say next time that she has style? . . . On my word of honor, I will say it."[80] Davison replied that he did not want Berlioz to lie. It was not Berlioz's criticism to which he objected, but his ironical tone, and all he asked was that Berlioz stay at home the next time the singer sang!

In a letter to A. F. Marmontel, Berlioz talks with despair about the problems involved in being a composer-critic.[81] Marmontel had recommended the work of a young composer and friend to Berlioz for review. Berlioz warns Marmontel that he cannot examine the work in depth and that he has strong prejudices against certain types of music, prejudices which might well be misguided. In short, Berlioz is worried about the possibility of not liking the music and consequently of upsetting his friend, though most probably some sort of compromise review could have been written.

As has already been mentioned, Berlioz was also aware of the advantages of being a composer-critic, in particular that of being able to propagate his personal ideals about music with the possible result of forming a public more receptive to his own compositions. On numerous occasions in his reviews Berlioz also wrote at length about the trials besetting the composer in Paris. At other times his personal interest as a composer in some issue led him to devote a disproportion-ate amount of space to it. The Gymnase Musical is a case in point.[82] He was personally interested in the Gymnase for two reasons. It was a venue for concerts—he held two concerts there on the fourth and twenty-fifth of June 1835—and Berlioz had hopes of becoming its musical director. This interest led him to write the best part of seven articles for *Le Rénovateur* alone and an unsigned article in the *Gazette Musicale* (31 May 1835) on the opening of the Gymnase. Berlioz's chances of becoming its director were dashed in 1836 when Thiers refused the theater permission to perform vocal music.[83]

The interaction between Berlioz's dual roles as critic and composer is indeed a subject in itself, and I shall restrict myself here to studying one example where Berlioz's objectivity as a critic seems to have been affected by his position as a composer.

Duponchel became director of the Opéra in August 1835. Six months before his appointment, in a conference with Bertin, Meyerbeer, and Berlioz, Dupon-chel had promised that if he were elected to office he would commission an opera from Berlioz. Berlioz did not believe Duponchel to be any more musical than Véron and said so in a letter to Humbert Ferrand.[84] Another letter to his sister shows that Berlioz was also wary about Duponchel keeping his word: "I know so well what these animals of directors are like that I would give [the significant sum of] a hundred écus for Duponchel's word."[85] Yet his first review on Duponchel's coming to office is full of praise and suggests that "musical art is going to regain the place at the Opéra it should never have lost,"[86] and an article for the *Journal des Débats* written some months later comments for some paragraphs on Duponchel's first administrative moves being the happy augury of a reaction in favor of music.[87]

Favorable comments about Duponchel in Berlioz's criticism are made all the more striking by the converse reactions of his fellow critics in, for instance, *Le National* (Louis Desnoyers), *Revue des Deux Mondes* (Blaze de Bury), *La Presse*, and *Revue de Paris*. The general feeling expressed by most critics towards Duponchel and the Opéra during this period was one of censure, mainly for the large number of nights with no performances (*relâches*), for the predominance of ballets, and for the trivial nature of many of the operas performed. As Blaze de Bury (signing Hans Werner) stated in the *Revue des Deux Mondes*:

> Now, unless *Stradella* suddenly shows M. Niedermeyer to be a man of genius, or M. Halévy has divine inspiration, or M. Auber regains the verve of *Le Philtre* or *La Muette*, all things which are at least very much subject to appeal, we must be patient, and build up our supplies for the coming times of musical paucity.[88]

Berlioz's failure to stress any of these shortcomings is perhaps a measure of his desire to have a work performed at the Opéra. Nor, presumably, did he want to criticize a friend of Meyerbeer—Meyerbeer had been instrumental in Duponchel's appointment to the Opéra. In a letter to his sister in 1836 Berlioz talks quite openly of the need to be conciliatory towards Duponchel. Bemoaning the obligation to provide free tickets to all the contemporary journals, Berlioz concludes:

> I normally do not take much notice of these petty little revenges, but the theater directors tremble before the least printed line, and my position with Duponchel, which is not one of the strongest in this regard, has made me bow my head and pay the tax.[89]

Obviously the journalists could not be trusted to give equitable reviews if denied their free tickets.

Despite Berlioz's direct support of Duponchel, he did make many indirect criticisms of the Opéra in his reviews of the period 1836 to 1837, of precisely the same issues criticized by his fellow critics. His criticisms are worded very circumspectly, to avoid giving offence, as can be seen in the following two quotations from an article for the *Journal des Débats*:

> Vocal and instrumental performance has no doubt made some progress at the Opéra, . . . but one must admit that there still remains a lot to be done in various regards.

> We do not deny the importance of the work needed by scores such as the last two [*La Juive* and *Les Huguenots*] appearing on our great lyric stage; however . . . it would not have been absolutely impossible to put on again at least one of the old masterpieces, already known by a large number of the singers.[90]

This instance of Berlioz's role as a composer impinging upon his critical role is thus not very serious—indeed Berlioz's praises for what Duponchel was going to achieve at the Opéra could be interpreted as merely wishful thinking.[91]

Adolphe Boschot in *Un Romantique sous Louis-Philippe* raises some doubts about Berlioz's integrity in his reviews of Duponchel and Meyerbeer.[92] Boschot's patronizing tone and lack of documentation are irritating, and it is easy to understand how he provoked the ire of Jacques Barzun. Nevertheless some of the points made by Boschot are valid and should not be too quickly passed over. For instance Boschot questions the integrity of Berlioz's 1834 reviews of the Théâtre Ventadour. He feels these reviews mirror Berlioz's personal relationship to the theater, that Berlioz's review for *Le Rénovateur* (13 June) of the theater's opening is not favorable because the theater had rejected a project proposed by Berlioz for a performance featuring his wife Harriet Smithson.[93] Harriet was engaged soon after this article, and Berlioz's next article on the Théâtre overflows with enthusiasm for the exciting possibilities of this new venue. I would tend to agree with Boschot. Although Berlioz may well have genuinely found the theater opening poor, but later felt that the prospects were better, his concern over Harriet's involvement with the theater would also have affected his criticism.[94]

Berlioz always referred to himself as an "honest critic," which indeed he was by the standards of the day.[95] As he said in his *Mémoires*, in his reviews of works he disliked the truth is almost always discernible, certainly to someone familiar with his style and beliefs, though perhaps not to the occasional reader. Those reviews where it is hard to tell exactly what Berlioz is thinking are almost without exception reviews of fairly insignificant works.

It is impossible for a composer-critic not to be influenced by his personal needs and interests. Berlioz even acquits himself well in this regard, since so often his digressions on the problems of the composer are attempts to achieve better conditions for all composers. But just as it is wrong to assume that Berlioz's "shady" reviews are symptomatic of a dishonest approach to criticism, so the attempt to whitewash Berlioz's involvement in any of the malpractices of the day needs to be corrected.

5

Attribution of Some Unsigned Articles of Berlioz in the *Revue et Gazette Musicale*, 1834–1837

To conclude the first part of this book I propose to examine a number of unsigned articles in the *Revue et Gazette Musicale* and explain why I attribute them to Berlioz. The full list of identified articles can be found in appendix B.

One of the journals to which Berlioz contributed most during his critical career was the *Revue et Gazette Musicale,* in which a number of unsigned articles of the 1830s show striking similarities to signed articles by Berlioz. The first aim of this chapter is to document and justify the reasons for attributing these articles to Berlioz. It was necessary to establish a workable method for identifying which articles were by Berlioz, a method that would raise questions of style, content, and the making of comparisons. The second, subsidiary aim was to establish why Berlioz wrote the articles.

As stated in chapter 3, Berlioz was an active collaborator for the *Revue et Gazette Musicale* from 1834 until 1859, and he contributed to it most extensively during the second half of the 1830s. It was common in 1834 for articles to remain unsigned, and there were many unsigned articles in the *Gazette Musicale* of 1834. The number diminished over the years however, and the period 1834 to 1837 proved the most productive in the search for unsigned articles by Berlioz. Over this same period the *Revue et Gazette Musicale* also published ninety-one of Berlioz's signed articles.[1]

Katherine Kolb Reeve confirms my view that there are a number of unsigned articles by Berlioz in the *Revue et Gazette Musicale.*[2] Reeve's articles for the *Berlioz Society Bulletin* prove that three of the unsigned *Revue et Gazette Musicale* articles are by Berlioz. These are the articles written in 1836 and signed "Un Vieillard stupide qui n'a presque plus de dents."[3] Berlioz is easily identifiable as the author of these articles since he repeats verbatim material from the first article (signed "Un Vieillard") in two subsequent signed reviews. Another five of the articles in my list can be shown to be by Berlioz simply by reference to his correspondence, in which he mentions them.[4] That is, he refers to having written them without, however, saying that they were unsigned.

More evidence is needed to show that the remaining unsigned articles from the *Revue et Gazette Musicale* (1834–37) are written by Berlioz, and the following method of identification was developed. It is based on three comparisons:

1. Comparison with reviews in other journals and newspapers of the time, both literary and political. The aim here is to see if other critics had written on the same subjects as those of the unsigned articles, and if so in what way their articles differed.[5]
2. Comparison with signed articles by Berlioz on the same subjects as the unsigned articles.
3. Examination of the style of the unsigned articles and comparison with the style of Berlioz's articles in general.

The first two comparisons provide convincing evidence by themselves; the third is only summarily applied. The second is the most convincing in nearly all cases.

A close examination of almost half the articles is presented, not including the articles mentioned in the correspondence and the "Vieillard" articles, showing why they are thought to be written by Berlioz. The remaining articles are merely listed (see appendix B). Of course the same process of identification could be applied to all articles, but the method has shown itself to be sufficiently workable and convincing without a full examination of each article being necessary.

Given its brevity, the examination remains fairly general. It aims to note points that will help in the identification of the articles and is not intended in any way as a comprehensive analysis of Berlioz's style.

Berlioz's narrative skill, his use of irony, his panegyrics for certain composers, and his tendency frequently to repeat certain personal opinions are the features of his literary style that have proved most useful in the process of identification.

Berlioz's mode of panegyric is often distinguished by a series of short phrases or sometimes even single words that explode in rapid succession for as much as a paragraph, occasionally interpolated by exclamation marks. He uses a number of words recurrently, such as "sublime," "poésie," "chef-d'oeuvre," "passion," "beau," "génie." This technique is merely a feature of Berlioz's mode of praise and when it occurs it is on the whole backed up by concrete evidence of why a work deserves praise. His mode of panegyric is usually reserved for a performance of the music of Beethoven, Gluck, or Weber, the writings of Shakespeare, or, to a lesser extent, Virgil, and occasionally for an exceptional performance of the work of another composer. While this mode of panegyric was not uncommon at the time, particularly in reference to Beethoven, it was not common for other Parisian critics to describe Gluck's or Weber's music in the same manner.

Once Berlioz has evolved a way of describing something or someone he often retains this description, reusing the same phrases. Thus, there are some expressions which become immediately identifiable as having been written by Berlioz.

This leads directly to the next feature of Berlioz's critical style, the repetition, frequently in the same words moreover, of certain opinions. This has been used the most extensively for purposes of identification. While other features of Berlioz's style have also been appealed to, they are more elusive and therefore more difficult to use as a tool.

Here are some concrete examples of opinions that Berlioz frequently repeated. They fall into two general groups, dislikes and eulogies. Things that Berlioz disliked are those which most often became formulae:

1. Vocalized "amens." They were usually spoken of as "those vocalized and fugal amens."[6] Berlioz's most enduring criticism of the "vocalized amen" is of course in the *Damnation de Faust,* where he has a group of drunken' students parodying it.
2. Italian cadence. This is most frequently referred to as "that most tired harmonic formula, the Italian cadence"[7] and seems to be a reference to a repeated $IV–V(^6_4)–V(^5_3)–I$ cadence at the end of a section or composition.
3. Scholastic use of the fugue, particularly in religious music. That is, use of the fugue just for the sake of showing that one knows how to write it, not because it is dramatically motivated. Schumann shared Berlioz's prejudice against the non-poetic fugue, saying that the best fugue was one whose mechanics were so concealed that it could be mistaken for a Strauss waltz.[8]
4. Parisian taste for the "romance, galop, *contredanse,* vaudeville, open air concerts, solos by—, one act *opéras-comiques,* Italian cavatinas, manufacturers of quadrilles, air and variations by—," et cetera. Berlioz usually quotes these items in a list. The list is not always the same but would normally include two or three of the above items.
5. "Chanteuses qui brodent" (singers who embroider their parts). Berlioz was by no means the only critic to complain about this phenomenon; his opinion was shared by his contemporary critics Edouard Fétis and Joseph Mainzer. What is distinctive about Berlioz's criticism of the "chanteuses" is his frequent use of the phrase "abominable roulade," written in italics, and best translated perhaps as "abominable vocal ornamentation."
6. *Concours* for the *Prix de Rome.* Berlioz particularly disliked both the system of examination—for instance the fact that the score was judged on the piano version—and the choice of Rome as a place for study.
7. Lack of acceptable concert halls in Paris.
8. Over-use of the "bass-drum" among contemporary composers. Again this was a common complaint among critics. Berlioz began to point to the

absence of the *grosse-caisse* in a work as a sign of merit. In such cases he invariably uses the phrase, "There is no bass drum" (again printed in italics).

Berlioz's eulogistic references to Gluck, Weber, Beethoven, and Shakespeare occur continually in all his writings, and although a large number of critics at the time spoke of both Beethoven and Shakespeare in eulogistic terms, none knew their works in the same depth or had analyzed them to the same degree as had Berlioz. Eulogies on Weber and Gluck are more characteristic of Berlioz than of anyone else. These distinctive likes and dislikes of Berlioz were a considerable aid in identifying the unsigned articles.

Examination of the Unsigned Articles

"De l'utilité d'un opéra-allemand à Paris" (6 July 1834)

Authorization for the performance of German Opera at the Ventadour Theater in July 1834 was not given much coverage by the music critics at the time. The *Journal de Paris* (5 July 1834) noted, "The license to perform German opera has just been granted to the director of the Ventadour Theater," but even a notice as brief as this was rare.[9] Towards the end of 1834 and at the beginning of 1835 several critics wrote articles on German opera and performers, with reference to the proposed revival of *Robin des bois* (the French version of *Der Freischütz*) at the Opéra-Comique. An article by André Delrieu for *Le Temps* (29 December 1834, 2) represents the suspicion common amongst many people at the time. He comments:

> For a public already not tempted much by the mellow, simple, and short recitatives of Italian composers, these interludes in a guttural and completely unfamiliar language will hold little attraction. The acting of the German artists is even more removed from our acting style than the declamation of the Théâtre Italien.[10]

Delrieu dutifully concludes by wishing the venture success. However, he clearly has misgivings about the appeal of German opera to a French audience. An article in the *Revue Musicale* (4 January 1835), unsigned but probably by Edouard Fétis, is more critical than Delrieu's article. The article disapproves of the performance of any foreign works at the Opéra-Comique, which the author felt should be reserved solely for French music.

Berlioz, however, was consistently enthusiastic about the coming of German opera, and particularly about the beneficial effect that the performance of German works could have on the musical education of the public, as is shown for example by his article for *Le Rénovateur* (2 July 1834). No other critic, at least none for the journals and newspapers examined, wrote on the subject in July

1834. Thus external evidence seems to point to Berlioz as the author of the *Gazette Musicale* article. Closer examination of the article confirms this impression.

A comparison between Berlioz's signed article on the subject and the unsigned *Gazette Musicale* article shows striking similarities. Compare for example:

> We were only able to hear Beethoven and Weber seven times a year at the rue Bergère concerts; from now on it will be possible to applaud these masterpieces daily.[11]
>
> *(Le Rénovateur, 2 July 1834)*

> The numerous worshippers of Beethoven and Weber are in ecstasy. The authorization to perform German opera has just been granted to the Ventadour Theater.[12]
>
> *(Gazette Musicale, 6 July 1834)*

> Ah! we are going once again to see *Fidelio* with Mme Schroeder! Let us also hope that we will not miss out on Haitzinger's vibrating voice.[13]
>
> *(Le Rénovateur, 2 July 1834)*

> We hope to see Fidelio again, acted by Madame Schroeder, also, probably [as] Florestan, Haitzinger whose marvelous voice has left such a strong impression on the habitués of the Salle Favart.[14]
>
> *(Gazette Musicale, 6 July 1834)*

The way in which the article discusses the Conservatoire concert audience—"the habitués of the Conservatoire, the elect of musical intelligence"—is very typical of the way Berlioz describes the Conservatoire audience.[15] To give just one example: "a choice, intelligent, and attentive public."[16] And the list of Parisian addictions listed in the article: "the *contredanses*, the galops, the waltzes, the vaudevilles et cetera"—is constantly repeated (with variations) by Berlioz.

"La Tempête, *ballet en 2 actes, précédé d'un prologue, de M. Coraly, musique de M. Schneitzoeffer, décors de MM. Ciceri, Feuchères, etc.*" *(7 September 1834)*

La Tempête was reviewed in all journals consulted.[17] The première of a new ballet was always considered worthy of review, even by the political newspapers, and particularly if one of the star ballerinas, in this case Fanny Elssler, was performing. Nearly every review of *La Tempête* concentrates on retelling the story in a humorous way. The reviews vary considerably in detail, though some incidents are recounted in all. The reviews in *La Quotidienne, Le Constitutionnel,* and *L'Artiste* barely mention the music, but dwell on the details of the *mise-en-scène* and the décor. The reviews for *Le National, Revue de Paris,* and *Le Ménestrel* mention the score briefly but only in order to condemn it. Apart from the obvious resemblances amongst all the articles in the retelling of the story, it is only the review in the *Revue Musicale* that bears any resemblance to the unsigned article in the *Gazette Musicale.*

Although the *Revue Musicale* article (signed "F. B."[unidentified]) expresses similar views to the unsigned article on the music of *La Tempête*, the similarities between Berlioz's *Le Rénovateur* article and the unsigned *Gazette Musicale* article are so strong as to make Berlioz's authorship of the unsigned article indisputable. Both articles remark sympathetically that M. Schneitzoeffer might have been obliged to change various sections of his music because of the demands of the master choreographer, and in praising the décor, both draw attention to the representation of the sea: "the imitation of the turbulent sea is also surprisingly true to life" (*Le Rénovateur*, 21 September 1834) and "the luxury of the *mise-en-scène* is truly royal; several effects, amongst others that of the turbulent sea whose waves break with a crash on the shore, covering it with flecks of foam . . . appeared both new and ingeniously rendered."[18]

There is also a striking comparison to another signed article by Berlioz, "L'Ile des pirates," *Le Rénovateur*, 16 and 17 August 1835. Here, Berlioz comments ironically on the intelligibility of pantomime, giving as an example "the man who in the *Sleeping Beauty* ballet carts onto the middle of the stage a large placard bearing the following words in enormous letters: *She will sleep for a hundred years.*"[19] The *Gazette Musicale* article refers to the same incident:

> Every time that it concerns an idea on which the meaning of the piece depends, it seems necessary to write it in big letters on a well-placed placard, where all the spectators can read, as in *Sleeping Beauty: She will sleep for a hundred years.*[20]

The ironical tone of the *Gazette Musicale* article is very similar to that adopted by Berlioz in many of his articles. The introduction of another character into the review besides the narrator is also a device used by Berlioz (and indeed by many other nineteenth-century writers such as E. T. A. Hoffmann, Schumann, and Jules Janin). The *Gazette Musicale* author's demonstrated acquaintance with the music of Spontini, Méhul, Grétry, and Mozart suggests someone with as broad a musical knowledge as Berlioz.

"Du mouvement musicale à Paris" (21 December 1834)

This article is a summary of recent musical events rather than a review of a specific concert and deals mainly with three issues: the construction of the Gymnase Musical (a new concert hall), the state of the Opéra and the Opéra-Comique, and the débuts of several singers. A large part of the article concentrates on the Gymnase Musical, on which Berlioz certainly wrote more articles than any other critic of the time. Before the opening of the Gymnase

Musical he wrote about its potential (*Le Rénovateur*, 17 May 1834), then later reviewed dress rehearsals (*Le Rénovateur*, 28 May 1834). He also reviewed the opening (*Gazette Musicale*, 31 May 1834) and many subsequent performances.[21]

The section on the Gymnase Musical in the unsigned *Gazette Musicale* article corresponds, in its description of the building, with the description that Berlioz gives in his article in *Le Rénovateur* (17 May 1835), the only difference being that by May 1835 the apprehensions about finding a suitable orchestra and choir had been resolved. Both articles comment on the interdiction of the *contredanse*: "the *contredanse* and the *galop* will be excluded" (*Le Rénovateur*), and "*the contredanse will not be on the program at all*" (*Gazette Musicale*).[22]

None of the other journals consulted discuss the formation of the Gymnase Musical at any length. An article in *Le Temps* (30 December 1834), which was unsigned but probably written by d'Ortigue, has two paragraphs on the formation of the Gymnase. But these are copied directly, and acknowledged as such, from the unsigned *Gazette Musicale* article: "There has been a question for some time now of the formation of a Gymnase Musical. The *Gazette Musicale* gives some curious information on this subject."[23] *Le Ménestrel* regularly followed the progress of the Gymnase, but mostly by snippets inserted in the Notes (*Nouvelles*) section; there were no full-length articles on the Gymnase.

None of the other critics consulted commented on the negligence of the performance at the Opéra of isolated acts from *Guillaume Tell* and *La Vestale*. They were more concerned with reviewing the ballets that these acts accompanied. On the other hand, the similarity between the *Gazette Musicale* article and a review by Berlioz in *Le Rénovateur* (14 December 1834), in which he does mention the careless performance of the second act of *Guillaume Tell* at the Opéra, is striking:

> I shall not speak of the musical execution [of the second act]; I want to address myself to the stagehand. Does he despise Rossini to the point of not caring at all about the décor for his works? It is hard to believe. However, at the end of the magnificent Grutli scene, when the woods, the waters, and the mountains must be inundated with floods of light, the sun did not appear; the canvas at the back, instead of rising little by little, stayed immobile, and the war-cry of the Swiss echoed in the dark.[24]
>
> (*Le Rénovateur*, 23 December 1834)

> In the second act of *Guillaume Tell* . . . everything was performed with such contemptuous slovenliness that even the stagehand did not think it necessary to stay at his post, so that at the end of the scene on the Grutli, when Arnold cries, "*Here is the day!*" the canvas at the back remained stationary and the sun did not appear.[25]
>
> (*Gazette Musicale*, 21 December 1834)

Other critics do refer to the débuts of singers; for instance the début of Mademoiselle Lebrun is commented on in the *Revue Musicale* (14 December

1834, 399, unsigned) and in *Le Ménestrel* (7 December 1834, 1, unsigned). These two reviews however do not show the same resemblance to the *Gazette Musicale* article as does an article by Berlioz in *Le Rénovateur* (14 December 1834). In this article Berlioz remarks on Mlle. Lebrun's weakness in sustained singing, "If I were her teacher I would make her do scales *adagio sostenuto* for a long, long, long time," and similarly the *Gazette Musicale* article comments "Mademoiselle Lebrun possesses a very fine contralto voice that she has used a lot in brilliant passages, but very little in sustained singing."[26] Both articles stress that more work was essential before any important role could be undertaken.

"Première représentation de Robin des bois*" (18 January 1835)*

All newspapers consulted had a review of *Robin des bois*.[27] Berlioz himself wrote a review for *Le Rénovateur* (18 January 1835). The merits of Castil-Blaze's version of *Der Freischütz* (*Robin des bois*), are commented on by three of the journals, all of which give the impression that they felt Castil-Blaze had been unjustly criticized. The *Gazette Musicale* article refers to the Castil-Blaze arrangement as the "monster of the Odéon," and although begrudgingly accepting the reason for the arrangement, the author complains trenchantly of the mutilations and corrections that still remain in the score. Berlioz's bitter attacks on Castil-Blaze's arrangements are well known, as is the fact that Berlioz himself later resurrected the score for a performance in 1841, restoring it to what he felt was as close as possible to Weber's original. The comments in the *Gazette Musicale* article on the faults still remaining in the score—something that no other critic had remarked upon—suggest that the article is by Berlioz.

In fact most things about the article suggest Berlioz. The ecstatic enthusiasm for Weber is very typical, as can be seen by the similarity between the following extracts, one from the *Gazette Musicale* article and one from a signed article by Berlioz:

> What invention! What ingenious work! What treasures this startling inspiration has made us discover! . . . There is nothing like it! It is divine art! It is poetry! It is love itself![28]
>
> (*Journal des Débats,* 16 June 1841)

> [Weber reduces me] to exclaim at each section, at each page, beautiful, sublime, prodigious, stupifying, incredible in its force, originality, grace, passion, reverie, [and] poetry, brimming over with inspiration.[29]
>
> (*Gazette Musicale,* 18 January 1835)

Though some of the other critics, in particular the reviewers for *Le Temps* and *L'Artiste,* were strong supporters of Weber, none was as extravagant in his praise as Berlioz. Fétis wrote a long article for *Le Temps* (1 February 1835, 2) entitled "Considérations sur la musique de Weber." The difference between his considered, pedantic tone and the flamboyance of that of Berlioz is well demonstrated by the following quotation from Fétis's article:

> To sum up, though it is easy to point out several serious faults in Weber's style, one cannnot deny that he has found many new things and that he was gifted with dramatic genius.[30]

A closer examination of the *Gazette Musicale* article reveals that whereas all the reviews commented enthusiastically on the German choir (except the critic for *Le Moniteur Universel* who felt that the choir lacked elevation in the religious passages) the author of the *Gazette Musicale* article had a quite specific complaint to make about the choir. It is surely significant that Berlioz makes the same complaint in his review for *Le Rénovateur:*

> The troupe of German singers . . . formed a formidable choir, whose studies unfortunately had not been directed in such a manner as to get the best out of them. . . . [T]he absence of musical feeling is noticeable everywhere, and certain passages that I thought would lead to a great success for the choir passed unnoticed.[31]
>
> *(Le Rénovateur, 18 January 1835)*

> The choir . . . performed several pieces very nicely; but in several others we found them a hundred leagues below what one has the right to expect from such a large number of voices. The reason must be attributed uniquely to the total lack of musical feeling in the conducting of the choir.[32]
>
> *(Gazette Musicale, 18 Jan. 1835)*

"Deuxième concert du Conservatoire" (8 February 1835)

The Conservatoire concerts were not considered to be of universal interest as was, for example, the première of a new ballet. Of the fourteen journals and newpapers consulted only four had reviews of the Conservatoire concerts: *Journal de Paris* (27 February, 2, signed "A. D." [Alphonse Duchesne]); *Le Temps* (7 February, 1–2, unsigned); *Revue Musicale* (8 February, 46–47, unsigned); and *L'Artiste* (vol. 9, no. 3, unsigned). The views expressed in these four newspapers are, with the exception of the *Journal de Paris*, surprisingly similar to one another, to the *Gazette Musicale* article, and to Berlioz's two signed articles on the concert for *Le Rénovateur* (8 February 1835) and *Journal des Débats* (12 February 1835). All the articles complain of the programming, point to the different expectations of the audience that attended the Conservatoire concerts, and underline the importance of performing works of consistently high quality. All reviews uniformly praise Beethoven.

Comparisons made between the vocabulary of the author of the *Gazette Musicale* article and by Berlioz in his two articles on the concert show striking similarities. A Fesca overture is variously described in the three articles as being "deprived of any real ideas" (*Le Rénovateur*), "a total eclipse of ideas" (*Journal des Débats*), and "deprived of ideas" (*Gazette Musicale*).[33] The author of the *Gazette Musicale* article felt that the Beethoven symphony produced more effect in this concert than in previous years. Berlioz expressed the same opinion in his article for *Le Rénovateur*.

To give just one more example, the opinion expressed and the vocabulary used in the description of Weber's *Oberon* overture are strongly suggestive of Berlioz: "Weber has never written anything that is more deliciously dreamy, more tender."[34]

"Troisième concert du Conservatoire" (22 February 1835)

The third Conservatoire concert was reviewed by the *Journal de Paris* (27 February, 2–3, "A. D."[Alphonse Duchesne]; *Le Temps* (22 February, 1–3, unsigned but possibly by d'Ortigue); *L'Artiste* (vol. 9, no. 6, 70, signed "R."); and by E. Fétis for the *Revue Musicale* (22 February, 60–61).

One of the most important features of these reviews is the expression of their attitude towards Haydn and Beethoven. It was undoubtedly fashionable at the time to find the symphonies of Haydn insipid in comparison to those of Beethoven. Mendelssohn, in a letter to Carl Zelter, commented disparagingly on this fashion, saying that the French denigration of Haydn showed a lack of understanding of Beethoven: "If they really appreciate what Beethoven had in mind, they must also know what Haydn was, and feel very small."[35]

Berlioz's early music criticism is strongly antagonistic towards Haydn, though he attempts to give a semblance of balance to his arguments, pointing out sections that he likes—for instance an unexpected modulation—and almost always holds the *Creation* to be a work of art.

The four reviews of the Conservatoire concert listed above represent a cross-section of typical attitudes towards Haydn. "A. D." for the *Journal de Paris,* though to a slight extent adopting the patronizing tone common at the time when writing on Haydn, clearly enjoyed the Haydn much more than the Beethoven, which he found complicated and disappointing. The critic for *L'Artiste*, "R.," reviews the third and fourth concerts together, concentrating on the fourth concert. One in fact gets the impression that he had not attended the third concert since his review of it centers on an exposition of the current opinions of Haydn and indeed could very easily have been adapted from one of Berlioz's reviews of the concert.

The critics for *Le Temps* and the *Revue Musicale* both appear to be reacting against the prevailing idolatry of Beethoven, though at the same time neither wishes to deny Beethoven's greatness. The *Le Temps* critic (22 February 1835, 2), for instance, comments, "Why make enemies of two first-rate artists just because, in the end, they belong to two different periods?"[36] The author expands on this point at some length, commenting also on the division in the audience between "romantics" and "classicists."

Edouard Fétis, writing for the *Revue Musicale,* comments mildly that the Conservatoire audience is unjust towards Haydn and Mozart "ever since the crowd of listeners has been taken up, quite justly to tell the truth, but with too much partiality, with fanatical admiration for Beethoven" (*Revue Musicale,* 22 February 1835, 60).[37] He concludes by stating that he found this particular Beethoven symphony—it was the eighth symphony—not as interesting as the Haydn.

Thus the *Gazette Musicale* article's scorn for the Haydn's supposed prosaicness and lack of passion, though very typical of Berlioz, is certainly not unique to him, but a common sentiment among certain artists of the time. A comparison between the section on Haydn in the *Gazette Musicale* article and corresponding sections in Berlioz's two reviews of this concert does show, however, very strong similarities of vocabulary and phrasing. Even more striking is the description in all three, of two of Berlioz's "bêtes noires," the "Italian cadence" and the "vocalized amen."

An "Italian cadence" appeared in the finale of the andante scherzando of the Beethoven symphony. Here are the corresponding sections describing it from each article:

> Unfortunately this admirable piece is a little shortened . . . and the end, astonishingly, is none other than the Italian cadence.[38]
>
> (*Le Rénovateur,* 17 February 1835)

> Could one believe that this ravishing idyll finishes with that of which, of all that is commonplace, Beethoven had the most horror, the Italian cadence![39]
>
> (*Journal des Débats,* 20 February 1835)

> The *Andante Scherzando,* where the violins are accompanied in such a piquant manner by the woodwind, would be one of the author's masterpieces if the end were not so curtailed. Besides, the two last measures comprise one of the most hackneyed harmonic forms, the Italian cadence.[40]
>
> (*Gazette Musicale,* 22 February 1835)

One other critic does mention the Italian cadence, but in such a way that it is clearly meant as a criticism of Berlioz. The critic for *Le Temps* comments:

> There are certain artists who will not forgive Beethoven for having employed a playful style in this andante, and especially for having finished with an Italian cadence. Everything is permitted the genius on the condition that he does it well. We have only one thing to say to the denigrators: Do as much yourselves. And their powerlessness will prove that it is no easier to imitate genius in the small things than in the great.[41]
>
> (*Le Temps,* 22 February 1835)

No other review comments on the "vocalized amen" at the end of the Beethoven *Gloria.* One doubts even if Edouard Fétis stayed until the end of the concert since he mistakenly states that the *Credo* was performed.

The question needs to be asked why Berlioz wrote these unsigned articles, and whether he wrote unsigned articles for any other journal or newspaper. As far as I can tell Berlioz did not write any unsigned articles for other journals or newspapers, except for the two autobiographical articles that he wrote for his friend d'Ortigue, who signed them in his own name.

As stated in chapter 1, the political newspapers had only sporadic music criticism at the beginning of the 1830s. As the decade progressed their music criticism became more regular, but also tended to be written by the one critic or perhaps shared by several, who signed or initialed their articles or occasionally still left them anonymous. The same is true of the majority of the literary journals. The only journal that continued to have a large number of unsigned articles was *L'Artiste.* Presumably, to insert an unsigned article in one of these newspapers or journals Berlioz would have had to have been acquainted with their editors. There is little evidence in his correspondence of this being the case, and although this does not exclude the possibility, it does not seem likely that there is a body of unsigned articles by Berlioz in any other journal of the time.

The major Parisian music journals of the time, apart from the *Gazette Musicale,* were *Le Ménestrel,* and, until November 1835 the *Revue Musicale.* At this time *Le Ménestrel* rarely had full-length articles on music; it was not a scholarly journal but catered chiefly to the devotees of the popular musical forms such as the romance and the *opéra-comique.* Berlioz's relationship with Fétis was not friendly, and Fétis would not have welcomed any articles from Berlioz, signed or unsigned. Thus the *Revue et Gazette Musicale* stands out as the most convenient magazine in which to insert anonymous articles on music, since Berlioz was on good terms with its editor, Maurice Schlesinger. Berlioz would not have written the unsigned articles for the *Revue et Gazette Musicale* for nothing, as he was too desperately in need of money, so Schlesinger must have been party to having Berlioz write them.

Two reasons could be suggested for why Berlioz himself might have wanted these articles to remain unsigned. First, many of them, as already shown, were on subjects about which he had already written, and they thus repeated ideas from other articles. Berlioz might have wished the articles to remain unsigned to avoid being accused of having duplicated material. Second, several of the articles, for instance the article "Du mouvement musical" of 1835, are provocative and strongly attack the musical establishment. Berlioz might have wished to remain anonymous in these cases, or alternatively Schlesinger might have thought it more appropriate that such articles remain unsigned. It is interesting that the article "Du mouvement musical" has an editorial note on the bottom that reads: "Without completely sharing the opinion on every issue of our spirited collaborator, we have made it our duty to insert this article."[42] Schlesinger was clearly aware how provocative these articles were.

In addition, since Berlioz wrote a very large number of articles for the *Revue et Gazette Musicale* during the 1830s, perhaps Schlesinger felt that his readers would object to too many articles signed "H. Berlioz," and consequently left some of them unsigned.

These are all reasonable explanations of the unsigned articles. It is a great pity that in his correspondence Berlioz does not mention leaving these articles unsigned and that there are no surviving autographs for any of them.

The quality of Berlioz's writing, combined with the extent of his knowledge of music, make his criticism superior to that of his contemporary Parisian music critics. It is unwise however to view his criticism in isolation from the work of his contemporaries. Study of these unsigned articles has shown that although Berlioz was often individualistic in his opinions he still shared many of his fellow critics' views. The very posing of the question, "Is this article by Berlioz?" shows that there was a body of music criticism forming during the 1830s with which Berlioz's criticism could be identified.

Part Two

Berlioz's Criticism of His Contemporaries

6

Vocal Music: *Opéra-Comique*

During his early years as a critic Berlioz reviewed a large number of *opéras-comiques*—the majority of which he disliked—for *Le Rénovateur* (1834 and 1835), the *Journal des Débats* (1835 to 1837), and the *Revue et Gazette Musicale* (1836 and 1837).

He wrote most of the reviews in the years 1834 and 1835 and virtually none in 1836. In 1836 Jules Janin covered *opéra-comique* for the *Journal des Débats*, and J. J. J. Diaz [Henri Blanchard] wrote the majority of reviews for the *Revue et Gazette Musicale*. Interestingly, that was also the year that Berlioz's three unsigned articles on *opéra-comique* appeared. These articles, while humorous, are much more acerbic than his signed *Revue et Gazette Musicale* articles on the genre. The following year, 1837, Berlioz began to review *opéras-comiques* again, and would often review the same work for the *Revue et Gazette Musicale*, *Journal des Débats,* and *Chronique de Paris*. His reviews in 1837, particularly his articles for the *Journal des Débats,* are slightly more overt in their criticism than in the earlier years.

A study of these *opéra-comique* reviews forms an interesting critical exercise because of the many different ways Berlioz avoids expressing his true feelings. His typical review of an *opéra-comique* is devious and ironical. Yet, with the aid of remarks made in his correspondence and in several straightforward articles, a more or less clear picture of his "true" impressions can be drawn from the web of rhetorical devices.

The *opéra-comique* of this period, the 1830s, comprised the works of Adam, Auber, Paer, Hérold, and others. It was to these works specifically that Berlioz objected, and not to the genre of *opéra-comique* itself. Indeed he talked with melancholy nostalgia of the *opéra-comique* of Monsigny, Dalayrac, Méhul, and Grétry (in particular *Richard Coeur de Lion*). Though not of the same stature as Gluck or Beethoven, these composers nevertheless represented for Berlioz a type of perfection within the limitations of their medium. He praises their simplicity and charm, the grace and perennial freshness of their melodies and their lack of pretension. He found the rapidity with which such works faded from the public's memory depressing and discouraging for contemporary artists, noting that "it is as though anything that is not part of the current concert and lyric theater repertoire has never occurred."[1] Since not much interest was expressed in these composers at the time, Berlioz's enthusiasm was unusual. His respect for earlier *opéra-comique* was further enhanced by the comparison to the *opéra-comique* of the 1830s. As he commented in an article for the *Revue et Gazette Musicale* of 1837:

> One could, it seems to me, grieve to see how real masterpieces languish in complete abandonment, while great attention and homage are paid to the myriad inane platitudes that appear each day, to squander arts' riches, buzz for an instant, then die.[2]

Berlioz's antipathy was not unusual. The average *opéra-comique* of the 1830s was seen by many critics as a distasteful element of the Parisian music scene. The following three quotations, from Deschamps, Berlioz, and Gautier respectively, show a striking similarity of opinion on the subject:

> The *opéra-comique* [is an] *eminently* national, but essentially bastard genre . . . [where] the mixture of spoken dialogue and music is no less fatal for art.[3]

> [The *opéra-comique* is] a bastard genre that tires the lovers of vaudeville by its musical exuberance as much as it irritates music lovers for its opposite faults.[4]

> For our part, we do not have any tender feelings towards the *opéra-comique*, a bastard and paltry genre, a mixture of two incompatible means of expression, where actors act badly under the pretext that they are singers, and sing out of tune under the pretext that they are actors.[5]

The Parisian *opéra-comique* was well known outside France and scorned by many outsiders. Mendelssohn, for example, self-righteously wrote to his father in 1831:

> None of the new libretti here would, in my opinion, be attended with any success if brought out for the first time on a German stage. One of the distinctive characteristics of all of them is precisely of a nature that I should resolutely oppose, although the taste of the present day may demand it, and I truly admit that it may, in general, be more prudent to go with the current than to struggle against it. I allude to that of immorality.[6]

And in a letter to Karl Klingemann he wrote,

> These ways and doings seem to me to smack of the devil; if a man does not pull himself together, he may as well hand over his soul (I mean his musical soul!) to that gentleman in comfort and pleasure. The superficialities are so tempting, people enjoy honors and money and decorations and cheers and orchestras, and lack absolutely nothing—if only they were not such execrably bad musicians![7]

In England the *opéra-comique* was frequently described as relatively harmless in comparison to the gross depravity of the opéra, about which the English music critic George Hogarth said that "the modern French public appear now to have a morbid appetite for horrid and revolting theatrical exhibitions."[8] During her visit to Paris in 1835 Frances Trollope recounted dutifully in her diary that the vaudeville and the *opéra-comique* were not nearly as morally depraved as she had been led to believe:

> It is certain, indeed, that, spite of all we say, and say in some respects so justly, respecting the corrupted taste of France at the present era, there never was a time when her stage could boast a greater affluence of delightful little pieces than at present. . . . Another proof that it is not necessary to be vicious in order to be in vogue at Paris, and that purity is no impediment to success, is the popularity of Madame Tastu's poetry.[9]

Berlioz's reviews of *opéra-comique* are a kaleidoscope of shifting tones and shades of meaning. He employs differing tactics in his approach to a work. Patterns emerge in these tactics however, which can be described as "quasi-methods," though there is no reason to suppose that Berlioz was conscious of them.

There were some *opéras-comiques* that Berlioz *did* like—small respite from the oppressive majority—and these shall be discussed too. It is immediately evident when Berlioz liked a work, and there is no need to decipher verbal games.

Two major patterns emerge in Berlioz's reviews of the *opéras-comiques* that he disliked, and they shall be discussed separately. The first pattern is that of devoting almost the entire review to recounting the libretto, with little or no commentary on the music. This pattern (already mentioned in the previous chapter) occurs chiefly in the 1834 articles for *Le Rénovateur*. Berlioz's retelling of the libretto is witty and entertaining and constantly mocks the nonsensical nature of the narrative. His ensuing comments on the music consist usually of a few standardized and ambiguous phrases, for instance: "This score is a treasure for the public for whom it was destined,"[10] and again: "The music with which M. Adam has embroidered this vaudeville lacks neither grace nor vivacity. It will soon be on pianos everywhere."[11] These platitudes carry a double meaning; their implication is obviously scorn for the music, which is not worthy of separate scrutiny.[12]

In various places Berlioz expressed his dislike of recounting the libretti of *opéras-comiques* and operas. This dislike became more openly expressed in his writings of 1835, and his review of *La Juive* for *Le Rénovateur* demonstrates this with some force.[13] The review opens with a condemnatory remark: "Another rude nightmare! I must recount you M. Scribe's libretto which you could buy for the modest sum of twenty sous."[14] Interestingly, Jules Janin's review of *La Juive* for the *Journal des Débats* starts in much the same way: "Unfortunately, before discussing the music of operas of this nature, it is necessary to discuss the libretto, and, again unfortunately, the libretto has to be a libretto of M. Scribe."[15] Franz Stoepel in his review of *La Juive* in the *Gazette Musicale* starts: "Let us start with the libretto, as is the custom in France."[16] "P." writes for *Le Moniteur Universel,* "The examination of an opera always raises an initial question for us. Is the libretto any good? This does not mean, especially when talking of M. Scribe, is it well written?"[17] These comments confirm that the recounting of the libretto was a convention considered necessary at the time and probably demanded of the critic by journal editors. Berlioz certainly implies in his reviews that he is under constant pressure to recount the libretto. His review of *La Juive* in *Le Rénovateur* continues:

> Thus many of my colleagues take little more trouble in analyzing the words of an opera than they would if it were a discourse of the Academy; and the readers, on seeing all this scribble, hasten to jump to the last column to see if, as usual, *the musician has shown great talent.* For the inequality with which the critic treats the poet and the musician is thoroughly worth noting. If the play is a flop, then the words are to blame; if successful, it is the musician who is to be praised. . . . But all this has nothing to do with *La Juive,* please believe me. My tirade was motivated only by the bad mood engendered by the obligation to write some sort of scenario, or if you prefer a bad extract from the new piece, that no one will read. So, on this occasion I hope to honor it at little cost. I shall be brief.[18]

The intention of being brief is of course not carried out and Berlioz launches once again into a detailed narration of the libretto.

In maligning reviews that always ended with some fatuous reference to the great talent displayed by the composer or musician, Berlioz was giving the lie to his own reviews that followed the same pattern. Having made clear his contempt for this technique, his own use of it demonstrated his lack of respect for the works on which he used it. Obviously it was necessary for him to be diplomatic about works he disliked, and his use of irony in this way was a convenient means for him to intimate his true feelings. At the same time he was able to mock his fellow journalists who worked to such a cliché. Of course, not all his fellow journalists wrote like this. In fact some of them, for instance Henri Blanchard, held views very similar to Berlioz on the subject:

> And do not believe that it is the score that concerns these gentlemen in a lyrical work: no, no! They direct seven or eight columns of indignation or irony at the author of the words, or the *poème,* as they call it, and to the author of the music, devote a little paragraph of ten or twelve lines in which they all say, in more or less identical fashion, "This lively and light music is worthy of the spirited composer."[19]

In a review in *Le Rénovateur* of 1834 Berlioz bemoans the tribulations of a critic and comments on the *opéra-comique, Le Chalet:*

> I have already said that the music of *Le Chalet* was very pretty, what more do you want? Must I list the modulations of each section, tell you how M. Adam goes from *D* to *E flat* or from *G* to *B*? Do you want a list of his woodwind instrumental effects, of his gracious songs?[20]

Thus he publicly admits to the paucity of his remarks on the music, hinting at the same time that an analysis of such music would be ridiculous. It must have been a tedious task recounting libretti. Occasionally Berlioz expresses relief when a libretto is too well known to demand detailed retelling: "The subject of the libretto is so well known that this time I can do away with the analysis."[21] However, the vivacity with which he recounts many of the libretti also seems to suggest he took some enjoyment in his task. Since reviewing *opéras-comiques* was an unavoidable task for the music critic of *Le Rénovateur,* Berlioz appears to have decided to make it as enjoyable as possible by turning his reviews into exercises in wit. These reviews are indeed extremely funny. As the critic Paul Smith commented: "The more a critic such as Berlioz is bored, the less he bores; the more vivacious and passionate he is, the more he formulates his stinging observations."[22] Underlying the humor, nevertheless, Berlioz's conviction of the basic triviality of the music is continually present.

As the author of the majority of these *opéra-comique* libretti (ninety-five in all), Scribe played an important role in the *opéra-comique* as well as in the opera of the 1830s.[23] Though Berlioz appears to have appreciated some of Scribe's libretti, in particular *Les Huguenots,* some of Berlioz's comments on Scribe's *opéra-comique* libretti are unmistakably ironical. The irony is very pronounced in Berlioz's unsigned review of Auber's *Actéon* in the *Revue et Gazette Musicale.* In this review Berlioz pretends to be under the impression that Auber has written the libretto and Scribe the music:

> Strictly speaking this is not bad for a musician. I well know that if M. Scribe had written the words instead of the music, he would certainly not have been happy with such a poor plot, nor employed such old-fashioned means; he would assuredly not have made Prince Aldobrandi so absolutely ridiculous without being also amusing. . . . But, on the whole, as I have just said, it is not bad for a musician.[24]

However, Berlioz's ironical comments on Scribe's *opéra-comique* libretti were just small darts to throw at someone who had attained the status of an institution, or had become, in Frances Trollope's words, "a national museum of invention."[25]

The second method emerging in these reviews is more difficult to elaborate. It could be said that many of Berlioz's reviews of *opéra-comique* are written in "bad faith"; that is, there are a number of reviews that give the appearance of being serious, objective articles, but which are in reality a tissue of semi-truths.

In these reviews Berlioz starts, as required, with a summary of the libretto, but he then proceeds to comment on the music. Following basically the method of Castil-Blaze outlined in chapter 3, Berlioz takes small sections of the score, elaborating on passages he likes and other passages he dislikes. This is such a common procedure that it is easy to read the article without digesting *what* it is that Berlioz likes. Closer examination shows that often the sections liked by Berlioz are very small compared with the sections he dislikes. To quote an example from his review of the *Cheval de bronze* by Auber:

> Several other pieces, amongst which I can draw attention to a duo and the overture, were also very much enjoyed. But the composer's verve did not serve him as well in the last act which is dominated by unmelodious roulade.[26]

Here, it is small passages such as a duo and overture which he likes while he dislikes the entire third act of the work. To quote another example, this time in a review of Godefroid's *La Diadesté* in the *Revue et Gazette Musicale* of 1836:

> In my opinion the overture is the best section of the piece. To be honest I do not like the little skipping theme in the middle, and the rest is rather dull; but it is all clearly arranged, and the beat is extremely regular.[27]

To quote a similar example from his review of Loïsa Puget's *Le Mauvais Oeil*:

> Her overture is not the best. I must admit that most of the phrases that comprise it are rather common; but the *coda* really has verve, enough, even, to excuse the author for her frightful bass-drum, an ignoble instrument that a young woman should never have used.[28]

This is not the only way he shows his derision. In other instances the sections he purportedly likes are qualified in such a way as to demonstrate quite clearly his scorn for them. To quote, again, from his review of Auber's *Cheval de bronze*:

> M. Auber was very inspired during the first two acts; from all sides rise the most droll little melodies. They will make the fortunes of our *contre-danse* hawkers.[29]

Berlioz's irony and condescension are here unmistakable. His use of the word "joli" is often equally condescending. Commenting on Auber's *Domino noir,* he says,

> In this unadventurous and unlikely, but lively and amusing piece, M. Auber has written one of his prettiest scores.[30]

While not as damning as some of the other comments, "jolie partition" is not very flattering; "joli" was not an adjective used by Berlioz to describe works he admired.

There are two words which immediately signal an article in "bad faith." These are the verbs "broder" ("to embroider"), and "brillanter" ("to load with florid ornament" or "to tart up"). If Berlioz starts an article by the words "The music with which M. x has embroidered this libretto" one knows that, whatever the number of small compliments that follow, Berlioz does not like the work. His review of the *Cheval de bronze,* for instance, starts: "The music with which M. Auber has ornamented this fantastic libretto is of a piquant character,"[31] and in his review of Loîsa Puget's *Le Mauvais Oeil* he writes, "Mademoiselle Puget has embroidered this little libretto."[32] Berlioz could never really respect music that he saw as only a decorative adjunct, and not as a dramatic expression of a text.

On the rare occasions when Berlioz discusses his criticism in his correspondence, proof is given of these conjectural remarks about his articles in "bad faith." The most striking occasion is the series of letters on Niedermeyer's opera *Stradella* mentioned in chapter 4. Another instance occurs in a letter in 1842, where, reviewing a work by Auber, Berlioz says, "I will say that it is *quite agreeable,* without adding *for dressmakers.*"[33] In 1839 Berlioz wrote with considerable bitterness of his critical role:

> The career of critic is odious to me; I have to manufacture a whole heap of platitudes that make me sick at heart. They pull me in apropos the most minor debutante, singer or pianist, for the most miserable *opéra-comique* that is not even worth an old cigar butt, for all the shameful sores of musical art, in such a way as to give me a frightful impression of the importance of the *Journal des Débats.* . . .
>
> I would be hated to death if I said only half of what I thought. Perhaps I will say it all. What a career![34]

I have elaborated a little on two of the ways in which Berlioz avoids expressing his true feelings. There are more, for his ingenuity is boundless. To give one more example of a different approach, I shall briefly discuss Berlioz's criticism of Ambroise Thomas's first *opéra-comique.*[35]

Ambroise Thomas's *La Double Echelle,* performed first in August 1837, presented Berlioz with a critical dilemma. In his writings he often deplored the fact that the winner of the *Prix de Rome* was never given the promised opportunity of having a work performed on his return to Paris. Ambroise Thomas, as a recently returned young *Prix de Rome* winner (1832), had already had a section from his "Italian" opera performed at a public concert at the Académie des Beaux-Arts.[36]

La Double Echelle was his first *opéra-comique.* Berlioz's sympathies were naturally inclined towards the young composer, and also he wished to encourage and applaud the authorities for performing the work of a "new" composer. However, the overall impression one gains from a study of his three reviews of *La Double Echelle* is that he did not like the work.[37]

His review in the *Chronique de Paris* is brief and outwardly favorable, but closer inspection reveals its ambiguities. We see this when he writes for instance, "*La Double Echelle,* a very amusing little comedy, where the music fits only too well the position that one couldn't refuse it, . . . will perhaps better serve the interests of M. Thomas's future than a less gay work would have done."[38] The majority of the review is taken up with a reiteration of the problems of the *Prix de Rome.*

The article in the *Revue et Gazette Musicale* is more comprehensive; Berlioz has obviously studied the work in close detail and he compliments Thomas on "a certain uncommon finesse in his dramatic intention, and a great deal of tact in his use of instrumental masses."[39] Berlioz finishes, however, by advising Thomas to find a more individual style.

The review for the *Journal des Débats,* published the same day as the article for the *Revue et Gazette Musicale,* more openly expresses Berlioz's lack of respect for the work. He comments, "This farce, this vaudeville, or if you want, this *opéra-comique,* has been a wild success."[40] The scorn here is unmistakable. Berlioz continues by complimenting Thomas for not choosing a heavy libretto which might have crushed his light score; but though Berlioz proceeds conscientiously to list the passages he liked, he has already shown his lack of appreciation. He suggests that further experience and reflection might develop a more individual style in Thomas, rather than the present vacillation between Italian and German styles of composition.

These reviews are interesting because they show Berlioz struggling *not* to show his true feelings in order to promote a cause, but finally not being able to resist hitting out. There is also an oblique criticism of Thomas for writing music to appeal to the *opéra-comique* public. Théophile Gautier on the other hand *praises* Thomas for this same reason: "It is a proof of spirit and tact for which one must be grateful to him. People sufficiently confident enough of themselves to become, if needs be, smaller than they are, are rare; and in doing this M. Thomas has proved that he understood his libretto, his theater, and his public."[41] Berlioz would not have agreed with this statement, even though he seemed to be facing the bitter realization that it was perhaps the only way a new composer could succeed.

Occasionally, in order to express a little of what he really thinks, Berlioz does not put his own name to an article, as in the articles in 1836 signed "Un Vieillard stupide."[42] In a review of Adam's *Micheline* in 1835, Berlioz pretends not to have been able to attend the work himself and to have taken the review from a friend. His friend is harsh in his judgments: "Again these nice little colorless musical phrases! Again a score void of thoughts! Again a little one-acter of M. Ad. Adam!"[43]

Because of the continual suppression and dissimulation of his feelings, when Berlioz does express his real views it comes as an explosion of vitriol. This really happens only once, and it is in his review for the *Journal des Débats* of

Zampa by Hérold.[44] Curiously, in his review of *Zampa* for the *Gazette Musicale* Berlioz is only mildly critical. The reason for this may have been that the protection of Bertin on the *Journal des Débats* gave Berlioz more confidence. The review for the *Journal des Débats* is very long. It is not an unthinking condemnation, for Berlioz carefully and conscientiously pulls the work to pieces. Often it seems as though his criticisms of *Zampa* are in fact the quintessence of his criticism of all *opéras-comiques* of this type:

> Hérold, without having a style of his own, is nevertheless neither Italian, French, nor German. His music very strongly resembles those industrial products manufactured in Paris, according to procedures invented elsewhere and slightly modified; it is Parisian music. . . . [H]owever we shall say in conclusion that this score fulfils all the conditions demanded of an *opéra-comique in Paris* today.[45]

Zampa is thus attacked both on its own terms and for all that it represents. Fortunately, though, Berlioz did like a few contemporary *opéras-comiques*.[46] For instance he liked the *opéras-comiques* of Gomis, a Spanish composer living in France, and, to a lesser extent, of the French composer Monpou.[47]

Berlioz wrote at length on the music of Gomis. It is interesting to study these reviews in a little detail, to see what it was that attracted Berlioz to Gomis's music, and what qualities he respected in an *opéra-comique* composer. Berlioz reviewed Gomis's *opéras-comiques, Le Revenant*[48] and *Le Portefaix*,[49] and also wrote Gomis's obituary notice for the *Revue et Gazette Musicale* in 1836.[50] In his criticism Berlioz would frequently put himself in the place of the composer and express what he felt the composer himself must have been wanting to express. The technique is effective in that the reader feels immediately involved in the review, yet obviously it can also lead to misinterpretation of the composer's aims and intentions.

Berlioz depicts Gomis as a brave fighter for higher values trying valiantly to lead the tastes of the *opéra-comique* public on to worthier paths; and as someone who, having failed in this attempt, has succumbed to the worthless desires of his audience and descended to their level. But from the little reading material available on Gomis—mostly other reviews of the time—one does not get the impression that he saw himself as the "revolutionary" of the Opéra-Comique as portrayed by Berlioz.

Berlioz's review of *Le Revenant* stands out strikingly from all his other reviews of *opéra-comique* for *Le Rénovateur,* as it takes the work seriously from beginning to end. His own identification with Gomis is evident throughout the article:

> M. Gomis is a scholarly musician, . . . he detests routine and old-fashioned traditions; he believes as much in his own judgment as in that of nobodies who want to impose their doctrines on him. Consequently what he produces is a work of art and must be treated with respect and consideration.[51]

Gomis's work is thus immediately raised on to a different level; it is not a vaudeville annotated by music but a work of art and must be treated appropriately. Having made this declaration Berlioz proceeds with a careful examination of the work, praising originality in rhythm, orchestration, and melody. Gomis's use of rhythm is highlighted, and Berlioz is particularly impressed by the use of what he calls binary rhythm in bars of triple time. The review is not entirely laudatory, however. Berlioz balances his praise with several minor criticisms, such as a lack of unity in the general plan and misuse of the ubiquitous trombones and bass-drum. However, he continually speaks as though he were Gomis, a fighter in the struggle for "true art" and even imputes a moral design or motive to some of the techniques used by Gomis. For instance, instead of simply saying that he does not employ square phrasing and monotonous rhythms, Berlioz says:

> He declared war on square-cut phrases whose ending could be anticipated from the very first beat; instead of the monotonous rhythm like that of a pendulum, the phrases of his music are arranged in a new order.[52]

It is interesting that Berlioz focuses on Gomis's adventurous use of rhythm, given that the decade of 1830s was probably the time when Berlioz himself was experimenting most with rhythm. As Hugh Macdonald comments, *Harold en Italie* (1834) reveals "rhythmic subtleties and novelties of all kinds, cross-rhythms, counter-rhythms, augmented and diminished rhythms, not to mention the sheer rhythmic energy which much more than thematic ideas propels the finale."[53] These reviews of Gomis are an obvious example of Berlioz's interests as a composer directing his critical discrimination.

Berlioz was not the only critic to praise Gomis. Naumann, for example, wrote two articles on *Le Revenant* in the *Gazette Musicale* (1834), describing the score as one of the most remarkable works of the time;[54] and an unsigned review in *Le Moniteur Universel* stated that *Le Revenant* "assigns M. Gomis a distinguished rank amongst our most talented composers," and further remarked, "The work, . . . by its forms, would seem to us to belong more to the stage of the Académie Royale de Musique than to that of the Opéra-Comique."[55]

In Berlioz's reviews of Gomis he gives the impression that despite general praise by critics *Le Revenant* was not popular. However, a survey of Maurice's *Courrier des Théâtres* shows that *Le Revenant* was performed frequently during 1834. Maurice mentions it continually during the month of January and each time with growing enthusiasm: for instance, on 2 January he states, "*Le Revenant* was perfectly played*," on 3 January, "The second performance of *Le Revenant* evoked a very favorable response yesterday and raised sweet hopes," on 5 January, "Another large audience yesterday for *Le Revenant,*" on 6 January,

"The musical success of *Le Revenant* grows from one performance to the next," and on 10 January, "The house was full."[56] In his obituary of Gomis, Berlioz gives the impression that the type of audience that would have appreciated *Le Revenant* was not that which frequented the Opéra-Comique and vice-versa; however this would not appear to be entirely true.

Gomis's next *opéra-comique, Le Portefaix,* was a disappointment for Berlioz. In his review of this work for *Le Rénovateur* he begins by pointing out that Gomis had his first two *opéras-comiques*—the first was *Diable à Seville* (1831)—performed only because of connections with theater directors. According to Fétis's *Biographie,* Gomis obtained a pension at the end of his life because of his friendship with Cavé.[57] In his reviews of *Le Portefaix* and in his obituary article Berlioz continues to identify with Gomis, outlining the image of a tormented man who is so depressed by the lack of appreciation of his music that in desperation he tries to write something in the popular style. Berlioz sympathizes with but chastises Gomis, and, adopting a pedagogical tone, writes a review that is more or less a personal address to Gomis, telling him not to abandon his ideals.

In both this article and in the obituary Berlioz elaborates a theory about composition, the essence of which is that it is almost impossible for a man of academic artistic talent like Gomis to be successful in the type of music demanded for a popular *opéra-comique.* Berlioz details passages in *Le Portefaix* where Gomis does succeed, but these are the passages where he uses an unusual rhythm or harmony. Where he fails most miserably is in his attempts to be frivolous. Skill in composition, according to Berlioz, does not mean that one will write a better *contre-danse* than the average *opéra-comique* composer; it means that one will write a worse one because it will be forced and lack the freshness and spontaneity that are the redeeming characteristics of such music:

> One creates popular art . . . because one cannot do otherwise. . . . Never . . . will a man of style manage to write common things with that ease, that abandon.[58]

Berlioz's whole perception of Gomis is permeated by a romantic image of him as a convention breaker, describing him as "one of those men who seem to be born to suffer and struggle throughout their short existence."[59] In the obituary Berlioz also talks of a new work by Gomis, *Comte Julien,* written for the Académie Royale de Musique. The article suggests this was a work written in accordance with Gomis's artistic ideals, not with the demands of the public. Berlioz gives no indication of having seen a copy of the score, and according to Fétis the authorities at the Académie royale de musique deemed the work not worthy of performance.[60] It is interesting that Berlioz makes no mention of another *opéra-comique* by Gomis, *Rock le barbu* (1836), which, judging by comments made in a review by J. J. J. Diaz [Henri Blanchard], seems to have been composed more in the style of *Le Portefaix* than of *Le Revenant*.[61] Jules Janin's ironical review of *Rock le barbu* in the *Journal des Débats* adds proof to Berlioz's claim that Gomis was disliked by some people for his scholarly approach:

> Thus, for this *bouffon* opera M. Gomis has written serious music. While M. Duport, his collaborator, provided him with gaiety, M. Gomis changed this gaiety into sadness. . . . M. Gomis and M. Paul Duport should have been able to come to an understanding, to cry together or laugh together, then, if M. Gomis was not so concerned at all times, and in all respects, and without knowing too much why, and without worrying too much how, with being a man of genius. To have genius is all very well, but it's also hard going. To have genius always is very tiring for everyone; what the devil! It is easier and more agreeable to be quite simply a man of talent. And then, what an idea to have genius in an *opéra-comique*! M. Gomis should have remembered that one does not need to take a paving stone to crush a fly.[62]

Berlioz's personal identification with Gomis resulted in a slightly distorted picture of his importance. Having begun by portraying him as a rebel, Berlioz then had to try to justify all of Gomis's compositions in the light of this original image.

Certainly Berlioz exaggerated Gomis's worth as a composer, particularly in his review of *Le Revenant*. Given the enormous quantity of similarly boring works Berlioz was required to review, one can see how easily he might overestimate the quality of a work that stood out from the rest just because it broke the monotony. Also, it is understandable that Berlioz was attracted towards works (again, in particular *Le Revenant*) that were inventive in the areas in which he himself was experimenting.

Berlioz liked other individual *opéras-comiques*—if not wholly, at least in part—such as Onslow's *Guise* (1837),[63] but no one else received the same eulogies as Gomis. Still, Berlioz's first review of the composer Monpou is highly commendatory. Monpou was well known at the time as a writer of romances, which were based particularly on the poetry of Hugo and Musset. He was self-consciously "romantic," to the point of heading some of his works "Je suis romantique"; he even attempted to set to music Lamennais's *Paroles d'un croyant*. His romances were atypical of the period, both in their choice of text, and in their musical style which often contained harsh dissonances and unconventional rhythms.[64] For *Le Rénovateur* in 1835 Berlioz reviewed a scene from Monpou's work called *Le Juif errant*. Berlioz commented on the work:

> The scene from *Le Juif errant*, extremely well interpreted by Dérivis, seemed to us to contain designs of great beauty and in general to have been written under the influence of a highly poetic feeling. This work should place M. Monpou high in the esteem of the musical public, were it ever possible for an artist who deviates from popular taste to be given the justice due him.[65]

I have found only one other reference to this work; d'Ortigue in his book *La Musique à l'église* comments, "We also owe sincere and merited praise to M. Monpou, whose *Juif errant* is full of melody and feeling."[66] I can find no other information on this composition, nor any evidence to suggest whether it was a full-scale work or not. The theme of *Le Juif errant* was popular at the time, and Monpou was most probably setting to music a well-known anonymous poem said to have been sung by the pilgrims of the Middle Ages.[67] Berlioz's elevated opinion of Monpou is gently retracted in subsequent reviews of his compositions. In reviews of Monpou's *Deux Reines* (1835) and *Piquillo* (1837) Berlioz notes original melodies, but also that these occur alongside banalities such as the nauseous "Italian cadence." In *Piquillo* Berlioz criticizes vocal parts that have awkward and ungrateful parts for the singers.[68]

In his reviews of 1834 Berlioz denigrates the public of the Opéra-Comique for its taste in music; the works performed might have been bad, but the audience's demand for and appreciation of them was even worse. But in 1835 he directs his scorn more towards the directors of the Opéra-Comique for continuing to produce such works. His article on the Opéra-Comique in 1836, "De L'Opéra-Comique," rather curiously supports the Opéra-Comique public—to the extent at least of saying it is ready to appreciate music other than what it is presented with. However, he also commented in his review of Puget's *Le Mauvais Oeil*:

> What one demands of them (I am speaking of the Opéra-Comique public) is quite simply a certain grace that is a little affected, a certain verve that is a little turbulent, a certain coloring that is a little crude, a certain invention that is a little common, all things that today virtually run the streets. With the union of these qualities, a little spirit and a little stage sense, one should easily manage to conquer the affections of a public which shows itself daily to be more benevolent.[69]

For a short period at the beginning of 1835 Berlioz was optimistic about the chances of improvement at the Opéra-Comique because of the forthcoming performances of *Robin des bois*. Even in its arranged form *Robin des bois* was still a "work of art"; and a German choir had been hired for the season.

Berlioz's reactions after the first performance were mixed. The German choir was badly directed and Mme. Casimir had been unable to resist the temptation to embellish her part with "roulades." The most important thing, however, was that the public liked it; it was a success. Berlioz hoped this success would prove to the directors that the public did appreciate music other than that of Adam and his ilk, and that they would henceforth enlarge their repertoire. No such transformation took place. Even a change of directors towards the end of 1835 made little difference; the Opéra-Comique continued to be dominated by the works of Adam and Auber.

By 1837 Berlioz's attacks on the Opéra-Comique directors were becoming fierce. In some reviews he implies that the directors have forced the composer to write a certain type of music in order to have his works included within the Opéra-Comique repertoire. When discussing various faults in Auber's *Le Domino noir*, Berlioz concludes:

> Perhaps these faults would be less remarked upon if one were willing to place oneself in the position of the musician who above all searches for the most appropriate style to use on the current public of the Opéra-Comique, and who seeks not to break from the musical circle in which the habits and the means of execution of this theater have enclosed the art, in such a way as not to allow him to escape them.[70]

Alongside his scorn for and mockery of the Opéra-Comique, Berlioz maintained serious concern for its present situation and future, and persistently presented plans for its reform. Apart from his distaste for the music performed at the Opéra-Comique, he was appalled at the low standard of the chorus[71] and the orchestra—his opinion of the chorus only became strongly antagonistic from 1835 onwards—and at the manner in which the principal singers often imitated the Italian style of embellishment. He held Mme. Casimir to be the main offender. He noted, realistically, that constant turnover of repertoire was a major cause of the low standards. Orchestral players and singers were exhausted by having to learn new works so rapidly and never had the time to learn how to perform one opera well. Berlioz was not alone in this observation. Many of his fellow critics were making similar remarks: a review of Monpou's *Les Deux Reines* for the *Gazette Musicale* comments that "the orchestra and the chorus as usual seemed overcome with tiredness and boredom."[72] However, an anonymous critic for *Le Ménestrel*, a journal that, at this time, perhaps more accurately reflected the general public's knowledge and taste gives a different view of the situation:

> A truth that escapes no one, but one that the stingy critic is often far too slow to remark upon, is that at no other time has such prodigious activity been seen at the Opéra-Comique than under the present administration. [See for example t]he numerous débuts following one another at this theater in the space of a year, . . . the series of new masterpieces with which it enlarges its repertoire, [and] the varied choice of revivals.[73]

This was the kind of response for which the Opéra-Comique directors were aiming.

By 1837 Berlioz became both more cynical and more pessimistic about the state of the Opéra-Comique chorus and orchestra. He began to express relief if a new *opéra-comique* had no or few choruses; they would have only been abominably sung anyway. He even ironically used the poor standard of the chorus to justify writing uninteresting choral parts. His review of Onslow's *Guise* says,

The voices almost always written in sustained chords, without striking designs, appear to be accompanying the orchestra rather than performing a principal part of the musical ensemble; but one has to consider the chorus of the Opéra-Comique a little, to understand how impossible it was for the composer to write for them in any other way than he did.[74]

In his review of Auber's *Le Domino noir* Berlioz comments at some length on the need for good choir schools like those in Germany, and on the efforts of Mainzer and Pastou to try to establish similar schools in France. Thoughout all his criticism Berlioz laments the death of Choron and the closing of his choir school, for which there had been no adequate replacement.[75] Berlioz's vision of the Opéra-Comique, though he was extremely uncertain of the feasibility of such a scheme, was that it should become a second Opéra house which would perform "works of art."[76]

In conclusion we can say that study of these reviews reinforces the points made in chapter 4, namely that Berlioz is able not only to evade saying what he thinks, but also to be dishonest in his criticism. However, seen within the context of editorial demands and the need for diplomacy towards popular composers, his deception is certainly understandable, perhaps even justifiable, as there was little else that he could have done short of refusing to review these works at all, which would have cost him his livelihood.

Furthermore, it was perhaps because he considered the genre, or rather the popular use of the genre, and its public to be inferior that Berlioz was prepared to stoop to such a degree of dissimulation, for, as his treatment of Gomis demonstrates, when Berlioz felt an *opéra-comique* composer was "serious" he treated him with respect. The question of betrayal of artistic principles is thus not really applicable here, and it is significant that Berlioz's group of reviews of the Opéra-Comique are very different in both style and content from his reviews of the Conservatoire concerts.

Berlioz's articles for *Le Rénovateur* are the most "dissimulating." Possibly this is because the reading public of *Le Rénovateur* would not have been highly informed about music and would probably even have missed the derogatory innuendoes of many of the articles. Anyone who knew Berlioz well would of course have seen through his deception.

One point in particular that remains perplexing is why, given that he disliked most *opéras-comiques* and disliked reviewing them, Berlioz should have written some unsigned articles on the subject in 1836. There are several explanations possible. One is that after the continual suppression of the 1834 to 1835 articles he wanted a chance to express more freely what he felt about the Opéra-Comique. Another is that he submitted the articles signed and that Schlesinger told him to sign them with a pseudonym or leave them unsigned. A third explanation—less likely perhaps—is that he had actually begun paradoxically to enjoy writing about the Opéra-Comique.

I shall conclude this chapter with a brief discussion of Berlioz's *opéra-comique, Béatrice et Bénédict*—of why he wrote in that genre. Berlioz first thought of *Béatrice et Bénédict* in 1833. He discusses the work in a letter to d'Ortigue: "I am going to write a very gay Italian opera based on Shakespeare's comedy *Much Ado about Nothing*."[77] He does not call *Béatrice et Bénédict* an *opéra-comique* at this stage, but an "Italian" opera, a term that seems to refer simply to something designed to be performed at the Théâtre Italien. Berlioz obviously was not seriously involved with the work in 1833, which was fortunate since nothing was to come of his contract. He appears to have viewed the project more as a stepping stone to other engagements. As he remarked optimistically to his father: "This door will open many others."[78]

A scenario entitled *Bénédict et Béatrix* exists in the Paris Bibliothèque Nationale collection of Berlioz autographs.[79] Hugh Macdonald in his notes for the *NBE* of *Béatrice et Bénédict* has dated this scenario 1852, through a study of the names of the singers listed by Berlioz under "Personnages."[80] A note in Legouvé's hand on the front page states that Berlioz had asked him to turn the scenario into a libretto. Once again this appears to have been an abortive project.

In 1858, for the opening of his new theater in 1860, Bénazet, the manager of the Casino at Baden-Baden, commissioned a work from Berlioz that was to be based on a libretto by Edouard Plouvier (1821–76). Berlioz had trouble starting composition; he wrote to the Princess Sayn-Wittgenstein, "I cannot tell you how upset I am to have been forced to sign an engagement contract with M. Bénazet—perhaps I am mistaken! Perhaps the fire will light up while I am composing."[81]

Bénazet's new theater was not ready by 1860, so Berlioz was not obliged to fulfil his contract. However, Bénazet seems to have been unwilling to let the contract drop: "M. Bénazet has never wanted to release me from my promise; he wants his opera, even if the project for the new theater doesn't come off, he will take his chances and keep our contract."[82] Finding the Plouvier manuscript unmanageable,[83] Berlioz asked Bénazet if he could exchange the libretto for that of *Béatrice et Bénédict,* Berlioz's own adaptation of Shakespeare's *Much Ado about Nothing.* Bénazet agreed and it was thus that *Béatrice et Bénédict* was performed for the opening of the theater, which finally took place in 1862.

Berlioz worked on *Béatrice et Bénédict* over the period 1860 to 1862. In his correspondence for these years *Béatrice et Bénédict* is now unequivocally referred to as an *opéra-comique.* Berlioz complains incessantly of the difficulty in finding time to work on it, but the work seems to have progressed at a steady rate. In October 1861 he wrote to Louis:

I worked for seven hours yesterday on a little one-act work that I have undertaken. . . . It is very pretty but very difficult to do well. I will still have a lot more work to do to the libretto; I so rarely have time to think about it consistently. Then it will be the music's turn.[84]

He must have worked remarkably quickly over the next few months for he wrote to Marc Suat on 7 December 1861 that he had just finished a two-act opera destined for the new theater at Baden-Baden:

> I am working a lot, I have just finished a two-act opera designed for the new theater at Baden-Baden. I have only the overture to do; but the feuilletons are going to stop me working on it.[85]

By March 1862 Berlioz was already involved with rehearsals, culminating in a big dress rehearsal of the singers on 12 July at the Paris Opéra-Comique. Berlioz went to Baden-Baden to rehearse the orchestra.

In all his dealings with Berlioz, Bénazet was extraordinarily accommodating, making sure that everything needed for a performance was provided regardless of expense. Berlioz was always appreciative of such generosity, but the fact that he was assured of the singers and orchestral players he wanted did not mean that he relaxed in his rehearsals. The preparations for *Béatrice et Bénédict* were particularly meticulous, and in his correspondence Berlioz often remarked on the difficulty of obtaining the necessary finesse in performance. For instance he writes in his summary of *Béatrice et Bénédict* in a much-quoted letter to the Princess Sayn-Wittgenstein, "A caprice written with the point of a needle and [which] requires the utmost delicacy of execution,"[86] and in another, later comment to the Princess, "In fact, in my opinion, this little work is much more difficult to perform musically than *Les Troyens,* since it has *humor.*"[87]

Berlioz was clearly pleased by the success of *Béatrice et Bénédict,* but at the same time did not think it indicated a major change in his position as a composer in Paris. He remarks wryly in a letter to Ferrand:

> You would laugh if you could read the stupid praise that the critics give me. They discover that I have melody, that I can be joyful and even comical. The astonishing story caused by *L'Enfance du Christ* begins again. They have realized, in *seeing* that there were no rowdy instruments in the orchestra, that I am not *noisy.* What patience I would need if I were not so indifferent![88]

He similarly remarks in a letter to the Princess, "There was a heap of enthusiastic hypocrites who importuned me with their demonstrations, whose *sincerity* I know perfectly well—I have to adopt a stupid air and look as if I believe."[89] The success at Baden-Baden did not of course entail immediate reception in Paris. A performance was suggested at the Opéra-Comique, and Berlioz commented to the Princess, "With the director of the Opéra-Comique we are looking at present for the means of reproducing this in Paris,"[90] but the lack of a suitable Béatrice was more than enough reason for the Opéra-Comique administration to prevaricate.

The nocturne from *Béatrice et Bénédict* was performed at the Société des

Concerts (24 March 1863), to an extremely enthusiastic audience,[91] but this success did not engender a performance of the entire work. The next performance was at Weimar, where the Duchess of Weimar commanded a performance for her birthday. Two performances were given, 8 and 10 April 1863, both using Richard Pohl's German translation. Once again the work met with acclaim.

How then can we reconcile Berlioz's own *opéra-comique, Béatrice et Bénédict,* with the bulk of his criticism of the average *opéra-comique* of the time?

First, it must be pointed out that *Béatrice et Bénédict* was not the first *opéra-comique* that Berlioz had aspired to write. As early as 1826 he was involved in plans for an *opéra-comique* called *Richard en Palestine* in conjunction with his friend Léon Compaignon. The choice of the *opéra-comique* genre in this case seems to have been merely opportunist, in that it would have been the most likely form in which to have a work performed given that the Opéra-Comique administration was more receptive towards new works than the Opéra administration. Many composers at the time directed their talent towards the Opéra-Comique (although better suited to the Opéra) in the hope that a success there might lead to a commission for the Opéra.[92] Berlioz writes to Compaignon, who was clearly worried about Berlioz's interpretation of the *opéra-comique* genre:

> Do not be afraid of excessive opposition to the genre of the *opéra-comique,* you must realize that our subject is completely that of grand opera; besides I have been well informed that Pixérécourt likes the grandiose genre a lot. . . . Make sure not to write me a ballad, nor romance, nor anything at all light for Blondel. . . . [W]rite for him a sort of Ossianic inspiration in a dreamy and wild style.[93]

Benvenuto Cellini, too, was originally intended for the Opéra-Comique but not accepted. As Berlioz commented: "I am regarded at the Opéra-Comique as an *underminer, an upsetter of the national genre,* and they do not want to have anything to do with me."[94]

Second, though *Béatrice et Bénédict* is written within the tradition of the French *opéra-comique,* Berlioz has to an extent divorced himself ideologically from the type of *opéra-comique* that he had been and still was reviling in his criticism. It is odd that in his correspondence of 1860 to 1862 he makes no direct reference to these *opéras-comiques*—he does not even attempt to differentiate *Béatrice et Bénédict* from, for instance, the *opéra-comique* of Adam. Yet perhaps this serves as further evidence of his alienation from the form as it was used by the majority of composers of the time.

Berlioz saw himself as composing a comedy, with a well-written libretto and interesting score. Originally, this comedy was meant to be an "Italian" opera, but instead it became an *opéra-comique.* It is interesting that some of the first reviews of *Béatrice et Bénédict* comment on the presence of early *opéra-comique* traits. Marie Escudier, for instance, remarks in his article for *La France Musicale* on "the *cabalette* in the style of the old *opéra-comique*," and how the accompaniment to the Duo "reminds one of Grétry."[95]

Berlioz's conception of the *opéra-comique* form was not a rigid one, as he remarked in a general article on the *opéra-comique*, "Is it strictly necessary to take the *opéra-comique* as an exclusive genre, circumscribed within certain limits?"[96] It is in this article that he asks why the theater of the Opéra-Comique could not be called the "second théâtre d'Opéra," saying that even if they forbade the performance of works that were entirely sung, there would still be a large repertoire,

> for a real opera loses hardly any of its value, nor does it descend below the rank assigned by its merit, simply because it's not sung from beginning to end, and because one substitutes for the running recitative a few lines of dialogue. *Fidelio* and *Der Freischütz* are illustrious proofs of this.[97]

While Berlioz does not refer to other *opéras-comiques* in his correspondence between 1860 and 1862, he does so in *Béatrice et Bénédict* itself, both directly and indirectly.

The care Berlioz took with his libretto and with the performance of his work points indirectly to two faults he deplored in the contemporary *opéra-comique*. First, with his simple well-written libretto based on Shakespeare, Berlioz demonstrates the value he placed on a good libretto, a characteristic he felt was neglected by the majority of *opéra-comique* composers. Second, the scrupulous care Berlioz took with the performance of his work points to his criticism of the standard of performance of most *opéras-comiques;* as he said in his correspondence, he felt a comedy demanded even more precision and delicacy in playing than a grand opera.

In the libretto of *Béatrice et Bénédict* itself, Berlioz refers mockingly to the predictable rhyming schemes of the typical *opéra-comique*.[98] In act 1, scene 4, Béatrice remarks sarcastically:

> Enough! Enough! Won't you soon stop singing to us, Glory and victory, Warriors and laurel wreaths? What rhymes! That's the aftermath of war![99]

And in act 2, scene 4, a dialogue between Béatrice et Bénédict runs:

> *Bénédict:*
> If—I could have your indulgence—never a heart—
>
> *Béatrice:*
> Go on.—Go on then! The rhyme is *constance.* Let fly a madrigal at me! You're capable of it, you're a poet! Ah! Ah! Ah![100]

Apart from its deliberate comedy, Somarone's inspired song is surely also an ironical criticism of the average *opéra-comique* drinking song: "From our island/ Of Sicily/ Long live this famous wine/ So fine/ But the most noble flame/ Sweet to the soul/ As to the heart/ Of the drinker/ Is the ruby liqueur/ Of the grape/ Of the vines of Marsala/ That has it!"[101]

Berlioz makes an interesting comment on *Béatrice et Bénédict* in a letter to M. and Mlle. Massart (19 April 1863): "The concert orchestra is a king placed on a throne. But then these great symphonic passions turn my heart a bit more brutally than the sentiments of a *demi-caractère* opera like *Béatrice*."[102] This quotation refers to a concert Berlioz was giving of his own works for the Prince Hohenzollern-Hechingen at Löwenberg.

Before any conclusions can be drawn here, the term "demi-caractère" has to be defined.

Castil-Blaze in his *Dictionaire de musique moderne* gives a rather confusing definition under the entry *caractère*:

> Of these characters, some are general, being relative 1. to our emotions, 2. to the degree to which we feel them, 3. to the tone in which we express them. The first creates a gay or sad style; the second, its vivacity or sweetness; the third, sublimity or simplicity. Each of these three states has a middle [mean] *character*. In combining them one gets a great number of mixed styles of which the principal ones are: 1. The *character* of the tragic style, which unites sadness with force and sublimity; 2. The buffoon, which unites gaiety with vivacity and familiarity; 3. Finally the *demi-caractère* which unites all the middle [mean] situations.[103]

In uniting all the "situations moyennes," "demi-caractère" would thus be a mixed genre, combining the "means" of gaiety and sadness, vivaciousness and gentleness, sublimity and simplicity—a very vague definition, capable of encompassing an enormous variety of works.

To return to the original quotation, two points need to be made. First, the fact that Berlioz refers here to *Béatrice et Bénédict* as an opera of "demi-caractère" shows that he did in fact distinguish it as something other than a straightforward *opéra-comique*. Second, without drawing any derogatory connotations from the term "demi-caractère" itself, Berlioz does nevertheless suggest here that his symphonic music meant more to him than a work such as *Béatrice et Bénédict*.

It was a challenge for Berlioz to see what he could do with a comedy, and with the *opéra-comique* form; a challenge that he obviously felt he had well met, as he commented in the postface to the *Mémoires*: "To my mind it is one of the liveliest and most original things I have done."[104]

He also appears to have been very well paid by Bénazet: "Bénazet, with his usual generosity, paid me at the rate of two thousand francs for the words of each act and the same for the music—eight thousand francs in all—and a further thousand to go back and conduct it the following year."[105] Perhaps Berlioz once again cherished the hope that the success of *Béatrice et Bénédict* might render *Les Troyens* more acceptable to the *Opéra*. *Béatrice et Bénédict* however could never have had the significance for him that *Les Troyens* had.

7

Vocal Music: Grand Opera

Grand opera was the dominating musical genre of the 1830s and one of the chief subjects of the contemporary music criticism. Its importance was such that it demands separate examination before it is studied in relation to Berlioz's criticism.

The period of grand opera is fairly clearly delineated; it covers works written for the Paris Opéra in the first half of the nineteenth century, particularly around 1830 to 1840. The term was used sometimes to refer to the Opéra house itself, as well as to the works performed there. The actual title was not much used by the composers or librettists themselves. The following works seem to have been generally classified as grand operas: Auber's *La Muette de Portici* (1828) (the progenitor of grand opera), Rossini's *Guillaume Tell* (1829), Meyerbeer's *Robert le diable* (1831), Auber's *Gustave III* (1833), Halévy's *La Juive* (1835), and Meyerbeer's *Les Huguenots* (1836). Other works that are often cited as grand opera are Meyerbeer's *Le Prophète* (1849) and *L'Africaine* (1865), Gounod's *Faust* (1859) and *Roméo et Juliette* (1867), Verdi's *Don Carlos* (1867) and *Aida* (1871), and even Berlioz's *Les Troyens* (1856–58).

Although the most important figures in grand opera were undoubtedly Meyerbeer and Scribe, Dr. Véron, director of the Opéra from 1831 to 1835 was an important figure too. Véron's high public profile and self-promotion at the time may have led to an exaggeration of his importance then and now. Evidence suggests that much of the ground work for grand opera had already been accomplished by the time of his arrival.[1] In Véron's *Mémoires* he outlines what he sees as the principal characteristics of grand opera.[2] Above all he stresses the importance of luxurious stage design, décor, and costumes. He sees the libretto as having the important role of providing dramatic situations and offering the possibility of many contrasts in décor and costumes, and he pays constant tribute to Scribe's mastery in this area. Véron does not mention demands placed on the composer. He implies, however, that the essential task was to draw the crowds by spectacular décor and scenery and that once captive they would have no choice but to become familiar with the music also. Music was certainly not portrayed as one of the important features of the opera; if anything it was the weak point in that it would possibly not be understood. Véron suggests for instance that it was the *mise-en-scène* that drew the crowds to *Robert le diable* and that they only began to appreciate the libretto and music later.[3] The essential conception of the grand opera was that of a multi-faceted work in which the various components combined to create an effective whole. The composer had to work in collaboration with both his librettist and stage producer in designing a grand spectacle. As Hugh Macdonald comments, "an art form which marshalled so many people and consumed so much artistic energy had to rely as much on generalship and efficiency as on inspiration."[4]

Opera was becoming a business as well as an artistic venture, and a successful business venture at that.[5] In the social life of the average bourgeois family of the day the opera played an important role. The advent of the upright piano and cheap sheet music meant that the opera could be enjoyed at home, and most of the famous arias of the day were arranged for piano and voice, often in simplified versions. W. L. Crosten argues that apart from Hollywood no other venture in history can compete with grand opera (particularly during the collaboration of Véron, Scribe, and Meyerbeer) in gauging so accurately the desires of the public.[6] To understand what was new about grand opera it is useful to examine separately the various components of libretto, décor, and music.

The libretti for the grand opera were almost exclusively the work of Scribe. Scribe is described with a great deal of scorn by many critics at the time. There is no doubt that his versification was banal and his characterization weak, yet, in his organization of material and choice of subject matter Scribe was both skilled and original. One of the best analyses of his libretti is in Patrick Smith's *The Tenth Muse*.[7] Smith outlines Scribe's talent as a "story planner and scene-and-act organizer—as a stage technician—and as a writer with a comprehensive mind and an endless facility for disguise."[8] Scribe's plots were simple and clear, and full of the action and dramatic contrasts so much sought after by Véron. The subject matter of his libretti was generally historical. There had been many operas before with historical libretti, but Scribe's libretti differed in their attempt to recreate the historical period. As Patrick Smith comments, an opera like Donizetti's *Anna Bolena* could really have been about any queen in any historical period, whereas with Scribe, in *Les Huguenots* for example, the story of Raoul and Valentine is set within a larger framework of the St. Bartholomew's day massacre.[9] Scribe's libretti are an example of the growing interest in history in the nineteenth century, of which a more important example is the pioneering work of historians such as Michelet and Quinet.

Some of Scribe's critics condemned him for not treating his historical subjects seriously enough, in degrading them with his romantic sub-plots. Gustave Planche's review of *Les Huguenots* ironically neglects to mention the words "Catholic" and "Huguenot" until halfway through the article, making the point that for Scribe the romantic story was more important than the historical facts.[10] Schumann was horrified at the way the St. Bartholomew's day massacre was recounted: "I am not a moralist, but it is too much for a good Protestant when he hears his most hallowed song bawled forth from the stage; too much for him when the bloodiest drama in the history of his church is reduced to a rustic farce simply to earn money and notoriety."[11] Scribe was indeed popularizing history, and to this end he was at times nauseatingly sentimental.[12] Yet his main concern was to appeal to his bourgeois public, and as a man of considerable experience in this area he correctly judged the right mixture of historical fact and sentimentality. The fact remains that Scribe was the first librettist to treat large-scale historical subjects in such a way that the interaction of political or religious forces was portrayed alongside the interaction of individuals. However, ultimately it must be acknowledged that the private intrigue was portrayed as the cause of the political action.[13]

Scribe designed his libretti with the latest developments in stage production in mind, being careful to create many opportunities for costume and scenery changes. The grand opera always included ballets and choruses and often, as Patrick Smith points out, a climax at the end of the fourth act over a specific historical event such as the St. Bartholomew's Day massacre (*Les Huguenots*), the Neapolitan revolt of 1647 (*La Muette*), or the assassination of Gustave III (*Gustave III*).[14]

Changes in the libretto were mirrored by similar changes in the stage production, décor, and costumes. Historical authenticity began to be an important concern in stage production, alongside an interest in realistic representation. This new interest in stage production started in the late 1820s. In 1827 Lubbert, the current director of the Opéra, set up a special committee to investigate new possibilities in production.[15] In *La Muette* (1828) much effort was put into presenting picturesque scenes of seventeenth-century Neapolitan life. For the famous explosion of Vesuvius on stage in the last act, Ciceri, who was later to become the most important figure in décor design, was sent to *La Scala* where in 1827 an eruption of Vesuvius had been performed on stage in Pacini's *L'Ultimo Giorno di Pompeia*. The details of costumes in the stage production booklet for *La Muette* stresses the use of Neapolitan colors: "Naples sky blue," "Naples lilac," "Naples bird of paradise."[16] How these colors differed from their Parisian equivalents is not specified; still the desire for authenticity is there in spirit. This stage production booklet concludes with some advice for provincial theaters, saying that if they wished to change the work from a grand opera to an *opéra-comique* they merely had to speak the recitatives and cut out anything else not designed as an air or ensemble piece.

Although the beginnings of the development of grand opera production must be placed before the 1830s, after 1830, under the directorship of Véron, the stage production became as important as—some even said more important than—the libretto and the music. Véron was aided by an extremely gifted team: for the décor, Ciceri assisted by Feuchères, Séchan, Diéterle, Despléchin, Philastres, and Cambon; for the stage production, Duponchel, and for the costumes, Lepaulle and Lorimier.

Main developments in décor involved the use of both light and perspective as an aid to realistic representation. The popular boulevard theaters had been experimenting for some time in both these areas, for instance, the panoramas and dioramas of Daguerre produced for the Panorama-Dramatique and later the Ambigu-Comique.[17] Gas lighting, introduced in 1822, was used in vaudeville theaters well before it was used at the Opéra. However, Véron began to exploit it as much as possible.

Ciceri and various members of his workshop had worked in many Parisian theaters and had thus encountered the work that was going on in the boulevard theaters. Ciceri was influenced a great deal by Daguerre's dioramas and also by the realistic historical dramas of Victor Hugo and Alexandre Dumas.[18] In *Robert le diable,* Véron's opening flourish, the décor was spectacular, in particular the extraordinary cloister scene of the third act where the nuns awake, rise from their tombs, and dance a seductive ballet. Catherine Join-Dieterle has noted that this scene had been suggested not by Meyerbeer but by Duponchel the stage producer[19] (as had the dramatic scene of the last act in the Palermo Cathedral)[20] or perhaps even by Scribe. It is revealing that the most famous scene of *Robert le diable* was the original idea of either the stage producer or librettist.

La Juive was the opera with the most extravagant and sensational décor and costumes. The costumes designer, Paul Lorimier, did extensive research on the opera's period—Southern Germany between 1400 and 1430—examining engravings, pictures, stained-glass windows, tapestries, and miniatures.[21] For the armor costumes he consulted a book by Pierre Palliot, *La Vraye et parfaite science des armoiries* (1660),[22] 30,000 francs were spent on the armor alone, out of a budget that totaled 150,000 francs.[23] The following description, taken from the stage production booklet, of a procession in act 1 of *La Juive* gives a good idea of the extravagance of the production:

[Act 1] *Procession crossing the stage during the singing*
1. The emperor's trumpeters, preceded by three guards on horseback, richly armed and equipped. 2. A banner carrier. 3. Twenty crossbow men. 4. A banner carrier. 5. Two cardinals followed by two clerics. 6. Two more cardinals followed by two more clerics. 7. A banner carrier accompanying bishops and masters from various professions. 8. A banner carrier accompanying two more masters and several of his colleagues. 9. Three aldermen . . . 10. One hundred and twenty soldiers richly armed and dressed in gold coats of mail. 11. Six trumpeters (the instruments bear banners richly ornamented by coats of arms) . . . 12. Six trumpeters. 13. Six banner carriers. 14. Twenty guards with crossbows. 15. Three cardinals followed by their pages and clerks. 16. Under a magnificent dais carried by four heralds (a fifth holds the horse's bridle), the CARDINAL BROGNY on horseback, followed by his pages and gentlemen and preceded by heralds carrying his pontifical clothes on rich velvet cushions. 17.

Ten soldiers. 18. Three armed heralds on horseback. 19. Twenty of the emperor's pages. 20. THE EMPEROR SIGISMOND in the most dazzling suit of armor. He rides a superb horse, harnessed and armor-plated with all the luxury imaginable. When he passes in front of the church, whose doors have been opened several moments before, a TE DEUM starts in the interior. From the steps of the church, children of the choir (eight at least) wave lit incense burners before the Emperor. The Emperor stops and bows before the house of God. The church bells ring with all their force. The organ is heard. This noise is mingled with the cries of joy and carols of the people.[24]

A comparison to what is supposed to be a spectacular scene from Rossini's *Moïse* shows the extent to which the stage production had developed in the grand opera:

[Act 3. Grand March]
ORDER OF THE MARCH
1) A chief and twelve guards . . .
2) Six ladies of the choir . . .
3) Six gentlemen of the choir . . .
4) Six ladies of the choir . . .
5) Six gentlemen of the choir . . .
6) Six ladies of the choir . . .
7) Six gentlemen of the choir . . .
8) Six gentlemen of the choir . . .
9) Oseride before four priests; they stop for Oseride's solo.
After the solo, Oseride and the four priests place themselves on the throne, stage left. They sit down. Here the march continues.
10) A chief and eight guards . . .

11)	Quadrille by	male	dancers	— in red
12)	"	female	"	— "
13)	"	male	"	— in blue
14)	"	female	"	— "
15)	"	male	"	— in brown
16)	"	female	"	— "

17) Pharaoh, Sinaide, Amenophis. Officers behind Pharaoh; his wife and his son, mount the throne on stage right, Pharaoh is in the middle. The priests rise when Pharaoh reaches the throne. When he is seated, the priests sit down again.)[25]

The décor for *Les Huguenots* was not so spectacular; indeed for the third act the stage production booklet indicates that the scenery and the décor of *Le Pré aux clercs* (an *opéra-comique* by Hérold and Planard of 1832) should be used. The goal of historical authenticity in décor of this period seems to have been more concerned with evoking a mood or creating an atmosphere than with a precise scientific reproduction of how things actually were. Nicole Wild, in her article on nineteenth-century stage production, makes a division between two types of historical authenticity. She calls one "synthetic," the desire to evoke the past, and the other "analytic," the desire to reconstitute history. The example she gives for the second type is the extraordinary six months of research that went into the costumes and sets for *Aïda*. Most of the grand opera up until 1840 could be classified under the "synthetic" heading. Though there was a desire for historical accuracy, attention to detail was not considered as important as obtaining an impressionistic overview.

The musical organization of grand opera, particularly of the works of Meyerbeer, showed a merging of Italian bel-canto and lyricism with the French declamatory style. This combination had already been present in Rossini's *Comte Ory* and *Guillaume Tell* and to a lesser extent in his *Moïse* and *Siège de Corinthe*. The chorus assumed a role of immense importance in the numerous crowd scenes. As Carl Dahlhaus quips, if the set "number" structure provided the skeleton of the grand opera, the crowd scene was its spinal column.[26] Although the basic structure was still that of a conventional "numbers" opera, there were fewer solo arias and the musical flow became more continuous with fewer breaks, organization being into large blocks rather than short sections. The impetus for the use of the chorus as a principal dramatic force came from Spontini's operas *La Vestale* (1807) and *Fernand Cortez* (1809), and Auber's *La Muette*, but it had indeed been a part of the French operatic tradition since Lully.

The orchestra, as has been widely documented, played an enormous role in the grand opera. Of particular note is the emphasis on percussion and brass instruments and on the exploration of unusual instruments (such as Meyerbeer's use of the *viole d'amour* in *Les Huguenots*) and on using instruments for unusual effects. At times the repetitive nature of Scribe's versification created problems for composers. As Hugh Macdonald comments, both Meyerbeer and Halévy found Scribe's versification difficult, and in their musical settings ended up emphasizing rather than disguising the sing-song quality of the verse. To quote Macdonald, "The predictability of Meyerbeer's music is its most severe shortcoming; it never sounds unfamiliar even when it is."[27]

The number of grand opera performances is enormous. *Robert le diable* was performed 558 times by 1893, *La Juive* 550 times by the same date, and *Les Huguenots* 1,080 times by 1914. Today not one of these works appears regularly in any opera house repertoire.[28] Meyerbeer, whose name was for many people synonymous with grand opera, was undoubtedly its major exponent. Reviews of his operas dominated the Parisian music criticism of the 1830s, and for many people he typified the spirit of the age. As it was the operas of Meyerbeer in which Berlioz was most interested and about which he wrote the largest number of articles, I shall be concentrating mainly on these articles and shall only occasionally refer to the other grand operas.

Berlioz's relationship to Meyerbeer is both complex and ambiguous. Two points need to be made about the relationship. First, having Meyerbeer as a friend was very important to Berlioz. Meyerbeer was a powerful and influential man at the time and one of the few musicians that Berlioz felt was really interested in and sympathetic to his music.[29] Of course Berlioz wished to maintain this friendship and it was perhaps inevitable and certainly understandable that his desire to please Meyerbeer played an important role in Berlioz's criticism of Meyerbeer's works.

Second, Berlioz did genuinely appreciate Meyerbeer's music—particularly *Les Huguenots*—and his grandiose treatment of historical themes. He found Meyerbeer's use of unusual instrumentation and mass vocal effects challenging for their intense dramatic power.

It is necessary, however, to bear in mind that Berlioz's reviews of Meyerbeer are as revealing in what they do not say as in what they do say; once again he adopts the tactic of "review by omission."

I shall examine Berlioz's reviews of Meyerbeer's operas *Robert le diable* and *Les Huguenots*. As said in chapter 3, Berlioz's article on *Robert le diable* for the *Gazette Musicale* of 1835 is not a review of the first performance of the work, but an article on one specific aspect of this opera, namely its orchestration. Since it was Meyerbeer's use of the orchestra that most interested Berlioz, and many other critics as well, this was a fairly safe area to choose. Berlioz could be enthusiastic in his praise and was spared the need to dwell on those other aspects of the work he enjoyed less. He was also spared the task of recounting the libretto.

Berlioz nevertheless briefly mentions aspects of the work other than the orchestra, qualifying each one with a commendatory adjective—for instance, "admirable melodies," "original harmonies," and "profound dramatic thought." Since the adulations are not expanded upon they remain fairly uninformative token tributes.

Berlioz obviously did think very highly of Meyerbeer's capabilities and inventiveness as an orchestrator. The *Traité d'instrumentation* includes several examples drawn from *Robert le diable,* quoting the "Resurrection des nonnes" twice.[30] This scene is described in the *Gazette Musicale* article as the "most prodigious inspiration of modern dramatic music."[31] Berlioz gives a vivid description of its novelty and the way in which Meyerbeer has created the effect of "half-death":

> The violins, violas, flutes, oboes and clarinets are silent. The horns, the valve trumpets, trombones, ophicleide, kettledrums, and tamtam alone are moaning several syncopated pianissimo chords, preceded on the strong beats by two pizzicato strokes in the violoncellos and double basses. Then, after each of these horrifying strophes, two solo bassoons begin to cluck a more animated rhythm.[32]

He stresses that the effect of this passage would be entirely different if any other instruments were used, for it is the particular choice and juxtaposition of instruments that was important and so original.

The orchestration is examined in terms of its dramatic and emotional effect. Berlioz not only acclaims its originality but also analyzes the reasons why it is effective. For instance, he comments admiringly on the effect of calm and freshness accompanying the entrance of Alice onto the stage, which is created both by the instrumentation of two flutes, two oboes, and two clarinets, and the contrast of these gentle woodwind instruments with the loud metallic frenzy of the preceding "infernal" scene with its percussion, brass, and full string tremolo. However, Berlioz criticizes Meyerbeer in one instance for banal instrumentation in the second act:

> I will however reproach the author for having introduced the trombones and the ophicleide towards the end where their presence is not motivated by any dramatic intention, and whose rough and violent timbre in the *forte* can do nothing but spoil the color of such a graciously gay piece.[33]

The use of drum and ophicleide in a dance air was common practice at the time but, according to Berlioz, dramatically incongruous and should have been avoided by someone of Meyerbeer's status.

The arias of Isabel in *Robert le diable* are decorated by innumerable roulades. Even Alice at times embroiders her otherwise straightforward lines. Berlioz makes no comment on these roulades which surely must have annoyed him intensely. If *Robert le diable* had been written by someone else, Hérold for instance, perhaps Berlioz would have unleashed one of his many tirades against roulades.

The *Gazette Musicale* article starts by noting the incredible success of *Robert le diable,* not only in France, but in the provinces and overseas. This provokes a lengthy digression on the state of orchestras in the provinces, a topic to which Berlioz often returns. In this particular instance it seems suspiciously like "padding," though Berlioz is also making a point about the precision and sophistication required for a Meyerbeer orchestra.

Given the paucity of Berlioz's commentary on aspects of *Robert le diable* other than the orchestration, it could be conjectured that he already harbored the rather dismissive view that he was later to print in the fifth evening of *Soirées d'orchestre*.[34] Here once again he does not mention any specific faults, but simply describes the work as a very uninspired modern French opera, during which everyone in the orchestra chatters except for the first violin, trombones, and bass drum (who presumably had the most to play). In the *Soirées* Berlioz classifies works by the amount of talking done by the members of the orchestra; if a work is very good then the orchestra is silent. *Robert le diable,* with several members quiet but the majority talking, would come into the category of the "mediocre."

In reviews of *Les Huguenots* in the *Revue et Gazette Musicale* (1836) and

Journal des Débats (1836) Berlioz firmly states his preference for this opera over *Robert le diable*. He found the style of *Les Huguenots* more serious, noble, and grandiose. Most other critics shared this preference, although not all. Castil-Blaze, for instance, felt that *Robert le diable* was more lively and fresh than *Les Huguenots*. Before examining Berlioz's reviews of *Les Huguenots*, I shall look at what some other critics said about the work.

Virtually all critics of the time felt obliged at some stage or other to write an article on *Les Huguenots*. From this wide choice of articles, I have chosen to study some written by the more "serious" critics and one by an unknown critic, which, typical of a number of reviews of the time, to an extent represents the "style admiratif" as described by Desnoyers (see chapter 1). The articles include four articles by Castil-Blaze in the *France Musicale* (1838);[35] two articles by Blaze de Bury in the *Revue des Deux Mondes* (1836), when he was aged sixteen, and the *Revue des Deux Mondes* (1859),[36] after he had become a good friend of Meyerbeer; two articles by Desnoyers in *Le National* (1836);[37] two articles by Mainzer in the *Monde Dramatique* (1836); an article by Planche in the *Chronique de Paris* (1836); George Sand's letter to Meyerbeer in her *Lettres d'un voyageur;* an article by Schumann on Meyerbeer; and an article by the unidentified "Ed. L." (Edouard Lerminier perhaps) in the *Nouvelle Minerve* (1836).[38]

An overview of these reviews shows a surprising amount of antagonism towards *Les Huguenots*, with the exception of George Sand (though she, too, has some reservations) and "Ed. L." Rather than analyze each article separately I shall examine them under the divisions of libretto, stage production, and music, used already in this section.

Scribe's libretto is unanimously decried by all the critics, but a slight division occurs between those critics who discuss the relationship between the music and the libretto and those who do not really make any connection between the two. Schumann for instance is morally outraged by the entire opera, including both libretto and music, between which he makes no differentiation. Castil-Blaze also makes no clear distinction, though he mentions several passages where he feels the music portrays perfectly the vulgarity of the libretto, such as Marcel's song in the first act, "A bas les maudits." Blaze de Bury's first article discusses Scribe's miserable profanations of religion and history.[39] In his second article he passes lightly over the libretto, saying that its poor literary quality was not reflected in the music. George Sand and Mainzer felt that Meyerbeer overcame the shortcomings of his libretto in the last acts, but not entirely in the first three acts. For Mainzer the music improved immensely as soon as there was some action in the libretto. He considers that the action starts in the third act but stops again completely in the last act.[40] Planche, though largely unconcerned with the relationship between the music and libretto, does question whether the reason for the poor chorus following the Septuor in the third act was that it was interpreting poor lyrics, and Desnoyers felt that Meyerbeer would have written a more profound work if he had had a more profound libretto. Finally, "Ed. L.," fulfilling the role of the stereotyped "critique littéraire," states that despite the appalling lyrics Meyerbeer overcame all—or nearly all, a slight exception being the second act—with his splendid music.

Thus for some critics the poor quality of the libretto did not infringe at all upon the quality of the music ("Ed. L." and Blaze de Bury's second article), for others it did so partially (George Sand, Mainzer, and Planche), or entirely (Desnoyers), and some criticize both the music and libretto, though one is not seen as a consequence of the other (Castil-Blaze and Schumann).

Not many of the critics discussed the *mise-en-scène* at any length, and those who do mention it are either slightly disparaging or disappointed. Planche was very critical of all the sets. He notes the borrowing of sets from *Gustave III* (as did Mainzer)[41] and found the lighting poor in both the third and fifth acts. Castil-Blaze was also critical, but more of the importance of the role assumed by the stage production in grand opera than of the specific production of *Les Huguenots*. He postulated that most of the effect of *Les Huguenots* was due to stage effects and not to the music. As might be expected, "Ed. L." praises the *mise-en-scène* highly:

> Shall I add that the success surpassed all that the opera administration could have been led to hope for by the composer's immense talent, [and] the luxury and brilliance of the decorations, amongst which one in particular in the second act showed a vast marble staircase, shadowed by enormous trees, the work of a meticulous, splendid, and intelligent *mise-en-scène*.[42]

This type of response was fairly typical of a number of reviews by minor critics of the time.

There is a common point of admiration in all discussion of the music of *Les Huguenots*: the "Bénédiction des poignards" and "Grand duo" of the fourth act, and it was these extracts that were performed as part of the program for the opening of the new Opéra in 1870. Even Schumann's condemnatory article, in which his emotional perturbation seems to make it difficult for him to put words down on paper, contains a begrudging though qualified respect for the "Bénédiction" and the "Duo." Reviews of recent productions of *Les Huguenots* still isolate these passages from the rest of the work. Yet other numbers were also appreciated by the critics of the time, in particular the page's romance from the first act, "Une Dame noble et sage," Marcel's "Chorale theme," the fifth act trio, and to a lesser extent the third act duo between Marcel and Valentine and the third act septet.

Meyerbeer's music was most fully examined by Castil-Blaze, whose articles on *Les Huguenots* are evidently the product of much research. Castil-Blaze first of all objected to Meyerbeer's prosody; he felt that Meyerbeer distorted the rhythms of the French language and at times even set words in such a way as to render them incomprehensible. Saint-Saëns made the same criticism of Meyerbeer at a later date.[43] Castil-Blaze was one of the first to criticize at length Meyerbeer's failure to develop melodies. He felt that Meyerbeer was unable to develop themes and attempted to unify the music by repetition of themes. However, Castil-Blaze's major contention with Meyerbeer concerns the question of borrowings; here, as the renowned arranger of other people's music, Castil-Blaze feels himself to be an unrivaled expert. His search for borrowings or "reminiscences" in *Les Huguenots* borders on the compulsive. He does not merely name passages and works that he thinks have been used—and he generously suggests that the borrowings could have been purely unconscious—but he also details the precise passages in question.

Both Desnoyers and Planche base their assessment of Meyerbeer's music on the common distinction of the time between talent and genius. They claim Meyerbeer to be a man of talent not genius, who worked hard but ultimately lacked inspiration.

Desnoyers saw *Les Huguenots* as a huge patchwork, with some good parts, some trivial, noble, or ugly ones, and all intricately and patiently joined together with the craftsmanship of a jeweler. He felt that Meyerbeer's gift for orchestration had been exaggerated, though his use of unusual instruments such as the *viole d'amour* was praiseworthy, and disliked his use of "jagged" rhythms and "bizarre" harmonies. Desnoyers's lack of tolerance for experimentation in rhythm and harmony is perhaps allied to his fervent support for Italian opera.

Mainzer also found *Les Huguenots* a mixture of good and bad qualities, had reservations about Meyerbeer's use of harmony and melodic inventiveness, but praised his instrumentation.

One of the most widespread opinions of Meyerbeer's music was that he reconciled the principal properties of Italian and German music and forged a new style, which could be classified as "French." This view was often quoted "parrot-fashion" by people with no knowledge of music at all. Blaze de Bury, in his second article on Meyerbeer (*Revue des Deux Mondes*, 1859), sees him as incorporating not only Italian and German music, but indeed all music and literature of the time. In reference to Meyerbeer's role at the time he cites Mephistopheles's statement to Faust, "One could, I see, call you Mr. Microcosm."[44] This tendency to confuse eclecticism with profundity was quite common. Meyerbeer was transformed into a symbol of the epoch and his eclecticism seen as a virtue. The popularity of Victor Cousin's philosophy is another instance of the favor held by theories of "eclecticism" at the time, and Cousin's philosophy has suffered the same decline as Meyerbeer's music.[45]

Gustave Planche was one of the few people to combat the notion of Meyerbeer's international French style. Planche saw Meyerbeer as attempting to merge Italian and German styles, but with the final result being not a reconciliation, but a loss of virility, a negative victory. Meyerbeer's "coat of arms belongs to all races. He . . . forgot only one thing, to give himself any ancestors."[46] Planche admits with a certain note of cynicism that Meyerbeer's method of writing was ideal for the French public, who always appreciated an easy victory.[47]

In his first article on Meyerbeer, Blaze de Bury complains of a lack of melody and abuse of modulation, despite excellent orchestration. In his second article he sees Meyerbeer as a great melodist, but then in this article Meyerbeer is faultless. After his *Revue des Deux Mondes* article of 1836, Blaze de Bury seems to have spent the rest of his life atoning for his early criticism, and his book on Meyerbeer even goes to some lengths to describe Meyerbeer's generosity in forgiving these early "rash" views.[48]

Unfortunately, only two critics, Planche and Castil-Blaze, comment at any length on the standard of performance, and they both thought the standard low. Castil-Blaze did not review the first performance, but the performances in 1838. He felt that the chorus and principal singers sang out of tune and that all the acts were marked by hesitations that sometimes developed into real breaks in the continuity. Castil-Blaze described the audience as completely cold and unenthusiastic until the fourth act.

Planche, reviewing the first performance in 1836, also noticed a timidity and indecisiveness in the chorus. He felt this was largely confined to the first act and due to the numerous last minute changes made by Meyerbeer, which caused confusion in the minds of the chorus. According to Planche both the orchestra and chorus were too loud and the soloists on the whole acted poorly. These criticisms are not echoed by other critics who, if they make any comment at all, tend to be more favorable. "Ed. L.," for instance, talks of "the concurrence of talented choristers and of this prodigious orchestra so admirably conducted by M. Habeneck."[49]

The overall pattern of these reviews is to talk first of the libretto, then of the music in either general or specific terms, and finally of the production and standard of performance. Several give a detailed description of the libretto (Mainzer, Planche, and "Ed. L." in particular), while others discuss it in more generalized terms. Many, for instance Desnoyers, Blaze de Bury, Schumann, and Planche, make an attempt to discuss Meyerbeer's historical role and evaluate his music as a product of the time. Discussions of the music make large divisions into harmony, melody, rhythm, and orchestration; and many critics at the same time mention individual sections that appealed to them. Only Castil-Blaze and, to a lesser extent, Planche offer detailed description of each act and recount the libretto at the same time.

One of the striking things about this collection of reviews is the number of critics who seemed to have been inspired to make quite lengthy digressions on the subject of criticism itself. Mainzer talks about the need for the critic to combat idolatrous praise, and, similarly, Desnoyers once again discusses the need to control the "style admiratif" in criticism, while Blaze de Bury discusses Meyerbeer as a social phenomenon and Planche expands on the properties of a man of talent. The digressions on the "role of the critic" were perhaps stimulated either directly or indirectly by the question of Meyerbeer's power over the press.

To draw some very general conclusions from this body of criticism, the two most striking points are the fierce antagonism towards Scribe's libretto and the ambivalent feelings about the music, in particular in the first two acts. All the critics have some worthwhile things to say; however Planche and Castil-Blaze stand out as the most interesting, as they both go into a great deal of detail. The attention Castil-Blaze gave to the score is even a little surprising given the fact that he fundamentally disliked the work, which he entitled "Luther's chorale [*Ein feste Burg*] put into music and in five acts by Meyerbeer!"[50] This ironical tone is pervasive in all of Castil-Blaze's articles on *Les Huguenots*.

Francis Claudon states that it is best to talk not just of Meyerbeer, but of the "cas Meyerbeer."[51] It is true that in reviewing Meyerbeer, critics were not only concerned with his music, but also with Meyerbeer as a "social phenomenon." This notion is examined at some length by Jane Fulcher in her article "Meyerbeer and the Music of Society." She claims that Meyerbeer's "stylistic eclecticism" became equated with social qualities. His eclecticism allowed him to speak a language which all individuals and groups could relate to, "full of historical suggestion and cultural associations," and in his use of massed musical forces rather than "individualistic melodies" (the phrase comes from Heine) he was symbolizing the "spirit of the people."[52] These are interesting observations and certainly seem true in terms of some of the criticism examined here, in particular that of Blaze de Bury. Other critics, however, lamented rather than praised the more prominent use of "mass forces" against "individualized melody."

Perhaps the "social force" of Meyerbeer's music helps explain its extraordinary public success at the time. In her dissertation on the press reception of *Robert le diable* and *Les Huguenots*, Marie-Hélène Coudroy concludes that "the success of these works was due even more to accidental causes that were already present in the public than to a determining influence of the press." Even the small sample of critics examined here would tend to suggest that this is true.[53] Although it is not of course unusual that "serious criticism" does not altogether reflect public taste, it is still surprising, given Meyerbeer's great public success, to find such a critical press.

Berlioz wrote five articles on *Les Huguenots* in 1836. The first three he wrote for the *Revue et Gazette Musicale* (6 March, 13 March, and 20 March) shortly after the première; the article of 6 March recounts the libretto and the others discuss the music. The two remaining articles were written for the *Journal des Débats* (10 November and 10 December) just after the publication of the score. In 1837 he wrote two articles, one for the *Revue et Gazette Musicale* (21 May) and one for the *Journal des Débats* (27 May), on the debut of Duprez in *Les Huguenots*.

Berlioz expresses basically the same opinions in both sets of 1836 articles, though, as might be expected, he gives much more detailed analysis in the *Journal des Débats* articles and discusses a greater number of individual movements. The articles for the *Journal des Débats* list more faults than do the *Revue et Gazette Musicale* articles, and this is obviously the result of a closer study of the written music. The *Revue et Gazette Musicale* articles, for instance, praise the first act chorus "A table amis," whereas the *Journal des Débats* (10 November) article, although appreciative of several good points in the chorus, also notes two small faults, one a laxness in prosody and the other a skipping theme in the worst "Italian style." The manner in which Berlioz details faults in his articles for the *Revue et Gazette Musicale* is more forthright and direct, while the *Journal des Débats* articles tend to try to find an excuse for the fault. A good example of this difference in approach can be found in a comparison of the opening of the second *Journal des Débats* article with the opening of the third *Revue et Gazette Musicale* article. Both articles discuss the fourth and fifth acts of the opera.

In the *Revue et Gazette Musicale* article Berlioz states with some relief that the fourth and fifth acts do *not* consist of light cavatinas ornamented with fioriture and vocalized passages, or of brilliant and picturesque vocal combinations that could be detached from the drama without its losing much of interest. Instead, states Berlioz, acts 4 and 5 comprise the drama of the opera for which the first three are just a prelude. The unmistakable inference here is that Berlioz found the first three acts inferior to the last two. In the *Journal des Débats* article Berlioz appears to be answering criticisms that had been directed against his article in the *Revue et Gazette Musicale,* criticisms made perhaps by Meyerbeer himself. The *Journal des Débats* article starts by saying that light cavatinas ornamented with fioriture are not easily given the grace and originality Meyerbeer gives them:

> One can write music that is brilliant and very advantageous for the singer, and that at the same time is devoid of any originality and entirely made up of commonplaces, I know. So, I was not trying to detract from the deserved merit of the composer in this task that is thankless and contrary to his practice.[54]

The tone is almost petulant, as though Berlioz resents having to qualify his former judgments. In fact he ends by drawing virtually the same conclusion as in the *Revue et Gazette Musicale* article, since he insists on a difference in quality between the acts; an "ingenious musician" could have written the first three acts but only a "genius" the last two.[55]

Throughout the *Journal des Débats* articles one senses that Berlioz is cautious not to criticize too strongly and is trying to temper every criticism with an antidote of some sort. To give a few examples, his criticism of the act 1 chorus, "L'Aventure est singulière," "The skipping rhythm that forms its basis is undistinguished," is followed by the comment, "One sees that the author has only written these pages against his better judgment."[56] The criticism of the act 3 tutti, "Que le ciel," "too many enharmonic modulations," is followed by the remark, "Many great harmonists like him have sometimes drawn this upon them."[57] Also the criticism of the fourth act where Saint-Bris and Valentine sing different words to the same tune is countered by the remark, "A moment of laxness will no doubt have caused the great composer to fall into a style that is not his own."[58] Berlioz's conciliatory manner is not confined to his reviews of Meyerbeer, but is used in other reviews as well, for instance in some of the reviews of Beethoven and Gluck, where it is somehow less objectionable. Perhaps this is because one can accept Berlioz calling Beethoven and Gluck "great composers" or "great harmonists," whereas with Meyerbeer it sounds too much like fawning. These *Journal des Débats* articles are more conciliatory than usual. As said before, the *Revue et Gazette Musicale* articles are more straightforward—perhaps too straightforward for Meyerbeer.

I shall now look at Berlioz's articles as a whole, using once again the general divisions of libretto, stage production, and score.

Perhaps one of the most striking points of comparison between Berlioz and the other critics is his praise of Scribe. Berlioz thought the libretto of *Les Huguenots* was good. To quote his general assessment: "M. Scribe's new libretto seems to us to be admirably arranged for music and full of incontestably dramatic situations."[59] His recounting of the story in the first *Revue et Gazette Musicale* article is serious and straightforward, not at all ironical. The only criticism Berlioz makes of the organization of the libretto is that in act 5 the passing across the stage of Marguerite de Valois's litter is a gratuitous contrast, not one motivated by the drama itself.[60] Of all the critics, Berlioz is the only one to have approved so wholeheartedly of the libretto in itself.

Berlioz was however led to question several other details of the libretto and its relation to the music. While other critics only at times mentioned a connection between the libretto and the music, for Berlioz they were intimately connected. For instance here is how he describes the second act of *Les Huguenots*:

> The second act has been judged very severely and very poorly in my opinion. The interest is not anywhere near as high as that of the rest of the play; but is this the musician's fault? And could he compose anything other than the gracious *cantilenas, cavatinas, roulades,* and the calm and sweet choruses on lines that only speak of *pleasant gardens,* of *verdant fountains,* of *sweet harmonies,* of *words of love,* of *folly,* of *coquetterie* and of *amorous strains* that *echo everywhere*? We do not think so; and indeed nothing less than a superior man was needed to manage as well with them.[61]

H. Robert Cohen has elaborated upon this point in his dissertation on Berlioz's criticism of opera, and he takes it to be one of the fundamental features of Berlioz's critical code:

> For Berlioz, an operatic composition can be no greater than its libretto: lack of variety and contrast in the drama prevents the good composer (one who follows the dramatic logic of the text) from attaining interesting musical results. . . .
>
> Berlioz is more concerned with the opportunities that a libretto offers for musical development than he is with the specific subject matter.[62]

This is a very valid point, and explains to a degree Berlioz's uncritical assessment of Scribe's literary ability; but to a degree only, because it is still puzzling how someone with Berlioz's appreciation of great literature and skill in writing (this applies not only to his criticism but to his libretti as well) should remain so uncritical of Scribe. In 1839 Berlioz even began negotiations with Scribe over a project for an opera called *La Nonne sanglante,* based on Lewis's *The Monk.*[63] Nothing final came of the collaboration, which as David Cairns puts it "was almost inevitably abortive, owing to fundamental lack of confidence on both sides."[64] In his *Mémoires* Berlioz portrays Scribe as an opportunist, and gives the impression that he had treated him badly over the affair with the *Nonne sanglante.* It is surprising then that in 1847 Berlioz could still ask Scribe if he would assist in turning the *Damnation de Faust* into an opera, with the name *Méphistophélès.*[65] Obviously, regardless of his personal opinions, Berlioz never lost sight of the practical and material advantages that could be gained from a collaboration with Scribe.

Other questions can be raised about Berlioz's attitude, expressed in his reviews of *Les Huguenots,* to the relationship between libretto and music. For instance, one might wonder how often he reasoned that a poor libretto meant poor music, to justify the music of other composers. Not very often in fact. He did not like the libretto of *La Juive,* for instance, nor much of its music, yet he does not offer Halévy the pretext that he offered Meyerbeer. The same point could be made about many other works.

So, the example in question, the second act of *Les Huguenots,* needs to be examined more closely. Berlioz wonders whether Meyerbeer could have composed different music for lines such as "pleasant gardens," "verdant fountains," and the like, thereby giving the impression that these lines appear over the course of the act. The libretto shows however that all the offending quotations come only from scene 1, Marguerite's opening air, and the following dialogue with her page Urbain. Berlioz asks whether anything other than cantilenas, cavatinas, and roulades could have been composed for these lines. There are only two cavatinas in the opera, in the first and fourth acts, and both are labeled. The opening section of Marguerite's air could, it is true, feasibly be called a cavatina also. Marguerite's air is certainly encumbered by roulades, but to such an extent that one can only wonder (as with Isabelle's roulades in *Robert le diable*) why Berlioz was not outraged. Castil-Blaze, not nearly as vigilant a detractor of roulades as Berlioz, commented on this air, "It is the most horrid and contorted collection of *vocalises* that has ever been destined to the *Bravore* of principal singers."[66] In the *Revue et Gazette Musicale* article of 20 March Berlioz comments on the entry of Raoul into the ballroom in the fifth act:

> Scarcely have the Protestants learnt of the massacre of their brothers than they are obliged to interrupt the messenger with a cry and race out of the hall without listening to the unimportant details. This is the librettist's fault, I know, and perhaps also the musician hasn't done all he could have to mitigate it. The more wordy the libretto is, the more rapidly the music needs to move.[67]

Talking about the same scene in the *Journal des Débats* article of 10 December, Berlioz states that the major fault with Raoul's air is the very fact that it is an air.[68] The point is that the composer does have a choice of form, he is not entirely bound by the libretto, and thus he too can be at fault. In a way, this contradicts the argument concerning the second act. This contradiction, coupled with Berlioz's slight distortion of facts about the layout of the second act and his failure to comment on issues for which his dislike was renowned, suggests that Berlioz was not saying what he really felt about the act. He develops his argument about Meyerbeer being cornered and unable to write anything but second-rate music as a cover-up for his distaste for the music; in this way he could criticize the music without criticizing Meyerbeer.

It is interesting that the faults in the second act later detailed by Berlioz, such as abrupt tonal transitions and too many enharmonic modulations, are purely *musical* faults, or in other words faults unrelated to the problem of the musical setting of the libretto.[69]

As said earlier, though Berlioz rarely discusses stage production or décor at any length, he usually devotes some attention to singers' interpretations and acting. The articles on *Les Huguenots* are no exception. Berlioz comments briefly on the production, "The ballets are short, luckily; the production and the costumes do M. Duponchel's wise taste great honor, and much of the scenery is magnificently effective."[70] Although he does not mention it, the fact that the production was less extravagant than *Robert le diable* could only have pleased Berlioz, which his remark on the ballets indicates. On the level of performance Berlioz remarks, "The actors, the chorus, and the orchestra rivaled each other's zeal and talent. On the level of both intelligence and precision the performance was one of the most remarkable."[71] Then follows a short enthusiastic appraisal of each of the performers in which particular attention is given to Nourrit and Falcon. All Berlioz's articles talk of the enormous success of the work: "Right from the first acts, two pieces were encored and the enthusiasm grew consistently until the end,"[72] and: "The success of this admirable work grows with every performance."[73] As shown in the previous section, the only other critic who goes into detail about the standard of performance and the reception of the first performances is Planche, and he is quite critical.

There would need to have been a greater number of critics saying the same things for us to take Planche's opinion in any way as a criterion. Yet it is still interesting that Berlioz's views are so different, given the high level of performance he usually demanded and his insistence on precision in the orchestra and choir. Berlioz's reviews of Duprez's debut in the 1837 production of *Les Huguenots* are more critical. Here he approaches Planche's, and also Castil-Blaze's, opinion of the 1838 performances, as he quite firmly criticizes the performance of the chorus: "Whether from negligence or memory lapses, it still remains that in many places in *Les Huguenots* they committed very grave errors," and to a lesser extent the orchestra: "The orchestra has also to be reproached for several peccadillos."[74] Berlioz felt that more rehearsals were needed and that the standard of performance would improve with time. It could be that he felt freer to comment on the performance once the success of the work was well assured. Even eight months made a difference to this freedom. In the *Revue et Gazette Musicale* articles of March 1836 Berlioz barely contemplates the possibility of anyone's disliking Meyerbeer, yet by November the *Journal des Débats* articles are discussing two rival schools, those who liked and those who disliked Meyerbeer.

Berlioz's approach to the music of *Les Huguenots* is more analytical and detailed than the approach of any of the other critics. He examines each act separately, noting which sections are good and at the same time mentioning anything he feels could be improved.

The particular sections Berlioz likes are roughly the same as those singled out by other critics: the act 1 Cavatina, "Une Dame noble et sage," the act 3 "Septuor," the act 4 "Bénédiction des poignards" and "Grand duo," and the chorale theme sung by Marcel. Berlioz adds more to the list however: Marcel's act 1 "A bas les maudits," the act 3 section of three choirs in ensemble, and the entire fourth act, not only two isolated numbers.

As said before, Berlioz joined the majority of critics in preferring *Les Huguenots* to *Robert le diable,* and he also joined them in preferring the last two acts of *Les Huguenots* to the first three, though he continually stressed that the first three acts also had their good points. Meyerbeer's use of instrumentation and of mass vocal effects, and the strength of his dramatic expression, shown particularly in the fourth act, were what impressed Berlioz most of all. He points out numerous passages where there is a striking use of an individual instrument, for instance, the *viole d'amour* accompaniment in the second act "Choeur des baigneurs," the cello interplay in the fourth act "Grand duo" (section "Tu l'as dit"), and the bass clarinet accompanying Marcel in the fifth act trio. He was impressed by Meyerbeer's ability to intensify dramatic expression by his careful and intelligent choice of instrument or instruments. The accompaniment to Marcel's first act aria, "A bas les maudits," was an instance described by Berlioz as a striking *combination* of instruments: the high piccolo coupled with the grave double-bass and pianissimo bass drum accompaniment. He uses the word "strange" to describe this instrumentation, and it is not really clear whether by this he did not also imply that it was a little odd.[75]

Berlioz does not talk about Meyerbeer's "lack of melody," yet he did not seem very taken with many of *Les Huguenots'* melodies, except for the cavatina, "Une Dame noble et sage." He was more impressed by Meyerbeer's manipulation of vocal effects—in particular the effect of the large chorus, but also of various interesting juxtapositions. For instance, he liked the third act dispute between two groups of women, which was animated by the "shock of the dissonances of minor and major seconds flung forcefully into the midst of a flowing, syllabic, tersely accentuated passage."[76] Berlioz enjoyed Meyerbeer's occasional use of syncopated rhythms, of an ostinato bass (in the third act duo and "Bénédiction des poignards"), and of counterpoint. One of his favorite passages was the contrapuntal juxtaposition of the three choruses in the third act, which he goes so far as to compare favorably with the three orchestras in the first act finale of *Don Giovanni*.[77] It is interesting that he particularly appreciated this passsage, given that he himself attempted something similar in combining three musical themes rather than three choruses in the finale of *Harold en Italie*.

In several places Berlioz notes original modulations which are effective because of their unexpectedness, for instance, in the assassin's song in the fifth act. In his description of the fourth act, however, every element is seen as excellent: unexpected harmony, original modulations, interesting rhythms, powerful use of massed voices, and exciting instrumentation. Berlioz describes in detail the entire climactic build-up of the act with such imagination and pacing that the words virtually spring off the page. To quote a short section:

> After several low-spoken words, the monks signal to those present to kneel, and, slowly passing amongst the various groups, they bless them. Then, in a paroxysm of fanatic exaltation, the whole choir takes up the first theme, "Pour cette cause sainte"; but this time, instead of dividing the voices into four or five parts as before, the composer joins them together in unison and in octaves, in a single compact mass, by means of which the thundering melody can brave the roar of the orchestra and dominate it completely. What is more, every two measures in the intervals of silence that separate each part of the phrase, the orchestra swells up to a *fortissimo* and, by means of intermittent attacks by the kettledrum seconded by a drum, produces a strange unparalleled death-rattle that instils consternation into the listener the most untouched by musical emotion.[78]

Although no critic neglects to mention the glories of this scene, no one managed to produce such a convincing description of why it was great.

Berlioz regrets several small points about *Les Huguenots,* the main one being the lack of an overture, upon which both Mainzer and Castil-Blaze also remarked. Given that Berlioz himself was to dispense with an overture in *Les Troyens,* he perhaps changed his mind on this issue. On other matters, too, Berlioz agrees with the disapproval of fellow critics, in particular Castil-Blaze.

For instance, in common with Castil-Blaze, Berlioz notes some problems with prosody in the act 1 "A table amis" (though not to anywhere near the same extent as Castil-Blaze does), some banal rhythms in the act 1 chorus, "L'Aventure est singulière," and, again, in "A table amis." Berlioz even comments very discreetly on Meyerbeer's lack of development of melody, noting "sometimes even melodies so piquant in their brevity, that one almost regrets not seeing them developed as real themes."[79] Other faults noted by Berlioz can be grouped under the three headings: faults of harmony, faults of dramatic consistency, and unspecified faults, that is ones that are noted but not elaborated upon.

Faults of harmony are very minor. Berlioz details abrupt tonal transitions in act 2 (which have already been mentioned), too many enharmonic modulations very close to one another, again in act 2 in the tutti "Que le ciel," and too many modulations in the act 4 duet.

The faults of dramatic inconsistency are clearly of the most importance to Berlioz. He details and expands upon four such faults. The first is in the finale of the third act where a second orchestra is placed on the stage. Berlioz comments that "the drama did not demand this extraordinary display of instrumental forces, and the music is not thereby sufficiently enhanced to justify it."[80] The second fault is in the fourth act, where Saint-Bris and Valentine sing very different words to the same tune: "The musical phrase to which the composer has put these words so different in character [is sung by] two people, one trembling and the other menacing."[81] Berlioz consistently objected to this practice, particularly in Italian opera.

The last two faults of dramatic inconsistency detailed by Berlioz are in the fifth act. The first, on which I have already commented, occurs when Raoul interrupts the ball with an aria to tell of the massacre, and the aria itself has to be interrupted as the Huguenots rush from the ballroom to aid their brothers. The other fault is also connected with Raoul's air, but this time it is the silences between verses to which Berlioz objects. These silences Berlioz takes as meaning to suggest Raoul's feeling of suffocation, yet he feels that "such a degree of truth is not fitting to a large theater like the Opéra, where the distance and the noise of the orchestra prevent the audience from noticing the expressions on the faces."[82] This type of error, unnoticed in this instance by any other critic, was often identified by Berlioz, especially where the music did not follow the dramatic implications of the text.

Finally, the unspecified faults noted by Berlioz are in the first, second, and third acts. He states that the accompaniment to Raoul's romance in the first act is much more interesting than the romance itself, thereby implying that he does not like the romance. About the second act finale he said:

> The finale, very dramatically conceived and full of striking orchestral effects, would make the fortune of any other composer, but for Meyerbeer it doesn't seem to me to be original enough, either in thought or form.[83]

Precisely what he thought about the "thought" and "form" he does not state. Several times Berlioz commented that Marcel's solo with harps, "Voyez le ciel s'ouvre," in the fifth act was not up to the standard of the rest of the opera, but once again he does not give any reasons why it was not.

The fault implied in all of these three instances is that of lapsing into a second-rate, "empty" style—a fault that was remarked upon by nearly all the other critics as well. Berlioz does not elaborate in these cases. Perhaps as part of his policy of minimizing faults he did not wish to draw attention to too many cases where Meyerbeer was writing "in a style not his own."

Berlioz's Meyerbeer articles concentrate very much on the music. He neither digresses at length on other areas nor tries to explain Meyerbeer's social and intellectual position.

Berlioz basically liked the same sections of *Les Huguenots* as the other critics. He had the same preferences regarding individual acts and disapproved of several of the same faults, such as abuse of harmony and Italianisms (in vocal ornamentation). Where he differed most, as has already been pointed out, is in his detailed analysis of the music and in his study of the opera as a vehicle of "dramatic expression." He thought the dramatic expression occasionally rang false, but culminated magnificently in the fourth act. A close examination of Berlioz's analysis of the music shows that in his appreciation of the opera the fourth act stands out well above the others. He has little good to say about the second act and sees the first, third, and fifth acts as being of mixed quality.

The general impression of the music of *Les Huguenots* given by the other critics is that of a flawed work with good and bad sections lying side by side. Although Berlioz says fundamentally the same thing, the overall impression he gives is different. Berlioz portrays *Les Huguenots* as a masterpiece in which there are several lapses, almost like slips of the tongue or pen, where Meyerbeer forgot himself or bowed momentarily to theatrical conventions. Berlioz aimed at toning down the lapses, and in the case of the second act he simply avoided detailing them altogether.

It is unlikely that Meyerbeer had ever bribed Berlioz. However, as mentioned in chapter 4, Meyerbeer's personal backing was of extreme importance to Berlioz, and the suspicion does remain that, for diplomatic reasons, in the case of *Robert le diable* and *Les Huguenots* he was not always saying what he really thought about the music or performance.

Despite these qualifications, there can be no doubt that Berlioz genuinely appreciated Meyerbeer's talents, in particular his inventive instrumentation. Two articles have been written insisting upon Berlioz's sincere liking for Meyerbeer, one by Patrick Besnier and the other by Charles Stuart.[84] Besnier expresses indignation at Boschot's implication that Meyerbeer was "paying Berlioz off."[85] He sees great similarities in Berlioz's and Meyerbeer's dramatic aspirations and even suggests that the reason why Berlioz's projected opera *La Nonne sanglante* was aborted was that Meyerbeer had already effectively covered the subject.

Stuart also feels that Berlioz and Meyerbeer were "within certain limits trying to achieve the same things in opera."[86] There is undoubtedly some truth in this statement. Berlioz was close to Meyerbeer in his love for the grandiose and his interest in instrumentation, but in certain fundamental respects Berlioz differed radically from Meyerbeer, such as in his powers of dramatic expression. Charles Stuart's article looks closely at Berlioz's review of *Le Prophète*, demonstrating how Berlioz's praise outweighs his criticism. Though this review is outside the scope of this study, it is worth looking briefly at what Berlioz says in his correspondence concerning *Le Prophète*.

First of all there is a series of odiously fawning letters from Meyerbeer to Berlioz expressing his concern at Berlioz's ill health and his hope that Berlioz can still come to the dress rehearsal. To quote one small extract from a letter written 15 April 1849 just before the first performance:

> I love you immensely, you know that. But this evening, I fear you even more than I love you, because of the desire that my score should make a good impression on you.
> A thousand compliments and thanks for attending the night before last.
> Your trembling and devoted
> > Meyerbeer[87]

Berlioz in a letter to his sister Nanci shortly after his review of *Le Prophète* says:

> Meyerbeer has the sense not to take too seriously the four or five qualifications that I introduced in my ten columns of eulogies. I would have liked to spare him the unpleasant impression these criticisms, expressed with a certain energy, gave; but there are some things that absolutely must be said; I cannot let it be thought that I approve or that I even tolerate these transactions of a great master with the poor taste of a certain public.[88]

This statement shows that Berlioz has been much sterner towards Meyerbeer than in previous reviews, his attitude of tolerance towards Meyerbeer's "weak patches" having turned to one of censure. His letter to Nanci continues:

> The score does nevertheless contain some very beautiful things alongside some extremely weak things and detestable fragments. But the incomparable magnificence of the spectacle will make it all alright. What a job it is today to make an opera succeed! What intrigues! What seductions to work, what money to spend, what dinners to give!—This makes me sick at heart. It is Meyerbeer who has caused all this and who has thus forced Rossini to give the game up.[89]

This is a cry of despair over the way musical advancement functioned, and shows Berlioz's resentment against Meyerbeer for his responsibility in the situation.

Meyerbeer, through his close friend the conductor Girard, had arranged for some scenes from Berlioz's *Damnation de Faust* to be performed at the prestigious Société des concerts (Conservatoire concerts), 15 April 1849. Was this an intelligent pre-première bribe?[90] Perhaps this gesture did affect Berlioz's judgment a little. If he were indeed aware of it, he might have moderated his criticism, but if so it would most probably have been unconscious, the impression given in the correspondence is that of someone who had taken great pains to be "honest." I would agree with Stuart that the tone of Berlioz's review of *Le Prophète* is straightforward and that he gives no hint of prevarication.

At the time of the première of *Les Huguenots* Berlioz was not overly concerned about Meyerbeer's method of opera production, but was rather very impressed by the amount of time taken in rehearsals. By 1849 he was understandably beginning to feel a little revolted by the whole rigmarole involved in producing a Meyerbeer opera. As time passed and Meyerbeer's fame solidified into legend—which led Heine to remark, "the mother of Meyerbeer was the second woman in history to see her son accepted as divine"[91]—Berlioz felt more able to state exactly what he felt about Meyerbeer.

To recapitulate, there is some doubt about Berlioz's sincerity in certain parts of his reviews of *Les Huguenots,* but less, perhaps none, in his later reviews of *Le Prophète.* Certainly Berlioz felt *Les Huguenots* was a much better opera than *Le Prophète.* His great admiration for *Les Huguenots* is shown by the number of examples he uses from it to demonstrate points in his *Traité d'instrumentation et d'orchestration.*[92] Although Berlioz's editors would have requested that he write on grand opera, it was clearly a genre that interested him (unlike the average *opéra-comique* of the day). It could be said of certain theoretical isssues he raises in his reviews of the genre, such as how much importance to give to personal relationships within the context of a historical drama, how best to portray crowd sentiments and a sense of historical inevitability, and how to manipulate multiple massed forces, that he was anticipating concerns that would later be of some importance to him when composing his opera *Les Troyens.*

8

Orchestral and Instrumental Music:
Conservatoire Concert Series

Berlioz's reviews of orchestral and instrumental music are dominated by those of the Conservatoire concert series. The 1830s were not a particularly flourishing time for performances of serious instrumental music, as the major emphasis of the day was on popular virtuosic compositions.

The Société des Concerts du Conservatoire (the official name of the Conservatoire concert series) was registered as a private organization, but received an annual government subsidy of two thousand francs and had free use of the Conservatoire hall. The orchestra was composed of faculty, students, and graduates, and the Société's "strictly professional management and performing practices made its orchestra the best anywhere."[1] It was renowned throughout Europe and envied even in Germany, the bastion of fine orchestras. Six concerts were scheduled each year during the winter season but usually several extra concerts were included. The subscription list for the series consisted of a chosen 1,100.[2] It is not known precisely how this list was chosen, but "social status and personal influence—and chiefly the former—must have governed the process."[3] The series was popular amongst Parisian literati: Balzac, Hugo, de Vigny, Fontenay, and the artist Eugène Delacroix were subscribers. The subscription was renewable each year, which meant that it was almost impossible for new subscribers to join.[4] As stated in the introduction, the Société was founded in 1828 by François Habeneck who conducted the orchestra until his death in 1849.[5] Berlioz saw the motivating force behind the establishment of the concert series to be the desire of a substantial number of people to become better acquainted with the music of Beethoven. Certainly Habeneck's main purpose in founding the Société appears to have been to promote Beethoven's music in Paris. This aim was fulfilled, as Beethoven became the most performed composer at the concerts. The following list gives the number of times each of Beethoven's nine symphonies were performed during the first thirty-one years of the society:[6]

Symphony No. 1	13 times
Symphony No. 2	26 times
Symphony No. 3	28 times
Symphony No. 4	24 times
Symphony No. 5	53 times
Symphony No. 6	51 times
Symphony No. 7	52 times
Symphony No. 8	14 times
Symphony No. 9	19 times

In the period of 1828 to 1871, 360 of the 548 symphonies performed were by Beethoven.[7] The concert programs were eclectic; a Beethoven symphony might be performed alongside an operatic aria, a solo fantasia, and sections from a requiem. The following program, that of the first concert, in March 1828, gives a good idea of this mixture of musical genres:

1. *Symphonie héroïque*—Beethoven.
2. *Duo* de l'opéra *Sémiramis*—Rossini.
3. *Solo* pour le cor à pistons, composé et exécuté par M. Meifred.
4. *Air*—Rossini.
5. *Concerto* nouveau de violon—Rode.
6. *Choeur* de *Blanche de Provence*—Cherubini.
7. Ouverture des *Abencerrages* [*sic*]—Cherubini.
8. *Kyrie* et *Gloria* de la *Messe du Sacre*—Cherubini (exécuté à grand choeur).[8]

Excerpts such as a scene from an opera or oratorio or one movement from a symphony were common, and chamber works were sometimes performed by the full orchestra. Jeffrey Cooper states for instance that Beethoven's Septet, op. 20, was performed with its original instrumentation in 1831, "but in its 46 representations from 1837 to 1869 it was usually rendered by string orchestra with doubled clarinets, bassoons, and horns (and often only *fragments* were played)."[9] Over the years fewer Italian operatic arias were performed, perhaps in response to criticism from the press. The audience for the concerts was necessarily small; it came to represent the elite of the musical intelligentsia and by its very exclusiveness attained a degree of prestige.

For Berlioz the Conservatoire concerts were manna. They provided him as a composer with the opportunity to hear the works of the composers he most respected, and as a critic with the opportunity to write about music that really inspired him. The vocabulary he used in describing the Conservatoire hall is quasi-religious; he would talk of "a sanctuary," of an "atmosphere embalmed in poetry."[10] Attending Conservatoire concerts was an act of devotion to what

Berlioz saw as the only musical institution in Paris dedicating itself solely to music. The enthusiasm of the audience was all the more impressive given the hall's uncomfortable seats and bad lighting.

Berlioz referred to the public attending the concerts as the only group of people capable of understanding truly great music and set them apart from the public that frequented the Opéra and the Théâtre Italien. With a paternal air he noted the growth in understanding of the Conservatoire concert audience, which had at one stage found Beethoven's music difficult and bizarre, but now responded to it with frenetic enthusiasm. He traces a similar development with respect to Gluck, though the resulting audience enthusiasm is milder than that for Beethoven. He considered that the audience's sensitivity, its openness to new forms and new emotions, made it receptive to further change. Berlioz does not portray the public as faultless however. For instance he writes "this public . . . often makes mistakes in spite of everything, since it often happens that it goes back on its own decisions."[11]

Within the general audience elite Berlioz once again positions the smaller elite of impassioned souls who like him are devoted to great music, who "sometimes instead of applause give tears or sighs of quite a different eloquence from the clapping of hands."[12] He observed the growing popularity of Beethoven's music during the 1830s with great satisfaction, but also with a few misgivings, in that in becoming well known, Beethoven was becoming "à la mode" and attracting the attention of dilettantes. In his review of a Conservatoire concert of 1835 Berlioz writes with distaste of a young dilettante who slept during the performance of the Beethoven symphony, but awoke for the Rossini aria; he had come to the concert because it was fashionable to do so, not because he liked the music of Beethoven. And again in a review of a 1837 concert he comments ironically about how a trio by Johann Pixis (1788–1874) was mistakenly announced as by Beethoven, and vice versa. The audience responded with enthusiasm to the Pixis and coldness to the Beethoven.[13] Berlioz wished that Beethoven could be spared such disrespect, and would have preferred that his music remain the domain of those few who really appreciated it. This "closet" attitude towards Beethoven is also reflected in Berlioz's attitude to the duration of the Conservatoire concert series itself.

In his first and last reviews of the Conservatoire concerts Berlioz usually makes a melancholy comment on the shortness of the season. He often counters this however by adding that perhaps it is a good thing that the season is so short since "music, like all pure and alive sensations, needs organs whose sensitivity has not been blunted by use."[14] On another occasion he commented that "one must hear them [Beethoven etc.] only at long intervals and this is why the rarity of the Conservatoire meetings is itself one of the conditions for their success."[15] This is a surprising view considering how Berlioz had complained so trenchantly elsewhere of the lack of good music performed in Paris. He is nevertheless quite adamant that the series should last only for a short season and maintained this opinion even in the face of attacks on the exclusiveness of the institution.

With regard to this last point Berlioz slightly changed his opinion over the 1830s. In an article in *Le Rénovateur* of 1835 he wonders whether there could indeed be more than 1,200 people in Paris capable of appreciating the music performed at the concert series.[16] By 1837 he is a bit more worried about the issue and feels some compunction for those who do not have the chance to attend the concerts: "Unfortunately it is a very limited public. The lay population is not admitted at all, and having only concerts which, with very few exceptions, are ridiculous or worthless, to develop and sustain its taste for music, conserves its prejudices and ignorance."[17] His answer to this problem is not to open the Conservatoire doors, but to encourage *artists* to break the barriers between institutions by playing Beethoven, for instance, in other venues. Liszt is cited as an artist who was breaking down such barriers by giving concerts variously at the Conservatoire, Opéra, Salle Erard, and elsewhere. Berlioz himself attempted to do the same with the concerts he was to give during the rest of his life, but he was emotionally bound to the preservation of the Conservatoire concert series as a select organization and dreaded its sanctity being broken by brash intruders drawn by curiosity, rather than devotion.

To Berlioz's gratification, in the second half of the 1830s the music of Gluck and Mozart began to be performed more frequently at the concerts. He was less happy though about the performances of Weber's music, which he felt were both too few in number and too limited in repertoire, complaining that only the *Euryanthe* overture was performed a great deal.[18] In fact Weber was the second most performed composer of instrumental works under Habeneck, although admittedly it was almost exclusively the overtures that were performed.[19] Berlioz's opinion of Mozart should be briefly mentioned at this point. As far as Mozart's symphonies were concerned, Berlioz basically would have agreed with the hierarchy outlined by E. T. A. Hoffmann in his essay on Beethoven's instrumental music, of Beethoven, Mozart, and Haydn, in descending order of merit. Berlioz appreciated Mozart's symphonies, but felt it was "crazy not to want to draw any sort of comparison between such symphonies [Beethoven's] and even the most admirable ones of Mozart; the struggle is . . . not equal."[20] Some of Mozart's operatic music however moved onto a different plane, in particular *Idomeneo* and certain scenes from the *Magic Flute*, "the religious March, Sarastro's Grand Air and the Chorus of Priests" he called "the most sublime musical manifestation of antique musical feeling."[21] So although in general, Mozart's symphonies did not approach the sublimity of Beethoven and Gluck, there were sections of his operas that did, and for this reason Berlioz sometimes includes Mozart in his list of "great masters."

Berlioz criticized the programs of the Conservatoire concerts for lack of variety.[22] His ideal program would have been a mixture of old and new music;

for instance he enthusiastically praised a program in 1837 that combined the music of Ries and Cherubini with the music of Beethoven and Gluck.[23] By "old" music Berlioz usually meant music of the recent past. He was not very familiar with much music earlier than the eighteenth century and mocked attempts to revive early music, such as Fétis's *Concerts historiques*. There may have been a degree of antagonism towards Fétis in his mockery, for one of the things that Berlioz lamented about the closure of Choron's Institution was the disappearance of the repertoire he taught and performed, which included composers such as Handel, Bach, Durante, Palestrina, Leo and Hasse. However, Berlioz does not often regret lack of exposure of these composers. It is as though he was conscious that such music was worthy of respect but had little interest in it himself.

Berlioz disliked the eclecticism of programs that combined the music of Beethoven with, for instance, popular arias; and he comments that the public, though initially accepting such practices, had begun expressing their discontent also. When in a concert in 1834 the violinist Haumann ended his fantasia on "La Prière de la Muette" with a set of fashionable pizzicato variations, Berlioz cried out against such degradation of music. Other audiences might expect such antics, he wrote, but not the Conservatoire audience.[24] Surprisingly, however, he appeared to enjoy some of the solo performances in between large works. These soloists were often members of the orchestra, such as the oboist Brod, the flautist Tulou, and the cellist Franchomme, who frequently performed fantasias or sets of variations of their own composition. Under Habeneck, Brod received thirteen performances, Franchomme nine and Tulou six.[25] Berlioz always mentioned these compositions, even if only briefly, and he remarks in one of his reviews of 1837 that a solo interspersed between works of great emotional content could give the audience time to rest.

In other instances he is not so charitable towards "solo fantasias "and indeed generally writes of them with displeasure, listing them as things to be avoided alongside "Italian cavatinas," "one-act *opéras-comiques*," "*contredanses*" et cetera. In another 1837 Conservatoire concert review he is very critical of a set of clarinet variations performed after a Beethoven symphony, and states that the solo virtuosi should realize the danger they run in performing alongside the music of Gluck and Beethoven and desist from playing in these concerts.[26] The context was obviously important; for instance the solos performed by artists at the Conservatoire concerts were more tasteful than some of the flashy arrangements of popular arias performed in the fashionable salons of the day. Yet despite the fact that Berlioz seemed to have enjoyed the occasional Conservatoire concert solo, ultimately he did not consider either these solos, or their showy counterparts, as appropriate to the concert series.

Beethoven and to a lesser extent Gluck were the two figures dominating Berlioz's reviews of the Conservatoire concerts. He frequently devotes more than half his review to their works, gives a detailed descriptive analysis of the music, and in the case of Gluck notes all the places where the performance diverged from the score. Since Gluck was not one of the most performed composers at this time, this emphasis on his music reflects Berlioz's own interest.

Berlioz was perhaps aware that the intensity of his enthusiasm for Beethoven's music laid him open to attack and so carefully notes passages where Beethoven could be said to have erred in some way. In a review in which he is clearly answering criticism accusing him of deifying Beethoven, Berlioz argues that he is merely stating the truth; he then points to those instances where he has, as he puts it, detailed the small faults that link Beethoven to humanity. The review continues with what Berlioz labels an unemotional and objective account of the Beethoven C-Minor Symphony, where he relates not his own but the audience's reaction, which is, needless to say, one of rapturous enthusiasm.[27]

A certain amount of new music was performed at the Conservatoire concerts, and while Berlioz always examined it conscientiously, it was rarely with great enthusiasm or at great length. It is difficult at times to discern what he felt about some of his contemporaries. As he himself said, there were "very few living composers about whom I can more or less frankly express my opinion."[28]

I shall briefly examine Berlioz's reviews of contemporary orchestral and instrumental music. I shall however expand the scope slightly to include some reviews of religious music and reviews other than those of the Conservatoire concerts.

We have already seen that Berlioz did not write extensively on the contemporary music performed at the Conservatoire concerts and other scattered instrumental or orchestral concerts. When he does discuss the work of young composers he frequently deals with the problems they faced as composers rather than with the quality of their works. The composers whose work Berlioz most appreciated and wrote about were Le Sueur, Liszt, Chopin, Cherubini, and Urhan. Other composers whose works, being occasionally performed, were reviewed by Berlioz were Hiller, Onslow (reviewed several times), Rousselot, Reber, Spohr, Turbry, Täglichsbeck, and Ries.

It is difficult to separate Berlioz's opinion of the compositions of Liszt and Chopin from his comments on their roles as virtuoso performers. I shall thus discuss Berlioz's examination of their music in the concluding section of this chapter, where I shall briefly examine his opinion of virtuosi.

Le Sueur was Berlioz's teacher and mentor and assumed a paternal as well as pedagogical role in Berlioz's early years in Paris.[29] In his articles (particularly in the obituary notice of 1837)[30] Berlioz conveys both respect for Le Sueur as an individual and admiration for his music.

Le Sueur's influence on Berlioz's ideas about music was extensive. Octave Fouque in his book *Les Révolutionnaires de la musique* comments at length on the similarities between Berlioz and Le Sueur. He mentions amongst other points Le Sueur's desire for each of his masses to be appropriate to the occasion, his wish to be able to write his own words, his sense of the grandiose, his dislike of unmotivated vocal fugues (such as fugal amens), and the lack of piano music in his repertoire.[31] Fouque extravagantly claimed that "if Berlioz is God, Le Sueur was surely his prophet," and that "Le Sueur's best work is Berlioz."[32] Certainly, in his reviews of Le Sueur Berlioz dwells noticeably on the above issues, in particular on the importance of writing music appropriate to the occasion and the text. He remarks in his review of Le Sueur's Oratorio *Noémi,* "The naïvety and mournful charm of these words can be found again in their entirety in the music,"[33] and often quotes Le Sueur's fugue "Quis enarrabit caelorum gloriam" as an example of a successful vocal fugue that is dramatically motivated.[34] However, as David Cairns comments, "Berlioz . . . disagreed fundamentally with Lesueur's Gluckian theory of music as the obedient servant of text and dramatic idea, believing instead in a Beethovenian symphonic ideal of music 'wholly in command.'"[35]

For Berlioz, Le Sueur represented most significantly "the sublime biblical style."[36] His skillful maneuvering of large forces and simplicity of forms and his cunning in evolving a method of composition that enabled his music to be properly heard in a cathedral filled Berlioz with admiration and surely acted as an inspiration for his own *Requiem.* It must have been a pleasure for him to analyze the work of a friend whose works he sincerely admired, despite the differences in their opinions.

When he boasted of his unbiased approach to the music of his enemies, Berlioz probably had Cherubini uppermost in his mind. Excerpts from Cherubini's music, largely religious, were often performed at the Conservatoire concerts. Berlioz responded to them with enthusiasm, to the extent of calling Cherubini's *Requiem* in C minor (in particular the "Marche de la communion" and "Agnus Dei") the work of a *poet* and musician—a high recommendation and one that he reserved normally for composers such as Beethoven and Gluck.[37] A performance of an air from Cherubini's opera *Les Abencérages* prompted Berlioz to place it in "the school of Gluck" and laud it for its "tragic depths, . . . its responsive orchestra and its forms that scorn meaningless ornamentation."[38] His reservations about Cherubini's music were connected with its dramatic inappropriateness. In particular he considered that Cherubini gave rough and bombastic interpretations of religious texts,[39] and also that he used repeated vocal "amens"[40] and dramatically unmotivated fugues.[41] In his two reviews of Cherubini's book *Cours de contrepoint et fugue* Berlioz scoffs at the idea that the fugue is the basis of all composition, to the neglect of melody, application of music to the drama, and the expression of the passions.[42] In his commentary on Cherubini's "Dies Irae" from the C-Minor *Requiem,* Berlioz suggests that the text could have been interpreted in a more complex and invigorating manner if the author had been able to break through the barriers of the orchestral organization to which he was bound. In other words Cherubini had gone as far as he could within the limitations of his orchestration, but it was possible to go still further (as Berlioz was to prove in his own *Requiem!*)[43] Though Berlioz makes this statement on Cherubini's orchestration in specific reference to one extract, surely it has implications for all of Cherubini's music. Thus without denying Berlioz's genuine appreciation of Cherubini's gift for expressive music, it can be said that he had misgivings not only about Cherubini's "dramatic improprieties," but also about the conservatism of his orchestration, which was in any case a related issue for Berlioz.

The works of Cherubini and Le Sueur reviewed by Berlioz were, with the exception of some of Cherubini's works for unaccompanied choirs, portions of works designed for large ensembles. Berlioz did not review Cherubini's chamber music. He did however attend odd concerts of chamber music. Although he eulogized over the music (chiefly that of Beethoven) performed by groups such as the Tilmant, Müller, and Baillot quartets[44] and various chamber groups organized by Liszt, Berlioz only occasionally elaborated on the actual performances.[45] Indeed, any discussion of the quartet members tended to examine their merits as interpreters of Beethoven.[46] On several occasions, however, he does devote major portions of articles to discussion of Beethoven's chamber music.[47] In an article on Beethoven trios and piano sonatas, Berlioz states that it is in his piano sonatas, not his symphonies, that Beethoven has his last word.[48] Berlioz's attitude to the sonatas is one of awe, concluding that they could be used as a benchmark by which to measure the development of musical intelligence.

A performance in 1834 of some of the chamber music of Henri Reber inspired Berlioz to write an article about Reber's music for *Le Rénovateur*. In the article he expresses admiration in general terms for Reber's instrumentation, expressiveness, and original harmonies.[49] Half the article is about the iniquities of the *Concours* for the *Prix de Rome,* and a great deal of the impetus behind Berlioz's enjoyment of Reber's music seems to be derived from the fact that he failed the *Concours*. Berlioz details the benefits of not being sent to Rome and comments on the consequent original style of Reber, "Nothing is more removed from the scholastic forms, or rather formulae, than the completely individual style that characterizes his compositions."[50] Berlioz does not review Reber's chamber music again, though in 1861 he wrote on the publication by Richault of Reber's four symphonies.[51]

The article in *Le Rénovateur* on Reber is in fact typical of several of Berlioz's reviews of contemporary composers in which the composer's work is used only as a springboard from which to launch an attack on the *Concours* and the conservatism of the Conservatoire. In general Berlioz finds the actual music of these contemporary composers uninspiring though relieved by interesting passages. The chief virtue of such music lies in its being the product of composers excluded from the system. This is the case with Berlioz's reviews of Rousselot,[52] who never even entered for the *Prix de Rome,* and Léfebure, who succeeded only in gaining a second prize.[53]

The most famous French composer of chamber music at the time was Georges Onslow.[54] Onslow is mentioned quite frequently by Berlioz, but with great reticence. He seems to have appreciated Onslow's use of rich harmonies most of all, but he rarely writes more than a few sentences about his music, either merely announcing that it was performed[55] or giving just a few phrases of moderate praise.[56] An excellent example of Berlioz's evasive style occurs in one of these reviews of Onslow's music: "The calm beauty of several of his *adagios* and the lively animation of most of his *finales* (prestos) prove the facility with which he manages the most opposing styles."[57] It is hardly an example of great facility with opposing styles to be able to write calm adagios and lively finales. Another composer of chamber music (mostly piano music) at this time, French pianist and composer Henri Bertini (1798–1876), is mentioned only once, in passing, by Berlioz during the period under consideration; he finds a sextet by Bertini "full of life and freshness."[58]

Apart from Beethoven's chamber music, the only chamber music Berlioz discusses at any length is that of Urhan.[59] Urhan's mystical Christianity and prudery were obviously the cause for some ridicule in the sophisticated musical circles of the day. Berlioz admired Urhan's strength of character, his sincerity, and the way all his activities, including his music, seemed to be an extension of his faith. Urhan was also a champion of Beethoven. An outstanding viola player, he performed the solo in *Harold en Italie* many times. In all his reviews of Urhan's music Berlioz comments on the peculiar intimacy of the works and the need for them to be performed in correspondingly intimate surroundings with a select audience of sympathetic intelligent listeners. Berlioz stresses that in order to appreciate Urhan's music the listener must be able to enter into the spirit of the music; this is particularly the case with his composition *Auditions*:

> For all the people who do not understand the author's point of view, *Auditions* is an absurd work; for those, on the contrary, who have enough religiosity in their soul to be able to understand the exaltation of an artist both pious and passionate like M. Urhan, this work, with its audacious simplicity, will be the source of the most vibrant emotions.[60]

Berlioz seems to feel some reticence in criticizing Urhan's music; it is almost as though he felt that in criticizing the music he would be criticizing the validity of the religious experience. Consequently, much of what Berlioz writes about Urhan takes the form of sympathetic reverie—but not all, however.

Urhan's composition *Auditions* was inspired by a mystical experience in which an angel accompanied by an Aeolian harp sang to him; his music attempts to convey that experience as precisely as possible. Berlioz applauds the attempt and describes in great detail the way the Aeolian harp is represented on the piano, but finally admits that he feels the harp would have been better represented by the *viole d'amour* (an instrument often used by Urhan) and the angel by a ten- to twelve-year-old boy rather than a female singer.[61] The only other direct criticism Berlioz makes of Urhan is of one of the pieces, "Orage," from Urhan's piano composition *Lettres à Elle,* in which Berlioz felt Urhan had mistakenly tried to represent a "storm" of the heart by sounds associated with a meteorological storm, depicting rather the "roar of a real tempest than the tumultuous movement of a storm of the heart."[62] Berlioz's appreciation of Urhan seems to stem from admiration for his integrity rather than from real involvement with his music. Indeed the very conditions that Berlioz says are required for an appreciation of Urhan's music hint at its limitations: music that could only be really appreciated by people with the same religious piety as Urhan was never going to attain the universal significance of, say, the music of Beethoven or even the works of Le Sueur. Berlioz nevertheless understood Urhan's desire to write for and perform to intimate gatherings only.

Performances of chamber music were certainly not a prominent feature of the musical life in Paris of the 1830s, and Berlioz assigned them a correspondingly small space. If he had wanted to write more extensively on chamber music, presumably the *Revue et Gazette Musicale* would have allowed him the space to do so. As was mentioned in chapter 3, when Berlioz was sent Schumann's music, he declared himself not capable of reviewing it, and passed it on to Liszt. Another reason behind the refusal may have been a fundamental lack of interest in the genre. Berlioz does not seem to have been motivated to make an effort to become more familiar with Schumann's piano music. Similarly he does not seem to have been motivated to became better acquainted with Schubert's music either. To the few works of Schubert's performed, which were almost exclusively songs and "La Religieuse" ("Die Nonne") in particular, Berlioz gave the highest praise, saying of "La Religieuse" that it was "of great poetic inspiration; not to mince words, it is sublime."[63] Berlioz writes little about any of the contemporary symphonies performed at the Conservatoire concerts, but there are three specific complaints that he makes. First, the music, though skilfully and carefully composed, is finally too scholastic and lacks excitement and originality;[64] second, the work resembled Beethoven or Haydn symphonies too strongly;[65] and third, the symphony needed to be heard again or be given more time for absorption before it could be examined properly. This last point appears to have been largely dissimulation in this context since it was unlikely that Berlioz would hear the works again, or at least not for some time.[66]

I shall comment briefly on the first two complaints. Berlioz's label of "scholastic" was not praise. There is an element of condescension for instance when he comments that a symphony by the German composer Täglichsbeck shows evidence of close study and often successful imitation of the masters. Berlioz elaborates on the symphony for the *Revue et Gazette Musicale,* saying that the first movement does not contain anything new, although everything is very nicely done, the Adagio (the movement where Berlioz looked for some sort of poetic inspiration) is cold and colorless, the Scherzo is just an imitation of Beethoven (a frequent complaint about scherzi) and he could not remember anything about the Finale. In his article on the symphony for the *Journal des Débats* Berlioz remembers enough about the Finale to call it a skillful tissue of notes without any firm color or intention. So much for scholastic music! Berlioz's other reviews of "scholastic" music are not so damning. Symphonies by Onslow and Spohr, for instance, are just summarized by a few bland statements on competent use of harmony, instrumentation, et cetera.

The second complaint, that of too closely resembling Beethoven or Haydn, is of course, closely allied to the first. Sometimes Berlioz feels a whole work is marred by being too closely based on a model. For instance he comments on a symphony by Ries that Beethoven is present in every note, even in details of instrumentation and harmonic progressions.[67] However, in a review of a symphony by Rousselot, Berlioz states that only two of the movements are spoiled by being too closely modeled on Beethoven and that one movement in particular, the Adagio, gives a glimpse of a more original, poetic sensibility. Berlioz's review of Rousselot is a little ambiguous. As already mentioned, Berlioz liked Rousselot's isolation from academic training; he called him a pupil of "the beautiful in music," his teachers being "Haydn, Beethoven and Weber." Berlioz comments sympathetically that Rousselot's symphony was barely applauded, noting how discouraging this was for an artist. Yet Berlioz's own comments on the symphony do not suggest that he himself felt the work, apart from the Adagio, to be particularly good. Berlioz encapsulates his attitude towards too close adherence to models in a review of the published score of a symphony by a M. Printemps from Lille. Berlioz notes the work's strict adherence to the model of a Haydn symphony and comments, "no doubt the model is beautiful," but "this makes it immensely difficult, not to say absolutely impossible, to excite new emotions by such means."[68] The only relatively detailed accounts by Berlioz of contemporary symphonies are in his reviews of Hiller.[69] Although he appreciates many features of Hiller's symphonies, such as "the distinguished melody, the always pure and clear harmony, and the general organization full of tact and taste,"[70] his praise is moderate and circumspect. Hiller represents another instance of the "correct" and academic approach with only the occasional flash of poetic inspiration, and was linked more to Haydn than to Beethoven.[71]

During the 1830s Liszt and Berlioz were good friends, corresponded regularly, and did what they could to help each other. Liszt's arrangements of Berlioz's *Symphonie fantastique, Lélio,* and sections from *Harold en Italie* played a role in making these compositions known to a wider public and provoking an interest in Berlioz's works outside Paris. Schumann's laudatory article on the *Symphonie fantastique* was based entirely on Liszt's piano transcription of 1835.[72] When in Weimar in 1852 and 1855, Liszt organized festivals of Berlioz's works, and in the second concert Berlioz himself conducted the *Symphonie fantastique* and the first performance of Liszt's Piano Concerto in E Flat with Liszt as soloist.[73] The question of whether his friendship with Liszt biased Berlioz's critical judgment is difficult to answer. Perhaps it affected him more in what he neglected to criticize, since it is surprising that Berlioz is not more critical of Liszt for his choice of program in the early 1830s and his abuse and distortion of scores.

Liszt's use of variation form and paraphrases of popular operas was not criticized by Berlioz, who felt that, in general, Liszt did not use the forms merely to display his technical skill:

> In a host of passages in these new works it is easy to recognize the highest intellectual merit, which produces an effect that is quite independent of the prestige of the performance. I cite, amongst other remarkable passages in this respect, the introduction to his *Fantaisie sur le pirate*, where a phrase of two beats is admirably treated, without ornaments, brilliant passages, or the help of any of the numerous means that musical pyrotechnicality puts at his disposal.[74]

This quotation comes from an article of 1836 in which Berlioz talks of a modification in Liszt's style as a performer, implying a corresponding modification in Liszt's compositional technique. That is, the rhetorical decorations added by Liszt to the music of others were also to be found in his own compositions of the time, for instance in his variations on Paganini's *La Campanella*. In 1837 Liszt himself wrote of the change in his compositional and performance style and of how in his early years everything he performed aimed primarily to highlight his virtuosity and serve his self-esteem.[75] Liszt's declaration seemed to liberate Berlioz, and two months later he wrote a direct criticism of Liszt's earlier style for the *Journal des Débats,* in which he disparages the way Liszt used to distort the Beethoven C-Sharp Minor Piano Sonata:

> Following the habit then adopted to make the fashionable public applaud, instead of those sustained notes in the bass, those dying voices in the upper parts, and the severe uniformity of rhythm that I have just mentioned, he put cadences and *tremoli,* he hurried and slackened the beat, thus disturbing by his passionate accents the calm of this sadness, and making thunder growl in this cloudless sky that darkened only with the sunset. . . . I suffered cruelly, I must admit, more even than I have ever suffered in listening to our unfortunate singers ornament the Grand Monologue of *Freischütz,* since to this torture was added the sorrow of seeing such an artist fall into the rut that ordinarily only mediocrities fall into.[76]

Berlioz's previous discussion of Liszt's mannerisms in performance had been much more circumspect. A review for the *Journal des Débats* in 1835 reproaches him gently: "It [the use of mannerisms] is the only improvement to which his talent seems susceptible,"[77] and a review in the *Revue et Gazette Musicale* of 1836 defends him: "Many bitter criticisms have been made of Liszt."[78] Berlioz does not make any direct criticism himself here, though he does suggest that attacks from the press had forced Liszt to reconsider his style.

Liszt had begun to drop his mannerisms from around 1832 onwards, and Berlioz was many times able to describe with great emotion an instance where Liszt's performance of the Beethoven C-Sharp Minor Sonata moved him to tears. It goes without saying that Liszt was not tampering with the text on this occasion.[79] Although Berlioz disliked being drawn into the contemporary game of comparing virtuosi, he clearly felt that because of the variety of his skills Liszt was the most outstanding performer of the time. Apart from his brilliant technical virtuosity, he also played with great expression: "He speaks *piano* like Goëthe speaks *German,* like Moore speaks *English,* like Weber speaks *orchestra.*"[80] He performed his own compositions magnificently, and interpreted the works of other composers with extraordinary empathy. As mentioned earlier, Berlioz came to view Liszt in a missionary light, as one devoted to "the beautiful and the useful,"[81] who spread the appreciation of great music by his expressive performances of Beethoven, and indeed of Berlioz himself, to so many different audiences. In 1836, when Liszt and Thalberg fought their public pianistic duel, Berlioz refused to cast his vote for one or the other. While his articles on the concert are measured in praise for both, he nevertheless expresses great admiration for Thalberg's taste, calm, poise, and technical skill; all qualities which caused many, including Fétis, to prefer him to Liszt. Commenting in an article for the *Chronique de Paris* of 1837, on the mania for assessing the respective talents of the two artists, Berlioz says quite casually, with regard to Liszt, "The advantage is incontestably on his side; this has always appeared to me as evident as it is unnecessary to say."[82] The same would have applied to a comparison with Chopin.

Liszt's arrangements of the *Symphonie fantastique, Lélio,* and sections from *Harold* were approved by Berlioz. He saw them not so much as sets of variations but as complete identifications with, and even to an extent developments of, his works. He was a little worried at times by what he saw as Liszt's penchant for the "enharmonic genre"[83] and his "abuse of enharmonic modulations"[84] in orchestral writing, and he wondered if the tendency was the result of Liszt's being a piano player: "Orchestral musicians are still not familiar with the modulations enjoyed by the pianists."[85] In comparison to the strong antagonism of critics such as Schumann,[86] Berlioz was relatively tolerant of virtuosi. He occasionally commented adversely on a number of the showy solo pieces popular at the time, objecting most strongly to their length and florid ornamentation. He also wrote about the ease with which a young virtuoso performer could attain fame in comparison to a young composer, but cynically noted at the same time the rapidity of the virtuoso's decline from fame.[87] There were a number of virtuosi, particularly violinists, whose playing Berlioz clearly enjoyed, though he never wrote about them at length, such as Ole Bull, Baillot, Ernst, and the harpist Labarre.[88] Amongst the host of pianist-composers in Paris at the time, Berlioz singled out the tasteful and refined compositions and playing of George Osborne[89] and the more adventurous piano works of Jules Benedict. In a review of a piano fantasy by Benedict on Goethe's *Faust,* Berlioz suggests that such a subject really demanded orchestral treatment.[90] The same is hinted at in an earlier review by Berlioz of a piano work by Benedict, *Notre-dame de Paris—rêverie musicale*: "[Benedict is] enclosed in a medium that is too narrow in our opinion. For a vast libretto, like that of Victor Hugo, a larger form was necessary."[91] Berlioz does not often discuss Chopin either as a performer or a composer. The occasions where he does are largely when Chopin had played in a public concert, for instance in one of Berlioz's own concerts or at benefit concerts.[92] The majority of Chopin's performances at this time were in salons.

The most negative remarks made by Berlioz about Chopin are on his use of rhythm. In the *Mémoires* Berlioz states that Chopin pushed rhythmic freedom too far and that the orchestra in his piano concertos was practically a superfluous accompaniment. In an article of 1837 for the *Chronique de Paris* he writes, "Perhaps the freshness and originality of these new forms would be felt more if in his performance Chopin produced fewer changes of movement, if he kept to the beat with a bit more regularity."[93] One could interpret Berlioz's classification of Chopin as a "salon artist" as implied criticism: "Chopin, again, was strictly the virtuoso of the elegant salon, the intimate gathering. For Ernst, vast halls, crowded theatres, the great pulsating public, hold no terrors,"[94] and similarly his description of *unicord* pianos:

> *Unicord* pianos [are] designed to perform the ravishing Mazurkas, the so ingenious Caprices of Chopin, in the elegant boudoirs of grand society, but they would not be able to withstand the thunderous performance of the more orchestral compositions of M. Liszt.[95]

Ernst and Liszt emerge triumphant from such comparisons.[96]

In his correspondence Berlioz's references to Chopin are few but generally affectionate; for instance in a letter to Liszt he mentions with satisfaction an article by Heine in which Chopin is praised: "Our friend Heine spoke of us two recently in the *Gazette Musicale,* with as much liveliness as irreverence, but with no nastiness all the same. On the other hand he wove a splendid crown for Chopin, which he has deserved for a long time moreover."[97] Though Chopin's music is not disparagingly spoken of by Berlioz, there is nevertheless a reserve in what he does say that makes it clear he did not regard Chopin as a major composer. Berlioz's first review of Chopin's music reveals a bemused fascination and describes the music as some exotic apparition: "His melodies impregnated with Polish forms have something naïvely wild that charms and captures one by its very strangeness. . . . [O]ne is tempted to approach the instrument and bend an ear to it as one would do at a concert of sylphs or sprites."[98]

However, the charms of the music are seen finally as ephemeral, since Berlioz clearly believed that the originality, the unexpectedness, and the nuances of the work were inherent in the performance:

> Unfortunately there is hardly anyone but Chopin himself who can play his music and give it that original touch, the unexpectedness that is one of its principal attractions; his performance is marbled by a thousand nuances of movement, that he alone has the secret of, and that one is unable to single out.[99]

A review of a Chopin piano concerto in 1834 talks briefly of "verve," "grace," and "ravishing arabesques,"[100] and he makes an unconvincing excuse for his lack of commentary on the music by saying that people might accuse him of praising Chopin through friendship: "I would have a lot to say about Chopin and his music, but I fear the banal reproach of friendship."[101] This excuse is specious, because this worry does not stop Berlioz from commenting at length on the music of Meyerbeer. The disinclination to talk about Chopin's music came perhaps from an unsureness about how to discuss it. In an article for the *Chronique de Paris* of 1837 Berlioz spoke of Chopin as being primarily a composer: "He frequently astonishes us by the capricious scintillation of his imagination; what one loves so much in him is less the pianist (though he has very few rivals for this title) than the composer."[102] Yet as already pointed out, Berlioz rarely examined Chopin's compositions. Perhaps the most appreciative comment made about Chopin's music is in an 1835 review of the Adagio from his Piano Concerto in F: "All that is most engagingly graceful is united with the most profound and religious thoughts."[103] The second part of this sentence uses words that imply a deeper level of appreciation by Berlioz. In his obituary notice on Chopin in 1849, Berlioz praises again Chopin's grace, his exquisite melodies and original system of ornamentation, giving most praise to the *Etudes*.[104] However, on the whole Berlioz seems to have appreciated Chopin's music as a sensory phenomenon enchanting him at that moment, but about whose ultimate value he was uncertain.

Though Berlioz rarely wrote at length on any of his contemporary composers, he certainly championed their cause—which was after all his own cause as well. Many times in his criticism he wrote about the seemingly insurmountable problems facing the young composer in Paris—problems of arranging performances of his works, hiring halls and musicians, copying parts, the awesome *Droit des pauvres* or "poor tax" (which took a quarter of the profits), and getting works published.[105] If the composer actually reached the stage of having a work accepted for performance, there was no guarantee that it would be performed as written. As Berlioz imaginatively puts it, the French government would never let a poor copy of Michelangelo's *Moses* be exhibited as the real thing, yet this is what constantly happened to the maligned composer.[106]

Conclusion

Skill at narration, frequent use of irony, and an unusually extensive and varied vocabulary are all notable features of Berlioz's literary style.

Berlioz's skill in narration is most noticeable in his reviews of opera and *opéra-comique*, where the libretto is adroitly retold with an accompanying commentary characterized by a degree of suspense that immediately involves the reader. He delights in parodying the stereotyped situations and characters and manages to do this at the same time as giving a straight outline of the story.

Berlioz's use of irony has several levels. His ironical comments on the musical tastes of the Parisian bourgeoisie, like his narrations of libretti, can be relatively light-hearted, but his ironical comments on certain Parisian musical authorities often have bitter undertones. For instance, his comments on the organization of the *Prix de Rome* are sometimes quite savage. In such cases Berlioz clearly preferred to express his feelings through a rhetorical use of irony rather than in a straightforward fashion.

Berlioz's vocabulary is unusually extensive—and J. M. Bailbé gives an excellent analysis of its sources in his book on Berlioz's *Mémoires*.[1] Bailbé notes the use of archaic scholarly words—medical words, foreign words, latinisms—and points particularly to Berlioz's liking for startling verbal juxtapositions, such as "Mozart was assassinated by Lachnith," or "a brigand suspected of having violated music."[2] The vocabulary used in the early feuilletons is perhaps less extensive than that of the *Mémoires*, though Bailbé's analysis is still valid.

If Berlioz's music criticism is viewed comprehensively, one can see that he uses a quite different vocabulary in discussing works he really likes, works he likes well enough, and works he dislikes. I have mentioned this vocabulary in specific instances in previous chapters and shall examine it more closely here, for it provides some guidelines to, and an overview of, Berlioz's judgments in music.

Berlioz's vocabulary of praise centers around his criticism of Beethoven, Gluck, and to a lesser extent Weber. As he said in a letter of 1838, "My most lively sympathies are for Gluck and Beethoven first, then for Weber."[3] The actual words used by Berlioz in describing the music of these three composers are not all commonly used as words of praise, but for him they perform that function and by association carry the connotations of praise when applied to other composers.

Berlioz uses certain words to convey the greatness of a piece of music or of a composer, and these words are often connected with size, for example "immense," "gigantic," "majesty," and "colossal." To describe the essence of the "great works," Berlioz employs words such as "genius," "passion," "poetry," "poetic thought," "truth of expression," "religious thought," and "sublime poetry," where the keyword is definitely "poetry."[4] When Berlioz is describing specific features of great works, the most striking aspect of his vocabulary is the strength and energy of the words: "the most striking oppositions," "the most unexpected contrasts," "full of ardor," "of anger," "of love," "overwhelming ending," "host of brilliant and energetic ideas."[5] Various musical elements are described as frank, original, forceful, and vigorous. Overall musical design shows grandeur, warmth, richness, amplitude, and use of imagination. Perhaps the points to highlight here are the importance he places on originality and of oppositions and contrasts. Berlioz describes the effect such music has on him in quite physical terms: the music "makes the heart beat," makes him "shudder," gives him "a nervous spasm," provokes "furious exclamations mixed with tears and shouts of laughter,"[6] or, to give a longer example from an 1837 *Revue et Gazette Musicale* article, "De la musique en général":

> The emotion, growing in direct proportion to the energy or grandeur of the author's ideas, produces in succession a strange agitation in the circulation of my blood; my arteries beat violently; tears, which ordinarily announce the end of a paroxysm, often indicate only a stage in the development that is going to be greatly surpassed. When this happens, there are spasmodic contractions of muscles, a trembling in all my limbs, *a total numbing of hands and feet*, a partial paralysis of the nerves of sight and hearing, I can no longer see, I scarcely hear, dizziness—half fainting.[7]

Berlioz's reactions to music that he loved are thus distinguished primarily by their dynamism, enthusiasm, and the continual use of certain keywords such as "poetry," "passion," "genius," and "sublime." These keywords formed a module of terms of praise from which Berlioz borrowed when wishing to intimate greater music, so that he could talk of a section of a composition that had a poetic tendency or expressed "passion," thus indicating that this section was superior.

As repeatedly stated, there is never any uncertainty when Berlioz really appreciated something; on the contrary his feelings are conveyed almost overwhelmingly. In *The Beautiful in Music* Edouard Hanslick denies music's ability to express any definite emotion, stating that it can express only the dynamics of emotion and be described by such qualifying adjectives as "elegant," "vigorous," "graceful," and "fresh."[8] Berlioz's vocabulary of "secondary praise" makes use of just such words; it could be said that for Berlioz, while great works expressed strong emotions and passions, lesser works expressed only the various dynamic properties of these emotions. Berlioz was at times quite specific about which emotions he felt music could express, listing, for instance, such emotions as "happy love, jealousy, active and carefree gaiety, modest agitation, menacing force, suffering and fear."[9]

As mentioned in previous chapters, Berlioz's mode of secondary praise can be reduced to a number of frequently used set phrases such as "distinguished melody," "melodic charm," "elegant simplicity," "distinguished harmony," and individual words such as "calm," "clear," "vivacious," "taste," "tact," "grace," "naïveté," "delicateness," and "gentle."[10] The "secondary" composer is usually a man of talent not genius, capable but not inspired, who writes with taste rather than passion, and is one of those people, to quote Berlioz, "of whom one speaks with esteem" but "who say nothing to the heart."[11] In one sense, for Berlioz this represented the difference between the eighteenth-century and the nineteenth-century composer and was typified by his comparisons between the symphonies of Haydn and Beethoven. Yet in another sense, of course Berlioz made no such crude dichotomies. He saw Gluck as expressing passions in the manner of Beethoven,[12] and many of his own nineteenth-century contemporary composers as bound by the same limitations as Haydn; he saw, that is, the expression of passion as timeless. Berlioz uses his phrases of secondary praise with great facility and to such an extent that they almost become formulae, and, as was said in chapter 4, they at times seemed to be used as a screen to disguise a lack of response to the music.

These two "modes of praise" are not mutually exclusive. Berlioz occasionally used the vocabulary of the second list in conjunction with stronger words of the first group (particularly when describing Weber or Beethoven adagios) and arrives at phrases such as "prodigious delicateness."[13] The tenderness of a Beethoven adagio for instance, is qualified as "surpassing all that the most *burning imagination* could ever dream of tenderness" (italics mine).[14]

When describing works he openly dislikes, Berlioz is curt and unambiguous. Typical phrases are "the salon style," "uninspired instrumentation," "flabby style," "vulgar phrase structure," "without fixed form," "lack of originality," "cold work," "common harmony," and "monotonous rhythm."[15] Of note is his continual use of words such as "vulgar" and "common" and his similar use, when distinguishing those who appreciate great music, of "musical aristocracy." In both cases he refers to a hierarchy of musical taste and ability.

Poor music also seems to have produced a physical effect on Berlioz. Although fortunately he does not mention it often, he does describe it vividly in the *Revue et Gazette Musicale* article, "De la musique en général":

> There is a vigorous contrast, . . . that of a *bad musical effect,* which produces the opposite of admiration and pleasure. No other music operates more strongly in this sense than that in which the principal fault appears to me to be platitude linked with false expression. Then I blush as with shame, real indignation takes hold of me; one could, on seeing me, think that I had just been the victim of an inexcusable outrage. To get rid of this impression there arises a general expulsion, an effort of excretion in all my body, like the efforts of vomiting when the stomach wants to get rid of a foul liquid. This is disgust and hatred taken to their most extreme limits. This music exasperates me, and I vomit it from all my pores.[16]

In this brief analysis of Berlioz's vocabulary his use of the terms "sublime" and "true" or "truth of expression" are worthy of particular attention. His use of the word "sublime" often carries with it the eighteenth-century connotations of awe and fear. A sublime work could defy judgment and paralyze the intellect. For instance a passage from Gluck's *Iphigénie en Tauride* is described (in the full *admiratif* mode) as "Prodigious! Admirable! Sublime! Inaccessible! Overwhelming! This is unsettling, it is impossible to breathe."[17] Berlioz would have agreed with Kant that the sublime "is that which indicates some capacity to transcend all empirical standards merely by thinking of it."[18] For Berlioz, the passions aroused by sublime music were often so strong that it was impossible to attempt any sort of analysis. He comments on the Trio at the end of the second act of *Guillaume Tell*: "It would be impossible for me to place the cold blade of the scalpel into the heart of this sublime creation. Analyze it?—What? Passion, despair, tears, the cries of a lost son learning that his father has been murdered? . . . I can only cry out like the crowd, Beautiful! Superb! Admirable! Heart-rending."[19]

In his book *Realism in Nineteenth-Century Music,* Carl Dahlhaus argues that the accentuation of the "true" instead of the "beautiful" is a possible characteristic of realism in music. In Berlioz's criticism, he does not oppose truth to beauty. "True" or "truth" are usually used in conjunction with words such as "expression." Describing music as displaying "truth of expression," for instance, implies that it is dramatically appropriate, or "true" to its dramatic nature. Berlioz defines "expression" as the reproduction of feelings and passions, and a work that displays "truth of expression" is one that corresponds to the character of the feelings it wishes to reproduce.[20] For Berlioz "truth" is more commonly linked with "beauty," as in his comment on Beethoven's piano sonatas that they possessed the quality of being "new without breaking from truth and beauty."[21] This statement suggests that there were some "new" or original works which Berlioz felt did break from his perception of "truth" and "beauty." There are instances when he comments on novel effects that are unsuccessful because of the composer's inexperience; for instance he quotes a passage from the conclusion of a Trio by Ferdinand Lavaine:

> This ending could create a good effect with a little more expansion in the second last chord and without the *D* flat that one hears in the preceding bar; as it is, it leaves the listener feeling indecisive, as it is impossible to know whether it finishes in *E* or on the dominant of *A*. This example proves however that M. Lavaine is looking for new forms; we don't doubt that with a little more experience he will do an excellent job with those that very probably he will be called upon to discover.[22]

In reviews of music, Berlioz usually covered various aspects of musical organization, mainly rhythm, instrumentation, harmony, and melody. He always acclaimed innovative or original use of rhythm, however slight. Rhythm was perhaps the musical parameter that he valued most in composition, although this was in part a reaction to the very conservative use of rhythm in much of his contemporaries' music. He strongly criticized the monotonous square-cut rhythms, "la carrure," that proliferated in, for instance, most of the *opéras-comiques* of the day. Berlioz complains that while people were quite ready to accept that with harmony, melody, and instrumentation, what is bad is simply that which produces a bad effect, they insisted upon tradition with rhythm. They could not admit that often lack of symmetry or rhythmic irregularity was precisely that which gave a musical phrase force and expression.[23] Berlioz details with gusto ways in which rhythm could be varied; one could accent the weak beat, quickly alternate duple and triple time, momentarily introduce a melody of triple time into a quadruple bar and vice versa. He outlines rhythmic consonances, rhythmic dissonances, rhythmic modulations, and so on.[24] Rhythm was not taught at the Conservatoire, and Berlioz constantly laments this fact as regards the training of both composers and performers. Yet he by no means advocated rhythmic anarchy and indeed was critical of composers who used rhythms that were too irregular, particularly in vocal music, where he felt it led to serious problems for the singers.[25] As is to be expected with Berlioz, any use of unusual rhythm had to be dramatically motivated. For instance, he applauds the attempt made by the composer Monpou to break from conservative rhythms, but obviously suspects that Monpou's motivation was one of rebellion against tradition rather than to answer any dramatic need. It was thus not successful in Berlioz's opinion.

Though critical of predictable use of harmonies, particularly antagonistic to repeated V–I cadences, and encouraging to composers who employed interesting modulations, Berlioz disliked compositions with too many modulations and abrupt changes of harmony.[26] As with dramatically unmotivated rhythmic experimentation, he gently chastised composers who he felt were trying to break from harmonic clichés and conventional modulations without having a dramatic motivation for doing so. He applauds the breaking of rules concerning consecutive fifths and octaves only if there is a dramatic reason for it: "their breach must be at least as well motivated as their observance, . . . the use of harmonic progressions prohibited by the rules of the school must have an obvious aim."[27] Thus a song by Marie Garcia de Bériot ("La Malibran") is criticized for having the vocal line form a series of seemingly unmotivated fifths with the bass,[28] but in the case of the consecutive fifths and octaves at the conclusion to Rossini's "Evening Prayer" from *Guillaume Tell,* "the naïve color of the piece . . . not only authorizes but makes this *breach of the ancients'* rules picturesque to the highest degree."[29]

As has been mentioned, Berlioz praised those composers who showed an interest in original instrumentation and explored the expressive possibilities of various instruments, and deplored the bombastic, noisy instrumentation of many of his contemporaries with their overuse of the bass drum and brass. He was later to pay homage to passages of instrumentation that he felt were interesting by including them in his *Traité d'instrumentation.*

All musical elements were ultimately judged in terms of their expressive qualities and capacity for dramatic nuances and contrasts—and this included melody, for even though it did not hold the supreme place in the musical organization it was still a major means of dramatic expression. Berlioz always praised originality in melody and criticized a work if there was little melody.

Berlioz's attitudes to these various musical parameters reflects to a degree his own musical interests and preferences. For instance, his interest in innovative rhythm and instrumentation, and the relative lack of experimentation in harmonic combinations in his music, show up in his criticism.

Berlioz's early criticism has two recurring concerns that call for some concluding comments. The first is the desire to be objective or, alternatively, to show that genius can make mistakes. This relates basically to the issue of dramatic motivation. The second concern is the role of the "elite" in Berlioz's aesthetics, which in turn bears upon his worship of "poetic" music.

Berlioz's habit of carefully detailing what he saw as faults in the works of composers he esteemed has already been mentioned in relation to Meyerbeer and to a lesser extent Beethoven. It occurs also in his reviews of Gluck, Cherubini, and Mozart. This habit is distinct in two ways from the mundane listing of faults that is a necessary part of the critic's chore. First, the faults are commented on very self-consciously, at times with an air of self-righteousness and at others with astonishment and surprise, or disappointment. Second, the faults revolve around certain issues, which in the main are the use of "Italian cadences," "vocalized amens," and "unmotivated fugues," as well as maladroit interpretations of texts, particularly of religious texts. With Gluck the faults noted are more specific. Berlioz notes small things such as inadequate instrumentation[30] and monotonous harmonies in some accompanied recitatives.[31]

To give a few examples, he found the "cadence italienne" in a scene from Mozart's *The Magic Flute,* in a Mozart motet, and in the slow movement of Beethoven's Eighth Symphony. Berlioz said of the "cadence italienne" in the Mozart motet: "It is regrettable to find in the middle . . . an Italian coda with its insipid cadence, which the author of *Don Juan* knew very well how to avoid elsewhere."[32]

The "vocalized amen" was found in, for example, the Beethoven "Resurrexit" and "Gloria" from the *Missa Solemnis.* Of the "Gloria" Berlioz wrote:

> Furthermore, this chorus finishes, God forgive me for saying it, with one of those fugal and vocalized *amens,* which I have already pointed out many times in other composers as a meaningless barbarity.[33]

Berlioz denigrated the practice as early as 1829 in an article for *Le Correspondant,* "Considérations sur la musique religieuse":

> I defy anyone gifted with musical feeling who listens without bias to a fugal *Amen* not to take the choir for a legion of devils incarnate turning the holy sacrifice into ridicule, rather than for a reunion of the faithful assembled to sing the praises of God.[34]

The problem of the vocalized amen was in fact just another aspect of the familiar problem of text interpretation. The question of text interpretation is a larger issue than the others just mentioned, and although it can be discussed here in terms of Berlioz's fault-finding it also needs a more general discussion relating to his set ideas on interpretation of texts.

Mozart and Cherubini are the composers whom Berlioz criticizes the most often for misinterpreting texts, and in nearly all cases it was in relation to their interpretation of religious texts. Berlioz admonishes Cherubini for his setting of the words *Da robur* in his unaccompanied "O Salutaris":

> I shall take the liberty of respectfully suggesting a remark to the author on the way in which to set the *Da robur fer auxilium.* The basses pronounce these words with an energetic and fierce phrase, the symbol of strength (*robur*). Of a hundred composers who have set this same subject since Gossec, there are only two perhaps who have avoided playing thus on the words instead of expressing their true sense. The *O salutaris* is a prayer, is it not? In it the Christian asks God for strength and courage. . . . It is therefore a weak being who prays, and his voice, in pronouncing the *Da robur,* must be as humble as possible, instead of breaking into syllables which hold more menace than supplication. This seems to me to be a palpable absurdity.[35]

This quotation is repeated verbatim in another article for the *Journal des Débats* of 1835.[36] Berlioz similarly attacks a chorus from Cherubini's *Requiem,* stating that the word "clamavi" should be interpreted quietly, being the voice of a penitent sinner, and not shouted. Berlioz's indignant criticism of the "Tuba

Mirum" from the Mozart *Requiem* is quite amusing if one bears in mind how Berlioz was later to interpret the words in his own *Requiem*:

> The *Tuba Mirum* starts with a sublime phrase that leads to nothing and whose instrumentation is feeble. Why is *a solo trombone* given the job of sounding the terrible call that should spread all over the earth and awaken the dead at the bottom of their tombs? Why make the other two trombones quiet when, instead of three, thirty, three hundred even, would not be too many? Would this be because the word *tuba* is in the singular and not the plural? It is an insult to Mozart to assume for even a moment that he could have held such a stupid idea.[37]

It has already been mentioned that Berlioz wrote with a certain glee in describing instances when Gluck and particularly Beethoven had broken "rules," notably of harmony. In other instances Berlioz clearly feels bewildered by some of Beethoven's harmonies, and though he makes an effort to understand why Beethoven used them he fails to find any real justification.[38] However, Berlioz incorporates these faults of harmony into his total vision of Beethoven, whose genius does not suffer an eclipse. As Berlioz says:

> Why take even the most defective qualities away from the physiognomy of a great man? Do you not think that the imperfections of these powerful natures offer real charm of originality to those who know how to understand them? And don't you know that enthusiasm is the brother of love?[39]

The sentiment expressed in this quotation seems to refer specifically to Beethoven's "unusual" harmonies and does not really represent Berlioz's attitude to the other "faults" that I have detailed; on the contrary he expressed many times his lack of understanding of, for instance, Beethoven's use of "cadences italiennes." As has been mentioned in chapter 7, Berlioz tried to excuse Meyerbeer's faults, and he occasionally does the same thing with the faults he finds in other composers, as for instance in this proviso about Mozart's use of a "cadence italienne": "The author was no doubt in a hurry to finish, because he has taken care in all his other works to avoid this stupid and tiring harmonic formula."[40] Clearly Berlioz felt that only unusual circumstances could have caused Mozart to use the cadence.

I would like to make two suggestions at this point. The first is that Berlioz's "fault-finding" may have come from a desire to prove his impartiality and objectivity; this would apply particularly to Gluck and Beethoven. Berlioz was clearly sensitive to attacks on his partiality and wished to establish the fact that his judgments were not "blind," and by pointing to faults in his "geniuses" he was proving his unbiased approach. Occasionally he goes to some lengths to prove his objectivity, giving excessively severe reviews of certain works of Weber and Beethoven, as in the following review of Weber's first symphony:

In fact one does not find there either the verve, the formal unexpectedness, the suddenness of movement, . . . or that irresistible melodic grace that one finds in *Obéron*. . . . [T]he style . . . is flabby, its phrase structure vulgar, its harmony common, its instrumentation uninspiring—so much so that one would think in listening to it that it had gained first Prize at the *Institut* competition. The first piece does however contain an attractive harmonic progression in the *coda*; but beside the emptiness of all that precedes this, one is disagreeably surprised to find a popular French air, . . . *la Pipe de tabac*. . . . The minuet is only a pale imitation of Mozart's and Haydn's minuets, and the finale is scarcely better. It would have been perhaps more suitable not to do such a scrupulously severe critique of this work and simply point it out as a production of little importance; but we thought it was our duty to express ourselves on this subject with even more frankness, since many people have accused us of infatuation over our outbursts of enthusiasm for Weber, and it was our duty in this case to give proof of impartiality.[41]

Berlioz gives a similarly severe review of the "Credo" from Beethoven's *Missa Solemnis*.[42]

The second suggestion is that Berlioz's criticism of faults in text interpretation (and this applies largely to criticism of Cherubini and Mozart) stems in a way from his fundamentally fixed ideas about text interpretation. His set ideas on the interpretation of religious texts have already been discussed; as early as 1829, Berlioz had outlined his basic objection to many interpretations of such texts:

Nothing is however more common, it is a style adopted by musicians, and what is even more inconceivable is that they call it the religious style. What a style, great God, that substitutes what one would think was the expression of a frenzied rage for the humble and touching sentiment of a prayer.[43]

This was a view that remained with him all his life. To give just one more example, in a review of a mass by Massimino, Berlioz comments:

What advantage is there in saying, "Peace! Peace! Peace! . . . on earth!" . . . instead of using natural phrasing? . . . Luckily the author put the monosyllable only on the soft notes, but how many others before him have thrown this unfortunate word on violent chords struck forcefully by the orchestra and the voices, in such a way that the singers, instead of representing angels wishing calm and happiness to all just men, seem to be crying out in anger "Peace!" like an exasperated schoolmaster restoring his pupils to silence.[44]

Occasionally Berlioz commented more specifically on faults that stemmed from a misunderstanding of the fundamental nature of a text, for instance the oriental and sacred subject of the "Flight into Egypt" demanded appropriately simple and calm harmonies, "the use of *perfect cadences,* in preference to chromatic harmonies and diminished sevenths."[45] Berlioz stated more baldly still that some subjects simply could not be set to music at all. Monpou, for instance, was misguided in trying to set the last scene of *Othello* to music, since it was not possible to do so: "These verses are not in any way made to be sung, and the scene is not arranged for music. In the face of such difficulties, all the efforts of art would be in vain; to try and surmount them is to pursue a chimera."[46] At a later date he appears to revise his opinion on this and lists the characters of Othello and Desdemona as susceptible to musical treatment:

> Love, enthusiasm, melancholy, joy, terror, jealousy, calm of the soul are feelings and passions perfectly suited to the development of musical forces; ambition, political intrigues, on the contrary, do not lend themselves to it in any way. That is why Romeo, Juliet, Tybald, the friar Laurence, Othello, Desdemona, Ariel, and Caliban himself could be admirable singing characters, whereas Richard III and Macbeth cannot figure in an opera without losing the principal character traits that Shakespeare has given them, or without uselessly tormenting music, by asking of it expressions that it does not possess.[47]

To say that there were dramatic improprieties in a composition however was not to deny its musical power. In a review of a Cherubini Mass in 1836, after attacking Cherubini's interpretation of the text of the mass, Berlioz reflects that if one thought of the work as a symphony with voices then it would have to be seen as one of Cherubini's best works.[48] That is, there was nothing technically wrong with the music, it was only its interpretation of the text that was at fault. Still, this was an important enough issue for Berlioz to criticize the work.

Berlioz's fixed ideas on text interpretation underlie his criticism and recur continually. His ideas on what was "beautiful" in music show a similar rigidity despite occasional protestations to the contrary.

In an apparently serious letter to his friend Edouard Rocher in 1833 Berlioz wrote:

> My father treats me like all fathers treat their sons; whereas I am, myself, an exception. Yes, an exception by my character, by my past life, by my heightened sensitivity, by my scorn of life and death, by my ideas on everything.[49]

Berlioz's correspondence during the 1820s is similarly full of anguished self-conscious statements; he saw himself pushed inexorably towards the career of a musician, it being the only outlet for his unusual sensitivity:

> I am drawn involuntarily towards a magnificent career.[50]

> There is a certain motivating power that I feel in me, a fire, an ardor that I am unable to define, that is directed so much towards a single point [namely] great dramatic or religious music, that I fail even to experience it for light music.[51]

> Even now I am capable of producing greatness, passion, vigor, and truth, and energetic things, and things of beauty too.[52]

It was as though Berlioz saw himself as called to fulfil a mission; certainly he came to view music as a religion, a "sacred art."

Although Berlioz admitted that "beauty" ("le beau") was not the same for every individual and that "relative beauty" ("beau relatif") was a necessary corollary, he himself obviously did believe in an "absolute beauty" ("beau absolu"). He at times made emotional outbursts such as: "I would rather be mad and believe in absolute beauty."[53] He coped with this seeming contradiction by defining music as *the art of moving by sound people who are sensitive, intelligent, informed, and gifted in admiration. It only speaks to them, and this is why it does not suit everyone,*"[54] thus suggesting that only people so defined were capable of understanding the "beau absolu." Berlioz's elite group, his "small band of the faithful"[55] mentioned throughout this book, presumably comprised believers in absolute beauty, to the extent that they all appreciated similar music so that any small differences could be put down to varying backgrounds.

The character Adolphe, in Berlioz's *nouvelle* "Le Suicide par enthousiasme," was destined to a life of suffering because he incessantly sought after an ideal of beauty, hating everything that did not resemble it.[56] There was an element of Adolphe in Berlioz. The increasing commercialism of music in the nineteenth century, the developing genre of "low art" music, the success of people for whom he had little respect while men of "genius" were pushed aside, even the relative lack of success of his own music, all contributed to Berlioz's feeling of encroaching mediocrity. In defense he adopted an idealist position, fiercely upholding the value of his cherished gods and clinging to his ideal of "beauty." Works of beauty were defined by the intensity of the feelings they expressed and Berlioz always responded to them with corresponding passion—he certainly did not advocate the calm contemplation of beauty.

Berlioz's criticism did aim to diffuse the love of "great music," to educate the public; in the words of Katherine Kolb Reeve, Berlioz aimed to form a listening public capable of appreciating the music of Beethoven and Gluck. At the same time I feel that Berlioz also enjoyed the sense of superiority and exclusiveness that being part of a small elite gave him. This is reflected not only in his attitude to the Conservatoire concerts, but also in certain attitudes towards the "great composers," he actually did not want Gluck and Beethoven to become popular, since this seemed necessarily to entail a cheapening of their "genius": "Perhaps Gluck will become fashionable again—by the eternal fire! If that happened, it would be necessary to wall up the Conservatoire door; it is already enough for him to have been subjected to that shame once."[57] Experience of the dilettantes of Italian opera obviously soured Berlioz's view of "popularity," which for him implied only superficial appreciation; it was better that great works remained the exclusive property of a chosen few than that they should be debased by ignorant enthusiasts.[58] There were other ways of furthering musical education, and Berlioz comments regularly and very encouragingly on the attempts made by various individuals to foster musical appreciation amongst the people. He pointed in particular to the work done by Joseph Mainzer and his choirs of working men in Paris[59] and the work of a certain Aubery du Boullay, who operated in Provence where he organized and inspired instrumental playing in numerous small towns. The towns would all join together several times a year for a grand "congrès philharmonique." Berlioz claimed that the success of these meetings was "a proof of the rapidity with which the taste for music is spreading in the lower classes of the population."[60] He also felt that the army should be taught singing in its spare time[61] and encouraged the efforts of a M. Beer to improve the standards of the military bands.[62] The introduction of choral teaching in primary schools in 1836 was seen as another step towards forming a musical public.[63] Romain Rolland said of Berlioz that "he despised the people."[64] Katherine Kolb Reeve makes a useful distinction between "the crowd" ("la foule") and "the people" ("le peuple"), "the former denoting the eternally repugnant *profanum vulgus,* the latter calling forth utopian fantasies of universal harmony and progress."[65] Rolland's comment makes more sense if we substitute "the crowd" for "the people," for Berlioz did seem to cherish some hopeful ideals about the possibility of educating "the people." It is not always easy to make the distinction, however. When, for instance, Berlioz says, "What disgusts me most is the certainty I have of the non-existence of beauty for the incalculable majority of human monkeys!"[66] there is a lurking suspicion that he could he referring to all of humanity.

In Berlioz's utopian vision of the ideal society, in his *nouvelle Euphonia,* the massed public is hand-picked; was Berlioz's vision of the ideal audience perhaps no more than a greatly expanded elite? There are suggestions throughout his criticism that this was the case. To give just one example, the following exclamation: "Ah! If one could only restrict the public to fifty intelligent and sensitive beings, what pleasure it would be to make art."[67]

Berlioz's position as a composer in the Paris musical world was never easy; his lifelong struggle for recognition and understanding is well-documented in his *Mémoires* and correspondence. By the early 1830s, however, he had a certain notoriety as a composer; his name would have been familiar to most of the concert-going public, and his criticism would presumably have aroused the curiosity of those people who knew his work as a composer. By the mid-1830s he was gaining a reputation as a critic quite apart from his reputation as a composer.

To an extent, Berlioz's music criticism provided an outlet for discussing some of the problems a composer faced at the time and also provided him with the opportunity to discuss and promote his musical ideals. Perhaps his criticism contributed to an improvement in taste, to a better understanding of Beethoven or Gluck. It is unlikely, however, that he contributed much to an amelioration in conditions for composers at the time. Berlioz's criticism nevertheless remains a vital documentary source on musical life in Paris; it provides information on all the major and many—perhaps all too many—of the minor works performed at the time. It also provides valuable information on concert life, on the role of the composer, and on performance practice in the nineteenth century.

What clearly emerges from the study of these early reviews is the degree of diplomacy involved in being a critic, and in particular a composer-critic. Whether it was a case of not offending a powerful friend, as with Meyerbeer, or of not offending fellow critics, discouraging young composers, or alienating theater directors or newspaper editors, Berlioz had at all times to strive for the delicate balance between honesty and loss of integrity.

Yet the most enduring image of Berlioz emerging from his criticism is that of an idealist whose love of music was so passionate, and governed his life to such an extent, that even the treadmill of daily criticism could not dull its ardor.

Appendixes

Appendix A

Press Regulations during the Restoration and Early Years of Louis-Philippe

Music criticism was not an area much affected by press censorship. However, a brief survey of the regulations governing the press provides a context for the otherwise isolated "musical feuilletons" of political journals.

Freedoms in the press introduced by the 1830 revised Charter were more apparent than real. Many of the Restoration press laws still existed under Louis-Philippe, the major difference between the two periods being that there were no *official* censorship laws during the July Monarchy. Both periods were marked by a dramatic event—the Restoration by the murder of the Duc de Berry (1820) and the July Monarchy by the attempted assassination of the king (1835)—which had the consequence of a tightening-up of the regulations governing the press.

The Restoration press regulations alternated between relatively repressive and liberal periods. A press law of 1814 established preliminary censorship for writings of fewer than twenty pages and preliminary authorization for newspapers.[1] From 1815 to 1819 the police controlled the press. A censorship committee was established which required a daily submission of copy from all newspapers, and failure to comply with the regulations led to suspension or suppression.[2] The criterion for censorship used by the committee was a law of November 1815 concerning seditious writing, which defined as "seditious" any writing that threatened an attempt on the person of the king or any member of his family; incited armed rebellion or the overthrow of the government; asked for change in the order of succession; tried to weaken the respect due to the king's authority; or spread rumors concerning restoration of national lands or feudal dues.[3] By January 1817 five newspapers had been suppressed, largely for Bonapartism, and twenty suspended, though most for a few days only.[4]

Police control was abolished in 1819, when the Government passed two new bills concerning freedoms of the press and dealing with the legal pursuit of newspapers. The first bill, passed 17 May 1819, proposed that any writer who provoked an action defined by the penal code as a felony or a misdemeanor should be punished as an accomplice. The second bill stated that these misdemeanors would be tried by jury in assize courts.[5] A third bill was then introduced which demanded that the founder of a newspaper should deposit caution money at the Treasury as guarantee for the payment of fines and declare the name of someone who would be responsible for the contents of the journal.[6] With the abolition of police control, opposition papers, in particular the liberal *Le Constitutionnel* and ultra-royalist *Drapeau Blanc,* flourished. In the provinces, too, local press became more lively, commercial, and politicized.

The murder of the Duc de Berry, 13 February 1820, however provoked such an outcry against the liberal press for supposedly inciting to violence against the king that a temporary censorship bill was re-introduced. This bill demanded much the same as the November 1815 law, namely authorization from the king for journals and periodicals dealing with political matters, and the submission of copy to a censorship committee with failure to do so resulting in fines or imprisonment. Copy could also be cited before courts and suspended or suppressed.[7] The censor was severe, striking heavily at the liberal papers and semi-periodicals. Journals such as *Le Constitutionnel* retaliated by leaving blanks where words or phrases had been censored. The liberal press was not alone in being subject to suppression, for the ultra-royalist papers were also attacked.[8]

In 1822 there was a change in the head of government. A M. Villèle succeeded M. Richelieu, who had been head of government since 1820. During 1822 there was an unprecedented number of lawsuits brought against newspapers, many for very trivial offenses.[9] In 1824 an extraordinary plan was proposed to Villèle by Sosthène de la Rochefoucauld; the scheme, "amortissement des journaux," was to buy up all the opposition newspapers published in Paris and place them under the direction of the ministry.[10] Three million francs, 450,000 of which came from Rochefoucauld's private funds, were spent on the project, which after a successful beginning collapsed when an aborted take-over of *La Quotidienne* ended in a disclosure of the whole plot and consequent discrediting of the ministry. Villèle tried other means of strangling the opposition press, such as increasing postal tariffs.[11] He was succeeded in government in 1828 by M. Martignac.

Martignac tried to establish more freedom in the press; for instance, he abolished the preliminary authorization for journals. In 1830 however Charles X in his coup d'état suspended the freedom of the press and proclaimed that no newspaper was to appear without the king's permission.[12] The 1830 Revolution began with a protest by journalists, drawn up by Thiers in *Le National* office, against this legislation. The presses of three papers, *Le National, Le Globe,* and *Le Temps,* remained working throughout the night of 26 July printing the journalists' declaration.[13] To quote Collins: "Louis-Philippe became king of the French as the result of a revolution started by the newspapers, but few of them had intended to make a revolution and . . . only the *National* had favored the idea of a new monarchy."[14]

Article Seven of the revised Charter of 1830 reaffirmed the right of Frenchmen to publish their opinions and stated categorically that censorship could never be restored. As journalists knew from their experiences during the Restoration, restrictions could be applied outside a system of censorship. Despite slight reductions in stamp duty and caution money, the government still had the possibility of bringing to trial any newspaper suspected of libel. The ministers varied in the vigor of their application of regulations. Lafitte, the first minister in 1830, was benevolent towards left-wing papers and more severe towards ultra-legitimists. Casimir Périer, who succeeded Lafitte, was equally severe on both groups. A bill of 1831 made it clear that political rights were to remain the exclusive possession of the wealthy.[15] This provoked considerable movement in the press. Papers such as *Le National,* which at the beginning of the July Monarchy had supported the king, became republican—openly so in January 1832. A spate of small republican papers, supported by republican secret societies in Paris, were founded in Paris and the provinces. Lamennais's paper *L'Avenir* called for universal suffrage and the separation of church and state as proposed in the Charter. The papers supportive of the Government were *Le Constitutionnel, Journal des Débats,* and *Courrier de France.*

By the end of 1834, 520 press cases had been heard in Paris, of which 332 were acquitted by lenient juries.[16] Irene Collins comments on a few surprising lapses in the control of the press at this period. She instances the period several weeks before the revolt in Lyons in 1834 when the newspapers openly incited rebellion, and the period immediately prior to the 1835 attempted assassination of the king when there was an unprecedented number of articles and caricatures setting him up to ridicule. So government control of the press during this period was not applied consistently.

The attempted assassination of the king frightened not only the government but the newspapers too. For instance Carrel, a journalist for *Le National,* was horrified at the thought that his articles could in any way induce people to such violence.[17] The government reacted by trying to silence both the legitimist and republican newspapers. In September 1835 a law was brought in which extended the list of seditious libels so that "it became a criminal offense to introduce the name of the king either directly, indirectly, or by allusion when discussing actions of his Government, or to express the wish, hope, or threat of the overthrow of constitutional monarchy or the restoration of the former dynasty."[18] A simple majority in trial by jury was to suffice for a verdict, and in certain cases, such as provocation to attack the person of the king, the charge could be classed as treason and tried by the peers. Fines were doubled, public subscriptions for collecting fines forbidden, caution money increased, and not even drawings could be published without permission from the Minister of the Interior.

The immediate result was the collapse of small papers with insufficient capital. For instance, some thirty small republican papers in the provinces folded because of new clauses regarding caution money. Papers such as *La Caricature*, founded in 1830, also folded because of the regulations concerning drawings.[19] In 1836 an important development in the press arose with the advent of Emile de Girardin's newspaper *La Presse*. The three major innovations of *La Presse* were that it halved the subscription price from eighty to forty francs, introduced advertisements, and introduced the serial story (*roman feuilleton*). The content of the journal consisted of more gossip and fashion notes than serious political articles, and its most successful element was the serial story. Eugène Sue was the genre's principal exponent, and his works were enormously popular.

Girardin's appeal to businessmen to place advertisements in *La Presse* was not successful because businesses were loath to advertise in a newspaper of low circulation. *Le Siècle*, founded by Dutacq, was another newspaper based on the same principles as *La Presse*. The majority of republican and legitimist newspapers abstained from the commercial tendencies of these newpapers. They were all however obliged to lower prices, except for the cunning *Journal des Débats*, which retained its high price but in 1837 introduced Eugène Sue's serial story *Les Mystères de Paris*, probably the most popular serial of the time.[20]

Thus the two important landmarks of the press of the July Monarchy were the September 1835 laws brought in after the attempt on Louis-Philippe's life and the advent of the cheap press. Though there was no censorship at this time, there were sufficient restrictions implemented by other means to enable one to say that freedom of the press did not vary dramatically between the two periods.

Appendix B

Unsigned Articles in the *Revue et Gazette Musicale* from 1834 to 1837 Attributed to Berlioz

1834

6 July
"De l'utilité d'un Opéra-Allemand à Paris" (*Gazette Musicale*), pp. 213–14. [K. R.][1]

7 September
"ACADEMIE ROYALE DE MUSIQUE. *La Tempête,* Ballet en 2 actes, précedé d'un Prologue, de M. Coraly, musique de M. Schneitzoeffer, décors de MM. Ciceri, Feuchères, etc." (*Gazette Musicale*), pp. 301–4. [K. R.]

7 December
"THEATRE NAUTIQUE. *La Dernière heure d'un Condamné,* Scène pantomime tragique de M. Henri, musique de M. Pugni" (*Gazette Musicale*), pp. 390–92. [Known: attributed to Berlioz in his correspondence; see *Correspondance générale* 2:174.]

21 December
"DU MOUVEMENT MUSICAL A PARIS" (*Gazette Musicale*), pp. 409–12. [K. R.]

1835

18 January
"THEATRE ROYAL DE L'OPERA-COMIQUE. Première représentation de *ROBIN DES BOIS*" (*Gazette Musicale*), p. 24. [K. R.]

8 February   "CONCERTS. DEUXIEME CONCERT DU CONSERVA-
TOIRE"
(*Gazette Musicale*), pp. 49–50.
"Revue critique. *LE MOINE,* paroles de M. Emilien Pacini,
musique de M. G. Meyerbeer" pp. 50–51.
[Berlioz mentions this article in his review "CHANTS
POUR LE PIANO, de Meyerbeer," *Gazette Musicale,* 18
October 1835, 343.]

22 February   "TROISIEME CONCERT DU CONSERVATOIRE"
(*Gazette Musicale*), p. 66.
[K. R.]

31 May   "GYMNASE MUSICAL. OUVERTURE"
(*Gazette Musicale*), pp. 183–85.
[Article identified by Prod'homme,[2] also listed in *Corre-
spondance générale* 2, "Chronologie 1835."]

9 August   "CEREMONIES DES INVALIDES ET DE NOTRE-
DAME"
(*Gazette Musicale*), p. 266.
[K. R.]

1836

31 January   "THEATRE DE L'OPERA-COMIQUE. *ACTEON,*
opéra-comique en un acte, de MM. Scribe et Auber.
(Première représentation)"
pp. 35–37.
Signed "UN VIEILLARD STUPIDE, qui n'a presque plus
de dents." [proved K. R.]

21 February   "LES CONCERTS"
pp. 59–60.
Signed *"Un amateur de bonne musique."*

6 March   "3ᵉ CONCERT DU CONSERVATOIRE"
pp. 79–80.
[Identified in Berlioz's correspondence. See letter to
Schlesinger, *Correspondance générale* 2:290, where he
says, "Demain je vous apporterai mon article sur la troisième
séance du Conservatoire."]

10 April	"DU CONSERVATOIRE DE MUSIQUE DE GENEVE" pp. 116–17. [Identified by Berlioz in his correspondence. See *Correspondance générale* 2:280.]
22 May	"DES ARTISTES ETRANGERS A PARIS" pp. 172–74. [K. R.]
29 May	"REVUE CRITIQUE. La musique simplifiée dans sa théorie et dans son enseignement" pp. 181–83. [Identified by Berlioz in his correspondence. See *Correspondance générale* 2:422.]
17 July	"CHRONIQUE MUSICALE" pp. 251–54. Signed "*Deuxième article du* VIEILLARD STUPIDE *qui n'a presque plus de dents.*" [K. R.]
28 August	"CHRONIQUE MUSICALE. NOTRE-DAME DE PARIS" p. 305. [K. R.]
11 September	"THEATRE DE L'OPERA-COMIQUE. *LE DIADESTE,* opéra-comique en deux actes, paroles de MM. Paul et Saint-Hilaire, musique de M. Jules Godfroy [*sic*]. (Première représentation)" pp. 319–20. [K. R.]
25 September	"ACADEMIE ROYALE DE MUSIQUE. *LA FILLE DU DANUBE.* Ballet-pantomime en 2 actes et en 4 tableaux, de M. Taglioni, musique de M. A. Adam, décors de MM. Ciceri, Dieterle, Feuchère [*sic*] Despléchin et Sechan. (Première représentation)" pp. 341–43. Signed "UN VIEILLARD STUPIDE qui n'a presque plus de dents." [K. R.]

1837

5 March   "THEATRE DE L'OPERA. Première représentation de *STRADELLA*, opéra en cinq actes"
pp. 79–80.
[Identified by Berlioz in his correspondence; see *Correspondance générale* 2:337.]

7 May   "CONCERT AU BENEFICE DES OUVRIERS LYONNAIS"
pp. 160–61.
[K. R.]

9 July   "ACADEMIE ROYALE DE MUSIQUE, PREMIERE REPRESENTATION DE *LES MOHICANS*, Ballet en deux actes de MM. LEON HALEVY et GUERRA, musique de M. Adam"
pp. 236–37.
[K. R.]

Appendix C

Music Criticism in the Major Parisian Newspapers, 1830–1839

In his article entitled "The Nineteenth-Century French Press and the Music Historian: Archival Sources and Bibliographical Resources," H. Robert Cohen describes the current situation where scholars, one after the other, scan the same newspapers for information relevant to their research.[1] The lack of any systematic listings of music criticism in the nineteenth-century press makes this rich source of material time-consuming to use. It is to be hoped that the formation of the *Répertoire internationale de la presse musicale au xix*[e] *siècle* (*RIPMxix*) will definitively resolve this problem.

The tables that I give below aim to make known to other researchers in the field the names of music critics of the major daily Parisian newspapers, whom I have come across in the course of my work on Berlioz's music criticism.

During this period (1830–39), critics often signed their names only with initials; I have tried in each case to identify these initials, although unfortunately a number of them remain unidentified.[2]

Apart from Berlioz, other music critics (as distinct from theater critics) writing for the major daily newspapers were Joseph d'Ortigue (*La Quotidienne, Journal de Paris, Le Temps*), François-Joseph Fétis (*Le Temps*), Castil-Blaze (*Journal des Débats, Le Constitutionnel*), and Joseph Mainzer (*Le National*). It must be said however that many literary critics also wrote interesting articles on music, for example, Théophile Gautier (*La Presse*) and Louis Desnoyers (*Le National*).

In the column headed "Contents" in my tables I have given the heading used in the newspapers, where one was used consistently, and enclosed it in quotation marks. The heading "Spectacles" encompasses reviews of all theaters not just those performing music. In cases where a variety of headings were used in the newspaper I have just given a brief general summary of the content without quotation marks. The heading "Théâtres lyriques" includes reviews of the Opéra, Opéra-Comique and Théâtre Italien. Each of the tables is followed by a few lines commenting on the value of the criticism for the period under consideration. At the end of this appendix I give a list of the initials I have managed to identify. I have examined twelve daily newspapers: *Le Constitutionnel, Le Courrier Français, La Gazette de France, Journal des Débats, Journal de Paris, Le Moniteur Universel, Le National, La Presse, La Quotidienne, Le Rénovateur, Le Siècle,* and *Le Temps.*

Le Constitutionnel

Year	Critic	Contents
1830–31	Not signed (Dumoulin, Evariste)*	"Spectacles" Théâtres lyriques
1832–33	Not signed (Dumoulin January–July 1832, then Castil-Blaze)**	Spectacles, January–July, then "Chronique musicale" (largely Théâtres lyriques)
1834	"XXX" (Castil-Blaze)	"Chronique musicale"
1835–36	"A."	Théâtres lyriques
1837–38	"A." "X. Y. Z."***	Théâtres lyriques A few articles on concerts
1839	"A." January–July, then "C. M." (Charles Merruau)	Théâtres lyriques

*According to *Entrées* listed in the Opéra-Comique *Registres* (vol. 248).
**The style of the "Chronique musicale" suggests Castil-Blaze.
***According to the Opéra *Registres* and the *Entrées* held at the Archives nationales, someone called Roussel was music critic for *Le Constitutionnel* during this period. Perhaps it is he who signed his articles "X. Y. Z."

Of mixed quality. Interesting on the whole, especially the work of Castil-Blaze. There are also several articles by Auguste Morel and "J. M." (Joseph Mainzer).

Le Courrier Français

Year	Critic	Contents
1830–31	Not signed (C. Moreau) (V. de Lapelouse)*	Opéra and Opéra-Comique Théâtre Italien
1832	Not signed (C. Moreau) January–July, then Artaud and Monnais Lapelouse	Théâtres lyriques Théâtre Italien

1833	Not signed (Monnais)	Théâtres lyriques and several articles on concerts
1834–38	"Ed. M." (Monnais)	Théâtres lyriques
1839	"Ed. M." (Monnais)	Théâtres lyriques
	"P. M." (Paul Merruau)	Concerts

*The criticism is not signed during the period 1831–33, but in the copy of the journal held at the Bibliothèque Nationale an anonymous hand has written in the names of the critics. These names correspond with the lists of *Entrées* at the Archives Nationales.

Quite interesting. Edouard Monnais perhaps was not asked to review anything other than the Théâtres lyriques. The areas he covered for the *Revue et Gazette Musicale* in the years 1838–39 are much more diverse. There also appear to be several articles written by Eugène Guinot during the period 1832–33.

La Gazette de France

Year	Critic	Contents
1830	"S." (C. de Sévelinges)	Théâtres lyriques (including the Théâtre Allemand)
1831	"S." January–May then unsigned (J. M. Brisset?)*	Théâtres lyriques
1832–33	Unsigned (Brisset?)	Théâtres lyriques
1834	Not signed January–July (Brisset?), then "A. D. L." and "X."	Théâtres lyriques
1835	"A. D. L." and "X."**	Théâtres lyriques
1836–39	"A."	Théâtres lyriques (and Berlioz concerts)

*"After the 1830 Revolution, he [Brisset] . . . came . . . onto the editorial staff of the *Gazette de France*, where he wrote political articles, . . . and did the theater criticism" ("Après la Révolution de 1830, il [Brisset] . . . entra . . . à la rédaction de la *Gazette de France*, où il a publié des articles politiques, . . . et fait la critique théâtrale" (*Larousse du XIXe siècle*).

**According to the *Entrées* of the Archives Nationales, Charles Beauregard was in charge of the theater criticism at the time. Perhaps it was he who signed his reviews "X."

Not very interesting. With the exception of a few reviews of concerts by Ernest Legouvé and "C. D." the bulk of the criticism is of the Théâtres lyriques only.

Journal des Débats

Year	Critic	Contents
1830–31	"XXX" (Castil-Blaze)	"Chronique musicale"
1832	Castil-Blaze January–July, then Jules Janin and J. E. Delécluze	"Chronique musicale" January–July, then Opéra, Opéra-Comique Théâtre Italien
1833	Janin Delécluze	Théâtres lyriques Théâtre Italien
1834–36	Berlioz (also signed H*****) Janin Delécluze	Concerts, Variétés musicales Opéra Théâtre Italien
1837–39	Berlioz Janin Delécluze	Concerts, Théâtres lyriques Ballet Théâtre Italien

Excellent, mainly because of Berlioz's criticism. The criticism of Castil-Blaze is at times also interesting. A very good coverage of musical events.

Journal de Paris

Year	Critic	Contents
1830	"S. C." (S. Champein [fils]	Nouvelles des Théâtres "Critique musicale" (mainly Théâtres lyriques)
1831	"S. C." January–July then "D." (Duchesne)	A bit of everything "Critique musicale"
1832	"D." (Duchesne) "ZZ."	Théâtre Italien, Opéra, Opéra-Comique
1833–35	"D." (signed A. Duchesne from September 1833) "ZZ."	Théâtre Italien, Opéra, Concerts Opéra-Comique
1836	"ZZ."	A bit of everything
1837	"A. B.," d'Ortigue, "ZZ."	A bit of everything

| 1838 | "A. B.," "B. de M."
(Bailleux de Marisy),
"A. M." (A. Morel) | A bit of everything |
| 1839 | "A. M." January–July,
then "Es." (Escudier) | A bit of everything |

Quite varied and on the whole interesting, especially the criticism of d'Ortigue, Morel, and Escudier.

Le Moniteur Universel

Year	Critic	Contents
1830–34	"P." (Sauvo)*	"Spectacles"
1835	"P." "H. P." (H. Prévost)	"Spectacles" Théâtre Italien
1836	"P."	"Spectacles"
1837	"P." "H. P." and Miel (also signed "E. F. M.")	"Spectacles" Théâtre Italien
1838	"P."	"Spectacles"
1839	"P."	"Spectacles"
	"P. V." (P.-A. Vieillard de Boismartin)	Théâtre Italien

*According to Brisson and Ribeyre, "the theater criticism . . .was skilfully and cheerfully carried out by M. Sauvo" ("la critique théâtrale . . . trouva dans M. Sauvo un interprète habile et bienveillant" [215]). Sauvo's name also appears in the *Entrées* of the Archives Nationales.

Not very specialized. The criticism is written almost exclusively by literary critics and, with the exception of a few reviews of concerts, reviews only the Théâtres lyriques. The periodical contains an excellent index.

Le National

Year	Critic	Contents
1830	"E."	Théâtres lyriques
1831	"E.," "A. R," "Z."	Théâtres lyriques, Concerts (a few articles)

1832	"Z.," "L. V." (L. Viardot), "L. D." (L. Desnoyers), "X." (H. Rolle)*	Théâtres lyriques
1833	L. Desnoyers "X."	Opéra, Théâtre Italien Opéra-Comique
1834–35	Desnoyers "X."	Opéra, Théâtre Italien, General articles on music Opéra-Comique
1836	Desnoyers January–July then J. Mainzer** (also signed "J. M.") "X."	Théâtres lyriques A bit of everything Opéra-Comique
1837	Mainzer "X."	A bit of everything Opéra-Comique, Ballet
1838	Mainzer "X.," "H. L." (H. Lucas)	A bit of everything Opéra-Comique, Ballet
1839	"X.," "H. L." (H. Lucas)	Opéra-Comique, Ballet ("H. L." for the Théâtres lyriques)

*According to the *Entrées* of the Archives nationales and Brisson and Ribeyre, "X." was Hippolyte Rolle.
**See also the music criticism of Mainzer (1834–35) in another very short-lived journal, *Le Réformateur*.

The music criticism for *Le National* is very interesting from 1833 onwards. Desnoyers's articles are well-written and the criticisms of Mainzer extremely interesting, covering areas that are not reviewed elsewhere.

La Presse

Year	Critic	Contents
1836	F. Soulié	Théâtres lyriques
1837	F. Soulié, T. Gautier, "G.-G." (T. Gautier and G. de Nerval)	Théâtres lyriques
1838	Gautier, "G.-G.," "G.-D." (T. Gautier and G. de Nerval)	Théâtres lyriques

1839	Gautier	Théâtres lyriques
	H. Berthoud	Several general articles on music

The first issue appeared in July 1836. Most of the articles are on the Théâtres lyriques except for a few articles on instrumental music by Stephen de la Madelaine in 1837, some reviews of Berlioz's concerts, and several anecdotal articles on musical life by Henry Berthoud. Information on music appears not only under the rubric of the *feuilleton musical,* but also in the column "Courrier de Paris," signed Vicomte Charles de Launay [Delphine Gay].

La Quotidienne

Year	Critic	Contents
1830–31	Not signed (Soulié)*	Théâtres lyriques, including the Théâtre Allemand
1832	"J. T." (J. T. Merle) D'Ortigue (from December)	Théâtres lyriques Concerts
1833–34	"J. T." D'Ortigue	Théâtres lyriques Concerts, a few general articles on music
1835	"J. T."	Théâtres lyriques
1836–38	"J. T.," d'Ortigue	Théâtres lyriques, Concerts, several general articles on music
1839	"J. T.," d'Ortigue	Théâtres lyriques, Concerts, several general articles on music, very few by d'Ortigue

*He is listed as critic for *La Quotidienne* for the years 1830–31 in the list of *Entrées* in the Opéra-Comique *Registres* (vol. 243).

Worth consulting, particularily for d'Ortigue's criticism.

Le Rénovateur

Year	Critic	Content
1833	"Z. Z." (Giueste?)* "H. B." (Berlioz) from December	A bit of everything Théâtres lyriques

| 1834 | Berlioz, "J." (d'Ortigue) | A bit of everything (d'Ortigue reviews only Berlioz's concerts) |
| 1835 | Berlioz | A bit of everything |

*According to the *Entrées* of the Archives nationales "Giueste" was Berlioz's predecessor for the *Rénovateur*.

Excellent because of Berlioz's criticism.

Le Siècle

Year	Critic	Contents
1836	"L. V." (L. Viardot) "Ed. L." (Lemoine)	Théâtres lyriques Opéra-Comique
1837	"L. V." A. Cler	Théâtres lyriques Opéra-Comique
1838	Viardot, January–July "H. L." (H. Lucas) A. Cler	Théâtres lyriques Théâtre Italien. Opéra-Comique
1839	A. Cler Viardot, Desnoyers*	Opéra-Comique Théâtres lyriques

*He also sometimes signed with his pseudonym L. D. Derville.

The first issue appeared in July 1836. The feuilleton of *Le Siècle* (run by Louis Desnoyers) was divided amongst many areas, "Théâtres," "Beaux-Arts," "Sciences physiques," "Finances" et cetera, and articles devoted to the theaters occurred only infrequently. Apart from the critics mentioned in this table, there were also a few articles on music signed by Eugène Briffault, Jules A. David, and Paul de Musset.

Le Temps

Year	Critic	Contents
1830	Not signed (Fétis)*	Théâtres lyriques including Théâtre allemand
1831	Not signed until November and then signed Fétis	Théâtres lyriques, Concerts
1832	Fétis, "L.-V." (Loève-Veimars), "Ch. L."	Théâtres lyriques, Concerts

1833	Fétis, "L.-V.," "Ch. L.," "A. G.," (A. Guéroult)	Théâtres lyriques, Concerts
1834	"L.-V.," A. Delrieu Fétis "A. G."	Théâtres lyriques A bit of everything Concerts
1835–36	"L.-V.," A. Delrieu Fétis, "A. G."	Théâtres lyriques, Concerts, Variétés musicales
1836	Fétis, d'Ortigue A. Delrieu C. Merruau A. Guéroult	Théâtres lyriques, Concerts, Variétés musicales
1837	C. Merruau, E. Pouyat (a few articles)	Théâtres lyriques, Concerts, Variétés musicales
1838	H. Panofka, C. Merruau	Théâtres lyriques, Concerts, Variétés musicales
1839	C. Merruau, "P. M." (Paul Merruau)	Théâtres lyriques, Concerts, Variétés musicales

*According to the Archives Nationales *Entrées* and judging by the general style of the articles, Fétis was the critic from 1830 onward.

The music criticism of *Le Temps* stands out as the best general coverage for the time. The paper had what amounted to a team of critics working for it. It is unfortunate that when the paper changed format in 1837 music criticism no longer held such an important position.

Music Critics of the Major Parisian Dailies, 1830–1839
Some Identified Initials

A. G.	Adolphe Guéroult (*Le Temps*)
A. M.	Auguste Morel (*Journal de Paris*)
B. de M.	Bailleux de Marisy (*Journal de Paris*)
C. M.	Charles Merruau (*Le Temps, Le Constitutionnel*)
D.	A. Duchesne (*Journal de Paris*)
Ed. L.	Edouard Lemoine (*Le Siècle*)
Ed. M.	Edouard Monnais (*Le Courrier Français*)
E. F. M.	E. F. Miel (*Le Moniteur Universel*)
Es.	Léon Escudier (*Journal de Paris*)
G.-D.	Théophile Gautier and Gerard de Nerval (*La Presse*)
G.-G.	Théophile Gautier and Gerard de Nerval (*La Presse*)
H. B	Hector Berlioz (*Le Rénovateur, Journal des Débats*)

H*****	Hector Berlioz (*Journal des Débats*)
H. L.	Hippolyte Lucas (*Le National, Le Siècle*)
H. P.	Hippolyte Prévost (*Le Moniteur Universel*)
J.	Joseph d'Ortigue (*Le Rénovateur*)
J. M.	Joseph Mainzer (*Le National*)
J. T.	Jean-Toussaint Merle (*La Quotidienne*)
L. D.	Louis Desnoyers (*Le National*)
L. V.	Louis Viardot (*Le National, Le Siècle*)
L.-V.	François-Adolphe Loève-Veimars (*Le Temps*)
P.	F. Sauvo (*Le Moniteur Universel*)
P. M.	Paul Merruau (*Le Temps, Le Courrier Français*)
P. V.	Pierre-Ange Vieillard de Boismartin (*Le Moniteur Universel*)
S.	Charles Louis de Sévelinges (*La Gazette de France*)
S. C.	Marie-François Stanislas Champein (fils) (*Journal de Paris*)
X.	Hippolyte Rolle (*Le National*)
XXX.	François Castil-Blaze (*Journal des Débats, Le Constitutionnel*)

Appendix D

Bibliography of Berlioz's Articles, 1823–1837

From 1823 to 1837 Berlioz contributed articles to the following journals:[1]

Le Corsaire	(1823–25, 1828)
Le Figaro	(1828)
Revue Musicale	(1828–32)
Le Correspondant	(1829–30)
Berliner Allgemeine Musikalische Zeitung	(1829)
Revue Européenne	(1832)
Revue de Paris	(1832)
L'Europe Littéraire	(1833)
Gazette Musicale	(1834–35)
Le Rénovateur	(1833–35)
Journal des Artistes	(1834)
Journal des Débats	(1834–37)
Le Monde Dramatique	(1835)
Revue et Gazette Musicale	(1836–37)
Chronique de Paris	(1837)

1823

Le Corsaire

12 August	"CORRESPONDANCE. POLEMIQUE MUSICALE" pp. 2–3. Signed "HECTOR B. . . ."

1824

Le Corsaire

11 January

"POLEMIQUE MUSICALE. LES DILET-
TANTI. MONSIEUR LE CORSAIRE"
p. 2.
Signed "H. B. . . ."

1825

Le Corsaire

19 December

"POLEMIQUE MUSICALE. Sur Armide et
Gluck. MONSIEUR LE REDACTEUR"
p. 2.
Signed "H. B."

1828

Le Corsaire

22 May

"CORRESPONDANCE. A MONSIEUR LE
REDACTEUR DU CORSAIRE"
p. 3.

Le Figaro

21 May

"CORRESPONDANCE. A M. Figaro"
p. 3.

Revue Musicale

16 May

"CORRESPONDANCE. Monsieur Le Rédac-
teur"
pp. 405–6.[2]

1829

Berliner Allgemeine Musikalische Zeitung

7 February

"Paris, Januar 1829. Aubers neueste Oper, 'la
Fiancée' (die Braut).
Text von Scribe"
pp. 46–48.
Unsigned.

6 June	"Paris den 21. Mai 1829. Erste Vorstellung der Oper 'les deux nuits,' von Bouilly und Scribe, Musik von Boieldieu." pp. 183–84. Unsigned.
27 June	"Die deutsche Oper in Paris" pp. 205–7. Signed "B."
11 July	"Paris, im Juni 1829. [*La Dame Blanche*]" pp. 224. Unsigned.
18 July	"Aus Paris. Königliche Akademie der Musik in Paris" pp. 226–28. Unsigned.
17 October	"Neue Pariser Opern. ("Zwei Nächte," Oper, von Scribe gedichtet und von Bojeldieu komponirt)" pp. 334–36. Unsigned.

Le Correspondant

21 April	"CONSIDERATIONS SUR LA MUSIQUE RELIGIEUSE" pp. 54–55. Signed "H."
4 August	"BEAUX-ARTS. BIOGRAPHIE ETRANGERE.—BEETHOVEN" pp. 179–80. Unsigned.
11 August	"BEAUX-ARTS. BIOGRAPHIE ETRANGERE.—BEETHOVEN" p. 187. Unsigned.
6 October	"BEAUX-ARTS. BIOGRAPHIE ETRANGERE.—BEETHOVEN. Suite et fin" pp. 251–52. Signed "H."

1830

Le Correspondant

22 October

"BEAUX-ARTS. APERCU SUR LA MU-SIQUE CLASSIQUE ET LA MUSIQUE ROMANTIQUE"
pp. 110–12.
Signed "H. B."[3]

1832

Revue Européenne

March-May, III

"LETTRE D'UN ENTHOUSIASTE SUR L'ETAT ACTUEL DE LA MUSIQUE EN ITALIE. Florence. Le théâtre de la Pergola. *I Montecchi ed i Capelli* [*sic*]. La *Vestale,* de Paccini [*sic*]. L'orchestre, les choeurs, les chanteurs. Service funèbre du jeune Napoléon Bonaparte. L'organiste.—Gènes. *L'Agnèse,* de Paer. Indifférence des Génois pour Paganini.—Rome. La fête *del Corpus Domini.* Le choeur de Castrati. La musique militaire. *Miserere* d'Allegri. Musique des églises. Théâtres. Chanteurs, choeurs et orchestre. Chant des montagnes romaines. Les Pifferari. L'institut de France et ses musiciens pension-naires à Rome.—Naples. Théâtre Saint-Charles. Théâtre *del Fondo.* Opéra buffa de Donizetti. Exécution du *Requiem* de Mozart. Conjectures sur Milan et Venise"
pp. 47–64.
Signed "H. B."[4]

La Revue Musicale

31 March

"LETTRE D'UN ENTHOUSIASTE SUR L'ETAT ACTUEL DE LA MUSIQUE EN ITALIE. (Extrait de *la Revue européenne.*) FLORENCE. Le théâtre de la Pergola. *I Montec-*

chi ed i Capelli [*sic*]. *La Vestale*, de Paccini [*sic*]. L'orchestre les choeurs, les chanteurs. Service funèbre du jeune Napoléon Bonaparte. L'organiste.—GENES. L'*Agnèse* de Paer. Indifference des Génois pour Paganini.—ROME. La fête *del Corpus Domini*. Le choeur de Castrati. La musique militaire. *Miserere* d'Allegri. Musique des églises. Théâtres. Chanteurs, choeurs et orchestre. Chant des montagnes romaines. Les Pifferari. L'Institut de France et ses musiciens pensionnaires à Rome. NAPLES. Théâtre *del Fondo*. Opéra buffa de Donizetti. Exécution du *Requiem* de Mozart. Conjectures sur Milan et Venise"
pp. 65–68.
Unsigned.[5]

9 April

"LETTRE D'UN ENTHOUSIASTE SUR L'ETAT ACTUEL DE LA MUSIQUE EN ITALIE. Suite"
pp. 73–75.
Unsigned.

Revue de Paris

23 December

"Galerie Biographique DES ARTISTES FRANCAIS ET ETRANGERS. V
—HECTOR BERLIOZ"
pp. 281–98.[6]

1833

L'Europe Littéraire (old series)

8 May

"JOURNAL D'UN ENTHOUSIASTE"
pp. 123–24.[7]

12 June

"ACADEMIE DES BEAUX-ARTS. CONCOURS ANNUEL DE COMPOSITION MUSICALE"
pp. 182–83.[8]

19 July

"CONCOURS ANNUEL DE COMPOSITION MUSICALE"
pp. 246–47.[9]

Le Rénovateur

9 July

"REVUE MUSICALE"
p. 1.
[extract from *L'Europe Littéraire* article, 19 July 1833]

8 December

"REVUE   THEATRALE.   ACADEMIE ROYALE DE MUSIQUE.—Première représentation de la *Révolte au Sérail*, ballet en 3 actes de M. Taglioni, décors de M. Ciceri, costumes de M. Duponchel, musique de M. Th. Labarre"
p. 1.
Signed "H. B."

15 December

"REVUE MUSICALE. CONCERTS" [Hiller, Liszt, Chopin]
p. 1.

20 December

"—Le concert annoncé pour dimanche prochain par M. Hector Berlioz doit piquer vivement la curiosité publique. Nous extrayons du libretto l'exposé de la représentation qui doit avoir lieu"
p. 1.
[K. Holoman attributes this unsigned announcement to Berlioz. It seems very probable to me also.]

29 December

"REVUE MUSICALE. CONCERTS. *Concerts Montesquieu.—Concerts Musard.*"
p. 2.

1834

Gazette Musicale

2 February

"INSTITUT. CONCOURS DE MUSIQUE ET VOYAGE D'ITALIE DU LAUREAT"
pp. 35–38.[10]

27 April

"CONCERTS DU CONSERVATOIRE. *Cinquième, sixième et septième concerts.*"
pp. 133–35.

1 June	"GLUCK" pp. 173–76.
8 June	"GLUCK. (SUITE ET FIN)" pp. 181–85.
20 July	"Le Suicide par enthousiasme. NOUVELLE" pp. 229–31.
27 July	"Le Suicide par enthousiasme. (SUITE)" pp. 237–39.
3 August	"Le Suicide par enthousiasme. (SUITE)" pp. 248–50.
10 August	"Le Suicide par enthousiasme. (SUITE ET FIN)" pp. 255–56.[11]
7 September	"SERVICE FUNEBRE DE CHORON" pp. 285–87.[12]
5 October	"UN BENEFICIAIRE ET RUBINI A CALAIS" pp. 317–19.[13]
12 October	"*GUILLAUME TELL*, DE ROSSINI" pp. 326–27.
19 October	"*GUILLAUME-TELL*, Second article" pp. 336–39.
26 October	"*GUILLAUME-TELL*, Troisième article.—2e acte" pp. 341–43.
2 November	"*GUILLAUME-TELL*, Quatrième article.—3e et 4e acte[s]" pp. 349–51.
2 November	"HISTORIQUE DE LA REPRESENTATION DE RUBINI A CALAIS" pp. 351–52.
9 November	"*Iphigénie en Tauride*" pp. 360–61.
16 November	"*Iphigénie en Tauride*. 1er acte.—2me article" pp. 365–67.
23 November	"*Iphigénie en Tauride*. 1er acte.—3me article" pp. 377–78.

7 December

"*Iphigénie en Tauride*. 3me [*sic*] et dernier article"
pp. 389–90.

Journal des Débats

10 October

"Rubini à Calais"
[With the note:] "Tel est le titre d'une anecdote que nous trouvons dans le dernier Numéro de la *Gazette musicale* racontée, avec autant d'esprit que de verve, par M. Hector Berlioz"
p. 1.

Le Rénovateur

5 January

"REVUE MUSICALE. *DON GIOVANNI.—LE REVENANT*. DON GIOVANNI, *Opéra de Mozart*.—LE REVENANT, opéra en 3 actes; paroles de M. Albert de Calvimont, musique de M. Gomis"
pp. 1–2.

12 January

"REVUE MUSICALE"
p. 1.

19 January

"REVUE MUSICALE. OPERA-COMIQUE. —THEATRE ITALIEN.—CONCERTS. OPE-RA-COMIQUE.—Le *Château d'Urtubi*, poéme de MM. Delurieu et Raoul, musique de feu Henri Berton fils. THEATRE ITALIEN.—*Gianni di Calais*, opéra de Donizetti. CONCERTS DU CONSERVATOIRE"
p. 1.

27 January

"REVUE MUSICALE ET LITTERAIRE. TRAITE DE COMPOSITION DE BEETHO-VEN"
p. 1.

2 February

"REVUE MUSICALE. *Premier Concert du Conservatoire.—Soirée musicale de Mme Stokausen.—L'Athénée musical.* OPERA-COMIQUE: *Une Bonne Fortune*"
p. 1.

9 February	"REVUE MUSICALE. LES LAUREATS DE L'INSTITUT.—M. Marliani. *Théâtre-Italien.* —*Il Bravo*" p. 1.
17 February	"REVUE MUSICALE. *Deuxième concert du Conservatoire*" p. 1.
23 February	"REVUE MUSICALE" p. 1.
2 March	"REVUE MUSICALE. 3ᵉ CONCERT DU CONSERVATOIRE.—*Symphonie pastorale*" pp. 1–2.
11 March	"REVUE MUSICALE ET THEATRALE. CONCERT DE M. HAUMAN.—*4ᵉ Concert du Conservatoire.*—OPERA. —*Don Juan,* musique de Mozart, paroles de MM. Emile Deschamps et Castil Blaze" p. 1.
16 March	"REVUE MUSICALE. OPERA—Première représentation de *Don Juan,* musique de Mozart, paroles de MM. Emile Deschamps et Henri Castilblaze, divertissemens de M. Coraly, décorations de MM. Ciceri, Léon Feuchère [*sic*], Filastre et Cambon" pp. 1–2.
23 March	"REVUE MUSICALE ET LITTERAIRE. *DON JUAN.*—(2ᵉ article)" pp. 1–2.[14]
30 March	"REVUE MUSICALE. CONCERTS.—*Cherubini et Mozart.*—*Les deux requiem*" p. 1.
8 April	"REVUE MUSICALE ET THEATRALE. SEPTIEME CONCERT DU CONSERVATOIRE" pp. 1-2.
13 April	"REVUE MUSICALE. SOUVENIRS D'ITALIE" p. 1.

20 April	"REVUE MUSICALE. LA CHAPELLE SIXTINE A ROME" pp. 1–2.[15]
27 April	"REVUE MUSICALE. CONCERTS.—*Beethoven, Cherubini, Haumann, Ponchard*" p. 1.
11 May	"REVUE MUSICALE ET LITTERAIRE" p. 1.
18 May	"REVUE MUSICALE. REPRISE DE *LA VESTALE*" p. 1.
25 May	"REVUE MUSICALE. SOUVENIRS D'ITALIE" pp. 1–2.
1 June	"REVUE MUSICALE. REOUVERTURE DE L'OPERA-COMIQUE.—Première représentation de *Lestocq;* paroles de M. Scribe, musique de M. Auber" p. 1.
8 June	"REVUE MUSICALE. LES DILETTANTI DE BORDEAUX ET BEETHOVEN" p. 1.
15 June	"REVUE MUSICALE. THEATRE NAUTIQUE.—OPERA-COMIQUE. Première représentation de l'*Aspirant de marine.*—Débutans" p. 1.
22 June	"REVUE MUSICALE" p. 1.
2 July	"REVUE MUSICALE. OPERA-ALLEMAND. —THEATRE VENTADOUR.—OPERA-COMIQUE" p. 1.
13 July	"REVUE MUSICALE. ACADEMIE ROYALE DE MUSIQUE.—La *Vestale.*—Mlle Falcon.—OPERA-COMIQUE.—L'*Angelus.*—Le *Petit Chaperon.*—Ponchard, Couderc, Mlle Massy.—Fête musicale de Londres" pp. 1–2.

20 July	"REVUE MUSICALE. *Quatuors,* M. Henri Reber" p. 1.
27 July	"REVUE MUSICALE. OPERA-COMIQUE.—Première représentation de *Un caprice de femme,* paroles de M. Lesguillon, musique de M. Paer.—Reprise du *Revenant*" p. 1.
3 August	"REVUE MUSICALE. *Fête musicale de Londres*" (Deuxième article) p. 1.
11 August	"REVUE MUSICALE. *Service funèbre de Choron*" p. 1.
16 & 17 August	"REVUE MUSICALE. ACADEMIE ROYALE DE MUSIQUE.—*La Vestale*" "THEATRE NAUTIQUE.—Le *Nouveau Robinson*" "OPERA-COMIQUE.—*Douze libretti,* avec cette épigraphe: *Tout pour la musique,* par F. L. Berthé" p. 1.
24 August	"REVUE MUSICALE. CONCERTS" p. 1.
31 August	"REVUE MUSICALE. OPERA-COMIQUE.—Première représentation de *Le Fils du Prince,* opéra-comique en deux actes, paroles de M. Scribe, musique de M. de Feltre" p. 1.
14 September	"REVUE MUSICALE. ACADEMIE ROYALE DE MUSIQUE.—*Guillaume Tell; Robert le diable*" pp. 1-2.
21 September	"REVUE THEATRALE. ACADEMIE ROYALE DE MUSIQUE.—Première représentation de la *Tempête,* ballet en deux actes de M. Coraly, musique de M. Schneitzoeffer, décors de MM. Ciceri, Feuchères et plusieurs autres" p. 1.

28 September	"REVUE MUSICALE. LES CHARMES DE PORTICI, rondo brillant." *NOTRE-DAME DE PARIS,* rêverie musicale, pour piano, dédiée à Victor Hugo, par Jules Benedict—*LE CHALET*" p. 1.
9 October	"REVUE MUSICALE. OPERA.—THEATRE ITALIEN—THEATRE DE L'OPERA-COMIQUE" p. 1.
14 October	"BOIELDIEU" p. 1.
18 October	"REVUE THEATRALE. THEATRE NAUTIQUE.—Première représentation de *Chao-Kang,* ballet, pantomime en 3 actes avec un épilogue par M. Henri" p. 1.
26 October	"REVUE MUSICALE. THEATRE VENTADOUR.—*Chao-Kang,* par M. Henri.—CONCERTS d'Haumann" p. 1.
2 & 3 November	"REVUE MUSICALE. OPERA-COMIQUE.—Première représentation de le *Marchand forain,* opéra en 3 actes, paroles de M. Planard, musique de M. Marliani" "*Avis aux lecteurs assez désoeuvrés pour lire mes feuilletons*" p. 1.
16 November	"REVUE MUSICALE. A ELLE, lettres pour le piano, par Chrétien Urhan, avec cette épigraphe. 'Peut-être dans la foule une ame [*sic*] que j'ignore, Aurait compris mon ame et m'aurait répondu' (LAMARTINE)" p. 1.
27 November	"REVUE MUSICALE. THEATRE-NAUTIQUE.—*La dernière Heure d'un Condamné.* CONCERTS" p. 1.

5 December

"REVUE MUSICALE. THEATRE-ITALIEN. —*Ernani,* musique de M. Gabussi.—OPE-RA-COMIQUE.—*La   Sentinelle   perdue,* paroles de M. Saint-George [*sic*], musique de M. Rifaut" pp. 1–2.

14 December

"REVUE MUSICALE. THEATRE-ITALIEN. —*Débuts de Mlle Brambilla.* OPERA-CO-MIQUE.—*Débuts de Mlle Annette Lebrun.*—THEATRE VENTADOUR.— Choristes allemands—" p. 1.

23 December

"REVUE MUSICALE. OPERA.—*Guillaume Tell.* OPERA-COMIQUE.—Reprise de *Zémire et Azor.*—CONCERTS" p. 1.

1835

La Gazette Musicale

11 January

"TELEMACO, *Opéra italien de Gluck*" pp. 10–13.

18 January

"PREMIER BAL DE L'OPERA" pp. 22–24.

1 February

"LETTRES A ELLE, pour le piano, par Chrétien Urhan. Prix: 4 fr. 50 c." pp. 40–41.

3 May

"CONCERT HISTORIQUE DE M. FETIS" pp. 155–56.

12 July

"DE INTRUMENTATION [*sic*] DE ROBERT LE DIABLE" pp. 229–32.

18 October

"CHANTS POUR LE PIANO, de Meyerbeer" pp. 342–43.

25 October

"CHANTS POUR LE PIANO, de Meyerbeer" (Deuxième et dernier article) p. 351.

Journal des Débats

25 January	"SOCIETE DES CONCERTS DU CONSERVATOIRE. PREMIER CONCERT" pp. 1–3. Signed "H . . ."
12 February	"DEUXIEME CONCERT DU CONSERVATOIRE" pp. 1–2. Signed "H."
20 February	"TROISIEME CONCERT DU CONSERVATOIRE. *Symphonie de Haydn.—Symphonie de Beethoven*" pp. 1–2. Signed "H."
22 March	"SOCIETE DES CONCERTS DU CONSERVATOIRE. 4e CONCERTS [*sic*]" pp. 1–3. Signed "Hxxx."
12 April	"CINQUIEME CONCERT DU CONSERVATOIRE. Symphonie en *si bemol* de Beethoven; grande Scène de Beethoven, chantée, par Mlle Falcon; Solo de violoncelle, par M. Franchomme; *Andante* de la symphonie en *la* de Beethoven; grande choeur *d'Euryanthe*, de Weber; ouverture de *Fidelio*, de Beethoven" pp. 1–2. Signed "H."
18 April	"SIXIEME CONCERT DU CONSERVATOIRE" pp. 1–2. Signed "H . . ."
25 April	"CONCERTS DE M. LISTZ [*sic*]. *Hôtel-de-ville (salle Saint-Jean)*" pp. 1–2. Signed "Hxxx."
23 June	"DERNIERES SEANCES DU CONSERVATOIRE.—GYMNASE MUSICAL" pp. 1–3. Signed "H . . ."

21 July

"DE LA MUSIQUE EN PLEIN AIR"
pp. 1–2.
Signed "Hxxx."

9 August

"LE REQUIEM DES INVALIDES ET LE TE DEUM DE NOTRE-DAME. MM. CHERUBI-NI ET LESUEUR"
pp. 1–3.
Signed "Hxxx."[16]

5 September

"DES MUSICIENS AMBULANS ALLE-MANDS ET ITALIENS"
pp. 1–3.
Signed "Hxxx."[17]

13 September

"SOUVENIRS D'UN HABITUE DE L'OPERA (1822–1823)"
pp. 1–3.
Signed "Hxxxxx."[18]

27 September

"DE LA PARTITION DE *ZAMPA*"
pp. 1–2.
Signed "Hxxxxx."[19]

2 October

"DU SYSTEME DE GLUCK EN MUSIQUE DRAMATIQUE"
pp. 1–2.
Signed "Hxxxxx."[20]

16 October

"DES DEUX *ALCESTES* DE GLUCK (Premier Article)"
pp. 1–3.
Signed "Hxxxxx."

23 October

"DES DEUX *ALCESTES* DE GLUCK (Deuxième et dernier Article)"
pp. 1–2.
Signed Hxxxxx."[21]

15 November

"DU DON JUAN DE MOZART"
pp. 1–2.
Signed "Hxxxxx."[22]

21 November

"MUSIQUE RELIGIEUSE. *Rachel, Noémi, Ruth et Booz*, oratorios de M. Lesueur. —*Auditions* de M. Urhan"
pp. 1–2.
Signed "Hxxxxx."[23]

22 December

"ENSEIGNEMENT MUSICAL. *Cours de contre-point et fugue,* de M. Cherubini.—*Traité de composition,* de Beethoven. Chez M. Maurice Schlesinger, rue de Richelieu, 97"
pp. 1–2.
Signed "Hxxxxx."

Le Monde Dramatique

June, vol. 1

"SPECTACLES DE PARIS. LE PORTEFAIX. Opéra comique en trois actes, musique de M. GOMIS"
pp. 84–86.

July, vol. 1

"SPECTACLES DE PARIS. DEBUT DE MADAME LAURI ET DE M. SERDA"
pp. 148–50.
[Article unsigned, however listed as by Hector Berlioz in the index.]

August, vol. 1

"DU REPERTOIRE DE GLUCK A L'ACADEMIE ROYALE DE MUSIQUE"
pp. 180–81.

August, vol. 1

"SPECTACLES DE PARIS. ACADEMIE ROYALE DE MUSIQUE. *L'ILE DES PIRATES* —Ballet-Pantomine, en quatre actes, par MM. Henry et xxx, musique de MM. GIDE, CARLINI, ROSSINI et BEETHOVEN; décorations de MM. PHILASTRE, CAMBON, DESPLECHIN, SECHAN, FEUCHERES et DIETERLE"
pp. 199–200.
[Unsigned, listed as "H. B" in the index. Prod'homme attributed it to Berlioz. I am still uncertain. It could be by Henri Blanchard.]

Le Rénovateur

5 January

"REVUE MUSICALE. CONCERTS" [Ernst-Francilla Pixis]
p. 1.

11 January

"REVUE MUSICALE" [Paisiello]
p. 1.

18 January	"REVUE MUSICALE. ACADEMIE ROYALE DE MUSIQUE—THEATRE ITALIEN —L'OPERA-COMIQUE.—Première représentation de *Robin des Bois*" p. 1.
25 January	"REVUE MUSICALE. CONCERTS.—*Concert de M. Hippolyte Monpou*" p. 1.
1 February	"REVUE MUSICALE. THEATRE ITALIEN.— *I Puritani*" p. 1.
8 February	"REVUE MUSICALE. ACADEMIE ROYALE DE MUSIQUE.—OPERA-COMIQUE. — CONCERTS. — *DEUXIEME CONCERT DU CONSERVATOIRE. — MATINEES DE M. TILMANT*" p. 1.
17 February	"REVUE MUSICALE" p. 1.
1 March	"REVUE MUSICALE. ACADEMIE ROYALE DE MUSIQUE.—Première représentation de *La Juive,* opéra en cinq actes, de M. Scribe, musique de M. Halevy [*sic*], décors de MM. Diéterle, Delplechin [*sic*], Sechan [*sic*] et Léon Feuchère [*sic*]" pp. 1–2.
5 March	"REVUE MUSICALE. THEATRE DE L'OPERA-COMIQUE.—*La Marquise,* paroles de MM. St-Georges et Lewen, musique de M. Adam.—Début de Mlle Fargueil.—THEATRE ANGLAIS" p. 1.
17 March	"REVUE MUSICALE. CONCERT DES ELEVES DE CHORON, *à l'Hôtel-de-Ville*" p. 1.
29 March	"REVUE MUSICALE. THEATRE ITALIEN: *Marino Faliero;* musique de M. Donizetti. —THEATRE DE L'OPERA-COMIQUE: *Le*

	Cheval de bronze; musique de M. Auber, paroles de M. Scribe" pp. 1–2.
5 April	"REVUE MUSICALE. CONCERTS" p. 1.
12 April	"REVUE MUSICALE ET THEATRALE. ACADEMIE ROYALE DE MUSIQUE.— THEATRE-FRANCAIS.—OPERA.—Bénéfice de Mlle Taglioni.—Première représentation de *Brezilia,* ballet en un acte, de M. Taglioni, musique de M. Gallemberg [*sic*]" pp. 1–2.
29 April	"REVUE MUSICALE. CONCERTS" p. 1.
13 May	"REVUE MUSICALE. OPERA-COMIQUE. Débuts de Mlle Camoin, de M. Riquier. Reprise du *Diable à quatre*" p. 1.
17 May	"REVUE MUSICALE" [*Gymnase Musical.* Arrival of Meyerbeer in Paris] p. 1.
28 May	"REVUE MUSICALE" [*Gymnase Musical*] p. 1.
7 June	"REVUE MUSICALE" [Début of Serda] p. 1.
14 June	"REVUE MUSICALE. GYMNASE MUSICAL" p. 1.
20 June	"REVUE MUSICALE. THEATRE DE L'OPERA-COMIQUE.—1re représentation du *Portefaix,* opéra-comique en 3 actes, musique de M. Gomis, paroles de M. Scribe" pp. 1–2.
29 June	"REVUE MUSICALE. *FIDELIO* A COVENT-GARDEN.—GYMNASE MUSICAL.—" p. 1.

12 July	"REVUE MUSICALE. THEATRE DE L'OPE-RA-COMIQUE.—*Micheline.*—*Alda.*—*Concerts Musard.*—*Cantiques de l'abbé Le Guillou*" pp. 1–2.
19 July	"REVUE MUSICALE. ACADEMIE ROYALE DE MUSIQUE.—FETES MUSICALES DE TOULOUSE" p. 1.
27 July	"REVUE MUSICALE" p. 1.
8 August	"REVUE MUSICALE. OPERA-COMIQUE. —Première représentation des *Deux Reines,* opéra-comique en un acte, musique de M. H. Monpou, paroles de MM. F. Soulié et Arnoud" pp. 1–2.
16 & 17 August	"REVUE MUSICALE. ACADEMIE ROYALE DE MUSIQUE.—Première représentation de l'*Ile des pirates,* ballet en quatre actes, de M. Henry; musique de MM. Carlini et Casimir Gide, décoration de MM. Despleschin [*sic*], Séchan, Feuchères, Diéterle, Philastre et Cambon" p. 1.
31 August	"REVUE MUSICALE. M. DUPONCHEL, LES CHOEURS DE L'OPERA" p. 1.
6 September	"REVUE MUSICALE. OPERA-CO-MIQUE.—Reprise de Zampa" p. 1.
21 September	"REVUE MUSICALE. PUBLICATIONS NOUVELLES—*Cours de contrepoint et fugue,* par M. Cherubini" pp. 1–2.
30 September	"REVUE MUSICALE. BELLINI" [Obituary] p. 1.
5 October	"REVUE MUSICALE" p. 1.

12 October	"REVUE MUSICALE ET THEATRALE" p. 1.
19 October	"REVUE MUSICALE. OPERA-COMIQUE: 1re représentation de *Cosimo,* opéra-bouffon en deux actes, de MM. Saint-Hilaire et Paul Duport, musique de M. E. Prévost" p. 1.
27 October	"REVUE MUSICALE. OPERA.—THEATRE-ITALIEN.—OPERA-COMIQUE.—GYMNASE-MUSICAL" p. 1.
5 November	"REVUE THEATRALE ET MUSICALE. OEUVRES POSTHUMES DE VICTOR LEFEBURE" p. 2.
3 December	"REVUE MUSICALE ET THEATRALE. ACADEMIE ROYALE DE MUSIQUE: Mlle Flecheux, Mme Baptiste Quiney. —OPERA-COMIQUE: La *Grande duchesse;* Mme Damoreau.—THEATRE ITALIEN. —*Concert* de MM. Allard et Chevillard" p. 1.
23 December	"REVUE MUSICALE. OPERA-COMIQUE: Première représentation de l'*Eclair,* opéra-comique en trois actes, de MM. Planard et Saint-Georges, musique de M. Halévy. —THEATRE-ITALIEN: *Norma.*—ACADEMIE ROYALE DE MU-SIQUE: *Le Siége* [*sic*] *de Corinthe*" p. 1.

1836

Journal des Débats

17 January	"OPERA-COMIQUE.—CONCERTS.—LES VIRTUOSES ET LES COMPOSITEURS" pp. 1–2. Signed "Hxxxxx."

24 February	"PREMIER CONCERT DU CONSERVATOIRE" pp. 1–2. Signed "Hxxxxx."
1 May	"CONCERTS DU CONSERVATOIRE. *La Flûte enchantée* et *les Mystères d'Isis.*—Le correcteur de Mozart" pp. 1–2. Signed "Hxxxxx."[24]
3 July	"ANTOINE REICHA" pp. 1–3. Signed "Hxxxxx."[25]
16 July	"BELLINI" pp. 1–2. Signed "Hxxxxx."[26]
23 July	"VARIETES MUSICALES—*Le Siége* [*sic*] *de Corinthe* à l'Opéra.—M. Ole-Bull.—M. Labarre et son école de harpe.—La musique des fêtes publiques.—Les Artistes et les Amateurs de Paris. Leur réunion en 1794 pour célébrer la victoire de Fleurus.—Les Dilettanti quêteurs en 1830.—Le choeur colossal de la galerie Colbert" pp. 1–2. Signed "Hxxx."[27]
2 August	"ITALIE PITTORESQUE" pp. 1–3. Signed "Hxxxx."
26 August	"CHRONIQUE MUSICALE. *M. Urhan.*—*Conservatoire de Genève*" pp. 1–2. Signed "Hxxxxx."
18 September	"DES PROGRES DE L'ENSEIGNEMENT MUSICAL EN FRANCE. M. JOSEPH MAINZER, M. AUBERY DU BOULLEY" pp. 1–2. Signed "Hxxxxx."
10 November	"*LES HUGUENOTS. La Partition.*—1er Article" pp. 1–2. Signed "Hxxxxx."[28]

10 December

"*LES HUGUENOTS. La Partition.*— (Deuxième et dernier Article)"
pp. 1–2.
Signed "Hxxxxx."[29]

Revue et Gazette Musicale

31 January

"PREMIER CONCERT DU CONSERVATOIRE"
pp. 38–39.

7 February

"BELLINI ET ROSSINI"
pp. 43–45.

14 February

"SECOND CONCERT DU CONSERVATOIRE"
pp. 54–55.

21 February

"LE CARNIVAL A ROME ET A PARIS. Du sentiment de l'art chez les masses, MATINEES MUSICALES DE MM. TILMANT"
pp. 57–59.

6 March

"*LES HUGUENOTS* (Première représentation), OPERA EN CINQ ACTES, Musique de M. MEYERBEER, paroles de M. SCRIBE, divertissemens de M. TAGLIONI, Décors de MM. SECHAN, FEUCHERES, DIETERLE et DESPLECHIN"
pp. 73–77.

13 March

"*LES HUGUENOTS*, 1er 2e 3e actes (Deuxième article)"
pp. 81–83.

20 March

"*LES HUGUENOTS*, 4e et 5e actes (Troisième article)"
pp. 89–91.

27 March

"5e CONCERT DU CONSERVATOIRE"
pp. 97–98.

3 April

"CONCERT DE MM. OSBORNE ET BENEDICT"
pp. 111–12.

24 April

"6e CONCERT DU CONSERVATOIRE"
pp. 133–35.

8 May	"SEPTIEME ET DERNIER CONCERT DU CONSERVATOIRE" pp. 151–53.
8 May	"A MONSIEUR HOFMEISTER, EDITEUR DE MUSIQUE A LEIPSICK [*sic*]" pp. 154–55.
12 June	"LISTZ [*sic*]" pp. 198–200.
19 June	"CONCOURS ANNUEL DE COMPOSITION MUSICALE A L'INSTITUT (Delenda et Carthago)" pp. 203–6.[30]
10 July	"CONCERT DE Mlle MAZEL A L'HOTEL-DE-VILLE" pp. 243–45.
7 August	"GOMIS" pp. 275–77.
18 September	"DE L'OPERA COMIQUE" pp. 323–25.
9 October	"THEATRE DE L'OPERA-COMIQUE. *LE MAUVAIS OEIL*, opéra-comique en un acte, paroles de MM. Scribe et Gustave Lemoine, musique de Mlle Loïsa Puget (Première représentation)" pp. 357–59.
16 October	"SEANCE PUBLIQUE DE L'INSTITUT. DISTRIBUTION DES PRIX" pp. 362–63.
23 October	"ENCORE UN MOT SUR LE CONCOURS DE COMPOSITION MUSICALE A L'INSTITUT, EN REPONSE AU DERNIER ARTICLE DE M. GERMANUS LEPIC" pp. 370–73.
30 October	"ENCORE UN MOT SUR LE CONCOURS DE COMPOSITION MUSICALE A L'INSTITUT, EN REPONSE AU DERNIER ARTICLE DE M. GERMANUS LEPIC. (Suite et fin)" pp. 377–80.

6 November	"THEATRE ITALIEN. Reprise du *Matrimonio Secreto* [*sic*]" pp. 389–90.
20 November	"ACADEMIE ROYALE DE MUSIQUE. *LA ESMERALDA*, opéra en 4 actes; paroles de M. Victor Hugo, musique de mademoiselle Louise Bertin, décors de MM. Philastre et Cambon (Première représentation)" pp. 409–11.
27 November	"REVUE CRITIQUE. Publications nouvelles pour piano seul, et chant avec piano et violoncelle, de M. Urhan" "*LE PELERIN*, ballade de M. Emilien Pacini, musique de M. H. Panofka.—*LA MORT DE GOMIS*, élégie dédiée à M. Cavé, paroles de M. E. Pacini, musique de M. J. Struntz" pp. 419–20.
4 December	"SOCIETE POLYTECHNIQUE. DISTRIBUTION DES PRIX" pp. 428–29.
18 December	"CONCERTS DE LA SOCIETE PHILOTHECNIQUE [*sic*]" p. 446.

1837

Chronique de Paris

19 March	"CHRONIQUE MUSICALE" pp. 191–93. Signed "...z."
7 May	"CHRONIQUE MUSICALE" pp. 309–11.
18 June	"CHRONIQUE MUSICALE" pp. 402–4.
30 July	"CHRONIQUE MUSICALE" pp. 71–73.
10 September	"CHRONIQUE MUSICALE" pp. 166–68.

8 October	"CHRONIQUE MUSICALE" pp. 223–24.

Journal des Débats

31 January	"REVUE MUSICALE DE L'ANNEE 1836" pp. 1–2. Signed "Hxxxxx."
5 March	"THEATRE DE L'OPERA. Première repré-sentation de *Stradella,* opéra en cinq actes, paroles de MM. Emile Deschamps et Emilien Paccini, musique de M. Niedermeyer, diver-tissemens de M. Coraly, décors de MM. Despléchin, Sechan [*sic*], Feuchères et Diéterle" pp. 1–2. Signed "Hxxxxx."
12 March	"SOIREES DE MM. LISZT, BATTA, ET URHAN. TRIOS ET SONATES DE BEETHO-VEN" p. 1. Signed "Hxxxxx."[31]
31 March	"THEATRE DE L'OPERA. Représentation au bénéfice de Levasseur" p. 1. Signed "Hxxxxx."
5 April	"THEATRE DE L'OPERA. *Représentation de retraite de Nourrit*" p. 1. Signed "Hxxxxx."
19 April	"THEATRE DE L'OPERA. *Guillaume Tell.*—Début de Duprez" p. 1. Signed "Hxxxxx."
17 May	"THEATRE DE L'OPERA—Débuts de Duprez dans *les Huguenots*" p. 1. Signed "Hxxxxx."
20 June	"DE QUELQUES ANCIENS COMPOSI-TEURS ITALIENS" pp. 1–2. [First article signed "H. BERLIOZ "for the *JD*.]

28 June

"THEATRE DE L'OPERA-COMIQUE. 1re représentation de *l'An Mil,* opéra-comique en un acte, paroles de MM. Paul Foucher et Mélesville, musique de M. Albert Grisar"
p. 1.

4 August

"PSAUMES DE BENEDETTO MARCELLO"
p. 1.

6 August

"THEATRE DE L'OPERA. Reprise de *la Juive.*—Duprez"
pp. 1–2.

13 August

"THEATRE DE L'OPERA-COMIQUE. Première représentation du *Remplaçant,* opéra-comique en trois actes, paroles de MM. Scribe et Bayard, musique de M. Batton"
p. 1.

27 August

"THEATRE DE L'OPERA. Début de Mme Stoltz dans *la Juive.* THEATRE DE L'OPERA-COMIQUE. Première représentation de *la Double-Echelle,* opéra-comique en un acte; paroles de M. Planard, musique de M. Ambroise Thomas"
p. 1.

10 September

"THEATRE DE L'OPERA-COMIQUE. Première représentation de *Guise ou les Etats de Blois,* opéra en trois actes, paroles de MM. Planard et de Saint-Georges, musique de M. Georges Onslow"
p. 1.

27 September

"THEATRE DE L'OPERA. Reprise de *la Muette de Portici.*—Duprez, Mlle Elssler, Mmes A. Dupont et Noblet. THEATRE DE L'OPERA-COMIQUE. Première représentation du *Bon Garçon;* paroles de MM. Lockroy et Anicet Bourgeois, musique de M. E. Prévost"
pp. 1–2.

15 October

"LESUEUR" [Obituary]
pp. 1–2.

2 November	"THEATRE DE L'OPERA-COMIQUE. Première représentation de *Piquillo*, opéra en trois actes de M. Alexandre Dumas, musique de M. Monpou" p. 1.
10 November	"STRAUSS. SON ORCHESTRE, SES WALSES.—DE L'AVENIR DU RHYTHME" pp. 1–2.
10 December	"THEATRE DE L'OPERA-COMIQUE. Première représentation du *Domino noir*, paroles de M. Scribe, musique de M. Auber" "ENSEIGNEMENT MUSICAL.—CONCERTS" pp. 1–2.

Revue et Gazette Musicale

1 January	"DE L'IMITATION MUSICALE" pp. 9–11.
8 January	"DE L'IMITATION MUSICALE. (2e et dernier article)" pp. 15–17.
22 January	"PREMIER CONCERT DU CONSERVATOIRE" pp. 29–31.
5 February	"QUELQUES MOTS SUR LES ANCIENS COMPOSITEURS, ET SUR GRETRY EN PARTICULIER" pp. 45–46.
5 February	"PREMIERE SOIREE MUSICALE DE MM. LISZT, BATTA ET URHAN. DEUXIEME CONCERT DU CONSERVATOIRE" pp. 50–51.
19 February	"A M. B. [*sic*] SCHUMANN, DE LEIPSICK [*sic*]" pp. 61–63.
19 February	"CONCERTS. (Troisième Soirée de MM. Liszt, Urhan, et Batta)" pp. 63–64.

26 February	"CONCERT DU CONSERVATOIRE" pp. 71–72.[32]
26 February	"*Rebecca,* paroles de M. E. Paccini, musique de Henri Panofka" p. 74.
12 March	"CONCERTS DU CONSERVATOIRE" pp. 88–89.
19 March	"REVUE DE LA QUINZAINE" pp. 95–96.
26 March	"CONCERT DU CONSERVATOIRE" pp. 101–3.
1 April	"JEAN-BAPTISTE BUONONCICI [*sic*]" pp. 114–15. [Signed "B," attrib. to Berlioz in index.]
9 April	"CONCERTS DU CONSERVATOIRE" pp. 121–23.[33]
23 April	"SEPTIEME CONCERT DU CONSERVATOIRE. Symphonie pastorale—Motet de Haydn.—Concerto de violon par M. Lafont.—Grande scène d'*Alceste*.—Ouverture de *Feychütz* [*sic*]" pp. 145–47.
30 April	"DERNIER CONCERT DU CONSERVATOIRE" p. 152.
21 May	"THEATRE DE L'OPERA. Début de Duprez dans les *Huguenots*" pp. 175–76.
11 June	"REVUE CRITIQUE. De l'art dans les provinces.—M. Ferdinand LAVAINE" pp. 203–6.
25 June	"ESQUISSES BIOGRAPHIQUES" pp. 219–21.
2 July	"REVUE CRITIQUE. DERNIERES PENSEES MUSICALES DE MARIE FELICITE GARCIA DE BENIOT [*sic*]" pp. 228–29. Signed "H. B. . . . .z."

6 August	"ACADEMIE ROYALE DE MUSIQUE. Reprise de la *Juive* (D'HALEVY)" p. 369.
20 August	"LES CONCERTS DES TUILERIES SOUS L'EMPIRE. SUSCEPTIBILITE SINGULIERE DE NAPOLEON; SA SAGACITE MUSICALE" pp. 379–80.[34]
27 August	"THEATRE DE L'OPERA-COMIQUE. PREMIERE REPRESENTATION DE *LA DOUBLE ECHELLE*, Opéra comique en un acte; paroles de M. PLANARD, musique de M. Ambroise THOMAS" pp. 389–90.
27 August	"NOTICE NECROLOGIQUE. CHARLES EBNER" p. 392. [Signed "H. B.," identified as by Berlioz in index.]
3 September	"REVUE CRITIQUE. MESSE A TROIS VOIX EGALES, DE M. MASSIMINO" pp. 400–401.
10 September	"DE LA MUSIQUE EN GENERAL" pp. 405–9.[35]
17 September	"THEATRE DE L'OPERA-COMIQUE. PREMIERE REPRESENTATION DE *GUISE, OU LES ETATS DE BLOIS*, Opéra en trois actes et en cinq tableaux, paroles de MM. PLANARD et DE SAINT-GEORGES, musique de M. ONSLOW" pp. 414–15.
17 September	"REVUE CRITIQUE. M. PRINTEMPS." pp. 415–16.
1 October	"LE PREMIER OPERA. NOUVELLE. Florence, 27 juillet 1555. ALFONSO DELLA VIOLA A BENVENUTO CELLINI" pp. 427–31.[36]

1 October

"ACADEMIE ROYALE DE MUSIQUE. RE-PRISE DE LA MUETTE DE PORTICI"
pp. 431–32.

8 October

"LE PREMIER OPERA. NOUVELLE. (Suite et fin.) BENVENUTO CELLINI A ALFONSO DELLA VIOLA. Paris, 10 juin 1557"
pp. 435–37.[37]

15 October

"NECROLOGIE.   JEAN-FRANCOIS LESUEUR"
pp. 443–45.[38]

22 October

"ACADEMIE ROYALE DE MUSIQUE. Première représentation de la *CHATTE META-MORPHOSEE EN FEMME*, Ballet en trois actes, De MM. CHARLES DUVEYRIER et CORALY, musique de M. MONTFORT"
pp. 459–60.

29 October

"CONCERTS DE LA RUE SAINT-HONORE, DIRIGES PAR M. VALENTINO"
pp. 470–71.

5 November

"THEATRE DE L'OPERA-COMIQUE. Première représentation de *PIQUILLO*, Opéra-comique en trois actes de M. ALEXANDRE DUMAS, musique de M. H. MONPOU"
pp. 478–79.

5 November

"GYMNASE MUSICAL, SOIREE DE VALSES DE STRAUSS"
pp. 479–80.

10 December

"THEATRE DE L'OPERA-COMIQUE. Première représentation du *DOMINO NOIR*, Opéra-Comique en trois actes, de MM. SCRIBE et AUBER"
pp. 541–43.

Notes

Preface

1. London: Fontana Paperback, 1985. Also published as *Contemplating Musicology: Challenges to Musicology* (Cambridge, Mass.: Harvard University Press, 1985).

2. Carl Dahlhaus, *Esthetics of Music,* trans. William W. Austin (Cambridge: Cambridge University Press, 1982), 99.

3. Dahlhaus, *Esthetics,* 100.

4. Dahlhaus, *Esthetics,* 99.

5. "Attribution of Some Unsigned Articles of Berlioz in the *Revue et Gazette Musicale de Paris (1834–1837),*" *Musicology Australia* 8 (1985): 39–49 (see ch. 5 and app. B) and "La Critique musicale dans les grands quotidiens parisiens de 1830–1839," *Revue Internationale de Musique Française,* no. 17 (June 1985): 19–28 (see appendix C).

Introduction

1. *Berlioz and the Romantic Century,* 2 vols. (New York: Columbia University Press, 1969). *NBE* is published by Bärenreiter-Verlag. Four volumes of the *Correspondance générale* have so far appeared; first volume (1972) and third volume (1978) ed. Pierre Citron, second volume (1975) ed. Frédéric Robert, and fourth volume (1983) ed. Pierre Citron, Yves Gérard, and Hugh Macdonald. All are published in Paris by Flammarion.

2. *Les Soirées de l'orchestre,* ed. Léon Guichard (1852; Paris: Gründ, 1968); *Les Grotesques de la musique,* ed. Léon Guichard (1859; Paris: Gründ, 1969); and *A travers chants,* ed. Léon Guichard (1862; Paris: Gründ, 1971).

3. *Festival Berlioz: Berlioz, biographie et autobiographie: Actes du colloque 1980* ([Lyons]: n.p., [1981]).

4. Peter A. Bloom, ed., *Music in Paris in the 1830s: La Musique à Paris dans les années 1830,* La Vie musicale en France au xixe siècle: Etudes et documents, vol. 9 (New York: Pendragon Press, 1987).

5. Katherine Kolb Reeve, "Hector Berlioz," in *European Writers,* vol. 6 (New York: Scribners, 1985).

6. H. Robert Cohen, *Berlioz on the Opera (1829–1849): A Study in Music Criticism* (Ann Arbor, Mich.: University Microfilms, 1973). Katherine Kolb Reeve, *The Poetics of the Orchestra in the Writings of Hector Berlioz* (Ann Arbor, Mich.: University Microfilms, 1978).

7. Dorothy Veinus Hagan, *French Musical Criticism between the Revolutions (1830–1848)* (Ann Arbor, Mich.: University Microfilms, 1965). See also her *Félicien David 1810–1876: A*

Composer and a Cause (Syracuse: Syracuse University Press, 1985). Peter A. Bloom, *François-Joseph Fétis and the "Revue Musicale" (1827–1835)* (Ann Arbor, Mich.: University Microfilms, 1972).

Dorothy Hagan's dissertation studies both the music and the music criticism of the July Monarchy in terms of their reflection of the age. She portrays the artistic imagination of the day as preoccupied with plans for social progress and utopian dreams, and the contemporary music criticism as a product of that imagination. A more recent dissertation dealing with music of this period and the influence of Saint-Simon is Ralph P. Locke's *Music and the Saint-Simonians: The Involvement of Félicien David and Other Musicians in a Utopian Socialist Movement* (Ann Arbor Mich.: University Microfilms, 1980). This is now revised as a book, *Music, Musicians and the Saint-Simonians* (Chicago: University of Chicago Press, 1986).

Peter A. Bloom's dissertation on Fétis is an essential guide when approaching the beginnings of serious musical criticism in Paris in the nineteenth century.

8. Gérard Condé, ed., *Hector Berlioz: Cauchemars et passions* (Paris: J.-C. Lattès, 1981), preface, 27. "Que faire si Berlioz commet une erreur de date (à condition, bien entendu, qu'il n'en tire aucune conclusion) . . . rectifier, comme l'auteur l'aurait fait lui-même?"

9. H. Robert Cohen, et al., ed., *La Critique musicale d'Hector Berlioz*, La Vie musicale en France au xixe siècle, vol. 6 (New York: Pendragon Press, forthcoming). This publication will include a 10 volume text and 2 volume critical apparatus.

10. I have included my own bibliography of Berlioz's articles of 1823 to 1837 in app. D.

11. Namely Dorothy Hagan (see n. 7) and Jane F. Fulcher's article "Le Socialisme utopique et la critique musicale en France sous le Second Empire," *Revue Internationale de Musique Française*, no. 14 (June 1984): 63–68.

12. Irene Collins, ed., *Government and Society in France, 1814–1848* (Great Britain: Edward Arnold, 1970), introd., 2–4.

13. Collins, *Government and Society*, 1.

14. A list given in the newspaper *L'Echo du Soir* of 1826 gives the total number of people subscribing to newspapers as 63,100, of which 21,000 were subscribers to the opposition paper *Le Constitutionnel*. (Quoted in Charles Ledré, *La Presse à l'assault de la monarchie: 1815–1848*, Kiosque series [Paris: Colin, 1960], 242n).

15. Subscriptions for the year 1836 total 84,466 (Ledré, *La Presse*, 244).

16. Ledré, *La Presse*, 16.

17. Collins, *Government and Society*, 6.

18. *Music and the Middle Class* (London: Croom Helm, 1975), 48.

19. This is according to Marie d'Agoult's *Mémoires*, quoted in Catherine Join-Dieterle, "L'Opéra et son public à l'époque romantique," *L'Oeil*, nos. 288–89 (July 1979): 33n.

20. "The Muddle of the Middle Classes," *Nineteenth-Century Music* 3 (November 1979): 175–85.

21. Weber, "The Muddle of the Middle Classes," 185.

22. Jeffrey Cooper, *The Rise of Instrumental Music and Concert Series in Paris 1828–1871* (Ann Arbor, Mich.: UMI Research Press, 1983), 7.

23. See Jeffrey Cooper, *The Rise of Instrumental Music*, ch. 2.

24. Some of the popular composers of romances during the July Monarchy were Loïsa Puget, Hippolyte Monpou and Antoine-Louis Clapisson.

25. Frances Trollope, *Paris and the Parisians in 1835*, vol. 1 (Paris: Baudry's European Library, 1836), 56. Musard was a violinist, conductor, orchestral leader, and composer of light music, in particular quadrilles. He lead many of the popular concerts, both indoor and outdoor.

26. Joseph Marc Bailbé, *Le Roman et la musique en France sous la monarchie de juillet* (Paris: Lettres modernes, 1969).

27. *Emile Deschamps: Dilettante* (Paris: Champion, 1921), vii. "Le *dilettante*, depuis la Restauration jusqu'à la fin du second Empire, c'est l'homme du monde, amateur passionné de musique italienne."

28. "Beaux-Arts. Théâtre Allemand. Etat actuel de la musique. *Eurianthe*. Les Choeurs. Madame Schroeder-Devrient," *Le Globe*, 17 June 1831, 676. Article is unsigned.

29. This evolution of the term corresponds well with its description in the Littré dictionary: "The lover of music, especially of Italian music, and by extension someone who is involved with something as an amateur" ("Amateur de musique, surtout de musique italienne. Par extension, celui qui s'occupe d'une chose en amateur.")

30. Edmond Hippeau remarks that the fanaticism of the dilettante was indeed very similar to the furious enthusiasms that Berlioz had for his idols Gluck and Beethoven. The difference lay in the manner in which Berlioz analyzed his emotions; he was interested in "dramatic truth instead of the art of singing" ("la vérité dramatique au lieu de l'art du chant"). Edmond Hippeau, *Berlioz et son temps* (Paris: P. Ollendorff, 1890), 50.

31. "Patterns in the Historiography of 19th-Century Music," *Acta Musicologica* 42 (1970): 77.

32. Cecilia Hopkins Porter, "The New Public and the Reordering of the Musical Establishment: The Lower Rhine Music Festivals, 1818–1867," *Nineteenth-Century Music* 3 (March 1980): 211–24.

33. "Celui qui trouve plaisir à quelque-chose." The *Trésor de la langue française* states that *dilettante* is an Italian word dating from the end of the fifteenth century or beginning of the sixteenth century, and was first used in France in 1740 by Ch. de Brosses in his *Lettres d'Italie*.

34. *RGM*, 8 May 1836, 151–52.

Chapter 1

1. François Henri Joseph Blaze (called Castil-Blaze) (1784–1857), French writer on music, librettist, and composer who contributed to many journals and newspapers including *JD*, *Revue de Paris*, *Le Constitutionnel*, *Le Ménestrel*, *RGM*, and *France Musicale*. He translated and adapted numerous operas such as *Le nozze di Figaro*, *Die Zauberflöte*, *Don Giovanni*, and *Il barbiere di Siviglia*. His books include *De l'Opéra en France* (1820) and a *Dictionnaire de musique moderne* (1821). An article by an "Equipe littérature-musique" from the Université de Paris 4 ("Les *Notes d'un dilettante* de Stendhal," *Revue de Musicologie* 67 [1983]: 187–208) argues that the first professional music criticism in Paris was the criticism written by Stendhal for the *Journal de Paris* (1824–26). Since Stendhal's criticism is almost exclusively of Italian opera, and by a professed dilettante at that, I would still maintain that Castil-Blaze was the first professional music critic. This is not to deny however that Stendhal's criticism is extremely interesting and deserves more recognition.

2. Some of his adaptations took the form of pastiches, for instance, *La Fausse Agnès*, *opéra-bouffon* en 3 actes, d'après Destouches, paroles ajustées sur la musique de Cimarosa, Rossini, Meyerbeer, Pucitta, Federici, etc., 1834. Léon Guichard quipped that "Choron servait la musique. Castil-Blaze s'en servit." Léon Guichard, *La Musique et les lettres au temps du romantisme* (Paris: Presses universitaires de France, 1955), 168.

3. Julien-Louis Geoffroy (1743–1814), French literary critic. In 1800 he took charge of the literary and drama feuilleton for the *JD*, changing the conception of the column in greatly broadening its scope. He was of classical orientation. His favorite genre was the *opéra-comique* of Grétry and he had little knowledge of music.

4. Pierre Duviquet (1766–1835), French writer and politician and, like Geoffroy, of strong classical orientation.

5. Quoted by Ernest Reyer, "La Critique musicale," in *Le Livre du centenaire du "Journal des Débats," 1789–1889* (Paris: Plon, 1889), 429. "Cette chronique sera exclusivement consacrée à la musique. Les opéras anciens et nouveaux y seront (uniquement sous le rapport musical) examinés, analysés avec soin et d'après les principes de la bonne école."

6. See for instance his article "Don Juan" (14 March 1821), in his *Chronique musicale du "Journal des Débats"* (Paris: Publ. by the author, 1830), 49–52. Despite its title the article discusses the literary music critic.

7. Castil-Blaze, "Concert spirituel. Retraite de juillet," *JD,* 30 April 1821, in Castil-Blaze, *Chronique musicale,* 67. "Dans le nouveau concerto de M. Viotti, les *tutti* en sont pleins de vigueur, le premier morceau est brillant, et de ce style large qui caractérise la manière de cet illustre violoniste. L'*adagio* est délicieux mais le rondeau n'a pas assez de noblesse."

8. François-Joseph Fétis (1784–1871), Belgian musicologist, critic, teacher, and composer. He was renowned for his *Biographie universelle des musiciens,* the most comprehensive biographical dictionary of its time. He had a special interest in early music, for example he ran *Concerts historiques* in Paris from 1832. In 1833 he was appointed head of the Conservatoire in Brussels. He wrote a large number of books, many pedagogically oriented, and helped to lay the basis for contemporary musicology and ethnomusicology.

9. Peter A. Bloom, *Fétis and the "Revue Musicale,"* 21. *Correspondance des amateurs musiciens* appeared in 167 numbers over the three-year period 1802–5. Both *Le Journal de Musique* (1770–77) and *L'Almanach Musical* (1775–83) had interruptions to their continuity.

10. Archives Nationales de Paris, AJ. 13, 218.

11. Free entries quickly became the music critic's prerogative. When, in 1854, a new director of the Opéra, Perrin, tried to withdraw the free entries, music critics declared a war of silence and refused to review the Opéra until their rights were restored. (Berlioz, letter of 1854, *CG* 4:575).

12. Quoted by Emile Faguet, "La Critique de 1820 à 1850," in *Histoire de la langue et de la littérature française,* ed. Petit de Julleville, vol. 7 (Paris: Armand Colin, 1899), 658. "Un petit cri de joie que nous arrache le spectacle du jour."

13. *Mém.* 2:169/435.

14. Ursula Eckart-Bäcker, *Frankreichs Musik zwischen Romantik und Moderne, die Zeit im Spiegel der Kritik* (Regensburg: G. Bosse Verlag, 1965), 17.

15. *La Mode* was a journal rather than a newspaper, but has been listed here because of its political leanings.

16. Jules Janin (1804–74), French literary critic and author. He wrote for *Figaro, La Quotidienne, Le Messager, JD, RGM,* and others; his feuilletons in the *JD* were more renowned for their spirit and verve than for their conviction and method. He was a very good friend to Berlioz. He wrote numerous books, the most interesting in relation to music being *Le Gâteau des rois* (1847) and *Les Symphonies d'hiver* (1857).

17. Quoted in Edmond Texier, *Histoire des journaux. Biographie des journalistes* (Paris: Pagnerre, 1850), 44. "Dit du mal de tout ce dont il avait dit du bien."

18. For instance, "P." [Sauvo] in *Le Moniteur Universel* and "J. T." [Jean-Toussaint Merle] in *La Quotidienne.* See app. C for reasons behind the identification of initials.

19. François Buloz (1804–77), French publicist and editor of journals. In 1831 he took over editorship of the *RDM* and in 1834 the *Revue de Paris.* He was gifted in detecting the budding talent of writers such as Musset and Sand.

20. "Lulli," parts 1 and 2, *Revue de Paris* 8 (August 1835): 73–98 and 145–69.

21. Louis Desnoyers (1802–68), French journalist and novelist. In 1829 and 1830 he founded various journals of a liberal tendency. In the 1830s he contributed to *La Caricature, Le Corsaire, Charivari,* and *Le National,* and in 1836 was put in charge of the literary feuilleton for *Le Siècle.* He published a book on the Opéra, *De l'Opéra en 1847* (1847), a collection of his *Le Siècle* articles.

22. *Bibliographie historique et critique de la presse périodique française* (Paris: Firmin-Didot, 1866), 368. "Déclara se 'vouer uniquement à la profession des vrais principes, au progrès des idées, au maintien de l'ordre et de la liberté, indépendamment des hommes et des partis qui triompheraient ou qui succomberaient. Recueillir des idées progressives, les mûrir, les développer, tels seraient sa tâche et l'esprit de sa polémique.'" *Le Temps* lasted from Oct. 1829 to June 1842 and was unrelated to the journal of the same name later in the century.

23. François-Adolphe Loève-Veimars (1801-54), French literary commentator. A fluent German speaker, he published numerous articles on German literature, for instance, his book *Résumé de l'histoire de la littérature allemande* (1826). He also translated Wieland and most importantly E. T. A. Hoffmann's *Contes fantastiques* and *Contes nocturnes* (1829–30). He wrote music criticism for *Le Temps* during the 1830s.

24. Adolphe Guéroult (1810-72), French politician, publicist, and journalist. An early sympathizer of Saint-Simon, he wrote literary and musical reviews for *Le Globe* and *Le Temps* during the 1830s. He was involved in founding several journals, including *La République* and *l'Opinion Nationale.*

25. *Le Temps,* 22 December 1834, 1–2.

26. "Revue. Chronique. Théâtres," *RDM,* 4th ser., 1 (1835): 595. "Que si vous nous trouvez sévères envers un homme de conscience et de talent, nous répondrons que devant la critique honnête et pure, il n'existe que les oeuvres bonnes ou méchantes, et que c'est son devoir de cultiver les unes, et de les émonder, afin qu'elles fleurissent au soleil, et d'arracher les autres sans pitié."

27. "Ch. L." [Delphine Girardin (Gay)] in an article "Société des concerts. Symphonies de Beethoven," 27 February 1834, 2. "Dieu me garde de me lancer dans l'analyse d'une symphonie à moins que je ne copie la *Revue musicale,* et que je ne dise après elle *que le retour dans le ton principal est préparé par un accord parfait sur* fa dièse, *dominant du ton de* si *naturel*: langage qui convient à merveille aux lecteurs spéciaux de la *Revue,* mais qui ne me va pas à moi, ignorant, qui ne va pas mieux à la majorité non spéciale des abonnés du *Temps.*"

Delphine Girardin—née Gay (1804–55), French poet, novelist and dramatist, who also worked as a journalist under the name of Vicomte de Launay.

28. Albert Tsugawa, *The Idea of Criticism,* Pennsylvania State University Studies, no. 2 (Pennsylvania: Pennsylvania State University, 1967), 11.

29. "Société des concerts du Conservatoire de musique," *L'Artiste* 7, no. 3 (1834): 26. The article is unsigned. "En effet, toutes les créations de Beethoven ne vous causent-elles pas et cette tristesse infinie et cette exaltation de l'ame [*sic*] qui éprouve le besoin de s'unir avec Dieu!"

30. "Société des concerts du Conservatoire de musique," *L'Artiste* 7, no. 1 (1834): 5. The article is unsigned. "Un public qui ne cherche pas à analyser après coup une ouverture ou une symphonie, qui comprend spontanément les pensées du compositeur."

31. Henri Blaze de Bury, [called Blaze de Bury] (1818–88), French literary figure, son of Castil-Blaze. He was music critic for the *RDM* and published numerous books among which were: *Musiciens contemporains* (1856), *Rossini et son temps* (1862), *Meyerbeer et son temps* (1865), and *Musiciens du passé, du présent et de l'avenir* (1880). In his early years he wrote under the name of Hans Werner and he also on occasion used his real name.

32. *De la littérature musicale en France* (Paris: Alfred Ikelmer, 1867), p. 29. "Dilettante passionné qui a pris la peine de réfléchir avant d'exprimer sa pensée." H. Robert Cohen categorizes Blaze de Bury as a "critic historian" (see "The Nineteenth-Century French Press," *Nineteenth-Century Music* 7 [Fall 1983]: 142) and perhaps he was to an extent; but he also wrote quite extensively on literature as well as music. He certainly could not be put in the same class as Fétis who was a true "critic historian."

33. Henri Blaze de Bury, *Musiciens contemporains* (Paris: Michel Lévy, 1856), x. "Juger c'est comprendre, comprendre c'est sentir."

34. Blaze de Bury, *Musiciens contemporains,* 32. "Ecoutez ces sons voilés des cors, cet exorde mystérieux si profondément empreint de cette vie mâle et forestière dont le tableau va se dérouler devant vous."

35. *History of Modern Criticism, 1750–1950,* 3:17. Gustave Planche (1808–57), French literary critic, who wrote on music and fine arts as well as literature. He wrote for *Le Globe* (1830–31), *RDM,* and *L'Artiste.* He was called the "adversaire des romantiques," whose works he judged severely, making enemies of such men as Victor Hugo. He remained friendly with Sand, de Vigny, and Balzac, for whom he relaxed his high critical standards. His most important book was *Etudes sur les arts* (1855).

36. "Du rôle de la critique," *L'Artiste* 10, no. 15 (1835): 166–68.

37. Catherine Portevin, "Le Langage de la critique musicale," *Revue Internationale de Musique Française,* no. 17 (June 1985): 102.

38. This is discussed in ch. 5.

39. See, in particular, Desnoyers's article, "Théâtre Italien. Récapitulation des premiers travaux de la saison. Considérations sur la critique musicale actuelle," *Le National,* 7 November 1834, 1–3, and d'Ortigue's "De la critique musicale. Dans ses rapports avec l'état actuel de l'art," *RGM,* 18 September 1836, 326–28, and 25 September 1836, 338–41.

40. Joseph Mainzer (1801–51), German music critic, teacher, and musician. He went into political exile in Paris in late 1833, where he worked as a critic and gave free singing classes for workers. The classes were stopped in 1839 and Mainzer left Paris and went to England where he continued his activities and founded *Mainzer's Musical Times* (which became the

present-day *Musical Times*). He worked as a journalist in Paris for a large number of papers, mainly the *RGM, Le Réformateur,* and *Le National* and published several books and many choruses designed for teaching purposes.

41. Desnoyers, "Considérations sur la critique musicale," *Le National,* 7 November 1834, 2. "Rien n'égale la beauté du spectacle, . . . le finale produit un effet impossible à décrire . . . [et] la mise en scène est d'une magnificence qui fait l'éloge de l'habile directeur."

42. Joseph d'Ortigue (1802–66), French writer on music, with a strong interest in religious and church music. He wrote for over twenty journals, also editing *Le Ménestrel* in 1863, and he took over from Berlioz on the *JD* (1864). His major books include: *De la guerre des dilettanti* (1829), *Le Balcon de l'Opéra* (1833), *Dictionnaire liturgique, historique et théorique de plain-chant et de musique de l'église* (1853).

43. Félicité de Lamennais (1782–1854), French priest and author. He began as a Royalist but changed after 1830 when he saw that injustices continued. In 1830 he founded a journal called *L'Avenir* in favor of separation of church and state, freedom of the press, and education. For the rest of his life he fought for humanitarian ideals and issues such as universal suffrage, with which he felt the church should be actively involved. His book, *Paroles d'un croyant* (1833), influenced artists such as Hugo, George Sand, Lamartine, and Vigny.

44. Hagan, *French Musical Criticism,* 18.

45. Hagan, *French Musical Criticism,* 19–20.

46. Discussed in d'Ortigue's articles for the *RGM,* "De la critique musicale."

47. Honoré de Balzac, *Le Chef-d'oeuvre inconnu. Gambara. Massimilla Doni,* introd. and notes Marc Eigeldinger and Max Milner (Paris: Flammarion, 1981), 92. "En ouvrant la *Symphonie en ut mineur* de Beethoven, un homme de musique est bientôt transporté dans le monde de la Fantaisie sur les ailes d'or du thème en sol naturel, répété en mi par les cors. Il voit toute une nature tour à tour éclairée par éblouissantes gerbes de lumières, assombrie par des nuages de mélancolie, égayée par des chants divins."

48. Henri Blaze de Bury, *Meyerbeer et son temps* (Paris: Michel Lévy, 1856), 4.

49. Joseph d'Ortigue, *Le Balcon de l'Opéra* (Paris: E. Renduel, 1833), vii.

50. Dahlhaus, *Esthetics of Music,* 27.

51. D'Ortigue, *Le Balcon,* vi. "La musique instrumentale réunit les diverses inspirations qui ont présidé aux différentes périodes de l'art, l'inspiration religieuse, l'inspiration dramatique, l'inspiration lyrique; elle absorbe à la fois la musique sacrée et la musique d'opéra; elle résume les traditions, s'élance dans les âges; elle mêle l'art catholique à l'art d'émancipation, la foi à la science; elle est sociale et individuelle; elle est tour à tour méditative, contemplative, mystique, sublime, pittoresque et colorée, passionnée et dévergondée."

52. D'Ortigue, *Le Balcon,* vii.

53. D'Ortigue, *Le Balcon,* 10.

54. Louis Desnoyers, *De l'Opéra en 1847* (Paris: E.-B. Delanchy, 1847).

55. Bailbé, *Le Roman et la musique,* 33. "De l'Opéra aux Italiens, on a l'impression d'avoir franchi un échelon dans le domaine de la pénétration et de l'intelligence musicale."

56. Peter A. Bloom, *Fétis and the "Revue Musicale,"* 239. Later in his life Berlioz attempted a reconciliation with Fétis. This is demonstrated by a letter Berlioz wrote to Fétis in 1860,

published by Ralph P. Locke in "New Letters of Berlioz," *Nineteenth-Century Music* 1 (July 1977): 71–84.

57. *De l'Opéra,* 53n. "Entre autres découvertes instrumentales, M. Berlioz a inventé ainsi un heureux instrument de rhétorique, qu'on peut appeler le calembour à jet continu."

58. Joseph Mainzer, "M. Berlioz," *Chronique Musicale de Paris,* No. 1 (1838): 1–95.

59. Bloom, *Fétis and the "Revue Musicale,"* 55.

60. Letter of 1837, *CG* 2:384. "Je redoute un article [sur le *Requiem*] dans *le National* de cet ours mal léché de Mainzer, parce que je n'ai pas employé ses choeurs d'ouvriers; il en a été très vexé, et il ne manquera pas de s'en venger." Mainzer states in his *Chronique* that Berlioz had requested his choirs and then not used them at the last moment.

61. Mentioned in d'Ortigue's book, *La Musique à l'église* (Paris: Didier, 1861): 244–53.

62. The article, "Galerie biographique, des artistes françaises et étrangers. 5. Hector Berlioz," *Revue de Paris,* 23 December 1832, 281-98, comes from the Berlioz autograph (Bibliothèque Nationale, *papiers divers,* no. 38). Over half the article is taken up by the direct transcription of this autograph.

63. D'Ortigue, *Le Balcon* (opinion on the Mozart *Requiem*), 55–57 (opinion on *Fidelio*), 214–22.

64. D'Ortigue, *Le Balcon,* p. 140. "Voilà ce qui a été dit, et bien dit."

65. For further information on d'Ortigue see Sylvia l'Ecuyer Lacroix, ed., *Joseph d'Ortigue: Ecrits sur la musique et les musiciens de son temps (1830–1866),* La Vie musicale en France au xixᵉ siècle, vol. 8 (New York: Pendragon Press, forthcoming) and Conrad Donakowski, *A Muse for the Masses* (Chicago: University of Chicago Press, 1972).

66. H. Robert Cohen, "The Nineteenth-Century French Press," *Nineteenth-Century Music* 7 (Fall 1983): 142. See n.32 above.

Chapter 2

1. Hagan, *French Musical Criticism* and Fulcher, "Le Socialisme utopique."

2. Ernest Renan, quoted in David O. Evans, *Social Romanticism in France 1830–1848* (Oxford: Oxford University Press, 1951): 52.

3. Quoted by Roger Fayolle, "Criticism and Theory," in *The French Romantics,* ed. D. G. Charlton, vol. 2 (Cambridge: Cambridge University Press, 1984): 264. "Peuple et poètes vont marcher ensemble. . . . L'art est désormais sur le pied commun, dans l'arène avec tous, côte à côte avec l'infatigable [*sic*] humanité."

4. See Louis Chevalier, *Classes laborieuses et classes dangereuses à Paris pendant la première moitié du xixᵉ siècle* (Paris: Librairie Plon, 1958).

5. An interesting discussion of this point can be found in Jane F. Fulcher, "Music and the Communal Order: The Vision of Utopian Socialism in France," *Current Musicology,* no. 27 (1979): 28.

6. In 1828 the movement had been tranformed into a "Church" ("Eglise") with two "supreme fathers" ("pères suprêmes"), Bazard and Enfantin.

7. *Aux artistes: Du passé et de l'avenir des beaux-arts. (Doctrine de Saint-Simon)* (Paris: A. Mesnier, 1830).

8. Barrault, *Aux artistes*, 84. "Les beaux-arts sont le culte, et l'artiste est le prêtre."

9. Barthélemy Prosper Enfantin (1796–1864), called "le père Enfantin," became the new leader of the Saint-Simonian movement after the death of Saint-Simon. He founded *Le Producteur* and created a model commune at Ménilmontant. From 1831 onward he turned to mysticism and lost many of his followers. He spent some time in Egypt where he had the idea of building a canal at Suez. He ended up as administrator of a railway company, the Lyons line.

10. Quoted in Bénichou, 292. "L'homme qui ramène toujours les autres à l'unité sociale. La sympathie sociale, en d'autres termes, l'*Amour* de Dieu, lui dicte seul ses actes et ses paroles." Bénichou felt that Enfantin's concept of the artist was more applicable to Enfantin himself than to people such as Delacroix or Hugo (p. 293).

11. Marguerite Thibert, *Le Rôle social de l'art d'après les Saint-Simoniens* (Paris: M. Rivière, 1926), 12–13.

12. Barrault defines poetry for example as the secret soul (*l'âme secrète*) of the arts, 15.

13. Barrault, 79. "Et nous aussi, nous sommes artistes!"

14. Barrault, 84. "Viennent, viennent donc à nous tous ceux dont le coeur sait aimer, et le front s'enflammer d'une noble espérance! associons nos efforts pour entraîner l'humanité vers cet avenir."

15. Préface, *Caliban, par deux ermites de Ménilmontant rentrés dans le monde* (Paris: 1833), xvii–xviii (quoted by Bénichou, 293, and 293n.88).

16. Locke, *Music, Musicians, and the Saint-Simonians*, 49–50.

17. Quoted in Locke, *Music, Musicians, and the Saint-Simonians*, 51.

18. Félicien David (1810–76), French composer and dedicated follower of Saint-Simon and Enfantin. He composed music for Enfantin's commune at Ménilmontant. His later sojourn in Turkey and Egypt influenced his music, including his most famous work, the *ode symphonie, Le Désert*.

19. Thérèse Marix-Spire, "Du piano à l'action sociale. Franz Liszt et George Sand, militante socialiste," *Renaissance Extrait*, 2 and 3, New York (1944–45): 187–216. Ralph P. Locke, "Liszt's Saint-Simonian Adventure," *Nineteenth-Century Music* 4 (Spring 1981): 209–27; ch. 9 of *Music, Musicians, and the Saint-Simonians*.

20. "De la situation des artistes et de leur condition dans la société," *GM*, 1835, rpt. in *Pages romantiques*, ed. Jean Chantavoine (Paris: Alcan, 1912), 1–83; "Lettres d'un bachelier ès-musique," *RGM*, 1837–40, rpt. in *Pages romantiques*, 97–288. The articles are controversial because they were thought for some time to be written by Marie d'Agoult. (See Emile Harazsti's article on Liszt, "Franz Liszt—Author Despite Himself: The History of a Mystification," *Musical Quarterly* 33 [1947]: 490–516.) It is now suggested that the *bachelier* articles were the result of an active collaboration by the two, Liszt's ideas expressed "in his companion's fluent prose" with passages of "pure d'Agoult" (see Locke's article on Liszt, 223). The discovery of the *Situation* articles' autographs has proved them to be by Liszt (see Edward N. Waters, "Sur la piste de Liszt," *Notes* 27 [1970–71]: 665–70).

21. "Liszt's Saint-Simonian Adventure," 211.

22. The Princess Carolyne Sayn-Wittgenstein also strongly influenced Liszt in his decision to abandon his virtuosic career.

23. Ralph P. Locke, "Liszt's Saint-Simonian Adventure," 226. An example of a benefit concert is a concert he gave with Nourrit for the workers at Lyons, 3 August 1837.

24. "Autour de la lettre à Duveyrier: Berlioz et les Saint-Simoniens," *Revue de Musicologie* 63 (1977): 55–77; and 64 (1978): 287.

25. Held at the Bibliothèque de l'Arsenal (*Fonds Enfantin*) in Paris.

26. *CG* 1:476–78. Charles Duveyrier (1803–66), French lawyer and writer, fervent Saint-Simonian and follower of Enfantin, collaborator for *Le Globe* in 1831 and 1832. This letter was thought to be the first reference to Berlioz's involvement with the Saint-Simonian movement. However, Ralph P. Locke has found one of Enfantin's letters showing that Berlioz was in fact in contact with the movement three months earlier ("Autour de la lettre à Duveyrier," *Revue de Musicologie* 64 [1978]: 287).

27. Dominique Tajan-Rogé (1803–78), French cellist and writer, spent many years in Russia, and was a dedicated Saint-Simonian. In replying to a letter from Rogé, in which Rogé had criticized Berlioz for his embarrassment over an affair with a working-class girl, Berlioz answered remorsefully, "One is so constantly surrounded by people of narrow and vulgar opinions that the idea never occurs to one that there are also a few straight and liberal spirits like your own" ("On est si constamment entouré de gens à opinions vulgaires et rétrécies, que l'idée ne se présente jamais qu'il y a aussi quelques rares esprits droits et libres comme le vôtre") (*CG* 3:498).

28. *Le Rén.*, 24 August 1834, 1. "L'*Adagio* en *la bémol* servant de repoussoir au *quadrille* de *la brise du matin!* Cela est indécent et ne peut exister que chez une nation aussi frivole que la nôtre, où la dignité de l'art et celle de l'artiste sont entièrement méconnues. Cette monstruosité ne peut paraître naturelle qu'à ces braves bourgeois qui *s'amusent* de tout et consentent volontiers à écouter un instant Beethoven dans les entr'actes du galop et de la valse parce qu'ils ont *entendu dire* que c'était un musicien allemand *très fort.*"

29. *Chronique de Paris*, 7 May 1837, 310. "C'est le temps moins que jamais de s'isoler, puisqu'il y a une oeuvre à faire, et que les éléments sont là."

30. Letter of 1839, *CG* 2:555. "Tout ce galimatias de théâtre, de théologie, de république et d'amour de la domination absolue dans l'art, me paraît prodigieusement absurde."

31. Letter of 1839, *CG* 2:555. "Cela touche cependant et agite beaucoup ceux qui ont connu intimement ce malheureux."

32. In Berlioz's correspondence of 1844 (*CG* 3) there is a letter from Berlioz to Emile Barrault (p. 208) and also a very friendly letter from Charles Duveyrier to Berlioz (pp. 209–10), both on the subject of Félicien David's work *Le Désert*, which Berlioz had praised in his feuilleton (*JD*, 15 December 1844). These letters show that Berlioz remained friendly with several prominent Saint-Simonians. Ralph P. Locke mentions in his article on Berlioz and Saint-Simonism (*Revue de Musicologie*, 1977) that Berlioz later (1855) retracted his opinion of *Le Désert*, calling it "enfantin" (p. 75).

33. Letter of 1830, *CG* 1:346. "Cette idée, que tant de braves gens ont payé de leur sang la conquête de nos libertés, pendant que je suis du nombre de ceux qui n'ont servi à rien, ne me laisse pas un instant de repos. C'est un supplice nouveau."

34. Letter of 1830, *CG* 1:358. "Heureusement, nous touchons à l'émancipation théâtrale; cette révolution est faite exprès pour la liberté des arts; je parviendrai dix fois plus tôt que je ne l'eusse fait sans elle."

35. Letter of 1834, *CG* 2:170. "Lamennais; le génie le sèche, le ronge, le brûle!! Quel diable d'homme! il m'a fait vibrer d'admiration."

36. *CG* 1:362.

37. Letter of 1832, *CG* 1:519.

38. Letter of 1833, *CG* 2:145. "Tu sais peut-être que je fais le feuilleton musical du *Rénovateur*, journal légitimiste. J'ai envie de te le faire envoyer. . . . Comme je me moque des opinions politiques, tu penses que la couleur du journal ne me fait absolument rien. Je ne touche jamais à ce qui est en dehors de mon domaine."

39. *CG* 1:510 n. 1.

40. Letter of 1848, *CG* 3:590. "Paris . . . [est] un *club* de fous et de drôles, hurlant, gesticulant, conspirant, écrivant, sans savoir ce qu'ils crient, ce qu'ils griffonnent, ce qu'ils menacent et ce qu'ils demandent."

41. Letter of 1848, *CG* 3:594. "Songer aux travaux paisibles de l'intelligence, à la recherche du beau dans la littérature et les arts, avec un pareil état de choses, c'est vouloir faire une partie de Billard sur un vaisseau battu par une tempête du Pôle antarctique, au moment où une voie d'eau s'est déclarée dans la cale et une insurrection de matelots dans l'entrepont."

42. *Le Producteur*, 1825–26, *L'Organisateur*, 1829–31, *Prédications* (basically information sheets).

43. *Le Globe*, founded 15 September 1824 by Dubois, was a doctrinaire liberal newspaper until the Saint-Simonians took it over.

44. "Théâtre Italien. Tancredi. Madame Raimbaux," 31 January 1832, 124, "Beaux-Arts. Théâtre Italien. Il Pirata, musique de Bellini," 7 February 1832, 151.

45. For example: "Beaux-Arts. Théâtre Royal Italien. Il Barbiere. M. Lablanche et Rubini; Madame Caradori," 7 October 1831, 1120, and "Théâtres. Théâtre Royal Italien. Bellini. La Sonnambula. Bénéfice de Madame Pasta," 1 November 1831, 1220.

46. See a discussion of this point in Locke, *Music, Musicians, and the Saint-Simonians*, 42.

47. "Concert pour les Polonais," 4 February 1831, 146.

48. "Concert pour les Polonais," 4 February 1831, 146. "Faire retrouver son coeur sous l'enveloppe glacée qui le serre et l'étouffe."

49. "Beaux-Arts. Jules Regondi, guitariste," 3 April 1831, 376.

50. "Beaux-Arts. Théâtre Allemand. *Oberon*," 26 May 1831, 587.

51. Cavel, "Politique. France. Les Evêques et l'opéra," 12 March 1832, 286.

52. "*Robert le diable*, grand opéra de M. Meyerbeer," *Le Globe*, 27 November 1831, 1325. Article is unsigned. "J'en étais là de mon récit, et je me laissais aller au goût et aux émotions de ce beau monde tout chargé de plumes, de fleurs et de pierreries, prenant plaisir à reproduire ainsi que je les ai senties les étranges beautés de ce grand drame où tous les prestiges des arts sont assemblés; mais voici qu'une nouvelle horrible a circulé. Les ouvriers de Lyon en plein révolte, le canon balayant les places et les rues; enfin le peuple tout mutilé et maître de la ville, faisant flotter sur les monuments publics cette devise d'un nouveau genre:

> Vivre en travaillant
> Ou mourir en combattant.

Je n'ai plus dans l'esprit ni Robert, ni mademoiselle Taglioni, ni les prodigieux décors de Ciceri. Le peuple hâve, amaigri, endolori; le peuple ignorant, maladif et grossier."

53. *Le Globe*, 27 November 1831, 1325. "O artistes! troupe brillante, exaltée; vous qui avez le génie de toutes les séductions et savez ravir les âmes affadies au spectacle de vos créations

merveilleuses; vous qui faites votre vie de charmer les ennuis et de multiplier les joies des heureux du siècle, ne vous unirez-vous jamais pour les attendrir, pour les enflammer de l'amour des masses souffrantes."

54. He also calls women to action to support the workers, saying that they too suffer the subordinate role of the proletariat; he is obviously influenced by Enfantin's ideas on sexual equality.

55. "Théâtres. Académie Royale de Musique. *Robert le diable,* opéra; musique de M. Meyer-Beer (2d article)," 3 December 1831, 1348. "Cet opéra nous prouve que la musique, la danse, la peinture appliquée à la scène; que tous les arts, en un mot, donc l'Académie royale est le foyer, se perfectionnent chaque jour, même dans la sphère étroite et glacée où l'absence complète d'inspiration sociale les emprisonne."

56. "Beaux-Arts. Paganini," *Le Globe,* 29 April 1831, 482. Article is unsigned. "Voici venir des chefs des nations, hommes puissants par le coeur, la tête et les bras, qui vous classeront selon votre capacité, vous aimeront en pères, vous combleront d'inspirations sociales, vous commanderont la gloire! Voyez autour de vous se grouper en choeur ces artistes nombreux pour prendre délicieusement avec vous, à la voix des pontifes de l'avenir, excitant les peuples à leur oeuvre pacifique, oeuvre créatrice de science et d'industrie."

57. Locke, *Music, Musicians, and the Saint-Simonians,* 60.

58. "Beaux-Arts. Théâtre Italien. Tancrède," *Le Globe,* 26 September 1831, 1075. Article is unsigned. "Est-ce ma faute si, à propos de *Tancrède,* au souvenir de cette charmante composition toute pleine de fraîcheur, de tendresse, d'exaltation chevaleresque, d'aussi sombres pensées me reviennent? Est-ce ma faute si je trouble par les cris de ceux qui meurent de faim, qui tombent pétrifiés, raides de froid, la béatitude de ceux qui se pâment d'enthousiasme aux accents harmonieux d'une musique qui n'est pas l'expression pathétique d'aussi déplorables misères?"

59. "Oh! combien je l'aime ce *Tancrède.*"

60. "Beaux-Arts. Théâtre Italien. Tancrède," 1075. "J'ai presque honte de céder au plaisir de me laisser bercer par ces délicieux accords."

61. Locke, *Music, Musicians, and the Saint-Simonians,* 58.

62. Locke, *Music, Musicians, and the Saint-Simonians,* 61.

63. "Beaux-Arts. Théâtre Allemand. Madame Rosner. *Fidelio,*" 20 May 1831, 566.

64. "Beaux-Arts. Théâtre Allemand. Etat actuel de la musique. *Eurianthe.* Les Choeurs. Madame Schroeder-Devrient," 17 June 1831, 676.

65. "Concert donné par M. F. Hiller," 7 December 1831, 1364. Ferdinand Hiller (1811–85), German pianist, composer, and conductor. He lived in Paris from 1828 for almost seven years and was a close friend of Berlioz's during this time.

66. Locke, *Music, Musicians, and the Saint-Simonians,* 106.

67. "C. N.," "Beaux-Arts. Société des concerts. Cinquième année," 12 February 1832, 172.

68. See Ch. Dufort, "Concerts du Conservatoire. Concert historique," *Revue Encyclopédique,* no. 54 (1832): 246.

69. Hippolyte Fortoul, "Bulletin dramatique," *Revue Encyclopédique,* no. 58 (1833): 589. "Cette idéaliste et intime partition de *Robert le diable,* il [le prolétaire] l'a aussi vraiment comprise et

aussi nettement jugée que les dilettanti. Conviez-le souvent à de semblables émotions, il rentrera chez lui plus grave, plus heureux, plus penseur, et plus moral."

70. Blaze de Bury, "Revue musicale," *RDM*, 1st. ser., 40 (1840): 603–4. Quoted (in translation) in Hagan, *French Musical Criticism*, 238.

71. Preface, *Mademoiselle de Maupin* (Paris: Bibliothèque-Charpentier, 1927), 18–19. "A quoi sert ce livre? Comment peut-on l'appliquer à la moralisation et au bien-être de la classe la plus nombreuse et la plus pauvre? Quoi! pas un mot des besoins de la société, rien de civilisant et de progressif! . . . La société souffre, elle est en proie à un grand déchirement intérieur (traduisez: personne ne veut s'abonner aux journaux utiles). C'est au poëte à chercher la cause de ce malaise et à le guérir. Le moyen, il le trouvera en sympathisant de coeur et d'âme avec l'humanité (des poëtes philanthropes! ce serait quelque chose de rare et de charmant)."

72. On the other hand, one must also remember Lamennais's influence on d'Ortigue.

73. Charles Merruau, "Musique. Cours gratuits de M. Mainzer. Choeurs d'ouvriers," *Le Temps*, 29 June 1837. "Le plus grand développement de l'intelligence, et qui touche aux arts par quelque endroit."

74. "Revue musicale de l'année 1836," *Le Monde*, 8 January 1837, 2. "Pendant que le monde élégant se presse chaque soir dans les salles resplandissantes de nos théâtres lyriques, au fond d'un faubourg, à la lueur de quelques quinquets appendus à quatre murailles nues, se rassemblent une fois la semaine, des hommes grossièrement vêtus, aux bras nerveux, à l'oeil intelligent, écoutant avec une soumission d'enfant les enseignemens d'un professeur qui se consacre avec dévouement à une noble et sainte tâche: celle de l'éducation musicale du peuple."

75. "M. Panofka. La Langue musicale. Cours d'ouvriers," *Le National*, 30 November 1837, 2.

76. Locke, *Music, Musicians, and the Saint-Simonians*, 16.

77. "Concerts Saint-Honoré," *Le National*, 21 November 1839, 1. "Sans musique vocale, tout répertoire est empreint de monotonie. . . . La musique instrumentale, si elle n'a pas la poésie pour appui, est vague, peu compréhensible. . . . [L]a musique instrumentale n'occupe que le second plan dans la domaine musicale."

78. Concerts of the Institution des Jeunes Aveugles were put on by students, graduates, and faculty of the Institution. There were thirty members in the orchestra in 1836, their concerts were irregular and the first known performance was 27 April 1836. (See Cooper, *The Rise of Instrumental Music*, 246.)

79. *Le National*, 29 April 1837, 1–3; 7 July 1837, 1–3; 23 September 1837, 1–2; *Revue et Gazette Musicale*, 19 June 1836, 206–9; 26 June 1836, 220–23.

80. *Le National*, 29 April 1837.

81. See David O. Evans, *Social Romanticism in France*, 76. For a discussion of the connections between social romanticism and utopian socialism see H. J. Hunt *Le Socialisme et le romantisme en France* (Oxford: Oxford University Press, 1935).

Chapter 3

1. *Le Corsaire*, 12 August 1823; 11 January 1824; and 19 December 1825.

2. Letter of 1824, *CG* 1:56.

3. Letter of 1824, *CG* 1:67 n. 3.

4. *Revue Musicale,* 16 May 1828, 405–6, *Le Figaro,* 21 May 1828, 3, and *Le Corsaire,* 22 May 1828, 3.

5. Letter of 1829, *CG* 1:254–58.

6. Letter of 1829, *CG* 1:253.

7. Mentioned in Berlioz, *Mém.* 1:167. All English translations of the *Mémoires* cited hereafter are by David Cairns (Cairns, *The Memoirs of Hector Berlioz* (1969; rpt, London: Panther Books, 1974)), and I shall give only their page numbers, separated from the French *Mém.* page number by a slash, "/."

8. Berlioz mentions this analysis in letter of 1829, *CG* 1:288–89.

9. Letter of 1828, *CG* 1:220.

10. The interview is mentioned in *CG* 1:234.

11. Letter of 1829, *CG* 1:253. "L'éditeur m'a fait prier par deux de ses rédacteurs de me charger des articles de musique, traité en grand [*sic*]. . . . Ces messieurs m'en ont fait beaucoup de compliments, ils m'écrivent toutes les semaines pour me demander le second article que je leur ai promis et que je fais attendre depuis longtemps. "Some distortion is perpetuated in the *Mém.* 1, ch. 21, also, where Berlioz states that the initiative to approach Carné came from Ferrand and not himself. As David Cairns states: "This does not . . . preclude Ferrand's having previously suggested that Berlioz should try his hand at criticism "(*Memoirs,* app. 3, 733).

12. Letter of 1829, *CG* 1:233 n. 3.

13. Letter of 1828, *CG* 1:221. "Les arts y occuperont une place distinguée."

14. Letter of 1829, *CG* 1:257. "La Prostituée trouve donc des amants même parmi les gens religieux."

15. Letter of 1829, *CG* 1:244.

16. Letter of 1830, *CG* 1:313. "Cette *faculté* de *souffrir* qui me tue."

17. Letter of 1830, *CG* 1:311. "Il y a en moi une *force d'expansion* qui agit violemment, je vois tout cet horizon, ce soleil, et je souffre tant, tant, que si je ne me contenais, je pousserais des cris, je me roulerais par terre. Je n'ai trouvé qu'un moyen de satisfaire complètement cette *avidité immense d'émotion,* c'est la musique."

18. *Le Correspondant,* 22 October 1830, 110-12.

19. The letter on classicism and romanticism, quoted in the *Revue Musicale,* 5A, no. 21 (November 1905): 531, is thought to be a fake.

20. Letter of 1831, *CG* 1:501. "Je reçois à l'instant une aimable lettre de *De Carné,* l'un des fondateurs du *Correspondant* et pour les talents duquel mon père professe beaucoup d'admiration; il m'écrit pour me demander quelque griffonage sur l'état actuel de la musique en Italie."

21. Mentioned in letter of 1843, *CG* 3:120.

22. At one stage in 1828 Berlioz was interested in writing a ballet on *Faust* based on a scenario by Bohain (letter of 1828, *CG* 1:217).

23. His very first article for the *JD,* "Rubini à Calais," 10 October 1834, 1, was only a reprint of an article from the *GM,* 5 October 1834, 317–19.

24. Books reviewed were for instance *Traité de composition de Beethoven* (27 January 1834, 1) and *Cours de contrepoint et fugue* by Cherubini (21 September 1835, 1–2).

25. The Théâtre Ventadour was also known as the Théâtre Nautique.

26. Letter of 1835, *CG* 2:229. "Je conserve toujours le *Rénovateur,* où je ne contrains qu'à demi ma mauvaise humeur sur toutes ces gentillesses."

27. For instance his article of 5 October 1835, 1. Reproduced in Gérard Condé, ed., *Hector Berlioz: Cauchemars et passions,* 37–39.

28. Henceforth, wherever reference is made to the *Revue et Gazette Musicale* in a general statement such as this one, reference is also being made to the *Gazette Musicale,* since the journal changed its name only in November 1835, and not its approach or contents.

29. *RGM,* 23 July to 20 August 1837.

30. "Le Suicide," *GM,* 20 July; 27 July; and 3 and 10 August 1834. "Un Bénéficiaire," *GM,* 5 October 1834.

31. Henri Blanchard (1791–1858), French violinist, dramatist, composer, and critic. From 1818 to 1829 he was conductor of the Théâtre des Variétés orchestra. He was a contributory editor of the *RGM* from 1836 until his death. He sometimes wrote under the alias of J. J. J. Diaz.

32. *Guillaume Tell* and *Le Barbier de Seville,* in particular the latter, were the two Rossini operas that Berlioz did appreciate.

33. The première of *Robert le diable* took place in 1831 when Berlioz was still in Rome.

34. A letter of 1836 to Bottée de Toulmon, the Conservatoire librarian, requests information on this subject: "I have been asked to provide some biographies of *Italian musicians* for a journal" ("On m'a fait promettre pour un journal des biographies de *Musiciens Italiens*") (letter of 1836, *CG* 2:313).

35. Letter of 1835, *CG* 2:232.

36. Berlioz had also been entrusted with the editorship of the paper in August of 1836 when Schlesinger went on a cure (*CG* 2:308). Schlesinger retook control at various stages in 1837, though Berlioz remained the chief editor for most of the year.

37. Louis-François Bertin, called "Bertin l'aîné" (1766–1841), took acquisition of the *JD* in 1800, and ran the paper in conjunction with his brother, Louis-François Bertin de Veaux (1771–1842), and son Armand (1801–54), who took over on his father's death in 1841. Another son, François-Edouard (1797–1871), took over on the death of Armand in 1854—very much a family-run affair.

38. Collins, *The Government and the Newspaper Press in France, 1814–1888* (London: Oxford University Press, 1959), 13.

39. See n. 23 above.

40. See *Mém.* 2, ch. 37, 18/287. Etienne Jean Delécluze (1781–1863). Delécluze was still in charge of reviews of the Théâtre Italien in 1851 when Berlioz wrote in a letter, "Since time immemorial, M. Delécluze has been in charge of recording . . . [its] ups and downs" ("C'est M. Delécluze qui depuis un temps immémorial est chargé d'en enregistrer . . . [ses] heureuses ou malheureuses péripéties") (letter of 1851, *CG* 4:48).

41. Letter of 1837, *CG* 2:333.

42. Letter of 1835, *CG* 2:232.

43. Letter of 1843, *CG* 3:120–21.

44. Letter of 1835, *CG* 2:229. "C'est une affaire importante pour moi; l'effet qu'ils produisent dans le monde musical est vraiment singulier; c'est presque un événement pour les artistes de Paris."

45. *VM* 2:414. "Et quel article tu vas me faire là-dessus dans le *Journal des Débats*! C'est une bonne fortune pour toi; ne va pas gaspiller un pareil sujet dans la *Gazette musicale*: non, un grand journal, dix-huit mille abonnés, voilà ton affaire." When Berlioz resigned from the *JD* in 1864, he commented in a letter, "It is so comical to see the disappointment and anger of those people who have been courting me for the past three months" ("Rien de plus comique que le désappointement et la colère des gens qui, depuis trois mois, me faisaient la cour") (*Corr. inéd.*, 306).

46. *Les Symphonies de l'hiver* (Paris: Morizot, 1858), 265. "Il nous avait choisis, il nous avait divinés, il nous avait encouragés, il nous avait adoptés, il nous avait fait libres, riches, honorés, indépendants de toutes les variations de la politique, et de tous les changements de la fortune."

47. His son Armand Bertin was Berlioz's chief friend and champion.

48. *Mém.* 2, ch. 48, 25/293. "Duponchel . . . me regardait comme une espèce de fou dont la musique n'était et ne pouvait être qu'un tissu d'extravagances. Néanmoins, pour être agréable au *Journal des Débats*, il consentit à entendre la lecture du livret de *Benvenuto*."

49. Mentioned in Henry Barraud, *Hector Berlioz* (Paris: Fayard, 1979), 75–76.

50. *Mém.* 2, ch. 54, 250/514.

51. At a later date Armand Bertin inadvertently published an article of Berlioz's which strongly attacked the Opéra. Berlioz commented, "Everyone at the Opéra is in uproar because of my latest feuilleton that Bertin passed *despite censorship* (inadvertently!!!!)" ("Tout l'opéra est en émoi à cause de mon dernier feuilleton que Bertin a fait passer *malgré la censure* [par mégarde!!!!]" (letter of 1852, *CG* 4:114).

52. *Chronique de Paris* ran from 3 August 1834 to 24 December 1837.

53. Letter of 1825, *CG* 1:98. The work was a *Messe solennelle;* only one of its nine movements, the "Et Resurrexit," still survives.

54. Letter of 1828, *CG* 1:192.

55. Letter of 1829, *CG* 1:284.

56. Letter of 1827, *CG* 1:160. "Le *Corsaire* et la *Pandore* m'ont donné des éloges, mais sans détails: de ces choses banales, comme on en dit, pour tout le monde. J'attends le jugement de Castil-Blaze, qui m'avait promis d'y assister, de Fétis et de l'*Observateur;* voilà les seuls journaux que j'avais invités, les autres étant trop occupés de politique."

57. Letter of 1828, *CG* 1:197. "Castil-Blaze, ne se trouvant pas à Paris, n'a pas pu assister à mon concert; je l'ai vu depuis; il m'a cependant promis d'en parler. Il ne se presse guère; heureusement, je puis m'en passer, et largement." Salle des Menus Plaisirs was the former name for the Conservatoire hall, built in 1806.

58. Letter of 1829, *CG* 1:284. "Castil-Blaze n'entre dans aucun détail; ces animaux ne savent parler que quand il n'y a rien à dire."

59. *Mém.* 1, ch. 21, 142/125. "En lisant les divagations d'un de ces fous je fus pris un jour de la tentation d'y répondre."

60. *Mém.* 1, ch. 21, 143/126. "La composition musicale est pour moi une fonction naturelle, un bonheur; écrire de la prose est un travail."

61. "The career of a critic is not all roses . . . [but] one must acknowledge that writing prose was an easy, if not agreeable, task for him" ("Tout n'est pas roses dans le métier de critique . . . [mais] on doit avouer qu'écrire de la prose était pour lui un travail facile, sinon agréable") (*Berlioz et son temps* [Paris: Ollendorff, 1890], p. 293).

62. Adolphe Jullien, *Hector Berlioz, sa vie et ses oeuvres* (Paris: Allison and Co., 1888), 335.

63. Barzun, *Berlioz and the Romantic Century* 2:259.

64. Letter of 1829, *CG* 1:254. "J'aurai bon besoin que cela me rapporte quelque argent, car je perds presque tout mon temps à copier des parties pour quelque chose que je prépare."

65. *Mém.* 1, ch. 21, 141/124. "L'idée d'une arme pareille mise entre mes mains pour défendre le beau, et pour attaquer ce que je trouvais le contraire du beau, commença aussitôt à me sourire, et la considération d'un léger accroissement de mes ressources pécuniaires toujours si bornées, acheva de me décider."

66. *Mém.* 2, ch. 47, 18–19/288. "Cette tâche toujours renaissante empoisonne ma vie. Et cependant, indépendamment des ressources pécuniaires qu'elle me donne et dont je ne puis me passer, je me vois presque dans l'impossibilité de l'abandonner, sous peine de rester désarmé en présence des haines furieuses et presque innombrables qu'elle m'a suscitées. . . . La seule compensation même que m'offre la presse pour tant de tourments, c'est la portée qu'elle donne à mes élans de coeur vers le grand, le vrai et le beau." In his correspondence Berlioz, in discussing the amount of time that his criticism took up, said, "But I must succeed at the Opéra, and this is my weapon for battering the door of this immense theater" ("Mais il faut arriver à l'Opéra, et c'est ma machine de guerre pour battre la porte de cet immense théâtre") (letter of 1837, *CG* 2:336).

67. Letter of 1837, *CG* 2:336. "A cause de la puissance que ses feuilles me donneront pour aider encore à l'influence si énergique des *Débats*."

68. Gérard Condé, introd., *Hector Berlioz*, 18.

69. "M. Berlioz le critique, se vengeant des échecs de M. Berlioz le compositeur," *Le Corsaire*, 22 August 1840, 1. Article is unsigned. "Mais au moyen de l'escopette que l'on nomme le *Journal des Débats*, M. Hector Berlioz parvient à faire jouer ses opéras acrobatiques et ses symphonies orichalciennes. Avec le *Journal des Débats*, M. Hector s'impose aux théâtres, aux cérémonies officielles, s'impose aux directeurs, aux ministres, au directeur des beaux-arts."

70. *Corr. inéd.*, 274. "Il faut pourtant m'obstiner à écrire pour gagner mes misérables cent francs, et garder ma position armée contre tant de drôles qui m'anéantiraient s'ils n'avaient tant de peur. Et j'ai la tête pleine de projets, de travaux, que je ne puis exécuter à cause de cet esclavage!"

71. "Berlioz's Personality," *Music and Letters* 50 (January 1969): 21.

72. Letter to the Princess Sayn-Wittgenstein, 21 September 1862, *SW*, 127. "J'ai l'ambition de ne plus être domestique, de ne plus monter derrière la calèche des sots et des idiots, et de pouvoir au contraire leur jeter des pierres, si cela me plaît. Mais les sorcières de *Macbeth* ne m'ont rien prédit. . . . [J]e louerai encore longtemps les hommes et les choses que je méprise le plus. Dieu le veut!"

73. *SW*, 1862, 127. "Je voulais n'avoir plus rien à faire, rien, absolument rien. J'y suis parvenu; et je puis à toute heure dire à la mort, cette abominable camarde: quand tu voudras!"

74. Letter of 1844, *CG* 3:167. "Il est dur d'être obligé d'avouer que je *n'ai pas le temps de travailler* et que je ne fais presque rien de ce dont je suis le plus capable!"

75. *SW*, 107–8, 110.

76. Cairns, introd., *Memoirs*, 11.

77. Gérard Condé, introd., *Hector Berlioz*, 19. "Son métier de critique a évité à Berlioz de devoir composer pour vivre. N'ayant pas la facilité d'un Auber ni l'opportunisme d'un Meyerbeer, il en aurait été d'ailleurs incapable: malgré ses illusions romantiques sur une éventuelle consécration populaire, il avait dû se rendre compte assez tôt que l'originalité de sa musique la réservait à une élite restreinte de connaisseurs ou d'esprits sensibles."

78. Letter of 1854, *CG* 4:569. "On ne dit plus 'que sais-je?' comme Montaigne, mais 'A quoi bon?' Je suis obsédé par des plans d'ouvrages, vastes et hardis que je me crois sûr de réaliser; je vais commencer et je m'arrête: Pour quoi entreprendre une pareille oeuvre, me dis-je, m'éprendre pour elle d'une effrayante ardeur? . . . Pour la voir livrée aux enfants ou aux brutes, ou enterrée vive."

79. David Cairns comments very movingly on this in his editor's epilogue to the *Memoirs*, 637–39.

80. Taking yet another standpoint on the issue, Hugh Macdonald takes the strong view that Berlioz's criticism was "ultimately counterproductive not only because he failed in his self-appointed task of winning readers to his views but also because his fame as a critic gradually impeded his role as a composer." See "Music and Opera," in *The French Romantics* 2:376.

Chapter 4

1. Letter of 1837, *CG* 2:335. "Je pense à ce que je vous ai demandé relativement à l'analyse de la pièce; je crois à présent que c'est inutile, le livret imprimé suffira; j'avais oublié, quand je vous ai parlé de m'en donner le contenu, qu'on pourrait se le procurer à la première représentation." In another, earlier review, Berlioz commented, "I must describe M. Scribe's libretto which you could buy" ("Il faut que je vous raconte le livret de M. Scribe que vous pourriez acheter") (*Le Rén.*, 1 March 1835, 1). Elizabeth Bartlett remarks in her article, "Archival Sources for the Opéra-Comique and its *Registres* at the Bibliothèque de l'Opéra," that in the early nineteenth century "printed libretti were not issued for the Paris première (and indeed sometimes never appeared)" (*Nineteenth-Century Music* 7 [Fall 1983]: 121). Perhaps the custom of issuing libretti at premières was just beginning in the 1830s—which would explain Berlioz's forgetfulness in his letter to Deschamps.

2. *RGM*, 7 February 1836, 44. "Il ne suffit pas de les [les véritables beautés] *énumérer*, il faut les démontrer, si toutefois le beau se démontre."

3. *JD*, 2 November 1837, 1. "Une première audition [est], je l'ai déjà dit, complètement insuffisante pour distinguer même les points saillans d'une partition. La nécessité de parler des ouvrages nouveaux immédiatement après leur apparition, nécessité imposée tant par les habitudes de la presse que par l'intérêt des théâtres, est fâcheuse pour les artistes comme pour les critiques."

4. *JD*, 10 November 1836, 2. The example refers to the sermon scene, "Devant vous nous jurons éternelle amitié."

5. *JD,* 2 November 1837, 1. "Ainsi, plusieurs morceaux des ouvrages que je viens de citer sont dessinés avec toute la symétrie et la carrure scholastique, le temps fort de chaque mesure y étant seulement déplacé. Mais ce déplacement n'est que pour l'oeil; on l'aperçoit en lisant la partition ou en regardant les mouvemens du chef d'orchestre; à l'audition il n'existe pas, la force du sentiment musical obligeant à leur insu les exécutans de remettre l'accent rhythmique à la place que la forme de la mélodie lui assigne naturellement."

6. See also ch. 7.

7. Katherine Kolb Reeve's dissertation, *The Poetics of the Orchestra,* gives an excellent account of the critic's response to music as an "independent medium."

8. Carl Dahlhaus, *Esthetics,* 29.

9. *RGM,* 27 April 1834, 134.

10. Guy Hocquenghem, "Minigraphie de la presse parisienne," pref., *Monographie de la presse parisienne* by Honoré de Balzac (1842; Paris: J.-E. Hallier/ Albin Michel, 1981), 14. "Le Service [service-rendu] est le vrai ciment de la Presse."

11. Balzac, *Monographie,* 147. "Entre l'argent à empocher et le gouvernement de la plus belle partie de l'intelligence, la presse n'a pas hésité: elle a pris l'argent et a résigné le sceptre de l'article de fond."

12. *CG* 4:351. "Je profiterai de tes avis pour Francfort, si je me décide à y aller; je me doutais déjà de l'existence de ces critiques de grands chemins, et de la nécessité où l'on est de jeter un sou dans leur chapeau quand on passe devant leur Escopette."

13. Quoted by Antoine Adam in his introduction to Balzac's *Illusions perdues,* xxviii. "Dont la spéculation financière est fondée sur la rançon qu'il tire sans pitié de quelque acteur ou actrice qui paient pour qu'il ne soit pas dit d'eux dans le feuilleton du lendemain qu'ils sont gauches, laids ou détestables."

14. Giacomo Meyerbeer, *Briefwechsel und Tagebücher,* vol. 2 (Berlin: Gruyter, 1970), 321. I have reproduced the French of the original. "Hier j'ai entendu [Ch. Maurice] dire—parlant à Caraffa, au foyer de l'Opéra, que la musique d'*Ali Baba* était encore au dessous de qu'on l'avait jugée, et ce matin, celui qui hier soir lui disait cela, a probablem[en]t été achété (car on là a bon marché) M. Charles Maurice a fait un article à l'opposé des paroles que j'ai entendu sortir de sa bouche. Il n'y a que le Moniteur qui ait osé dire qu'on l'avait sifflé, le fait est vrai et c'est un ouvrage passablement ennuyeux."

15. Maurice's full name was Jean Charles François Maurice Descombes (1782–1869), but he was commonly known as Charles Maurice.

16. Charles Maurice, *Histoire anecdotique du théâtre, de la littérature et de diverses impressions contemporaines,* 2 vols. (Paris: H. Plon, 1856).

17. Maurice, letter of 10 March 1835, 2:120. "Mon *Marino Faliero* . . . sous la protection de votre talent."

18. Maurice, letter of 11 August 1835, 2:124. "Veuillez, nous vous prions, monsieur, nous protéger comme vous l'avez fait jusqu'à présent." The Elssler sisters, Fanny and Thérèse, were two Austrian ballet dancers. Fanny became one of the most famous ballerinas of the time.

19. Maurice, letter of 1836, 2:154. "Vouloir bien prendre sous votre protection mon début de compositeur dans la carrière dramatique."

20. Maurice, letter of 18 February 1837, 2:156. "Je n'ai trouvé qu'un journaliste qui fît de la haute critique théâtrale; et ce journaliste c'est vous."

21. Mentioned in Auguste Ehrhard, "L'Opéra sous la direction Véron (1831-1835)," *Extrait de La Revue Musicale de Lyon,* 1907, 40.

22. Introd., *Illusions perdues,* xxvii n. 3. "Si l'on veut apprécier la vertu de Janin, qu'on lise, dans le journal du comte Apponyi, ces étonnantes confidences du journaliste: 'Je suis comme une femme entretenue, je suis à la mode, il faut que j'exploite la folie; dans un an, je serai peut-être à cent sous.' Pour le moment—1834—il 'était' à mille francs l'article de louange."

23. 20 June 1864. "Un grand critique musical très versé dans les mystères du son—de l'or." Quoted in Marie-Hélène Coudroy's dissertation, "La Critique parisienne face aux créations du *Prophète* et de *l'Africaine* de Meyerbeer," Doctorat du 3ᵉ cycle, Université de Paris 4, 1982, 194. Fiorentino (1806–64), wrote music criticism for *Le Corsaire, Le Constitutionnel, Le Moniteur Universel* (under the pseudonym of A. de Rovray), and *La France.*

24. Quoted in Ehrhard, 41. "La bourse ou la vie!"

25. Introd., *Illusions perdues,* xxvii. "Balzac avait compris que le caractère essentiel de son temps, c'était la toute-puissance de l'argent. La librairie, le théâtre, le journalisme, les belles-lettres étaient dominés par cette nouvelle et abjecte tyrannie."

26. Berlioz discussed Court de Fontmichel (1789–1862) in his unsigned article for the *RGM,* 17 July 1836. The name of Fontmichel's *opéra-comique* was *Le Chevalier de Canolle.* On another occasion Berlioz spoke of a M. Cohen who had paid money in order to have his work, *Le Moine,* rehearsed: "M. Cohen gave a thousand francs to the society, as indemnity for the rehearsals. You can imagine that such an argument could not be resisted" ("M. Cohen a donné mille francs à la Société comme indemnité pour les répétitions. Vous concevrez qu'on ne pouvait résister à cet argument") (letter of 1851, *CG* 4:53).

27. *Der Fall Heine-Meyerbeer* (Berlin: W. de Gruyter, 1958).

28. Heine turned against Meyerbeer after a financial misunderstanding explained in Becker, *Der Fall Heine-Meyerbeer.*

29. See Henri [Heinrich] Heine, *De tout un peu* (Paris: Michel Lévy, 1890). In a series of confidential letters addressed to A. Lewald, director of the *Revue Théâtrale de Stuttgart* (reprinted in the above), Heine describes Meyerbeer as timorous etc. See, in particular, p. 278.

30. Heine, *De tout un peu,* 279–80. Peter Conrad remarks about the image of the cathedral in the nineteenth century that it was "an image of art in the service of faith . . . [proclaiming] the notion of an art which was dogmatic and epic, not romantically self-divided and self-communing, it was naturally the object of artistic assaults in a later period: Debussy sinks his cathedral under the sea. Monet makes his molten in a dazzling light" (Peter Conrad, *Romantic Opera and Literary Form* [Berkeley: University of California Press, 1981], 15). This is an interesting observation, to which I would like to add the point that Heine's comparison of Meyerbeer's work with a Gothic cathedral also reflects the influence of Saint-Simonism, where the Gothic cathedral represented the ultimate art-form.

31. Heine, *De tout un peu,* 272.

32. *Lutèce: Lettres sur la vie politique, artistique et sociale de la France,* 5th ed. (Paris: Michel Lévy, 1859), 196–97. This work is a collection of letters originally written for the *Gazette d'Augsbourg,* 1840–43.

33. Heine, *Lutèce*, 196. "L'art d'employer toute sorte d'hommes comme instruments."

34. *New Grove Dictionary of Music and Musicians*, s.v. "Meyerbeer."

35. "Friends and Admirers: Meyerbeer and Fétis," *Revue Belge de Musicologie* 32–33 (1978–79): 185.

36. Gilbert Duprez, *Souvenirs d'un chanteur* (Paris: C. Lévy, n.d.), 149–50.

37. Louisa Bertin (1805–77), French composer, daughter of Louis Bertin (of the *Journal des Débats* dynasty) and sister of Armand Bertin. She wrote several operas: *Guy Mannering* (1825), *Le Loup-garou* (1827), *Fausto* (1831), and *Esmeralda* (1836). After the failure of *Esmeralda* she wrote no more operas, her music thereafter consisting mainly of a series of cantatas that were performed only in private. She also published two volumes of poetry.

38. Puget also wrote some light-weight *opéras-comiques*.

39. Hans Werner [Henri Blaze], "De la musique des femmes," *RDM*, 8, 4th ser. (1836): 625. "D'ailleurs est-ce bien l'oeuvre d'une femme de soulever les tempêtes de l'orchestre et de faire mouvoir les choeurs? . . . Trouver la voix des larmes et du coeur, c'est là une assez belle tâche pour occuper les loisirs d'une femme."

40. Letter of 1836, *CG* 2:285. "C'est la puissance seule du *Journal des Débats* qui fait accepter cet ouvrage par l'administration de l'Opéra."

41. "Courrier de Paris," *La Presse*, 24 November 1836, 1–2. "On ne va pas à l'Opéra pour y compter les amis et les ennemis du *Journal des Débats*." It is significant that this critic was a woman, Delphine Gay, who wrote for *La Presse* under the name of Vicomte Charles de Launay. See n. 27, ch.1.

42. Janin's articles were 17 November (8 1/2 col.), 21 November (5 col.), and 19 December (2 1/2 col.).

43. "Despotisme du *Journal des Débats*," *La Mode*, no. 8 (1836): 215–16. Article is unsigned.

44. Frédéric Soulié, "Théâtres. Opéra [*Esmeralda*]," *La Presse*, 14 November 1836, 1. "Ouvert les portes, forcé les comités de lecture, [et] marqué la mesure aux chanteurs et à l'orchestre."

45. Soulié, "Théâtres. Opéra [*Esmeralda*]," *La Presse*, 21 November 1836, 1–2. "Pour la gloire d'un duo vous avez insulté à l'église; pour l'honneur d'un récitatif vous avez sali le prêtre. . . . [L]es vers de M. Hugo pouvaient alarmer la réligion, mais on les a fait chanter en choeur parce qu'ils étaient utiles à la dynastie des Bertin. Il résulte de tout ceci que . . . les *Débats* sont plus fort que Dieu."

46. Letter of 1836, *CG* 2:319. "A bas les Bertin! à bas le *Journal des Débats*!"

47. Letter of 1836, *CG* 2:318.

48. The first article was 28 August 1836, 305, and the second 20 November 1836, 409–11.

49. Letter of 1836, *CG* 2:306. "Il y a vraiment dans cette partition des choses bien remarquables, et les gens impartiaux seront fort surpris." In his *Mémoires* he wrote that *Esmeralda* suffered from a certain indecisiveness of style and from the rather naïve character of some of its melodies, but that it contained some fine things and passages of great interest (*Mém.*, 2:23–24/292).

50. In a letter to his sister (1836, *CG* 2:319) Berlioz reaffirms that this air really was by Louisa Bertin, saying, "my collaboration was limited to indicating to the author an end more worthy of the beginning" ("ma collaboration s'est bornée à indiquer à l'auteur une péroraison plus digne de l'exorde.")

51. Letter of 1852, *CG* 4:330–31. "Je crois donc que le mieux, si vous voulez dire quelque chose dans le *Journal des Débats*, serait d'annoncer seulement que la *première représentation* a eu lieu samedi dernier, sous ma direction, en présence de la Reine, qui est restée jusqu'à la dernière note du dernier choeur; que plusieurs morceaux ont été redemandés et que l'exécution et la mise en scène ont été fort remarquables. Obligez-moi de mettre ces quelques lignes."

52. Letter of 1852, *CG* 4:331–33. Gemmy Brandus became the editor of the *RGM* in 1846.

53. In a letter to Janin on the failure of *Benvenuto Cellini* in Paris, Berlioz wrote, "The orchestra massacred the overture which they had not rehearsed, but you must not say so" ("L'orchestre a massacré l'ouverture qu'il n'avait pas répétée, mais, il ne faut pas le dire") (letter of 1839, *CG* 2:518).

54. Balzac, *Monographie*, 128.

55. *De l'Opéra en France* (Paris: Janet et Cotelle, 1820), vol. 2, 198. "Il faudrait au moins s'en acquitter avec adresse, en passant légèrement sur les endroits faibles, garder un silence absolu lorsqu'il s'agit des défauts et signaler avec éclat les beautés, les traits remarquables, les passages que l'on peut, sans crainte, montrer en première ligne."

56. For instance, in a letter to a Russian friend in 1852, Berlioz said, "You cannot imagine what happens with these feuilleton affairs and how much nonsense we are forced to talk about before being able to study the important things" ("Vous ne pouvez savoir comment ces affaires de feuilletons s'arrangent et de combien de niaiseries nous sommes forcés de parler avant de pouvoir étudier les choses importantes") (*CG* 4:103) and in a letter to his sister (1854): "And then my damned feuilleton that obliges me to spend my time on so many uninspired horrors and often even to speak of them with a sort of deference!" ("Et puis mon maudit feuilleton, qui m'oblige à m'occuper de tant de plates vilenies et souvent même à en parler avec une sorte de déférence!" (*CG* 4:569).

57. I have given only one example here, though numerous others could be given. To mention one other, of an opera performed in 1857 by a M. Billeta, Berlioz commented in a letter to his friend Auguste Morel, "Do not believe a word of my eulogies in this morning's feuilleton, and believe, on the contrary, that I had to use strong control to write as calmly as I did" ("Ne croyez pas un mot des quelques éloges que contient sur cette musique mon feuilleton de ce matin, et croyez, au contraire, que je me suis tenu à quatre pour en faire aussi tranquillement la critique") (*Corr. inéd.*, 249).

58. *CG* 2:333. "C'est une position bien difficile à conserver sans de vilaines concessions. Ainsi dans quelques jours je vais avoir à dire passablement des bêtises *indulgentes* pour une *énorme* niaiserie musicale appelée *Stradella*, dont j'ai vu la répétition hier soir à l'Opéra. . . . Mais je te préviens de ne rien croire de ce que je dirai de la musique car depuis 15 ans que j'en entends, je n'ai encore rien rencontré d'aussi *tranquillement plat*."

59. *RGM*, 5 March 1837, 80. "M. Niedermeyer dans cet ouvrage a fait preuve de beaucoup de talent; mais ce talent, à en juger d'après une première impression, se fût exercé probablement avec plus d'avantages sur un sujet moins vaste et plus en harmonie avec sa nature tranquille et ses douces habitudes."

60. *JD*, 5 March 1837, 2. "Il s'est borné à exprimer ce qu'il sentait, sans ambitionner dans l'art de nouvelles conquêtes, ni chercher un mieux qu'on dit ennemi du bien."

61. Some time later in a letter (25 November 1856) Berlioz expresses concern at his fellow critic Adolphe Samuel whom he felt was taking criticism too seriously: "I can only view with some disquiet all the pain that you are causing yourself by the seriousness of your criticism. Just

look at what has resulted from my rare fits of frankness" ("Je ne vois pas sans inquiétude tous les chagrins que vous vous préparez par le sérieux de votre critique. Voyez tout ce qui est résulté pour moi de mes rares boutades de franchise") (quoted in Condé, *Hector Berlioz,* 34).

62. "H. W." [Henri Blaze], "Revue Musicale," *RDM* 9 (March 1837): 767.

63. "Bulletin," *Revue de Paris* 39, n.s. (1837): 77. "La musique . . . manque fréquemment de force, toujours de caractère; mais souvent elle a du charme, de la vivacité."

64. *Mém.*, 2:19/288. "Chaque mot mensonger, écrit en faveur d'un ami sans talent, me cause des douleurs navrantes."

65. *Mém.*, 2:20/289. "La violence que je me fais pour louer certains ouvrages, est telle, que la vérité suinte à travers mes lignes, comme, dans les efforts extraordinaires de la presse hydraulique, l'eau suinte à travers le fer de l'instrument."

66. *Chronique de Paris,* 19 March 1837, 191-93.

67. Letter of 1835, *CG* 2:229. "Je n'ai pas voulu, malgré l'invitation de M. Bertin, rendre compte des *Puritani,* ni de cette misérable *Juive;* j'avais trop de mal à en dire; on aurait crié à la jalousie." At a later date Berlioz also refused to review the Paris première of *Tannhäuser.*

68. His review of *La Juive* was on 1 March 1835 after its première on 23 February; he reviewed *I Puritani* 1 February 1835 after its première on 25 January.

69. Théophile Gautier, *Histoire de l'art dramatique,* vol. 1 (Leipzig: Hetzel, 1858), 21. "Au plus haut rang des compositeurs modernes."

70. Letter of 1848, *CG* 3:594. "C'est vraiment bien. . . . J'ai dit *ce que je pensais* dans mon feuilleton."

71. *JD,* 26 December 1861.

72. *Le Rén.*, 1 February 1835, 1. "A part les choristes qui se tenaient presque constamment à une distance respectueuse du *temps* frappé par l'orchestre, l'exécution a été magnifique"; "Bellini connaît son monde, et s'il a par fois eu le courage de rebaisser son style et de parler à son auditoire une langue plus à sa portée, il ne l'a fait sans doute que pour *faire passer les belles choses.*"

73. *CG* 2:191. "Un article contre ne vous irait pas." A footnote to this letter erroneously gives Berlioz's review of the opera as appearing in the *Journal des Débats* instead of *Le Rénovateur* (27 July).

74. *CG* 2:348. "Tu es le seul, ce me semble, qui puisses le faire d'une manière complète."

75. *CG* 3:162. "J'ai donc recours à tous ceux de nos confrères qui ont montré et qui montrent journellement de la bienveillance pour moi, afin de donner à cette oeuvre toute la publicité possible."

76. *RGM,* 10 April 1836 (unsigned), 116–17, and *JD,* 26 August 1836, 1–2.

77. *RGM,* 18 December 1836, 446.

78. *Mém.*, 2:19/289. "N'oublions pas le mal que vous font au coeur, quand on a comme moi le malheur d'être artiste et critique à la fois, l'obligation de s'occuper d'une façon quelconque de mille niaiseries lilliputiennes, et surtout les flagorneries, les lâchetés, les rampements, des gens qui ont ou auront besoin de vous."

79. "Concerts," *JD,* 7 April 1861, 1. Herz's letter to Berlioz was written on 17 March 1861 and was kindly shown to me by Thérèse Husson, secretary of the Berlioz Association. "Je n'ai pas

pu assister au concert de Henri Herz, mais j'ai su que, malgré le *great excitement* causé par une soirée antimusicale . . . la salle de Herz n'a pu contenir tous les auditeurs que l'affiche de son concert avait attirés. J'ai su que le nouveau concerto de piano de Herz avait obtenu un brillant succès. Tout se sait, malgré les efforts de certains artistes à dérober leurs triomphes à la connaissance du public."

80. Letter of 1854, *CG* 4:653. "Qu'importe d'ailleurs un mensonge de plus ou de moins? Veux-tu que je dise, à la prochaine occasion, qu'elle a du style. . . . Parole d'honneur, je le dirai."

81. Letter of 28 March 1863, published in the *Revue de Musicologie*, no. 66–72 (1938–1939): 140–41, and translated in Barzun, *Berlioz and the Romantic Century*, 2:262.

82. The Gymnase Musical was an orchestral society established in 1834 to perform serious music. Its conductor was Tilmant aîné and its repertoire consisted of orchestral works, particularly symphonies and overtures of composers such as Beethoven, Weber, and Spohr. Programs were to emphasize both old and new works that were little known in Paris (see Cooper, *The Rise of Instrumental Music*, 243).

83. According to Berlioz, the only way the theater could survive was to be granted permission to perform vocal as well as instrumental music—thus when this was refused the theater had no choice but to close, which it did in January 1836. Berlioz also suggested that the Gymnase closed because it could not afford to pay the crippling poor tax. See *CG* 2:278 and 281. Berlioz's major articles that deal with the Gymnase musical are *Le Rén.*: 17 May, 28 May, 7 June, 14 June, 29 June, 12 October, and 27 October 1835; *JD*, 23 June 1835; and *GM*, 31 May 1835.

84. *CG* 2:248. "Véron n'est plus à l'Opéra. Le nouveau directeur, Duponchel, n'est guère plus musical que lui."

85. *CG* 2:246. "Je sais si bien ce que c'est que ces animaux de directeurs, que je donnerais pour cent écus la parole de Duponchel."

86. *Le Rén.*, 31 August 1835, 2. "L'art musical va reprendre le rang d'où il n'aurait jamais dû descendre à l'Opéra."

87. *JD*, 15 November 1835, 2.

88. "Revue Musicale," *RDM* 9, 4th ser. (January 1837): 117. "Or, à moins que *Stradella* ne révèle subitement un homme de génie dans M. Niedermeyer, que M. Halévy ne soit tout à coup inspiré du ciel, et que M. Auber ne retrouve sa verve du *Philtre* et de *la Muette*, toutes choses au moins fort révocables, nous pouvons prendre patience, et faire nos provisions pour les temps de disette musicale qui vont s'ouvrir."

89. Letter of 1836, *CG* 2:317. "Je ne fais pas grand cas d'ordinaire de ces ignobles petites vengeances, mais les directeurs de théâtres tremblent devant la moindre ligne imprimée, et ma position avec Duponchel, qui n'est pas des plus hardis à cet égard, m'a fait baisser la tête et payer l'impôt."

90. *JD*, 31 January 1837, 1. "L'exécution vocale et instrumentale a fait sans doute des progrès à l'Opéra . . . mais il faut avouer qu'il reste beaucoup à faire sous plusieurs rapports." *JD*, 31 January 1837, 1. "Nous n'ignorons pas l'importance des travaux nécessités par des partitions comme les deux dernières qui ont paru sur notre grande scène lyrique; pourtant . . . il n'eût pas été tout-à-fait impossible de remonter au moins un de ces anciens chefs-d'oeuvre, déjà connus d'une partie des chanteurs."

91. Berlioz was not always concerned with keeping on good terms with the director of the Opéra. Indeed in 1846 he was on very bad terms with the then Opéra director, Pillet, and aware that

his animosity would count against the possibility of a performance of the *Damnation de Faust*: "I will have some difficulties in getting it performed, very probably, because of the merciless war that I have declared in my feuilletons on the Opéra, and especially on the administration of this great idiot of a theater" ("J'aurai quelques difficultés pour l'exécution, très probablement, à cause de la guerre sans merci ni trève que j'ai déclarée dans mes feuilletons à l'Opéra et surtout à la direction de ce grand imbécile de théâtre") (*CG* 3: 349).

92. *Un Romantique sous Louis-Philippe* (Paris: Plon, 1908). See chapter 5, "Vers l'Opéra."

93. See *CG* 2:173. Berlioz here discusses the project with the conductor Girard. Boschot states, "In *Le Rénovateur*, the review of the opening evening was a serious set-down. A few days later, Harriet was engaged" ("Dans *Le Rénovateur*, le compte rendu de la soirée d'ouverture, ce fut un coup de caveçon. Peu de jours après, Harriet était engagée") (*Une Vie romantique* [Paris: Plon-Nourrit, 1919], 148).

94. Berlioz ended up losing money over the Théâtre Ventadour, since the director was declared bankrupt and unable to pay his debts. Berlioz brought a lawsuit against him, but to no avail because the director of the Théâtre went into hiding. See *CG* 2:276.

95. A typical statement for instance is, "My position as honest critic has made me a host of enemies in Paris" ("Ma position de critique honnête m'a fait à Paris une foule d'ennemis") (letter of 1852, *CG*:121).

Chapter 5

1. He wrote nineteen articles in 1834, eight in 1835, twenty-seven in 1836, and thirty-seven in 1837.

2. Katherine Kolb Reeve also compiled a list of unsigned articles while engaged in more general research on Berlioz's music criticism.

3. Katherine Kolb Reeve, "A Berliozian Spoof," parts 1 and 2, *Berlioz Society Bulletin* 103 (Spring 1979): 2–8, 106; (Winter 1979–80): 4–10 and 111; and (Spring/Summer 1981): 2–6. These articles are included in my list (see app. B).

4. These articles are referred to in my list.

5. The following journals and newspapers for the period 1834 to 1837 have been consulted for the purpose of comparison to the unsigned articles: *L'Artiste, Le Constitutionnel, Journal de Paris, Journal des Débats* (only for 1834 as Berlioz became the music critic in 1835), *Le Ménestrel, Le Moniteur Universel, Le National, La Presse, La Quotidienne, Le Siècle, Le Temps, Revue de Paris, Revue des deux Mondes, Revue Musicale* (from 1834 until its merger with the *Gazette Musicale* in 1835).

6. *Journal des Débats*, 20 February 1835. "Ces amens vocalisés et fugués."

7. *Journal des Débats*, 20 February 1835. "Plus usée des formules harmoniques, celle de la cadence italienne."

8. Quoted in Reeve's thesis, 306n.

9. "Le privilège de jouer l'opéra allemand vient d'être accordé au directeur du théâtre Ventadour."

10. "Pour un public que les récitatifs des compositeurs italiens, si moelleux, si faciles, et si courts, ne séduisent pas déjà trop, on comprend que ces intermèdes dans une langue gutturale et nullement familière, auront très peu d'attrait. Le jeu des artistes allemands s'éloigne d'ailleurs encore plus des habitudes de notre scène que la déclamation du Théâtre-Italien."

11. "Nous ne pouvions entendre Beethoven et Weber que sept fois par an aux concerts de la rue Bergère; il nous sera désormais loisible d'applaudir journellement ces sublimes conceptions."

12. "Les nombreux adorateurs de Beethoven et de Weber sont dans la joie. L'autorisation de jouer l'opéra allemand vient d'être accordée au théâtre Ventadour."

13. "Ah, nous allons donc revoir Fidelio avec Mme Schroeder! espérons aussi que la voix frémissante de Haitzinger ne nous fera pas défaut."

14. "Nous espérons revoir Fidelio sous les traits de madame Schroeder, probablement aussi Florestan [*sic*] Haitzinger, dont la voix merveilleuse a laissé de si profonds souvenirs aux habitués de la salle Favart."

15. "Les habitués du Conservatoire, les élus de l'intelligence musicale."

16. *Le Rénovateur*, 25 January 1835. "Un public choisi, intelligent et attentif."

17. *Journal de Paris* (18 September, 1–2, signed A. Duchesne); *Le Ménestrel* (21 September, 4, unsigned); *Revue Musicale* (21 September, 300–302, signed "F. B."); *Revue de Paris* (vol. 9, n.s., 210–12, signed "L. G."); *Le Constitutionnel* (17 September, 1–2, signed "XXX" [Castil-Blaze]); *La Quotidienne* (20 September, 1–2, signed "J. T." [Jean-Toussaint Merle]); *Le National* (17 September, 1–2, signed "X" [Rolle]); *L'Artiste* (vol. 8, no. 8, 90–91, unsigned). For reasons behind identification of initials see app. C.

18. "L'imitation de la mer en fureur est aussi d'une vérité surprenante." "Le luxe de la mise en scène est vraiment royal; plusieurs effets, entre autres celui de la mer agitée, dont les flots viennent se briser avec fracas sur la grève qu'ils couvrent de flocons d'écume . . . ont paru aussi nouveaux qu'ingénieusement rendus."

19. "Cet homme qui, dans le ballet de *la Belle au bois dormant*, apporte au milieu de la scène un grand écriteau où sont tracés les mots suivans en lettres énormes: *Elle dormira cent ans*."

20. "Toutes les fois qu'il s'agit d'une idée d'où l'intelligence générale de la pièce dépend, on se voit forcé de l'écrire en toutes lettres sur quelque tableau placé bien en évidence, où les spectateurs peuvent lire, comme dans *La Belle au bois, dormant: Elle dormira cent ans*."

21. *Le Rénovateur*, 14 June 1834, 29 June 1834, 27 October 1834, and *Journal des Débats*, 23 June 1834.

22. "La contredanse et le galop sont exclus," "*la contredanse n'y figurera point*."

23. "Il est question, depuis quelque temps, de la formation d'un Gymnase musical. *La Gazette Musicale* donne de détails curieux à ce sujet."

24. "Je ne parlerai pas de l'exécution musicale [du deuxième acte]; c'est au machiniste que je m'adresse. Est-ce qu'il méprise Rossini au point de ne pas s'occuper des décors de ses ouvrages? C'est peu croyable. Cependant, à la fin de la magnifique scène du Grutli, au moment où les bois, les eaux et les montagnes doivent être innondés de torrens de lumière, le soleil n'a point paru, la toile du fond au lieu de se lever peu à peu est restée immobile, et le cri de guerre des Suisses a retenti dans l'obscurité."

25. "[Dans] le second acte de *Guillaume Tell* . . . tout y était exécuté avec un laisser-aller si dédaigneux, que le machiniste lui-même n'a pas cru nécessaire de rester à son poste, de sorte qu'à la fin de la scène sur le Grutli, quand Arnold s'écrie: '*Voici le jour!*' la toile du fond est demeurée immobile et le soleil n'a pas paru."

26. "Si j'étais son maître, je lui ferais faire des gammes *adagio sostenuto* pendant long-temps, long-temps, long-temps." "Mademoiselle Lebrun possède un fort beau contralto qu'elle a beaucoup exercé dans les traits, fort peu dans le chant soutenu."

27. *Journal des Débats* (19 January, 2, signed J. Janin); *Le Constitutionnel* (19 January, 1–2, signed "A."); *Journal de Paris* (18 January, 1–2, signed "ZZ."); *Le Ménestrel* (18 January, 4, unsigned); *Revue Musicale* (18 January, 20–21, unsigned); *Le Moniteur Universel* (19 January, 136, signed "P." [Sauvo]); *La Quotidienne* (19 January, 1–2, signed "J. T." [Merle]); *Le Temps* (23 January, 1–2, signed "L. V." [Loève-Veimars]) .

28. "Quelles inventions! Quelles recherches ingénieuses! Quels trésors qu'une inspiration soudaine fit découvrir! . . . Il n'y a rien de pareil! c'est l'art divin! c'est la poésie! C'est l'amour même!"

29. "[Weber me réduit] à écrier à chaque morceau, à chaque page, beau, sublime, prodigieux, stupéfiant, incroyable de force, d'originalité, de grâce, de passion, de rêverie, de poésie, débordant d'inspiration."

30. "Au résumé, bien qu'il soit facile de signaler quelques défauts assez graves dans le style de Weber, on ne peut nier qu'il a trouvé beaucoup de choses nouvelles, et qu'il était doué au génie dramatique."

31. "La troupe des choristes allemands . . . formait un choeur formidable, dont les études malheureusement n'ont pas été dirigées de manière à en tirer parti. . . . [L]'absence de sentiment musical se faisait remarquer partout, et certains passages que je croyais devoir amener un succès pour le choeur, ont passé inaperçus."

32. "Les choeurs . . . ont exécuté quelques morceaux avec beaucoup de tact; mais, dans plusieurs autres, nous les avons trouvés à cent lieues en dessous de l'effet qu'on avait droit d'attendre d'un aussi grand nombre de voix. La raison doit en être attribuée uniquement à l'absence totale de sentiment musical dans l'enseignement et la direction des choristes."

33. "Dépourvue d'idées véritables," "éclipse totale d'idées," "dépourvue d'idées."

34. "Weber n'a rien écrit de plus délicieusement [*sic*] rêveur, de plus tendre."

35. Felix Mendelssohn, *Letters,* 15 February 1832, 192.

36. "Pourquoi vouloir faire des ennemis de deux artistes du premier ordre, uniquement, au fond, parce qu'ils appartiennent à deux époques distinctes?"

37. "Depuis que la foule de leurs auditeurs s'est éprisé, fort justement en verité, mais avec trop de partialité d'une admiration fanatique pour Beethoven."

38. "Malheureusement cet admirable morceau est un peu écourté . . . et la fin (chose incroyable) n'est autre que la cadence italienne."

39. "Croirait-on que cette ravissante idylle finit par celui de tous les lieux communs pour lequel Beethoven avait le plus d'horreur, par la cadence italienne!"

40. "L'*Andante scherzando,* où les violons sont accompagnés d'une façon si piquante par les instrumens à vent, serait un des chefs d'oeuvre de son auteur, si la fin n'en était aussi écourtée; en outre, les deux dernières mesures se composent de la plus usée des formules harmoniques, celle de la cadence italienne."

41. "Il est certains artistes qui ne pardonnent pas à Beethoven d'avoir employé le style badin dans cet andante, et surtout de l'avoir terminé par une formule à l'italienne. Tout est permis au génie à la condition de faire de l'effet. Nous n'avons qu'une chose à dire aux dénigrateurs: Faites-en autant. Et leur impuissance prouvera qu'il n'est pas plus aisé d'imiter le génie dans les petites choses que dans les grandes."

42. "Sans être tout-à-fait du même avis sur tous les points avec notre spirituel collaborateur, nous nous faisons un devoir d'insérer cet article."

Chapter 6

1. *RGM*, 5 February 1837, 45. "Tout ce qui ne fait pas partie du répertoire courant des concerts et des théâtres lyriques est à peu près comme non avenu."

2. *RGM*, 5 February 1837, 45–46. "On peut, ce me semble, s'affliger de voir le complet abandon où languissent de véritables chefs-d'oeuvre, pendant qu'on accorde toute attention et tout hommage à ces myriades de niaises platitudes que nous voyons éclore chaque jour, pour gaspiller les richesses de l'art, bourdonner un instant et mourir."

3. Emile Deschamps, "Lettres sur la musique française (1835)," in *Oeuvres complètes, Prose* 4 (Paris: A. Lemerre, 1873), 24. "L'Opéra-Comique [est un] genre *éminemment* national, mais essentiellement bâtard . . . [où] le mélange du dialogue parlé et de la musique n'en est pas moins mortel pour l'art."

4. Berlioz, *RGM*, 18 September 1836, 323. "[L'*opéra-comique* est] un genre bâtard qui fatigue les amateurs de vaudevilles par son exubérance musicale autant qu'elle irrite les partisans de la musique par les défauts opposés."

5. Théophile Gautier, *Histoire de l'art dramatique en France*, 2:142. "Nous n'avons, pour notre part, aucune tendresse à l'endroit de l'opéra-comique, genre bâtard et mesquin, mélange de deux moyens d'expressions incompatibles, où les acteurs jouent mal sous prétexte qu'ils sont chanteurs, et chantent faux sous prétexte qu'ils sont comédiens." Even Jules Janin spoke of the *opéra-comique* as "that so precious and ridiculous drug one calls an *opéra-comique*" ("cette drogue si précieuse et si ridicule, qu'on appelle un opéra-comique") (*JD*, 8 August 1836).

6. Felix Mendelssohn, *Letters*, ed. and trans. G. Selden-Goth (1945; rpt. New York: Vienna House, 1973), 180.

7. Mendelssohn, *Letters*, 182.

8. George Hogarth, *Memoirs of the Opera* (London: 1851; rpt. New York: Da Capo, 1972), vol. 2, 268–69.

9. *Paris and the Parisians in 1835*, 1:180–81.

10. Review of *Lestocq* by Auber, *Le Rén.*, 1 June 1834, 1. "Cette partition est un trésor pour le public auquel elle a été destinée."

11. Review of *La Marquise* by Adam, *Le Rén.*, 5 March 1835, 1. "La musique dont M. Adam a brodé ce vaudeville ne manque ni de grace ni de vivacité. Elle sera bientôt sur tous les pianos."

12. For other reviews that follow this pattern in *Le Rénovateur* of 1834, see the reviews of Adam's *Une Bonne Fortune* (2 February), Auber's *Lestocq* (1 June), Labarre's *L'Aspirant de marine* (15 June), Paer's *Un Caprice de femme* (27 July), Feltre's *Le Fils du prince* (31 August), Adam's *Le Chalet* (28 September), and Rifault's *Sentinelle perdue* (5 December) .

13. *Le Rén.*, 1 March 1835.

14. *Le Rén.*, 1 March 1835, 1. "Encore un rude cauchemar! Il faut que je vous raconte le livret de M. Scribe que vous pourriez acheter pour la modique somme de 20 sous."

15. Jules Janin (signed "J. J."), "Première représentation de *la Juive*, opéra en cinq actes, paroles de M. Scribe, musique de M. Halévy, décorations de MM. Filastre, Cambon, Séchan, Diéterle, Despléchin et Feuchères," *JD*, 25 February 1835, 1. "Malheureusement avant de

parler de la musique de tout opéra de ce mode, il faut parler du poème, et malheureusement
encore le poème est de toute nécessité un poème de M. Scribe." I am translating both "poème"
and "livret" as libretto, since they refer to the same thing here.

16. "Académie Royale de Musique. *La Juive,*" *GM,* 1 March 1835, 72. "Commençons par le
poëme; l'usage le veut ainsi en France. "The article is unsigned but listed as by Franz Stoepel
in the index.

17. "P." [M. Sauvo, see app. C]. "Spectacles. Académie Royale de Musique. *La Juive,* opéra en
cinq actes, paroles de M. Scribe, musique de M. Halévy," *Le Moniteur Universel,* 28
February 1835, 458. "L'examen d'un opéra soulève toujours pour nous une première
question. Le poëme est-il bon? Ce qui ne veut pas dire, surtout en parlant des vers de M.
Scribe: est-il bien écrit?"

18. *Le Rén.,* 1 March 1835, 1. "Aussi beaucoup de mes confrères ne mettent-ils guère plus de soin
à l'analyse des paroles d'un opéra qu'ils n'en mettraient à celles d'un discours académique, et
les lecteurs, à l'aspect de tout ce griffonage, s'empressent-ils de sauter à la dernière colonne
pour voir si, comme à l'ordinaire, le *musicien a fait preuve de beaucoup de talent.* Car c'est
une chose tout-à-fait digne de remarque que l'inégalité avec laquelle la critique traite le poète
et le musicien. Si la pièce est tombée, les paroles seules en sont cause; si elle a obtenu du
succès, c'est au musicien qu'il faut en faire honneur. . . . Mais tout cela n'a point trait à *La
Juive,* je vous prie de le croire; ma tirade n'a été motivée que par la mauvaise humeur que me
cause toujours l'obligation d'écrire une espèce de scenario ou si vous aimez mieux un mauvais
extrait de la pièce nouvelle, qu'on ne lira point. Aussi espérai-je m'en tirer cette fois à peu de
frais. Je serai bref." English translation up until the ellipsis marks is based on Robert Cohen's
translation given in his dissertation on Berlioz's music criticism, *Berlioz on the Opera,* p. 33.
I shall acknowledge all further use of Cohen's translations by the words "Cohen, trans."
followed by the page number of his dissertation.

19. Henri Blanchard (signed J. J. J. Diaz), "Théâtre de l'Opéra-Comique. *Les Chaperons blancs,*
opéra-comique en trois actes, musique de M. Auber, libretto de M. Scribe," *RGM,* 17 April
1836, 124. "Et ne croyez pas que ce soit la partition qui préoccupe ces messieurs quand il
s'agit d'un ouvrage lyrique: non, non! ils dirigent sept ou huit colonnes d'indignation ou
d'ironie contre l'auteur des paroles ou du poème, comme ils appellent cela, et consacreront à
l'auteur de la musique un petit paragraphe en dix ou douze lignes, dans lequel ils disent tous,
et d'une manière à peu près identique: Cette musique vive et légère est digne du spirituel
compositeur."

20. *Le Chalet, opéra-comique* by Adam. *Le Rén.,* 9 October 1834, 1. "Je vous ai déjà dit que la
musique du *Châlet* était fort jolie, que voulez-vous de plus? Faut-il énumérer les modulations
de chaque morceau, vous dire comment M. Adam passe de *re* en *mi bémol* ou de *sol* en *si*?
Voulez-vous la liste de ses effets d'instruments à vent, de ses chants gracieux?" *Le Rénovateur*
writes *Chalet* with a circumflex.

21. *Le Rén.,* 29 March 1835, 1. "Le sujet du libretto est trop connu pour que je ne puisse, cette
fois, en esquiver l'analyse."

22. Paul Smith [Edouard Monnais], "Littérature musicale. *A travers chants,* par Hector Berlioz,"
RGM, 21 September 1862, 308. "Plus un critique tel que Berlioz est ennuyé, moins il ennuie;
plus il a de verve et de chaleur, plus il formule ses piquantes observations."

23. Karin Pendle, in her book *Eugène Scribe and the French Opera of the Nineteenth Century*
(Ann Arbor, Mich.: UMI Research Press, 1979) analyzes and systematizes Scribe's entire
opus.

24. *RGM*, 31 January 1836, 37. "A la rigueur, ceci n'est point mal pour un musicien. Je sais bien que si M. Scribe eût écrit les paroles au lieu de la musique, il ne se serait certes pas contenté d'une intrigue aussi pauvre, il n'eût pas employé d'aussi vieux moyens; il n'aurait assurément pas fait du prince Aldobrandi un personnage aussi volontairement ridicule sans être amusant. . . . Mais en somme, comme je viens de le dire, ce n'est pas mal pour un musicien." The article is signed "Un Vieillard stupide qui n'a presque plus de dents."

25. Frances Trollope, 1:180.

26. *Le Rén.*, 29 March 1835, 2. "Plusieurs autres morceaux, parmi lesquels nous signalerons un duo et l'ouverture, ont également été fort goûtés. Mais la verve du compositeur ne l'a pas aussi bien servi au dernier acte. La roulade sans mélodie y domine."

27. *RGM*, 11 September 1836, 320. The article is unsigned (see app. B). "L'ouverture est à mon avis le meilleur morceau de la pièce, je n'aime pas il est vrai le petit thème sautillant du milieu, et le reste est assez terne; mais tout y est clairement disposé et la coupe en est fort régulière."

28. *RGM*, 9 October 1836, 359. "Son ouverture n'est pas ce qu'il y a de mieux; la plupart des phrases qui la composent sont bien communes, il faut le dire; mais la *coda* a réellement de la verve, assez même pour faire pardonner à l'auteur son affreuse grosse caisse, instrument ignoble dont une jeune femme n'aurait pas dû se servir."

29. *Le Rén.*, 29 March 1835, 2. "M. Auber a été bien inspiré pendant les deux premiers actes; de tous côtés surgissent les plus droles [*sic*] de petites mélodies, qui feront la fortune de nos marchands de contre-danses."

30. *RGM*, 10 December 1837, 542. "M. Auber a écrit sur cette pièce tant soit peu risquée et invraisemblable, mais vive et amusante, une de ses plus jolies partitions."

31. *Le Rén.*, 29 March 1835, 1. "La musique dont M. Auber a brillanté ce livret fantastique est d'une piquante physionomie."

32. *RGM*, 9 October 1836, 359. "Mademoiselle Puget a brodé ce petit *poëme*."

33. Letter of 1842, *CG* 2:714. "Je dirai que c'est *assez agréable*, sans ajouter *pour* les *modistes*."

34. Letter of 1839, *CG* 2:552 and 554. "Le métier de critique m'est odieux, il faut que je ménage un tas de platitudes qui me font mal au coeur. On me circonvient à propos de la plus mince débutante, chanteuse ou pianiste, pour le plus misérable opéra-comique qui ne vaut pas un vieux bout de cigare, pour toutes les plaies honteuses de l'art musical, de manière à me donner une idée effrayante de la puissance du *Journal des Débats*. . . . On va me haïr à la mort, si je dis seulement la moitié de ma pensée. Peut-être la dirai-je tout entière. Quel métier!"

35. Ambroise Thomas (1811–96), French composer.

36. This is mentioned by Berlioz in an article in the *JD*, 27 August 1837.

37. *RGM*, 27 August 1837, *JD*, 27 August 1837, and *Chronique de Paris*, 10 September 1837.

38. *Chronique de Paris*, 10 September 1837, 166. "*La Double Echelle*, petite comédie fort amusante, où la musique n'a que tout juste la place qu'on ne pouvait lui refuser, . . . servira peut-être mieux les intérêts de l'avenir de M. Thomas, que ne l'eût faut un ouvrage moins gai."

39. *RGM*, 27 August 1837, 390. "Une certaine finesse d'intentions dramatiques peu commune, et beaucoup de tact dans l'emploi des masses instrumentales."

40. *JD,* 27 August 1837, 1. "Cette farce, ce vaudeville, ou, si l'on veut, cet opéra-comique, a obtenu un succès de fou rire."

41. *Histoire de l'art dramatique,* 1:28. "C'est une preuve de tact et d'esprit dont il faut lui savoir gré. Les gens assez maîtres d'eux pour se faire, au besoin, plus petits qu'ils ne sont, sont rares, et, en faisant ainsi, M. Thomas a prouvé qu'il comprenait son poëme, son théâtre et son public."

42. See app. B.

43. *Le Rén.,* 12 July 1835, 1. "Encore de gentilles petites phrases musicales incolores! Encore une partition vide de pensées! Encore un petit acte de M. Ad. Adam!"

44. *JD,* 27 September 1835, 1–2.

45. *JD,* 27 September 1835, 1. "Hérold, sans avoir un style à lui, n'est cependant ni Italien, ni Français, ni Allemand. Sa musique ressemble fort à ces produits industriels confectionnés à Paris d'après des procédés inventés ailleurs et légèrement modifiés; c'est de la musique parisienne. . . . [N]ous disons en finissant que cette partition remplit cependant toutes les conditions qu'on exige aujourd'hui *à Paris* d'un véritable opéra-comique."

46. He always retained an affection for Auber's *La Muette de Portici,* even if he deplored the Italian influence Auber underwent in his later works. Though this is a Grand Opera, not an *opéra-comique,* it is important to mention it here, to show that Berlioz did not dislike all of Auber's works. Berlioz reviewed it in *JD,* 27 September 1837, *RGM,* 1 October 1837, and *Chronique de Paris,* 8 October 1837.

47. José Melchor Gomis (1791–1836), Spanish composer, who was a political exile in Paris from 1823, where he remained for almost all the rest of his life; he wrote chiefly *opéras-comiques.* Hippolyte Monpou (1804–41), French composer. He was a pupil of Choron, and composed principally songs and *opéras-comiques.*

48. *Le Rén.,* 5 January 1834, 1–2.

49. *Le Rén.,* 20 June 1835, 1–2.

50. *RGM,* 7 August 1836, 275–77.

51. *Le Rén.,* 5 January 1834, 1. "M. Gomis est un savant musicien, . . . il déteste la routine, les vieilles traditions; il croit autant à son propre jugement qu'à celui des inconnus qui veulent lui imposer leurs doctrines. En conséquence, ce qu'il produit est oeuvre d'art et doit être traité avec respect et considération."

52. *Le Rén.,* 5 January 1834, 1. "Il a declaré la guerre aux phrases carrées dont la désinence se prévoit dès la première mesure; au lieu de ce rhythme, monotone comme celui d'un pendule, les phrases de sa musique sont disposées dans un ordre nouveau."

53. Hugh Macdonald, *Berlioz* (London: J. M. Dent, 1982), 103.

54. Naumann, "Théâtre Royale de l'Opéra-Comique. *Le Revenant,* opéra-fantastique en deux actes et en cinq tableaux; paroles de M. Calvimont, musique de M. Gomis," parts 1 and 2, *GM,* 12 January, 14–16, and 19 January, 24–25.

55. "Spectacles: Opéra-Comique," *Le Moniteur Universel,* 13 January 1834, 90. Unsigned. "Assigne à M. Gomis un rang distingué parmi nos plus habiles compositeurs," "L'ouvrage, . . . par ses formes, nous semblerait devoir appartenir davantage à la scène de l'Académie Royale de Musique qu'à celle de l'Opéra-Comique."

56. Charles Maurice's column (p. 4) in the *Courrier des Théâtres*, 2, 3, 5, 6, and 10 January 1834. "*Le Revenant* a été parfaitment joué," "La seconde représentation du *Revenant* a causé, hier, le plus heureux effet et autorisé de douces espérances," "Nouvelle affluence, hier au *Revenant*," "Le succès musical du *Revenant* grandit d'une représentation à l'autre," "La soirée a été complète."

57. Cavé was the *Commissaire-Secrétaire de la Commission de l'Académie Royale de Musique.* John Dowling in his book *José Melchor Gomis: Compositor Romantico* (Madrid: Editorial Castalia, 1973) elaborates on Gomis's friendship with Cavé, who called him the "Rossini espagnol," 45.

58. *RGM,* 7 August 1836, 276–77. "On fait de l'art populaire . . . parce qu'on ne peut faire autrement. . . . Jamais . . . un homme de style ne parviendra à écrire des choses communes avec cette aisance, cet abandon."

59. *RGM,* 7 August 1836, 275. "Un de ces hommes qui semblent nés pour souffrir et lutter pendant toute la durée de leur courte existence."

60. This is according to Fétis' *Biographie universelle des musiciens.* The *NG* article on Gomis states that *Comte Julien* was performed at a later date with great success. However, John Dowling suggests that the work was never performed (*Gomis,* 77).

61. J. J. J. Diaz [Henri Blanchard], "Théâtre de l'Opéra-Comique. Rock le barbu, libretto en un acte, paroles de MM. Paul Duport et Deforges, musique de M. Gomis," *RGM,* 22 May 1836, 174–75.

62. "Théâtre de l'Opéra-Comique. Rock le barbu, opéra-comique en un acte, paroles de MM. Paul Duport et Deforge, musique de M. Gomis," *JD,* 16 May 1836, 1–2. "Donc à propos de cet opéra bouffon, M. Gomis a écrit de la musique sérieuse. Pendant que M. Duport, son collaborateur, lui faisait de la gaîté, M. Gomis changeait cette gaîté en tristesse. . . . M. Gomis et M. Paul Duport avaient pu s'entendre pour pleurer ensemble ou pour rire ensemble, et ensuite, si M. Gomis ne tenait pas tant à être toujours et à tout propos, et sans trop savoir pourquoi, et sans trop s'inquiéter comment, un homme de génie. Avoir du génie, c'est bien beau, mais c'est bien pénible. Avoir du génie toujours, c'est une grande fatigue pour tout le monde; que diable! il est plus facile et plus agréable d'être tout simplement et tout bonnement un homme de talent. Et puis quelle idée d'avoir du génie en opéra-comique? M. Gomis aurait dû se souvenir qu'il ne faut pas prendre un pavé pour écraser une mouche." Janin was not at all sympathetic to the majority of the *opéras-comiques* performed. This review is of course tongue in cheek.

63. *Guise, ou les Etats de Blois,* words by MM. Planard and St. Georges, music by M. George Onslow. Berlioz reviewed it in *JD,* 10 September 1837, *RGM,* 17 September 1837, and *Chronique de Paris,* 8 October 1837.

64. E. F. Jensen, "Hippolyte Monpou and French Romanticism," *The Music Review* 45 (1984): 122–34.

65. *Le Rén.,* 17 March 1835. "La scène du *juif errant,* fort bien rendue par Dérivis, nous a paru renfermer des intentions de la plus grande beauté, et avoir en général été écrite sous l'influence d'une impression poétique fort élevée. Cet ouvrage devrait placer haut M. Monpou dans l'estime du public musical, s'il était jamais possible à un artiste qui s'écarte de la grande route battue par la foule, d'obtenir dans les premiers temps la justice qui lui est due."

66. Joseph d'Ortigue, *La Musique à l'église* (Paris: Didier, 1861), 121. "Nous devons aussi des éloges sincères et mérités à M. Hippolyte Monpou, dont le *Juif errant* est plein de mélodie et de sentiment."

67. To give just two examples of settings of the theme, see Scribe and Halévy's opera, *Le Juif errant* (1852), and Eugène Sue's book, *Le Juif erran*t (1845).

68. *Piquillo* was an *opéra-comique* in 3 acts, with words by Alexandre Dumas. See *RGM*, 5 November 1837, 478–79.

69. *RGM*, 9 October 1836, 358. "Ce qu'on exige d'eux (je parle du public de l'Opéra-Comique), c'est tout simplement une certaine grâce un peu minaudière, une certaine verve un peu turbulante, un certain coloris un peu cru, une certaine invention un peu commune, toutes choses qui aujourd'hui courent presque les rues. Avec la réunion de ces qualités, un peu d'esprit et un peu d'entente de la scène, on doit parvenir aisément à conquérir les affections d'un public qui se montre plus bénévole de jour en jour."

70. *JD*, 10 December 1837, 2. "Peut-être ces défauts seraient-ils moins remarqués si l'on voulait se placer au point de vue du musicien qui cherche, avant tout, le style le plus propre à agir sur le public actuel de l'Opéra-Comique, et à ne pas sortir du cercle musical dans lequel les usages et les moyens d'exécution de ce théâtre ont enfermé l'art pour ne plus lui permettre d'en sortir."

71. Choruses in general had a bad reputation in Paris at this time, as A. Cler remarked: "Chorus-singers resemble asparagus, which has value only in a bunch; one must never look at and certainly not listen to them individually. . . . In France, with only a few exceptions, the chorus only sings out of habit" ("Le choriste ressemble aux asperges, qui n'ont de valeur qu'en boîte; il ne faut jamais le regarder et surtout l'écouter individuellement. . . . En France, à peu d'exceptions près, les choristes ne chantent que par routine") (A. Cler, *Physiologie du musicien* [Paris: Aubert and Co., 1841], 51).

72. "*Les Deux Reines,* musique de M. Monpou, paroles de MM. Soulié et Arnoud," *GM*, 9 August 1835, 265. Signed "N**" [Naumann?] "L'orchestre et les choeurs nous ont paru comme à l'ordinaire accablés de fatigue et d'ennui."

73. "Opéra-Comique," *Le Ménestrel*, 28 June 1835, 1, unsigned. "Une vérité qui n'échappe à personne, mais que l'avare critique est souvent trop lente à constater, c'est qu'à aucune époque il n'a été déployé une aussi prodigieuse activité à l'Opéra-Comique que depuis l'administration actuelle. [Voir par exemple l]es nombreux débuts qui se sont succédé à ce théâtre dans l'espace d'un an, . . . la série des chefs-d'oeuvre nouveaux dont elle a grossi son répertoire, [et] le choix varié des ouvrages repris."

74. *Chronique de Paris*, 8 October 1837, 234. "Les voix presque toujours écrites en accords plaqués, sans dessins saillants, ont l'air d'accompagner l'orchestre plutôt que d'exécuter la partie principale de l'ensemble musical; mais il faudrait penser un peu à ce que sont les choristes de l'Opéra-Comique, et l'on comprendrait alors l'impossibilité où se trouvait le compositeur d'écrire pour eux autrement qu'il ne l'a fait."

75. See for instance *JD*, 10 December 1837, 2. Alexandre Choron (1771–1834), French writer on music, teacher, publisher, and composer. He founded the Institution Royale de Musique Classique et Religieuse, and his work had a "widespread influence on teachers, organists, choralists, and those who were awakening to the importance of music history" (*NG*, s.v. Choron).

76. *RGM*, 18 September 1836, 323.

77. *CG*, 2:68. "Je vais faire un opéra italien fort gai, sur la comédie de Shakespeare (Beaucoup de bruit pour rien)."

78. Letter of 1833, *CG* 2: 72. "Cette porte en fera ouvrir bien d'autres."

79. *Fonds du Conservatoire,* Berlioz, *Papiers divers,* no. 44.

80. Hugh Macdonald notes, "On the 'Personnages' page Berlioz has penciled the names of suggested singers. All were engaged at the Opéra-Comique, and the only period when all five singers were there was between December 1851 and the summer of 1853, dates when the tenor Dufresne respectively joined and left the company. The reference to Mendelssohn's Symphony in A on the last page suggests that the scenario was in Berlioz's hands shortly before 28 May 1852, the date on which he conducted the Italian Symphony in London" (App. 1, *NBE, Béatrice et Bénédict,* 299).

81. *SW,* 10 March 1859, 88. "Je ne saurais vous dire le chagrin que je ressens d'avoir été forcé de souscrire cet engagement avec M. Bénazet—peut-être m'abusé-je! peut-être le feu s'allumera-t-il en composant."

82. *SW,* 20 June 1859, 98. "Bénazet n'a jamais voulu me rendre ma parole; il veut son opéra, lors même que le projet du nouveau théâtre ne se réaliserait pas, il en court les chances, et garde notre traité."

83. The libretto was passed on to Henry Litolff (1818–91), whose opera *Le Chevalier Nahel ou La Gageure du diable* was produced at Baden-Baden, 10 August 1863 (see H. Macdonald, foreword, *NBE, Béatrice et Bénédict,* viii).

84. *Corr. inéd.,* 21 October 1861, 283. "J'ai travaillé hier pendant sept heures à un petit ouvrage en un acte que j'ai entrepris. . . . C'est très joli, mais très difficile à bien traiter. J'aurai encore longtemps à travailler au poème; il m'arrive si rarement de pouvoir y songer avec suite. Puis la musique aura son tour."

85. Letter to Marc Suat, 7 December 1861, kindly shown to me by Thérèse Husson, secretary of the Berlioz Association. "Je travaille beaucoup, je viens de finir l'opéra en deux actes destiné au nouveau théâtre de Bade. Il me reste à faire l'ouverture; mais les feuilletons vont m'empêcher de m'en occuper."

86. *SW,* 22 July 1862, 123. Translation by Hugh Macdonald, foreword *NBE, Béatrice et Bénédict,* ix. "Un caprice écrit avec la pointe d'une aiguille et qui exige une excessive délicatesse d'exécution."

87. *SW,* 21 September 1862, 126. "En somme, à mon sens, ce petit ouvrage est beaucoup plus difficile d'exécution musicale que les *Troyens,* parce qu'il y a l'*humour.*"

88. *Lettres intimes,* 21 August 1862, 238. "Vous ririez si vous pouviez lire les sots éloges que la critique me donne. On découvre que j'ai de la mélodie, que je puis être joyeux et même comique. L'histoire des étonnements causés par L'*Enfance du Christ* recommence. Ils se sont aperçu que je ne faisais pas de *bruit,* en *voyant* que les instruments brutaux n'étaient pas dans l'orchestre. Quelle patience il faudrait avoir si je n'étais pas aussi indifférent!"

89. *SW,* 21 September 1862, 125. "Il y a eu un tas de Tartuffes d'enthousiasme qui m'ont obsédés de leur démonstrations dont je connaissais parfaitement la *sincérité*—Il m'a fallu prendre l'air nias et avoir l'air de croire."

90. *SW,* 21 September 1862, 125–26. "A présent, nous cherchons avec le directeur de l'Opéra-comique les moyens de reproduire cela à Paris."

91. This concert is reviewed by G. Chouquet, *L'Art Musical,* 26 March 1863, 132; E. Viel, *Le Ménestrel,* 29 March 1863, 133; and Léon Durocher, *RGM,* 29 March 1863, 99–100.

92. See E. F. Jensen, "Hippolyte Monpou and French Romanticism."

93. Letter of 1826, *CG* 1:123. "Ne craignez pas l'excès opposé au genre de l'opéra-comique, figurez-vous bien que notre sujet est tout à fait du grand opéra, d'ailleurs Pixérécourt aime beaucoup mieux le genre grandiose, j'en suis bien informé. . . . Gardez-vous bien de me faire ni ballade ni romance, ni quoi que ce soit de léger pour Blondel . . . [F]aites-lui une espèce d'inspiration Ossianique en style rêveur et sauvage."

94. Letter of 1838, *CG* 2:197. "On me regarde à l'opéra-comique *comme un sapeur, un bouleverseur du genre national*, et on ne veut pas de moi."

95. Marius [Marie] Escudier, "Théâtre de Bade. *Bénédict et Béatrice,*" *La France Musicale,* 17 August 1862, 259. "La cabalette, dans le style du vieil opéra-comique," "fait penser à Grétry."

96. *RGM,* 18 September 1836, 323. "Est-il rigoureusement nécessaire de supposer à l'Opéra-Comique un genre exclusif, circonscrit dans certaines limites?"

97. *RGM,* 18 September 1836, 324. "Car un véritable opéra ne perd guère de son prix et ne descend point au-dessous du rang que son mérite lui assigne, par cela seul qu'il n'est pas chanté d'un bout à l'autre, et qu'on substitue au récitatif courant quelques lignes de dialogue. Fideleo et le Freyschütz en sont d'illustres preuves."

98. Libretto, *Béatrice et Bénédict, opéra-comique en 2 actes. Paroles et musique d'Hector Berlioz* (1906; Paris: Rolland, 1976).

99. *Béatrice et Bénédict,* act 1, scene 4, p. 9. "Assez! assez! aurez-vous bientôt fini de nous chanter: Gloire et victoire, Guerriers et lauriers? Quelles rimes! Voilà les suites de la guerre!"

100. *Béatrice et Bénédict,* act 2, scene 4, p. 60.
    Bénédict:
    Si—je pouvais trouver en vous quelque indulgence—jamais un coeur—
    Béatrice:
    Allez!—Allez donc! La rime est: *constance.* Décochez-moi un madrigal! vous en êtes capable, vous êtes poète! Ah! ah! ah!

101. Libretto, *Béatrice et Bénédict,* act 2, scene 1, p. 49. "De notre île/ De Sicile/ Vive ce fameux vin/ Si fin! /Mais la plus noble flamme/ Douce à l'âme/ Comme au coeur/ Du buveur/ C'est la vermeille liqueur/ De la treille/ Des coteaux de Marsala/ Qui l'a!"

102. This letter was shown to me by Thérèse Husson. "L'orchestre de concert est un roi placé sur un trône. Et puis ces grandes passions des symphonies me retournent le coeur un peu plus brutalement que les sentiments d'un opéra de demi-caractère comme *Béatrice.*"

103. Castil-Blaze, *Dictionnaire de musique moderne,* rvd. 3rd ed. (Brussels: Cantaerts, 1828), 36. "De ces *caractères,* les uns sont généraux, étant rélatifs 1. à nos affections, 2. au degré dans lequel nous les ressentons, 3. au ton sur lequel nous les exprimons. Le premier donne le caractère gai ou triste; le second, la vivacité ou la douceur; le troisième, la sublimité ou la simplicité. Chacun de ces trois états a un *caractère* moyen. En les combinant on aura un grand nombre de *caractères* mixtes dont voici les principaux: 1. Le *caractère* du style tragique, qui réunit la tristesse avec la force et la sublimité; 2. le bouffon, qui réunit la gaîté avec la vivacité et la familiarité; 3. enfin le *demi-caractère,* qui réunit les situations moyennes."

104. *Mém.* 2:348/608. "A mon sens, c'est une des plus vives et des plus originales [choses] que j'aie produites."

105. *Mém.* 2:348/608. "M. Bénazet, avec sa générosité ordinaire, me la paya deux mille francs par acte, pour les paroles, et autant pour la musique, c'est-à-dire, huit mille francs en tout. De plus, il me donna encore mille francs pour en venir diriger la représentation l'année suivante."

Chapter 7

1. It should not however be forgotten that *La Muette* was produced under Lubbert, and *Les Huguenots* under Duponchel. Duponchel and Ciceri in their roles of stage producer and set designer respectively were also extremely important figures.

2. Louis Véron, *Mémoires d'un bourgeois de Paris*, vol. 3 (Paris: de Goret, 1854).

3. Véron, 3:236.

4. "Music and Opera," in *The French Romantics*, 2:356.

5. This is the major thesis of W. L. Crosten in *French Grand Opera—An Art and a Business* (1948; rpt. New York: Da Capo, 1972).

6. W. L. Crosten, *French Grand Opera*, 5.

7. Patrick Smith, *The Tenth Muse: A Historical Study of the Opera Libretto* (New York: Alfred. A. Knopf, 1970). See also Karin Pendle's book on Scribe, mentioned in the previous chapter.

8. Smith, *The Tenth Muse*, 211.

9. Smith, *The Tenth Muse*, 211–12. The libretto of *Anna Bolena* was written by Felice Romani (1788–1865).

10. Gustave Planche, "Théâtres. Académie Royale de Musique: Première représentation des *Huguenots*," *Chronique de Paris*, 3 March 1836, 250–53.

11. Robert Schumann, "*The Huguenots*," in *The Musical World of Robert Schumann: A Selection from His Writings*, trans. and ed. Henry Pleasants (London: Victor Gollancz, 1965), 138.

12. Gautier mocks Scribe's obvious coquetry aimed at various sections of the bourgeoisie, quoting lines such as "Ah what pleasure to be a soldier! Oh! the charming career of being a wig-maker! What sweet destiny, to be a confectioner!" ("Ah quel plaisir d'être soldat! Oh! le charmant métier, Que d'être perruquier! Quel sort plein de douceur, Que d'être confiseur!") (Gautier, *Histoire de l'art dramatique*, 1:256).

13. See discussion of this issue in Carl Dahlhaus, *Realism in Nineteenth-Century Music*, trans. Mary Whittall (Cambridge: Cambridge University Press, 1985), 82–84.

14. Smith, *The Tenth Muse*, 222.

15. Mentioned in Yves Ozanam, "Recherches sur l'Académie Royale de Musique (Opéra Français) sous la seconde restauration 1815–1830," Dissertation, Ecole Nationale des Chartes, vol. 3, Paris 1981, 569.

16. Solomé, *Indications générales et observations pour la mise en scène de la Muette de Portici, Grand Opéra en cinq actes, paroles de MM. Scribe et G. Delavigne, musique de M. Auber* (Paris: E. Duverger, 1828).

17. The principle of a diorama was to paint a canvas on both sides, with transparent colors on the front and reliefs in black and white on the back. Only the light was mobile—in illuminating the canvas from in front or behind, one could make one or other of the two drawings appear. The graduation of light enables one to obtain effects of night and day and especially of movement, for instance, flames, sunset, and the ebb and flow of the sea. (This description comes from an article by Nicole Wild, "La Recherche de la précision historique chez les décorateurs de l'Opéra de Paris au xixe siècle," in *Report of the Twelfth Congress of the International Musicologial Society*, Berkeley, California, 1977, session on "Nineteenth-Century Staging and Romantic Visual Symbolism," 456.)

18. Wild, "La Recherche de la précision historique," 453.

19. Catherine Join-Dieterle, "*Robert le diable*: premier opéra romantique," *Romantisme*, Nos. 28–29 (1980): 157.

20. Join-Dieterle, "*Robert le diable*," 162.

21. Wild, "Recherche de la précision historique," 454.

22. Wild, "Recherche de la précision historique," 454.

23. Marvin A. Carlson, *The French Stage in the Nineteenth Century* (Metuchen, New Jersey: Scarecrow Press, 1972), 77.

24. "Livret de mise-en-scène de *la Juive*, opéra en 5 actes de M. E. Scribe, musique de F. Halévy," in Louis Palianti, *Collection de mises en scène de grands opéras et d'opéras-comiques* (Paris: Chez l'Auteur et chez MM. les correspondants des Théâtres, n. d.), no. 49, 5.

    [Acte 1]: *Cortége défilant pendant le chant*
    1. Les sonneurs de trompe de l'empereur, précédés de trois gardes à cheval richement armés et équipés. 2. Un porte bannière. 3. Vingt arbaletiers. 4. Un porte bannière 5. Deux cardinaux suivis de deux clercs. 6. Deux autres cardinaux suivis de deux clercs. 7. Un porte bannière accompagné d'évêques et des maîtres de différents métiers. 8. Un porte bannière accompagné de deux autres évêques et de quelques supérieurs de confréries. 9. Trois échevins. . . . 10. Cent vingt soldats richement armés et couverts de cottes et de juste au corps en maille d'or. 11. Six trompettes. (Les instruments sont ornés de tabliers richement armoiriés). . . . 12. Six trompettes. 13. Six porte bannières. 14. Vingt gardes arbaletiers. 15. Trois cardinaux suivis de leur pages et de leur clercs. 16. Sous un magnifique dais porté par quatre héraults (un cinquième tient la bride du cheval). Le CARDINAL BROGNY à cheval, suivi de ses pages et de ses gentilshommes et précédé des héraults portant sur les riches coussins de velours les vêtements pontificaux. 17. Dix soldats. 18. Trois héraults d'armes à cheval. 19. Vingt pages de l'Empereur. 20. L'EMPEREUR SIGISMOND, sous une armure des plus éblouissantes. Il monte un superbe cheval harnaché et cuirassé avec tout le luxe imaginable. Lorsqu'il passe devant l'église, dont les portes se sont ouvertes quelques instants avant, on attaque dans l'intérieur le TE DEUM. Des enfants de choeur (huit au moins) sur les marches du temple, agitent alors devant l'Empereur les encensoirs allumés. L'Empereur s'arrête et s'incline devant la maison du Seigneur. Les cloches sonnent à toute volée. Les orgues se font entendre. A ce bruit se mêlent les cris de joie et les NOEL du peuple.

25. "Livret de mise en scène de *Moïse*," Palianti, *Collection de mises en scènes*, no. 64, pp. 5–6.
    [Acte 3. Grande Marche]
    ORDRE DE LA MARCHE
    1) Un chef et douze gardes . . .
    2) Six dames des choeurs . . .
    3) Six hommes des choeurs . . .
    4) Six dames des choeurs . . .
    5) Six hommes des choeurs . . .
    6) Six dames des choeurs . . .
    7) Six hommes des choeurs . . .
    8) Six hommes des choeurs . . .

9) Oséride, devant quatre prêtres. Ils s'arrêtent pour le solo d'Oséride.
Après le solo, Oséride et les quatres prêtres vont se placer sur le trône côté Jardin. Il s'asseyent. Ici la marche continue.
10) Un chef et huit gardes . . .
11) Quadrille d'hommes du ballet—En rouge
12)   "   de dames " "   En rouge
13)   "   d'hommes " "   En bleu
14)   "   de dames " "   En bleu
15)   "   d'hommes " "   En brun
16)   "   de dames " "   En brun
17) Pharaon, Sinaïde, Aménophis. Officiers derrière Pharaon; sa femme et son fils montent sur le trône côté Cour, Pharaon est au milieu. Les prêtres se lèvent lorsque Pharaon est arrivé sur son trône. Lorsqu'il est assis, les prêtres se rasseyent.

26. Dahlhaus, *Realism in Nineteenth-Century Music*, 84.

27. "Music and Opera," in *The French Romantics*, 2:359.

28. Alfred Loewenberg, *Annals of Opera: 1597–1940*, 2d rev. ed. (Geneva: Societas bibliographica, 1955), cols. 736, 766, and 777.

29. Letter of 1835, *CG* 2:231.

30. Berlioz, *Traité d'instrumentation et d'orchestration, suivie de l'Art du chef d'orchestre*, (Paris, Brussels: Henry Lemoine and Co. [1855]; Gregg Intern. Reprint, 1970), no. 31, p. 130, and no. 65, p. 280.

31. Berlioz, *GM*, 12 July 1835, 232. "Plus prodigieuse inspiration de la musique dramatique moderne."

32. *GM*, 12 July 1835, 231–32 (Cohen trans., 120, modified). "Les violons, altos, flûtes, hautbois et clarinettes se taisent. Les cors, les trompettes à pistons, trombonnes, ophicléide, timballes et tamtam, gémissent seuls quelques accords sincoppés pianissimo, précédés sur le temps fort de deux coups pizzicato des violoncelles et contrebasses. Puis après chacune de ses horribles strophes, deux bassons seuls viennent glousser un rythme plus animé."

33. *GM*, 12 July 1835, 231 (Cohen trans., 116–17, modified). "Je reprocherai cependant à l'auteur d'y avoir introduit vers la fin les trombonnes et l'ophicléide, dont la présence n'est motivée par aucune intention dramatique, et dont le tymbre rude et violent dans le forte, ne peut qu'altérer la couleur d'un morceau aussi gracieusement gai."

34. *SO*, 87.

35. François Castil-Blaze, "*Les Huguenots*," *France Musicale*, 13 May 1838, 1–2; 20 May 1838, 1–2; 27 May 1838, 1–3; and 10 June 1838, 1–3.

36. Blaze de Bury, using his real name Henry[i] Blaze, "*Poètes et musiciens de l'Allemagne*. M. Meyerbeer," *RDM* 5 (March 1836): 678–7ll, and, under the name of Henri Blaze de Bury, "De l'ésprit du temps. A propos de musique. M. Meyerbeer," *RDM* 23 (October 1859): 645–73.

37. Louis Desnoyers, "Théâtres de l'opera. Les Huguenots," *Le National*, 3 March 1836, 1–3, and 16 March 1836, 1-3.

38. Joseph Mainzer, "Académie Royale de Musique. Première représentation des *Huguenots*, opéra en cinq actes de MM. Scribe et Meyerbeer," parts 1 and 2, *Le Monde Dramatique* 2 (1836): 234–38, 247–53.

Gustave Planche, "Première représentation des *Huguenots*," *Chronique de Paris*, n.s., 3 March 1836, 250–53, and 6 March 1836, 261–64.

George Sand, "A Meyerbeer. La Musique, *Les Huguenots*," *Lettres d'un voyageur* (1863; rpt. Paris: Michel Lévy, 1869), 313–35.

Robert Schumann, *"The Huguenots,"* in *The Musical World of Robert Schumann: A Selection from His Writings*, 137–40.

"Ed. L.," "Théâtres. Académie Royale de Musique. Première représentation des *Huguenots*," *Nouvelle Minerve* 4 (1836): 323–28.

39. Blaze de Bury, *RDM* (1836): 708.

40. Mainzer, *Monde Dramatique*, 1836: 249–51.

41. They must both be mistaken here, since according to the *Livret de mise-en-scène* it was the *Pré aux clercs* that was used, and not in this act anyway.

42. "Ed. L.," *"Les Huguenots,"* *Nouvelle Minerve* (1836): 327. "Ajouterai-je que le succès a dépassé toutes les espérances qu'avaient pu faire concevoir à l'administration de l'Opéra et l'immense talent du compositeur, [et] le luxe et l'éclat des décorations, parmi lesquelles on doit distinguer celle qui, au second acte, nous montre ce vaste escalier de marbre qu'ombragent des arbres magnifiques, les soins d'une mise en scène minutieuse, riche et intelligente."

43. Camille Saint-Saëns, "Meyerbeer," *Ecole buissonnière: Notes et souvenirs* (Paris: Lafitte, 1913), 278.

44. Blaze de Bury, *RDM* (1859): 646. "On pourrait, je le vois, vous appeler le seigneur Microcosme."

45. Victor Cousin (1792–1867), French philosopher who developed a theory of philosophy that he himself called *electicism* that was based chiefly on the ideas of Descartes and Kant. His most well known work was *Du vrai, du beau et du bien* (1853).

46. Planche, *Chronique de Paris*, 1836, 253. "Blason appartient à toutes les races. Il . . . n'a oublié qu'une chose, de se donner des ancêtres."

47. Planche, *Chronique de Paris*, 1836, 253.

48. Blaze de Bury, *Meyerbeer et son temps* (Paris: Michel Lévy, 1856).

49. "Ed. L.," *"Les Huguenots,"* *Nouvelle Minerve* (1836): 327. "Le concours de choristes habiles, et de ce prodigieux orchestre si admirablement conduit par M. Habeneck."

50. Castil-Blaze, "Giacomo Meyerbeer. *Les Huguenots*," *France Musicale*, 13 May 1838, 2. "Le choral de Luther mis en musique et en cinq actes par Meyerbeer!"

51. Francis Claudon, "G. Meyerbeer et V. Hugo: Dramaturgie comparée," in *Regards sur l'Opéra. Ballet comique de la Reine à l'Opéra de Pékin*, Publications of the University of Rouen (Paris: Presses universitaires de France, 1976), 101.

52. "Meyerbeer and the Music of Society," *Musical Quarterly* 67 (1981): 214, 227, 225.

53. "Les Créations de *Robert le diable* et des *Huguenots* de Meyerbeer face à la critique," Dissertation, Conservatoire Supérieur de Musique de Paris, 1979, 208. "Le succès de ces ouvrages tient plus encore à des causes accidentelles qui préexistaient dans le public qu'à une influence déterminante de la presse."

54. *JD*, 10 December 1836, 1 (Cohen trans., 163, modified). "On peut écrire de la musique brillante et avantageuse pour le chanteur, qui soit en même temps dépourvue de toute invention et tissue tout entière de lieux-communs; je le sais. Aussi ne cherchai-je point à diminuer le mérite réel du compositeur dans ce travail ingrat et antipathique à ses habitudes."

55. *JD*, 10 November 1836, 1.

56. *JD*, 10 November 1836, 1 (Cohen trans., 155, modified). "Le rythme sautillant qui en fait le fond est peu distingué," "On voit que l'auteur n'a écrit ces quelques pages qu'à contre-coeur."

57. *JD*, 10 November 1836, 1 (Cohen trans., 159). "Un trop grand nombre de modulations enharmoniques," "Beaucoup de grands harmonistes comme lui l'ont quelquefois encouru."

58. *JD*, 10 December 1836, 1 (Cohen trans., 167, modified). "Un instant de lassitude aura sans doute fait glisser le grand compositeur dans cette voie qui n'est pas la sienne."

59. *RGM*, 6 March 1836, 76 (Cohen trans., 146, modified). "Le nouveau livret de M. Scribe nous paraît admirablement disposé pour la musique et plein de situations d'un intérêt dramatique incontestable."

60. *RGM*, 6 March 1836, 76.

61. *JD*, 10 November 1836, 1 (Cohen trans., 156, modified). "Le second acte a été jugé très sévèrement, et fort mal à mon avis. L'intérêt n'en est pas à beaucoup près aussi grand que celui du reste de la pièce; mais la faute en est-elle au musicien? Et celui-ci pouvait-il faire autre chose que de gracieuses cantilènes, des cavatines à roulades et des choeurs calmes et doux, sur des vers qui ne parlent que de *rians jardins, de vertes fontaines, de sons mélodieux, de flots amoureux, de folie, de coquetterie,* et *de refrains d'amour* que *répètent les échoes d'alentour*? nous ne le croyons pas; et certes, il ne fallait rien moins qu'un homme supérieur pour s'en tirer aussi bien."

62. Cohen, *Berlioz on the Opera*, 38, 41.

63. Some of Berlioz's music for *La Nonne sanglante* still survives (*La Nonne sanglante, partition d'orchestre*, MS fol. autograph, Paris, Bibliothèque Nationale). In his article "Berlioz's Bleeding Nun" (*Musical Times* 107 [July 1966]: 584–88) A. E. F. Dickinson analyzes the fragments. He seem to me to overestimate the value of the music, and I tend to agree with Hugh Macdonald's assessment of the music in his article in the *New Grove* as "undistinguished." Gounod eventually took over the libretto and his opera *La Nonne sanglante* was performed 18 October 1854 at the Opéra.

64. *Memoirs*, Glossary, 706.

65. *CG* 3, 1847, 473, 489.

66. "*Les Huguenots*," *France Musicale*, 27 May 1838, 3. "C'est le plus pénible et le plus contourné de tous les recueils de vocalises qu'on ait jamais destinées à la *Bravoure* des premières chanteuses."

67. *RGM*, 20 March 1836, 90. "A peine les protestans ont-ils appris le massacre de leur frères, qu'ils doivent interrompre par un cri le porteur de la nouvelle, et se précipiter hors de la salle sans écouter d'inutiles détails. Ce défaut est du poète, je le sais, peut-être aussi le musicien n'a-t-il pas fait pour le pallier tout ce qu'il aurait pu. Plus le libretto est prolixe, plus la partition devrait marcher rapidement."

68. *JD*, 10 December 1836, 2.

69. *JD*, 10 November 1836, 2. Thus Berlioz's system, though usually adhered to, does occasionally break down, and he criticizes works, such as those of Wagner, that are nevertheless dramatically perfectly consistent. As Katherine Kolb Reeve states in her dissertation: "Even when presented with a lucid and unequivocal dramatic 'reason' Berlioz pronounced himself undeterredly against certain musical gestures and practices" (Reeve, *Poetics*, 216).

70. *RGM*, 6 March 1836, 77 (Cohen trans., 150). "Les ballets sont courts, fort heureusement: la mise en scène et les costumes font le plus grand honneur au goût savant de M. Duponchel, et plusieurs décors sont d'un effet magnifique."

71. *RGM*, 6 March 1836, 77 (Cohen trans., 149.) "Les acteurs, les choeurs et l'orchestre ont rivalisé de zèle et de talent. L'exécution a été des plus remarquables, sous le double rapport de l'intelligence et de la précision."

72. *RGM*, 6 March 1836, 73 (Cohen trans., 136). "Dès les premiers actes, deux morceaux ont été redemandés, et l'enthousiasme croiss[ait] jusqu'à la fin."

73. *RGM*, 13 March 1836, 81. "Le succès de cet admirable ouvrage croît à chaque représentation."

74. *JD*, 27 May 1837, 1. "Soit négligence, soit défaut de mémoire, toujours est-il qu'en maint endroit des *Huguenots* ils ont commis les erreurs les plus graves," "L'orchestre a bien aussi quelques peccadilles à se reprocher."

75. *RGM*, 13 March 1836, 82.

76. *JD*, 10 November 1836, 2 (Cohen trans., 161, modified). "Choc des dissonnances de seconde mineure et majeure, jetées avec force sur un débit syllabique brusquement accentué."

77. *JD*, 10 November 1836, 2.

78. *JD*, 10 December 1836, 2 (Cohen trans., 168, modified). "Après quelques mots prononcés à voix basse, les moines font signe aux assistans de se mettre à genoux et les bénissent en traversant lentement les différens groupes. Alors, dans un paroxisme d'exaltation fanatique, tout le choeur reprend le premier thème, *Pour cette cause sainte;* mais cette fois, au lieu de diviser les voix en quatre ou cinq parties, comme auparavant, le compositeur les rassemble à l'unisson et à l'octave, en une seule masse compacte, au moyen de laquelle la tonnante mélodie peut braver les cris de l'orchestre et les dominer tout-à-fait; en outre, de deux en deux mesures dans les intervalles de silence qui séparent chaque membre de la phrase, l'orchestre se gonfle jusqu'au *fortissimo*, et, au moyen d'une attaque intermittente des timballes secondées d'un tambour, produit un ralement étrange, inoui, qui frappe de consternation l'auditeur le plus inaccessible à l'émotion musicale."

79. *RGM*, 13 March 1836, 82. "Quelquefois même de mélodies si piquantes dans leur laconisme, qu'on regrette presque de ne pas les voir développées comme de véritables thèmes."

80. *JD*, 10 November 1836, 2 (Cohen trans., 162). "Le drame n'exigeait pas ce déploiement extraordinaire de forces instrumentales, et la musique n'y gagne pas assez pour le justifier."

81. *JD*, 10 December 1836, 1 (Cohen trans., 166). "La phrase musicale sous laquelle le compositeur a placé ces paroles de sentimens si opposés, [est chantée par] deux personnages dont l'un tremble et l'autre menace."

82. *JD*, 10 December 1836, 2 (Cohen trans., 170). "Un pareil degré de vérité n'est pas celui qui convient à un grand théâtre comme l'Opéra, où l'éloignement et le bruit de l'orchestre empêchent le spectateur de remarquer l'expression du visage."

83. *RGM*, 13 March 1836, 82. "Le final, fort dramatiquement conçu, et plein d'effets d'orchestre saisissans, ferait la fortune d'un autre compositeur, mais pour Meyerbeer il n'est pas ce me semble d'une assez grande originalité sous le double rapport de la pensée et de la forme."

84. Patrick Besnier, "Berlioz et Meyerbeer," *Revue de Musicologie* 63 (1977): 35–40. Charles Stuart, "Did Berlioz *Really* Like Meyerbeer?" *Opera* 3 (December 1952): 719–25.

85. See Adolphe Boschot, *Un Romantique sous Louis-Philippe*.

86. Stuart, "Did Berlioz *Really* Like Meyerbeer?" 723.

87. Letter of 1849, *CG* 3:620. "Je vous aime immensément, vous le savez. Mais ce soir, je vous crains encore plus que je vous aime, par le désir que j'éprouve que ma partition vous impressionne en bien.

     Mille compliments et mille remerciements de ce que vous êtes venu avant-hier soir.

     Votre tout dévoué et tremblant

     Meyerbeer."

88. Letter of 1849, *CG* 3:624. "Meyerbeer a le bon esprit de ne pas trop mal prendre les quatre ou cinq restrictions que j'ai introduites dans mes dix colonnes d'éloges. J'aurais voulu lui épargner la pénible impression que ces critiques exprimées avec une certaine énergie, lui ont fait éprouver; mais il y a des choses qui doivent absolument être dites; je ne puis pas laisser croire que j'approuve ou que je tolère seulement ces transactions d'un grand maître avec le mauvais goût d'un certain public."

89. Letter of 1849, *CG* 3:624–25. "La partition néanmoins contient de très belles choses à côté de choses très faibles et de fragments détestables. Mais la magnificence incomparable du spectacle fera tout passer. Quelle tâche aujourd'hui que celle de faire réussir un opéra! Que d'intrigues! que de séduction à opérer, que d'argent à dépenser, que de dîners à donner! . . . Cela me fait mal au coeur. C'est Meyerbeer qui a amené tout cela et qui a ainsi forcé Rossini d'abandonner la partie."

90. Mentioned by Boschot, Stuart, and others.

91. Quoted in Bernard Van Dieran, *Down among the Dead Men* (London: Oxford University Press, 1935), 144.

92. Five of the major examples in the *Traité* come from *Les Huguenots*.

Chapter 8

1. William Weber, *Music and the Middle Class*, 69.

2. Berlioz repeatedly gives the figure 1,200 as the number of subscribers, for instance in his article in *Le Rén.*, 25 January 1835. William Weber gives the figure 1,100 (p. 70), which is the figure that I have taken to be more correct, given that both Antoine Elwart, *Histoire de la société des concerts* (Paris: Castel, 1860), 115–16, and Arthur Dandelot, *La Société des concerts du Conservatoire de 1828 à 1897* (Paris: G. Havard, 1898), 8, give 1,078 as the number of tickets available.

3. Weber, *Music and the Middle Class*, 70.

4. Weber, *Music and the Middle Class*, 71.

5. François-Antoine Habeneck (1781–1849), French violinist, conductor, and composer.

6. The following list is quoted in Elwart, 309.

7. Cooper, *The Rise of Instrumental Music*, 29.

8. Quoted in Elwart, 130–31.

9. Cooper, *The Rise of Instrumental Music*, 28.

10. "Un sanctuaire," "atmosphère embaumée de poésie."

11. *RGM*, 22 January 1837, 29–30. "Ce public-là . . . se trompe souvent malgré tout, puisqu'il lui arrive maintes fois de revenir sur ses propres décisions."

12. *Le Rén.*, 14 June 1835, 1. "Donne parfois au lieu d'applaudissemens des pleurs ou des frémissemens d'une bien autre éloquence que celle des claqemens de mains."

13. *RGM*, 19 February 1837, 63–64.

14. *RGM*, 27 April 1834, 133. "La musique, comme toutes les sensations pures et vives, veut des organes dont l'habitude n'ait pas émoussé la sensibilité."

15. *RGM*, 30 April 1837, 152. "Il ne faut les entendre [Beethoven etc.] qu'à de longs intervalles; et voilà pourquoi la rareté des séances du Conservatoire est elle-même une des conditions de leur succès."

16. *Le Rén.*, 25 January 1835, 1.

17. *Chronique de Paris*, 7 May 1837, 310. "Malheureusement c'est un public fort restreint. Le peuple des amateurs n'y étant point admis, et n'ayant pour alimenter ou développer son goût pour la musique que des concerts, à très-peu d'exceptions près, ridicules ou mesquins, conserve ses préjugés et son ignorance."

18. *RGM*, 12 March 1837, 89.

19. Cooper, *The Rise of Instrumental Music*, 30.

20. *RGM*, 27 March 1836, 98. "Folie de ne vouloir établir aucune espèce de comparaison entre de telles symphonies et celles mêmes les plus admirables de Mozart; la lutte n'est pas égale."

21. *RGM*, 4 February 1836, 55. "La marche religieuse, le grand air de Sarastro et le choeur des prêtres," "la plus sublime manifestation musicale du sentiment religieux antique."

22. *RGM*, 14 February 1836, 55.

23. *RGM*, 26 March 1837, 101.

24. *Le Rén.*, 11 May 1834, 1.

25. Cooper, *The Rise of Instrumental Music*, 30. Henri Brod (1799–1839), French oboist and composer. Auguste Franchomme (1808–84), French cellist and composer. Jean-Louis Tulou (1786–1865), French flutist.

26. *RGM*, 12 March 1837, 89.

27. *JD*, 18 April 1835, 1–2.

28. Letter of 1838, *CG* 2:434. "Fort peu de compositeurs vivants sur lesquels je puisse exprimer à peu près franchement ma pensée."

29. Jean-François Le Sueur (1760–1837), French composer and writer on music. One of the most prominent musicians during the Revolution, the Empire, and the Restoration, he distinguished himself as a composer of religious music and operas, the most famous of which was *Ossian ou les bardes* (1830). He taught composition at the Conservatoire from 1818 to 1837 and also

devoted the last years of his life (1830–37) to theoretical writings. See Jean Mongrédien, *Jean-François Le Sueur: Contribution à l'étude d'un demi-siècle de musique française (1780–1830)*, 2 vols. (Berne: P. Lang, 1980).

30. *JD*, 15 October 1837, 1–2.

31. Octave Fouque, *Les Révolutionnaires de la musique* (Paris: C. Lévy, 1882).

32. Fouque, 9, 180. "Si Berlioz est Dieu, Lesueur assurément fut son prophète," "le meilleur de l'oeuvre de Lesueur est Berlioz." Fouque writes *Le Sueur* as one word.

33. *JD*, 21 November 1835, 2. "La naïveté et le charme douloureux de ces paroles se retrouvent en entier dans la musique."

34. *JD*, 9 August 1835, 3.

35. Cairns, *Memoirs*, Glossary, 686.

36. "La sublimité du style biblique." Berlioz at times however found the forms inadequate when performed in an orchestral hall: "these *simple, too simple* combinations produced the saddest effect" ("ses *simples, trop simples* combinaisons, ont produit le plus triste effet") (letter of 1829, *CG* 1:252).

37. *Le Rén.*, 30 March 1834, 1, and *GM*, 27 April 1834, 134.

38. *Le Rén.*, 27 April 1834, 1. "Ecole de Gluck," "profondeur tragique, . . . son orchestre parlant et ses formes dédaigneuses de futiles ornemens."

39. *JD*, 23 June 1835, 1, and *RGM*, 6 March 1836, 79. The article is unsigned (see app. B).

40. In Cherubini's *Pater noster, JD*, 12 February 1835, 2.

41. *JD*, 9 August 1835, 3.

42. *Le Rén.*, 21 September 1835, 1–2, and *JD*, 22 December 1835, 1–2.

43. *JD*, 9 August 1835, 3.

44. *Tilmant Concerts* 1833–?1838: Théophile Tilmant (1799–1878), French violinist and conductor, formed a quartet with his cellist brother Alexandre. According to Cooper, the Tilmant Concerts were a short series of Sunday matinées, usually at biweekly intervals, announced in Autumn 1833. No mention of the series can be found after 1838. Apart from the Tilmant brothers, other players were Claudel (2d vn, 1835–37), Croisilles (2d vn, 1836), Urhan (va) and Duriez (db). They mainly performed works by Beethoven, Mozart, Haydn, and Onslow (Cooper, 272–73). Berlioz discusses the Quartet in *Le Rén.*, 8 February 1835, 1.

    Müller: German family of musicians, four brothers of which (Carl, Georg, Gustav, Theodor) formed a string quartet that toured all over Europe from about 1832 to 1855. Haydn, Mozart, and Beethoven were their principal repertoire. They performed in Paris at soirées held by Maurice Schlesinger.

    Baillot Quartet: Pierre Baillot (1771–1842), French violinist and composer, organized various chamber music concerts in Paris from 1814 to 1836 and later. The members of his quartet were Baillot, Vidal (vn), Urhan (va), and Norblin (vc/db). Other participants included Vaslin (vc), Baudiot (vc), Chevillard (vc), Norblin (vc/db), Mialle (pf), Hiller (pf) (see Cooper, 221).

45. Franz Liszt Concerts: Four weekly soirées, 28 January–18 February 1837, held at the Salle Erard. Other participants were Urhan (vn), Batta (vc), and the vocalists MM. Geraldi and Nourrit. (Cooper, 248). See Berlioz reviews, *RGM*, 5 February 1837, 50–51 and 19 February 1837, 63–64.

46. A most striking example of this occurs in Berlioz's review of the Tilmant Quartet for *Le Rén.*, 12 January 1834, where he discusses each performer separately in relation to the role of their particular instrument in a Beethoven quartet. Another example can be found in the *RGM*, 5 February 1837, 50–51.

47. For example, *Le Correspondant*, 6 October 1829, 215, and *JD*, 12 March 1837, 1.

48. *JD*, 12 March 1837, 1.

49. *Le Rén.*, 20 July 1834, 1. Henri Reber (1807–80), French composer and teacher. He attended the Paris Conservatoire where he studied harmony under Reicha and composition under Le Sueur. He wrote several works for theater, largely *opéras-comiques*, though his main interest was in instrumental music. He taught at the Conservatoire from 1862 and is remembered chiefly for his *Traité d'harmonie* (1862). Frédéric Robert (author of the *NG* article on Reber) gives the date of Reber's first chamber works as circa 1835. Berlioz's *Le Rén.* article of July 1834 shows that in fact these chamber pieces were written at an earlier date.

50. *Le Rén.*, 20 July, 1834. "Rien de plus éloigné des formes ou plutôt des formules scholastiques, que le style tout individuel qui caractérise ses compositions."

51. *JD*, 23 July 1861. See *ATC*, 341–47.

52. Scipion Rousselot (1804– ?), French composer and cellist. By 1831 his list of works had reached twenty-six opus numbers, of which most were chamber music. He was mainly known in Paris through the occasional performances of at least one symphony (Cooper, 182). See *Le Rén.*, 17 February 1834, 1.

53. Victor Léfebure (1811–40), French pianist and composer. *Le Rén.*, 5 November 1835, 2.

54. Georges Onslow (1784–1853), French composer of English descent. He studied theory and composition with Reicha at the Conservatoire and wrote a number of songs and piano variations and three operas, but his major output was his chamber music, which included thirty-four string quintets and thirty-five string quartets. His chamber music was performed in Paris and some of it was printed in the late 1830s by Breitkopf & Härtel.

55. *RGM*, 6 March 1836. Article is unsigned see app. B.

56. *RGM*, 27 March 1836, 98.

57. *JD*, 10 September 1837. "La beauté calme de plusieurs de ses *adagio* et de la verve pétulante de la plupart de ses *finales* (presto) témoignent de la facilité avec laquelle il manie les styles les plus opposés."

58. *Le Rén.*, 5 April 1835, 1. "Plein de verve et de fraîcheur."

59. Chrétien Urhan (1790–1845), French violist, violinist, and composer of German descent, well-known for his improvisation and sight-reading on many instruments, and above all for his viola playing. He was a member of the Baillot quartet and played the viola in Anton Bohrer's quartet (German brothers Anton and Max Bohrer visited Paris in 1830–31 and performed the late Beethoven string quartets with Tilmant and Urhan).

60. *JD*, 21 November 1835, 2. "Pour toutes les personnes placées hors du point de vue de l'auteur, les *auditions* sont une oeuvre absurde, pour celles au contraire qui ont assez de religiosité dans l'âme pour pouvoir comprendre l'exaltation d'un artiste à la fois pieux et passionné comme M. Urhan, cet ouvrage, dans son audacieuse simplicité, sera la source des plus vives émotions."

61. *JD*, 26 August 1836, 1.

62. *JD*, 26 August 1836, 1. "Mugissemens d'une tempête véritable que les mouvemens tumultueux d'un orage du cœur." The same point is also made in *Le Rén.*, 16 November 1834, 1.

63. *RGM*, 19 February 1837, 64. "D'une haute inspiration poétique; tranchons le mot: c'est sublime."

64. See for instance his reviews of Thomas Täglichsbeck (1799–1867), German violinist and composer, in *RGM*, 31 January 1836, 38, *JD*, 24 February 1836, 2, and *RGM*, 9 April 1837, 123, and his review of Louis Spohr (1784–1859), German composer, violinist, and conductor, in *JD*, 23 June 1835, 3.

65. See his reviews of Rousselot in *Le Rén.*, 17 February 1834, and of Ferdinand Ries (1784–1838), German pianist, composer, and copyist, in *RGM*, 26 March 1837, 101, and of J. J. Printemps, *RGM*, 17 September 1837, 415–16.

66. See his reviews of François Turbry (1795–1859), French composer, in *Le Rén.*, 12 October 1835, 1, and Onslow in *Le Rén.*, 8 April 1834, 1, and *GM*, 27 April 1834, 134.

67. *RGM*, 26 March 1837.

68. *RGM*, 17 September 1837, 416. "Sans doute le modèle est beau . . . De là une difficulté immense, pour ne pas dire une impossibilité absolue, d'exciter par de tels moyens de nouvelles émotions."

69. Major reviews of Hiller are in *Le Rén.*, 29 December 1833, and *JD*, 25 April 1835.

70. *JD*, 25 April 1835, 1. "La mélodie distinguée, l'harmonie toujours pure et claire, et l'ordonnance générale pleine de tact et de goût."

71. The article in the *JD*, 25 April 1835, distinguishes the last two movements of Hiller's first symphony as being superior to the rest of the work because of "a poetic tendency more in keeping with the demands of the time" ("Une tendance poétique plus en harmonie avec les exigences de l'époque").

72. Written for the *Neue Zeitschrift für Musik* of 1835.

73. Quoted in the "Register of Persons" in Alan Walker, ed., *Franz Liszt* (London: Barrie & Jenkins, 1976), 373.

74. *RGM*, 12 June 1836, 200. "Dans une foule de passages de ces nouvelles oeuvres, il est aisé de reconnaître le plus haut mérite purement de pensée, d'où résulte un effet absolument indépendant du prestige de l'exécution. Je citerai, entre autres parties remarquables sous ce rapport, l'introduction de sa Fantaisie sur le pirate, où une phrase de deux mesures est traitée avec un art admirable, sans ornements, sans traits, sans le secours d'aucun des nombreux moyens que la pyrotechnie musicale mettait à sa disposition."

75. He wrote about the change in his articles "Lettres d'un bachelier ès-musique," *RGM*, 1837. Cited in chapter 2.

76. *JD*, 12 March 1837, 1. "Suivant l'usage alors adopté pour se faire applaudir du public fashionable: au lieu de ces longues tenues des basses, au lieu de ces voix mourantes des dessus, au lieu de cette sévère uniformité de rhythme et de mouvement dont je viens de parler, il plaça des cadences, des *tremoli*, il pressa et ralentit la mesure, troublant ainsi par des accens passionnés le calme de cette tristesse, et faisant gronder le tonnerre dans ce ciel sans nuages qu'assombrit seulement le départ du soleil. . . . Je souffris cruellement, je l'avoue, plus

encore qu'il ne m'est jamais arrivé de souffrir en entendant nos malheureuses cantatrices broder le grand monologue du Freyschütz; car à cette torture se joignait le chagrin de voir un tel artiste donner dans le travers où ne tombent d'ordinaire que les médiocrités."

77. *JD*, 25 April 1835, 3. "C'est le seul perfectionnement dont son talent nous paraisse susceptible."

78. *RGM*, 12 June 1836, 199. "Bien des critiques amères avaient été adressées à Liszt."

79. For just one reference, see *RGM*, 12 June 1836, 200.

80. *Le Rén.*, 11 March 1834, 1. "Il parle *piano* comme Goëthe parlait *allemand*, comme Moore parle *anglais*, comme Weber parlait *orchestre*."

81. "Le beau et l'utile."

82. *Chronique de Paris*, 19 March 1837, 193. "L'avantage est donc incontestablement de son côté; cela nous a toujours paru aussi évident qu'inutile à dire."

83. *Le Rén.*, 29 April 1835, 1.

84. *JD*, 25 April 1835, 1. "Abus de modulations enharmoniques."

85. *Le Rén.*, 29 April 1835, 2. "Les musiciens d'orchestre sont encore peu familiarisés avec ces modulations dont se jouent les pianists."

86. Discussed in Leon B. Plantinga, *Schumann as Critic* (New Haven: Yale University Press, 1967), 196–218.

87. *JD*, 17 January 1836, 1.

88. Ole Bull (1810–80), Norwegian violinist and composer. For Baillot, see n. 44 above. Heinrich Ernst (1814–65), Moravian violinist and composer. Théodore Labarre (1805–70), French harpist and composer.

89. George Alexandre Osborne (1806–93), Irish pianist and composer. *RGM*, 3 April 1836, 111–12.

90. *RGM*, 3 April 1836, 111–12. Jules Benedict (1804–85), English composer, conductor, and pianist of German descent.

91. *Le Rén.*, 28 September 1834, 1. "[Benedict est] renfermé dans un cadre trop étroit à notre avis. Pour un vaste poème, comme celui de Victor Hugo, il fallait une forme plus grande."

92. *Le Rén.*, 15 December 1833.

93. *Chronique de Paris*, 18 June 1837, 404. "Peut-être l'originalité et la fraîcheur de ces nouvelles formes seraient-elles plus senties, si dans l'exécution Chopin prodiguait moins les altérations du mouvement, s'il conservait à la mesure un peu plus de régularité."

94. *Mém.* 2, ch. 56, 276/538. "Chopin d'ailleurs, était uniquement le virtuose des salons élégants, des réunions intimes. Ernst ne redoute point les théâtres, les vastes salles, le grand public, la foule."

95. *JD*, 25 April 1835, 1. "Pianos *unicordes*, [sont] destinés à exécuter dans les boudoirs élégans du grand monde les ravissantes Mazurkas, les Caprices si ingénieux de Chopin, mais qui ne résisteraient pas à l'exécution foudroyante, aux compositions plus orchestrales de M. Liszt."

96. Katherine Kolb Reeve expresses a similar opinion to this in her dissertation, p. 120.

97. Letter of 1838, *CG* 2:411. "Notre ami Heine a parlé dernièrement de nous deux dans la *Gazette Musicale* avec autant d'esprit que d'irrévérence, mais sans méchanceté aucune toutefois; il a en revanche tressé pour Chopin une couronne splendide qu'il mérite au reste depuis longtemps."

98. *Le Rén.*, 15 December 1833, 1. "Ses mélodies toutes imprégnées des formes polonaises, ont quelque chose de naïvement sauvage qui charme et captive par son étrangeté même. . . . [O]n est tenté de s'approcher de l'instrument et de prêter l'oreille comme on ferait à un concert de sylphes ou de follets."

99. *Le Rén.*, 15 December 1833, 1. "Malheureusement il n'y a guère que Chopin lui-même qui puisse jouer sa musique et lui donner ce tour original, cet imprévu qui est un de ses charmes principaux; son exécution est marbrée de mille nuances de mouvement dont il a seul le secret et qu'on ne pourrait indiquer."

100. *Le Rén.*, 23 February 1834, 1. "Verve," "grâce," and "ravissantes arabesques."

101. "J'aurais beaucoup à dire sur Chopin et sa musique; mais je craindrais le reproche banal de camaraderie."

102. *Chronique de Paris*, 18 June 1837, 403. "Il étonne souvent par le scintillement capricieux de sa fantaisie; ce qu'on aime tant en lui, c'est moins le pianiste (bien qu'à ce titre il ait très peu de rivaux) que le compositeur."

103. *Le Rén.*, 5 January 1835, 1. "Tout ce que la grâce a de plus engageant est réuni aux pensées les plus profondes et les plus religieuses."

104. *JD*, 27 October 1849.

105. To name just two of the reviews where he discusses these problems, see *Le Rén.*, 15 December 1833, and *Le Rén.*, 22 June 1834.

106. *Le Rén.*, 22 June 1834, 1.

Conclusion

1. *Berlioz, artiste et écrivain dans les "Mémoires"* (Paris: Presses universitaires de Paris), 1972.

2. Bailbé, 36. "Mozart a été assassiné par Lachnith," "un brigand soupçonné d'avoir violé la musique."

3. *CG* 2:433. "Mes sympathies les plus vives sont pour Gluck et Beethoven d'abord, pour Weber ensuite."

4. "Immense," "gigantesque," "majesté," "colossal," "génie," "passion," "poésie," "pensée poétique," "vérité d'expression," "pensée religieuse," "poésie sublime," "poésie." In comparing two Beethoven trios, one of which he preferred to the other, Berlioz wrote, "It is magnificent prose, that is true, but beautiful poetry is more beautiful still" ("C'est de la prose magnifique, il est vrai; mais la belle poésie est plus belle encore") (*RGM*, 19 February 1837, 64).

5. "Oppositions les plus saisissantes," "contrastes les plus imprévues," "pleine de fougue," "de colère," "d'amour," "péroraison foudroyante," "foule d'idées brillantes et énergiques."

6. "Fait battre le coeur," "frémir," "un spasme nerveux," "exclamations furieuses mêlées de larmes et d'éclats de rire."

7. *RGM*, 10 September 1837, 406–7. "L'émotion croissant en raison directe de l'énergie ou de la grandeur des idées de l'auteur, produit successivement une agitation étrange dans la circulation du sang; mes artères battent avec violence, les larmes qui d'ordinaire annoncent la fin du paroxysme, n'en indiquent souvent qu'un état progressif, qui doit être de beaucoup dépassé. En ce cas, ce sont des contractions spasmodiques des muscles, un tremblement de tous les membres, un *engourdissement total des pieds et des mains,* une paralysie partielle des nerfs de la vision et de l'audition, je n'y vois plus, j'entends à peine; vertige . . . demi-évanouissement."

8. Edouard Hanslick, *The Beautiful in Music,* trans. G. Cohen, ed. Morris Weitz (New York: Bobbs-Merrill, 1957).

9. *RGM*, 8 January 1837, 16. "L'amour heureux, la jalousie, la gaîté active et insouciante, l'agitation pudique, la force menaçante, la souffrance et la peur."

10. "Mélodie distinguée," "charme mélodique," "simplicité élégante," "harmonie distinguée," "calme," "clair," "vivacité, " "goût," "tact," "grâce," "naïveté," "délicatesse," "doux."

11. *RGM*, 27 April 1834, 134. "Dont on parle avec estime . . . qui ne disent rien au coeur."

12. In an article for the *RGM*, talking of Gluck, Berlioz writes, "Truth of expression . . . is eternal" ("La vérité d'expression . . . est de tous les temps") (*RGM*, 26 February 1837, 71).

13. "Prodige de délicatesse."

14. *RGM*, 4 February 1836, 55. "Surpasse tout ce que l'imagination la plus brûlante pourra jamais rêver de tendresse."

15. "Le style de salon," "instrumentation plate," "style flasque," "phraséologie vulgaire," "sans forme arrêtée," "manque d'originalité," "travail froid," "harmonie commune," "monotone rythme."

16. *RGM*, 10 September 1837, 407. "Il y a un vigoureux contraste, . . . celui du *mauvais effet musical,* produisant le contraire de l'admiration et du plaisir. Aucune musique n'agit plus fortement en ce sens, que celle dont le défaut principal me paraît être la platitude jointe à la fausseté d'expression. Alors je rougis comme de honte, une véritable indignation s'empare de moi, on pourrait, à me voir, croire que je viens de recevoir un de ces outrages pour lesquels il n'y a pas de pardon; il se fait, pour chasser l'impression reçue, un soulèvement général, un effort d'excrétion dans tout l'organisme, analogue aux efforts du vomissement, quand l'estomac veut rejeter une liqueur nauséabonde. C'est le dégoût et la haine portés à leur terme extrême; cette musique m'exaspère, et je la vomis par tous les pores."

17. *GM*, 16 November 1834, 367. "Prodigieux! admirable! sublime! inaccessible! écrasant! cela confond, on ne peut respirer."

18. Kant, *Kritik der Urteilskraft* (part 1, book 2, section 25) quoted in Peter Le Huray and James Day eds., *Music and Aesthetics in the Early Eighteenth and Nineteenth Centuries* (Cambridge, Cambridge University Press, 1981), 225.

19. *GM*, 26 October 1834, 343. "Il nous est impossible de porter la froide lame du scalpel au coeur de cette sublime création. Analyser? . . . quoi? la passion, le désespoir, les larmes, les cris d'un fils éperdu apprenant le meurtre de son père? . . . Je ne puis que m'écrier comme la foule, beau! superbe! admirable! déchirant!"

20. See *RGM*, 10 September 1837, 407.

21. *JD*, 12 March 1837, 1. "Nouveau sans sortir du vrai et du beau."

22. *RGM,* 11 June 1837, 205. "Cette terminaison pourrait être d'un bon effet avec un peu plus de largeur dans l'avant-dernier accord et sans le *ré* bémol qu'on entend dans la mesure précédente; présentée de la sorte, elle laisse l'auditeur dans l'indécision, et il est impossible de savoir si le morceau finit en *mi* ou sur la dominante de *la.* Cet exemple prouve cependant que M. Lavaine cherche les formes nouvelles; nous ne doutons pas qu'avec un peu plus d'expérience, il ne tire un excellent parti de celles qu'il est très-probablement appelé à découvrir."

23. *JD,* 10 November 1837.

24. *JD,* 10 November 1837, 2.

25. He mentions this in his reviews of Monpou, *Le Rén.,* 17 March and 8 August 1835, and of Louisa Bertin, *RGM,* 20 November 1836.

26. This is mentioned in his reviews of Monpou, Liszt, and Bertin.

27. *RGM,* 2 July 1837, 229. "Leur infraction doit être au moins aussi bien motivée que leur observation, . . . l'emploi des mouvements harmoniques prohibés par le code des écoles doit avoir toujours un but évident."

28. *RGM,* 2 July 1837, 229.

29. *RGM,* 26 October 1834, 342. "La couleur naïve du morceau . . . non seulement autorise, mais rend pittoresque au plus haut degré cette *infraction aux ordonnances des anciens.*"

30. *GM,* 16 November 1834, 365–66.

31. *GM,* 25 November 1834, 378.

32. *JD,* 1 May 1836, 1. "On regrette de trouver dans le milieu . . . une *coda* italienne avec son insipide cadence, dont l'auteur de *Don Juan* a su si bien se garantir partout ailleurs." See ch. 5 for three other examples of the "cadence italienne."

33. *JD,* 20 February 1835, 2. "D'ailleurs ce choeur finit, Dieu me pardonne de le dire, par un de ces *amen* vocalisés et fugués que j'ai déjà signalés maintes fois chez d'autres compositeurs comme un contresens barbare."

34. *Le Correspondant,* 21 April 1829, 54. "Je défie quiconque est doué du sentiment musical et écoute sans préventions une fugue sur *Amen,* de ne pas prendre le choeur pour une légion de diables incarnés, tournant en ridicule le saint sacrifice, plutôt que pour une réunion de fidèles assemblés pour chanter les louanges de Dieu."

35. *Le Rén.,* 8 April 1834, 1. "Je me permettrai de soumettre respectueusement à l'auteur une observation sur la manière de dire le *Da robur fer auxilium.* Les basses prononcent ces mots sur une phrase énergique et fière, symbole de la force *(robur).* Sur cent compositeurs qui ont traité le même sujet depuis Gossec, il n'y en a pas deux peut-être qui aient évité de jouer ainsi sur les mots au lieu d'en exprimer le véritable sens. L'*O salutaris* est une prière, n'est-ce pas? Le chrétien y demande à Dieu de la force et du courage. . . . C'est donc un être faible qui prie, et sa voix, en prononçant le *da robur,* doit être aussi humble que possible, au lieu d'éclater en accens qui tiennent plus de la menace que de la supplication. Cela me semble une absurdité palpable."

36. *JD,* 23 June 1835, 1.

37. *Le Rén.,* 30 March 1834, 1. "Le *Tuba mirum* débute par une phrase sublime, qui n'aboutit à rien et dont l'instrumentation est impuissante. Pourquoi *un seul trombonne,* est-il chargé de sonner l'appel terrible qui doit retentir par toute la terre et réveiller les morts au fond de leurs

tombeaux. Pourquoi faire taire les deux autres trombonnes? quand, au lieu de trois, trente, trois cent même ne seraient pas de trop? serait-ce parce que le mot *tuba* exprime le singulier et non le pluriel? C'est faire une injure à Mozart que de lui supposer un instant une aussi sotte idée."

38. Katherine Kolb Reeve gives an excellent account of Berlioz's reaction to Beethoven's breaking of "rules" in her chapter "Freedom and Its Limits" in her dissertation, *Poetics of the Orchestra*.

39. *JD*, 22 March 1835, 2. "Pourquoi enlever à la physionomie d'un grand homme ses traits mêmes les plus défectueux? Croyez-vous que les imperfections de ces natures puissantes n'offrent pas un charme réel d'originalité à qui sait les comprendre? Et ne savez-vous pas que l'enthousiasme est frère de l'amour?"

40. *RGM*, 14 February 1836, 55. "L'auteur était sans doute pressé de finir, car il a eu bien soin, dans tous ses autres ouvrages, d'éviter cette sotte et fatigante formule harmonique."

41. *JD*, 23 June 1835, 2–3. "On n'y rencontre en effet, ni cette verve, ni cet imprévu dans les formes, ni cette soudaineté de mouvemens, . . . ni cette grâce mélodique irrésistible qu'on trouve dans *Oberon*. . . . [L]e style . . . est flasque, sa phraséologie vulgaire, son harmonie commune, son instrumentation plate, tellement qu'on dirait à l'entendre qu'elle a remporté le grand prix de composition au concours de l'Institut. Le premier morceau contient cependant une progression harmonique d'un beau caractère à la *coda;* mais outre la nullité de tout ce qui précède, on est désagréablement surpris de retrouver là un air populaire français, . . . *la Pipe de Tabac*. . . . Le menuet n'est qu'une pâle imitation des menuets de Mozart et de Haydn, et le final ne vaut guère mieux. Il eût été peut-être plus convenable de ne pas faire de cet ouvrage une critique aussi minutieusement sévère et de le signaler tout simplement comme une production de peu d'importance; mais nous avons cru devoir exprimer notre pensée à ce sujet avec d'autant plus de crudité que bien des gens ont taxé d'engouement nos élans d'enthousiasme pour Weber, et qu'il était de notre devoir en ce cas de faire preuve d'impartialité."

42. *JD*, 18 April 1835, 2. He retracts this opinion of the *Credo* at a later date, though making no reference to the earlier opinion expressed in the *JD* article.

43. *Le Correspondant*, 21 April 1829, 54. "Rien n'est pourtant plus commun, c'est un style adopté par les musiciens, et ce qu'il y a de plus inconcevable, c'est qu'ils l'appellent style religieux. Quel style, grand Dieu, que celui qui substitue au sentiment humble et touchant de la prière ce qu'on croirait l'expression d'une rage forcenée."

44. *RGM*, 3 September 1837, 401. "Quel avantage y a-t-il à dire: 'Paix! paix! paix! . . . sur la terre' . . . au lieu d'employer la phraséologie naturelle? . . . Heureusement l'auteur n'a placé le monosyllabe que sur des notes douces; mais combien d'autres avant lui avaient jeté ce malheureux mot sur de violents accords frappés avec force par l'orchestre et les voix, de sorte que les chanteurs, au lieu de représenter les anges souhaitant le calme et le bonheur aux hommes justes, semblaient s'écrier avec colère: Paix! comme un magister impatienté qui imposerait silence à ses élèves."

45. *RGM*, 11 June 1837, 204. "L'usage des *accords parfaits*, de préférence à celui des harmonies chromatiques et des septièmes diminuées."

46. *Le Rén.*, 25 January 1835, 1. "Ces vers ne sont point faits pour être chantés, et la scène n'est pas coupée musicalement. Devant de pareilles difficultés, tous les efforts de l'art seraient vains; chercher à les surmonter c'est poursuivre une chimère."

47. *JD*, 10 September 1837, referring to Ferdinand Lavaine's work, *La Fuite d'Egypte.* "L'amour, l'enthousiasme, la mélancolie, la joie, la terreur, la jalousie, le calme de l'âme sont des sentimens et des passions parfaitement propres au développement des forces musicales; l'ambition, les intrigues politiques, au contraire, ne s'y prêtent en aucune façon. Voilà pourquoi Roméo, Juliette, Tybald, le frère Laurence, Othello, Desdémona, Ariel et Caliban lui-même pourront être d'admirables personnages chantans, quand Richard III et Macbeth ne sauraient figurer dans un opéra sans perdre les principaux traits du caractère que leur a donné Shakspeare [*sic*], ou tourmenter inutilement la musique, en lui demandant des expressions qu'elle ne possède pas."

48. *RGM*, 21 February 1836. See appendix B.

49. *CG* 2:90. "Mon père me traite comme tous les pères traitent tous les fils; tandis que je suis, moi, une exception. Oui, exception par mon caractère, par ma vie antérieure, par ma sensibilité exaltée, par mon mépris de la vie et de la mort, par mes idées sur tout."

50. Letter of 1824, *CG* 1:64. "Je suis entraîné involontairement vers une carrière magnifique."

51. Letter of 1825, *CG* 1:85. "C'est une certaine puissance motrice que je sens en moi, un feu, une ardeur que je ne saurais définir, qui se dirige tellement vers un seul point: la grande musique, dramatique ou religieuse, que je ne l'éprouve pas même pour la musique légère."

52. Letter of 1825, *CG* 1:101. "Même actuellement je suis capable de produire du grand, du passionné, de l'énergique, du vrai, du beau enfin."

53. *ATC*, 47. "J'aimerais mieux être fou et croire au beau absolu."

54. *Le Correspondant*, 22 October 1830, 110. "*L'art d'émouvoir par des sons les êtres sensibles, intelligents, instruits et doués d'admiration.* Elle ne s'adresse qu'à eux, et voilà pourquoi elle n'est pas fait pour tout le monde."

55. "Petit nombre de fidèles."

56. *GM*, 20 July–10 August 1834.

57. *RGM*, 24 April 1836, 135. "Peut-être que Gluck redeviendra à la mode . . . par le feu éternel! Si cela arrivait; il faudrait murer la porte du Conservatoire; c'est déjà bien assez pour lui d'avoir subi cette honte une fois."

58. See ch. 8.

59. *JD*, 18 September 1836; *JD*, 31 January 1837, 2; and *RGM*, 4 December 1836. Berlioz's reviews in 1838 of Mainzer's classes are more pessimistic (*JD*, 6 July 1838; *RGM*, 6 May 1838). He felt that this movement had not lived up to its expectations and he strongly criticized the insipid music that the choir sang, saying that instead they should be becoming acquainted with "well-written" music. Since Mainzer himself was the author of the majority of compositions performed, there is obviously some personal animosity underlying these comments.

60. *JD*, 31 January 1837, 2. "Une preuve de la rapidité avec laquelle se répand le goût de la musique dans les classes inférieures de la population."

61. *JD*, 9 August 1835, 2.

62. *JD*, 18 September 1836, 2.

63. *JD*, 31 January 1837, 2.

64. Romain Rolland, *Musiciens d'aujourd'hui*, 19th ed. (Paris: Hachette, 1949), 6. "Il méprise le peuple."

65. *Poetics of the Orchestra,* 105.

66. *Corr. inéd.,* 1857, 240. "Ce qui me dégoute le plus, c'est la certitude où je suis de la non-existence du beau pour l'incalculable majorité des singes humaines!"

67. *RGM,* 2 November 1834, 351. "Ah! si l'on pouvait réduire le public à une assemblée de cinquante personnes sensibles et intelligentes, quel bonheur alors de faire de l'art!"

Appendix A

1. Irene Collins, *The Government and the Newspaper Press in France, 1814–1888* (London: Oxford University Press, 1959), 3–4.

2. Collins, *Government and the Press,* 10.

3. Collins, *Government and the Press,* 12.

4. Collins, *Government and the Press,* 11.

5. Collins, *Government and the Press,* 23. This bill was introduced by De Broglie.

6. Collins, *Government and the Press,* 24. This Bill was introduced by Guizot. Caution money remained a feature of the press legislation up till 1881.

7. Collins, *Government and the Press,* 31–32.

8. Collins, *Government and the Press,* 33.

9. Collins, *Government and the Press,* 38.

10. Collins, *Government and the Press,* 42–43.

11. Collins, *Government and the Press,* 45–48.

12. Collins, *Government and the Press,* 58.

13. Collins, *Government and the Press,* 59.

14. Collins, *Government and the Press,* 60.

15. Collins, *Government and the Press,* 67.

16. Collins, *Government and the Press,* 77–79.

17. Irene Collins, "The Government and the Newspaper Press During the Reign of Louis-Philippe," *English Historical Review* 69 (April 1954): 277.

18. Collins, *Government and the Press,* 82.

19. Collins, *Government and the Press,* 84.

20. Collins, *Government and the Press,* 88–91.

Appendix B

1. Care has been taken to reproduce the exact title of these articles. K. R. in square brackets indicates articles also included in Katherine Kolb Reeve's list (see ch. 5).

2. J.-G. Prod'homme, "Bibliographie berliozienne," *Revue Musicale,* No. 233 (1956): 4–13.

Appendix C

1. *Nineteenth-Century Music* 7 (Fall 1983): 136–142.

2. For this work I have used the following sources: general references on the press, of which the most useful were Félix Ribeyre and Jules Brisson, *Les Grands Journaux de France* (Paris: Marlé, 1863) and Edmond Texier, *Histoire des journaux: Biographie des journalistes* (Paris: Pagnerre, 1850); Dictionaries of pseudonyms; *Entrées* of the Opéra conserved at the Archives Nationales (Aj 13, 218); and lists of *Entrées* found in the Opéra *Registres* (old numbers, vol. 606: 287–89; new numbers, vol. 158–61) and Opéra-Comique *Registres* (vol. 225, 243–67, 272, 278).

Appendix D

1. Care has been taken to reproduce the exact title of each of these articles.

2. Pierre Citron (*CG* 1:165) suggests that an article that appeared in *L'Album* (18 December 1828), "La Jeune France," is possibly by Berlioz. I think it is not by Berlioz, but possibly by Henri Blanchard.

3. Reproduced in part in *VM* 1:241-60.

4. Reproduced in *Mém.*, chs. 35, 39, and 41, and, in part, in *VM* 2.

5. Exact reproduction of preceding article in *Revue Européenne*.

6. Although this article is signed by d'Ortigue, it was prepared from an autograph in Berlioz's hand (held at the Paris Bibliothèque Nationale papiers divers no. 38). Reproduced in part in *Mém.*, ch. 12, and d'Ortigue, *Le Balcon de l'Opéra*.

7. Reproduced in *Mém.*, ch. 36, *VM* 2:121–25, and *SO*, no. 1, 47–52.

8. Reproduced in *VM* 2:5–13, and *Mém.*, ch. 22.

9. Reproduced in *VM* 2:17–29 and 33–43, and *Mém.*, ch. 23.

10. Reproduced in part in *Mém.*, chs. 22, 30, and 41.

11. Reproduced in part in *SO*, no. 12, 175–96, and *VM* 2:311–40.

12. Reproduced in *Journal des Artistes*, 5 October 1834, 216–20. Article is reproduced exactly except for the omission of several paragraphs towards the end.

13. Reproduced exactly in *JD*, 10 October 1834.

14. In this review, and in most of those following which have *Revue musicale et théâtrale* or *littéraire*, the theater or literature section is not done by Berlioz.

15. Reproduced in *Mém.*, ch. 39, and *VM* 2:153–76.

16. Reproduced in *Mém.*, ch. 13.

17. Reproduced in *Mém.*, chs. 41 and 39.

18. Reproduced exactly in *Le Ménestrel*, 10 April 1836, except for omission of last few paragraphs. See also *VM* 1:385–99, and *Mém.*, ch. 15.

19. Reproduced in *MM*, 131–41.

20. Reproduced in *VM* 2:265–77, and *ATC*, 173–79.

21. Reproduced in *VM* 2:281–307, and *ATC*, 180–88.

22. Reproduced in *MM*, 3–13.

23. Reproduced in *MM*, 59–67.

24. Reproduced in *Mém.*, ch. 16, and *MM*, 14–21.

25. Reproduced in *Mém.*, ch. 13.

26. Reproduced in *MM*, 167–79.

27. Reproduced in *Mém.*, ch. 29.

28. Reproduced in *MM*, 83–94.

29. Reproduced in *MM*, 95-105.

30. Reproduced in *Mém.*, ch. 22.

31. Reproduced in *VM* 1:359–65, and *ACT*, 81–85.

32. Reproduced in part in *Mém.*, chs. 1 and 8.

33. Reproduced in *VM* 1:279–88, and *ACT*, 40–44.

34. Reproduced in *SO*, no. 20, 285–89.

35. Reproduced in *VM* 1:241–60, and *ATC*, 21–34.

36. Reproduced in *VM* 2:229–49.

37. Reproduced in *VM* 2:251–62, and *SO*, no. 1.

38. Reproduced in *Mém.*, ch. 13, and *MM*, 68–79.

Bibliography

Primary Sources

Writings of Berlioz

Les Années romantiques, 1819–1842. Correspondance. Ed. Julien Tiersot. Paris, 1904.
Au Milieu du chemin, 1852–1855. Correspondance. Ed. Julien Tiersot. Paris, 1930.
Béatrice et Bénédict, opéra-comique en 2 acts. 1906; Paris: Rolland, 1976.
Briefe von Hector Berlioz an die Fürstin Carolyne Sayn-Wittgenstein. Ed. La Mara. Leipzig, 1903.
Correspondance générale 1, 1803–32. Ed. Pierre Citron. Paris: Flammarion, 1972.
Correspondance générale 2, 1832–42. Ed. Frédéric Robert. Paris: Flammarion, 1975.
Correspondance générale 3, 1842–50. Ed. Pierre Citron. Paris: Flammarion, 1978.
Correspondance générale 4, 1850–55. Ed. Pierre Citron, Yves Gérard, and Hugh Macdonald. Paris: Flammarion, 1983.
Correspondance inédite de Hector Berlioz 1819–1868. Ed. Daniel Bernard. Paris: C. Lévy, 1879.
Evenings with the Orchestra. Trans. and ed. Jacques Barzun. Chicago: University of Chicago Press, 1969.
Les Grotesques de la musique. Ed. Léon Guichard. Pref. by Henri Sauget. 1859; Paris: Gründ, 1969.
Hector Berlioz: Cauchemars et passions. Ed. Gérard Condé. Paris: J. C. Lattès, 1981.
Lettres inédites de Berlioz à Thomas Gounot. Ed. L. Michould and G. Allix. Grenoble, 1903.
Lettres intimes. 2d ed. Pref. by Charles Gounod. Paris: C. Lévy, 1882.
Mémoires. 2 vols. Ed. Pierre Citron. 1870; Paris: Garnier-Flammarion, 1969.
The Memoirs of Hector Berlioz. Trans. and ed. David Cairns. 1969; London: Panther Books, 1974.
Le Musicien errant, 1842–1852. Correspondance. Ed. Julien Tiersot. Paris, 1919.
Les Musiciens et la musique. Ed. with an introduction by André Hallays. Paris, n. d. [1903. Articles published in the *Journal des Débats.*]
New Letters of Berlioz 1830–1868. Ed. Jacques Barzun. New York: Columbia University Press, 1954.
Le Retour à la vie, mélologue, faisant suite à la symphonie fantastique intitulée: Episode de la vie d'un artiste, paroles et musique de M. Hector Berlioz. (Montagnes d'Italie. Juin 1831). Paris: Schlesinger, 1832.
Les Soirées de l'orchestre. Ed. Léon Guichard. Pref. by Henry Barraud. 1852; Paris: Gründ, 1968.
Traité d'instrumentation et d'orchestration. Nouvelle édition suivie de l'Art du chef d'orchestre. Paris and Brussels: Henri Lemoine et Co., n. d. [1855] (Gregg International Reprint, 1970).
A travers chants. Ed. Léon Guichard. Pref. by Jacques Chailley. 1862; Paris: Gründ, 1971.
Voyage musical en Allemagne et en Italie, études sur Beethoven, Gluck, et Weber. Mélanges et nouvelles. 2 vols. Paris: J. Labitte, 1844.

Books and Articles

Adam, Adolphe. *Souvenirs d'un musicien.* Paris: Michel Lévy, 1857.

Balzac, Honoré de. *Le Chef-d'oeuvre inconnu. Gambara. Massimilla Doni.* Introd. and notes Marc Eigeldinger and Max Milner. Paris: Flammarion, 1981.

――――. *Illusions perdues.* Introd. and notes Antoine Adam. 1855; Paris: Garnier, 1961.

――――. *Monographie de la presse parisienne.* Pref. Guy Hocquenghem. "Minigraphie de la presse parisienne." 1842; Paris: J.-E Hallier/Albin Michel, 1981.

――――. *Traité de la vie élégante.* Paris: Librairie nouvelle, 1853.

Barbier, Auguste. *Souvenirs personnels et silhouettes contemporaines.* Paris: Dentu, 1883.

Barrault, Emile. *Aux artistes: Du passé et de l'avenir des beaux-arts. (Doctrine de Saint-Simon).* Paris: A. Mesnier, 1830.

"Beaux-Arts. Jules Regondi, guitariste." *Le Globe,* 3 April 1831, 376.

"Beaux-Arts. Paganini." *Le Globe,* 29 April 1831, 482.

"Beaux-Arts. Théâtre Allemand. Etat actual de la musique. *Eurianthe.* Les Choeurs. Madame Schroeder-Devrient." *Le Globe,* 17 June 1831, 676.

"Beaux-Arts. Théâtre Allemand. Madame Rosner. *Fidelio." Le Globe,* 20 May 1831, 566.

"Beaux-Arts. Théâtre Allemand. *Oberon." Le Globe,* 26 May 1831, 587.

"Beaux-Arts. Théâtre Italien. *Il Pirata,* musique de Bellini." *Le Globe,* 7 February 1832, 151.

"Beaux-Arts. Théâtre-Italien. *Tancredi." Le Globe,* 26 September 1831, 1075.

"Beaux-Arts. Théâtre Royal Italien. *Il Barbiere.* MM. Lablanche et Rubini; Madame Caradori." *Le Globe,* 7 October 1831, 1120.

Blanchard, Henri. "Des acteurs dramatiques et lyriques." *Revue et Gazette Musicale,* 14 July 1839, 235–37.

――――– [J. J. J. Diaz, pseud.]. "Théâtre de l'Opéra-Comique. *Les Chaperons blancs,* opéra-comique en trois actes, musique de M. Auber, libretto de M. Scribe." *Revue et Gazette Musicale,* 17 April 1836, 124–26.

――――. "Théâtre de l'Opéra-Comique. *Rock le barbu,* libretto en un acte, paroles de MM. Paul Duport et Deforges, musique de M. Gomis." *Revue et Gazette Musicale,* 22 May 1836, 174–75.

Boigne, Charles de. *Petits mémoires de l'Opéra.* Paris: Libraire nouvelle, 1857.

Briffault, Eugène. "L'Opéra." *Extrait du livre des cents et un.* Paris: Ladrocat, 1834.

"Bulletin [*Stradella*]." *Revue de Paris* 39, n.s. (1837): 73–79.

Buloz, François. "Revue. Chronique. Théâtres." *Revue des Deux Mondes,* 4th ser., 1 (1835): 595.

Bury, Henri Blaze de [Henri Blaze]. "De l'ésprit du temps: A propos de musique. M. Meyerbeer." *Revue des Deux Mondes* 23 (1859): 645–73.

――――. *Meyerbeer et son temps.* Paris: Michel Lévy, 1856.

――――. *Musiciens contemporains.* Paris: Michel Lévy, 1856.

――――. [Hans Werner, pseud.] "De la musique des femmes." *Revue des Deux Mondes* 8, 4th ser. (1836): 611–25.

――――. (Signed Henry Blaze.) "Poètes et musiciens de l'Allemagne. M. Meyerbeer." *Revue des Deux Mondes* 5 (March 1836): 678–711.

――――. (Signed "H. W.") "Revue Musicale [*Stradella*]." *Revue des Deux Mondes* 9 (March 1837): 760–72.

Castil-Blaze, François [François Blaze]. *Chronique musicale du "Journal des Débats."* Paris: Publ. by the author, 1830.

――――. *Dictionnaire de musique moderne.* Rvd. 3rd edition. Brussels: Cantaerts, 1828.

――――. "*Les Huguenots." France Musicale,* 13 May 1838, 1–2, 20 May 1838, 1–2, 27 May 1838, 1–3, 10 June 1838, 1–3.

――――. "Lulli," parts 1 and 2. *Revue de Paris* 8 (August 1835), 73–98 and 145–169.

――――. *Mémorial du Grand-Opéra.* Paris: Publ. by author, 1847.

———. *De l'Opéra en France.* 2 vols. Paris: Janet et Cotelle, 1820.

———. *Théâtres lyriques de Paris. L'Opéra-Italien, de 1548 à 1856.* Paris: Publ. by the author, 1856.

Castille, Hippolyte. *Les Journaux et les journalistes sous le règne de Louis-Philippe.* Paris: F. Sartorius, 1858.

Cavel. "Politique. France. Les Evêques et l'Opéra." *Le Globe,* 12 March 1832, 286.

Cler, Albert. *Physiologie du musicien.* Paris: Aubert and Co., 1841.

"Concert donné par M. F. Hiller." *Le Globe,* 7 December 1831, 1364.

"Concert pour les Polonais." *Le Globe,* 4 February 1831, 146.

Delacroix, Eugène. *Journal* New rev. ed. Notes and introd. A. Joubin. Foreword by Jean-Louis Vaudoyer. Vol. 1 (1822–52). Paris: Plon, 1960.

Deschamps, Emile. "Lettres sur la musique française (1835)." In *Oeuvres complètes. Prose* 4. Paris: A. Lemerre, 1873.

Desnoyers, Louis. "Académie de Musique. *La Juive.*" *Le National,* 27 February 1835, 1–3, and 7 March 1835, 1–2.

———. *De l'Opéra en 1847: A propos de Robert Bruce.* Paris, E.-B. Delanchy, 1847.

———. "Théâtre de l'Opéra. *Les Huguenots.*" *Le National,* 3 March 1836, 1–3, and 16 March 1836, 1–3.

———. (Signed "L. D.") "Théâtre Italien. Récapitulation des premiers travaux de la saison. Considérations sur la critique musicale actuelle." *Le National,* 7 November 1834, 1–3.

"Despotisme du *Journal des Débats.*" *La Mode,* No. 8 (1836), 215–16.

Diaz, J. J. J. [See Blanchard, Henri.]

Dufort, Ch[arles]. "Concerts du Conservatoire. Concert historique." *Revue Encylopédique, no.* 54 (1832): 246–50.

Duprez, Gilbert. *Souvenirs d'un chanteur.* Paris: C. Lévy, n. d.

Escudier, Léon and Marie. *Dictionnaire de musique théorique et historique.* 5th ed. Pref. by M. F. Halévy. Paris: E. Dentu, 1872.

Escudier, Marie. (Signed Marius Escudier.) "Théâtre de Bade. *Béatrice et Bénédict.* " *La France Musicale,* 17 August 1862, 257–59.

Fétis, François. *Biographie universelle des musiciens et bibliographie générale de la musique.* 8 vols. 2nd ed. Paris: Firmin-Didot, 1860–78. *Supplément et complément.* Ed. Arthur Pougin. 2 vols. Paris: Firmin-Didot, 1878–81.

———. *La Musique mise à la portée de tout le monde.* 3rd ed. Paris: Brandus, 1847.

Fiorentino, Pier Angelo. [A. de Rovray pseud.] "Revue Musicale. Théâtres lyriques [*Béatrice et Bénédict*]." *Le Moniteur Universel,* 24 August 1862, 1.

Forster, Charles de. *Paris et les parisiens ou quinze ans à Paris (1832–1848).* 2 vols. Paris: Firmin Didot, 1848–49.

Fortoul, Hippolyte. "Bulletin dramatique." *Revue Encyclopédique, no.* 58 (1833): 586–602.

Gail, Jean François. *Réflexions sur le goût musical en France.* Paris: Paulin, 1832.

Gautier, Théophile. *Histoire de l'art dramatique en France depuis vingt-cinq ans.* Vols. 1 and 2. Leipzig: Hetzel, 1858.

———. *Histoire du romantisme suivie de notice romantique et d'une étude sur la poésie française, 1830–68.* Paris: G. Charpentier and Co., 1874.

———. *Mademoiselle de Maupin.* Paris: Bibliothèque Charpentier, 1927.

———. *La Musique.* Paris: E. Fasquelle, 1911.

Gay, Delphine. (Signed Vicomte Charles de Launay.) "Courrier de Paris." *La Presse,* 24 November 1836, 1–2.

———. (Signed Ch. L[aunay].) "Société des Concerts. Symphonies de Beethoven." *Le Temps,* 27 February 1834, 1–3.

Girardin, Delphine. [See Gay, Delphine.]

Halévy, Jacques François Fromental. *Souvenirs et portaits, études sur les beaux-arts*. Paris: Michel Lévy, 1861.

Heine, Henri [Heinrich]. *De Tout un peu*. Paris: Michel Lévy, 1890.

————. *Lutèce. Lettres sur la vie politique, artistique et sociale de la France*. 5th ed. Paris: Michel Lévy, 1859.

Hogarth, George. *Memoirs of the Opera in Italy, France, Germany, and England*. Vol. 2. London: 1851; rpt. New York: Da Capo, 1972.

Houssaye, Arsène. *Les Confessions, souvenirs d'un demi-siècle*. Paris: E. Dentu, 1885.

Janin, Jules. *Le Gâteau des rois: Symphonie fantastique*. Introd. and notes J. M. Bailbé. 1847; Paris: Lettres modernes, 1972.

————. *Les Symphonies de l'hiver*. Paris: Morizot, 1858.

————. (Signed "J. J.") "Théâtre de l'Opéra. Première représentation de *la Juive*, opéra en cinq actes. Paroles de M. Scribe, musique de M. Halévy, décorations de MM. Filastre, Cambon, Séchan, Diéterle, Despléchin et Feuchères." *Journal des Débats*, 25 February 1835, 1–2.

————. "Théâtre de l'Opéra-Comique. *Rock le barbu*, opéra-comique en un acte, paroles de MM. Paul Duport et Deforge, musique de M. Gomis." *Journal des Débats*, 16 May 1836, 1–2.

Jouvin, B. "Théâtre de Bade [*Béatrice et Bénédict*]." *Le Figaro*, 17 August 1862, 1–2.

"Ch. L[aunay]." [See Gay, Delphine.]

"Ed. L." "Théâtre. Académie Royale de Musique. Première représentation des *Huguenots*. " *Nouvelle Minerve* 4 (1836): 323–28.

La Rochefoucauld, Sosthène de. *Mémoires*. Vol. 8. Paris: Michel Lévy, 1862.

Launay, Vicomte Charles de. [See Gay, Delphine.]

Legouvé, Ernest. *Soixante ans de souvenirs*. 2 vols. Paris: J. Hetzel and Co., 1886–87.

Liszt, Franz. *Pages romantiques*. Ed. and introd. Jean Chantavoine. Paris: Alcan, 1912.

————. (Acknowledged as being by Marie d'Agoult.) "Revue musicale de l'année 1836." *Le Monde*, 8 January 1837, 1–3.

Mainzer, Joseph. "Académie Royale de Musique. Première représentation. *Les Huguenots*, opéra en cinq actes de MM. Scribe et Meyerbeer." Parts 1 and 2. *Le Monde Dramatique* 2 (March 1835) [1836], 234–38 and 247–53.

————. "Concerts Saint-Honoré." *Le National*, 21 November 1839, 1.

————. "Début de M. Duprez dans *Les Huguenots*. Ecole chorale à Nantes." *Le National*, 19 May 1837, 1.

————. "Education musicale. Concert des jeunes aveugles." *Le National*, 29 April 1837, 1–3.

————. "M. Berlioz." *Chronique Musicale de Paris*, no. 1 (1838): 1–95.

————. "M. Panofka. La Langue musicale. Cours d'ouvriers." *Le National*, 30 November 1837, 2.

Maurice, Charles. *Epaves. Théâtre, histoire, anecdotes, mots*. Paris: Alcan-Lévy, 1865.

————. *Histoire anecdotique du théâtre, de la littérature et de diverses impressions contemporaines. Tirée du coffre d'un journaliste avec sa vie à tort et à travers*. 2 vols. Paris: H. Plon, 1856.

Mendelssohn, Felix. *Letters*. Ed. and trans. G. Selden-Goth. 1945; rpt. New York: Vienna House, 1973.

Merruau, Charles. "Musique. Cours gratuits de M. Mainzer. Choeurs d'ouvriers." *Le Temps*, 29 June 1837, 1.

Meyerbeer, Giacomo. *Giacomo Meyerbeer, Briefwechsel und Tagebücher*. Ed. Heinz Becker. 3 vols. Berlin: Verlag Walter de Gruyter & Co., 1960–75.

Monnais, Edouard [Paul Smith, pseud.]. *Esquisses de la vie d'artiste*. 2 vols. Paris: J. Labitte, 1844.

————. [Paul Smith, pseud.] "Littérature musicale: *A travers chants*, par Hector Berlioz." *Revue et Gazette Musicale*, 21 September 1862, 307–8.

Musset, Alfred de. "Mélanges de littérature et de critique." Vol. 10 of *Oeuvres complètes*. Paris: Bibliothèque-Charpentier, 1907.

"N**" [Naumann?]. *"Les Deux Reines,* musique de M. Monpou, paroles de MM. Soulié et Arnoud."
Revue et Gazette Musicale, 9 August 1835, 265.

"C. N." "Beaux-Arts. Société des concerts. Cinquième année." *Le Globe,* 12 February 1832, 172.

Naumann. "Théâtre Royal de l'Opéra-Comique. *Le Revenant,* opéra-fantastique en deux actes et en
cinq tableaux; paroles de M. Calvimont, musique de M. Gomis." Parts 1 and 2. *Gazette Musicale,*
12 January 1834, 14–16, 19 January 1834, 24–25.

Nettement, Alfred. *Histoire du "Journal des Débats."* Paris: Dentu, 1842.

―――. *Histoire politique, anecdotique et littéraire du "Journal des Débats.* "Paris: Aux bureaux
de *l'Echo de France,* 1838.

"Opéra-Comique." *Le Ménestrel,* 28 June 1835, 1.

d'Ortigue, Joseph. *Aperçu sommaire de la littérature et de la bibliographie musicale en France.*
Paris: Dubuisson, 1855.

―――. *Le Balcon de l'Opéra.* Paris: E. Renduel, 1833.

―――. "De la critique musicale. Dans ses rapports avec l'état actuel de l'art." *Revue et Gazette
Musicale,* 18 September 1836, 326–28, 25 September 1836, 338–41.

―――. *Du Théâtre Italien et de son influence sur le goût musical français.* Paris: Au Depôt central
des meilleurs productions de la presse, 1840.

―――. *La Musique à l'église.* Paris: Didier, 1861.

―――. "Nécrologie-Meyerbeer." *Le Ménestrel,* 8 May 1864, 177–78 and 188–90.

―――. *La Sainte-Baume.* 2 vols. Paris: E. Renduel, 1834.

"P." "Spectacles. Académie Royale de Musique. *La Juive,* opéra en cinq actes, paroles de M. Scribe,
musique de M. Halévy." *Le Moniteur Universel,* 28 February 1835, 458.

Palianti, Louis. *Collection de mises en scène de grands opéras et d'opéras-comiques. Représentées
pour la première fois à Paris.* Paris: Chez l'auteur et chez MM. les correspondants des théâtres, n.
d.

Planche, Gustave. "Du rôle de la critique." *L'Artiste* 10, no. 15 (1835): 166–68.

―――. *Etudes sur les arts.* 2 vols. Paris: Michel Lévy, 1855.

―――. "Théâtres. Académie Royale de Musique: Première représentation des *Huguenots.* "
Chronique de Paris, n.s., 3 March 1836, 250–53 and 6 March 1836, 261–64.

"Robert le diable, grand opéra de M. Meyerbeer." *Le Globe,* 27 November 1831, 1325.

Roqueplan, Nestor. "Théâtres [*Béatrice et Bénédict*]." *Le Constitutionnel,* 18 August 1862, 1–2.

Rovray, A. de [See Fiorentino, Pier Angelo].

Sainte-Beuve, Charles-A. *Mes poisons: Cahiers intimes inédits.* 2nd ed. Introd. and notes Victor
Giraud. Paris: Les Oeuvres représentatives, 1926.

―――. *Nouveaux lundis.* 2nd ed. Vol. 2. Paris: Michel Lévy, 1866.

Saint-Saëns, Camille. *Ecole buissonnière: Notes et souvenirs.* Paris: Pierre Lafitte and Co., 1913.

Sand, George. "A Meyerbeer. La Musique, *Les Huguenots."* *Lettres d'un voyageur.* 1863; rpt. Paris:
Michel Lévy, 1969, 313–35.

Schumann, Robert. *The Musical World of Robert Schumann: A Selection from his Writings.* Trans.
and ed. Henry Pleasants. London: Victor Gollancz, 1965.

―――. *Sur les musiciens.* Trans. Henri de Curzon. Pref. and notes Rémi Jacobs. 1894; Paris:
Stock, 1979.

Scribe, Eugène. *Les Huguenots: Opéra en cinq acts.* Paris: C. Lévy, 1898.

Scudo, Paul. *Critique et littérature musicales.* Paris: Amyot, 1850.

Séchan, Charles. *Souvenirs d'un homme de théâtre 1831–1855.* Ed. Adolphe Badin. Paris: C. Lévy,
1883.

Second, Albéric. *Les Petits Mystères de l'Opéra.* Paris: G. Kugelmann, 1844.

"Société des concerts du Conservatoire de musique." *L'Artiste* 7, no. 1 (1834): 5–6.

"Société des concerts du Conservatoire de musique." *L'Artiste* 7, no. 3 (1834): 26–27.

Smith, Paul [See Monnais, Edouard].

Solomé. *Indications générales et observations pour la mise en scène de la Muette de Portici, Grand Opéra en cinq actes, paroles de MM. Scribe et G. Delavigne, musique de M. Auber.* Paris: E. Duverger, 1828.

Soulié, Frédéric. "Théâtres. Opéra [*Esmeralda*]." *La Presse,* 14 November 1836, 1–3.

――――. "Théâtres. Opéra [*Esmeralda*]." *La Presse,* 21 November 1836, 1–3.

"Spectacles. Académie Royale de Musique. *La Juive,* opéra en cinq actes, paroles de M. Scribe, musique de M. Halévy." *Le Moniteur Universel,* 28 February 1835, 458.

"Spectacles: Opéra-Comique." *Le Moniteur Universel,* 13 January 1834, 90.

Stoepel, Franz. "Académie Royale de Musique. *La Juive.*" *Revue et Gazette Musicale,* 1 March 1835, 72–75.

Trollope, Frances. *Paris and the Parisians in 1835.* 2 vols. Paris: Baudry's European Library, 1836.

Véron, Louis. *Mémoires d'un bourgeois de Paris.* Vol. 3. Paris: G. de Goret, 1854.

――――. *Paris en 1860: Les Théâtres de Paris depuis 1806 jusqu'en 1860.* Paris: A. Bourdilliat, 1860.

Weber, Johannes. *Meyerbeer, notes et souvenirs d'un de ses secrétaires.* Paris: Fischbacher, 1898.

Werner, Hans. [See Blaze de Bury, Henri.]

Secondary Sources

Abraham, Gerald. "Weber as Novelist and Critic." *Musical Quarterly* 20 (January 1934): 27–28.

Allevy, Marie Antoinette. *La Mise en scène en France dans la première moitié du XIXe siècle.* Paris: E. Droz, 1938.

d'Alméras, Henri. *La Vie parisienne sous le règne de Louis-Phillipe.* Paris: A. Michel, 1911.

d'Ariste, Paul. *La Vie et le monde de boulevard (1830–1870): Un dandy: Nestor Roqueplan.* Paris, Jules Tallandier, 1930.

Aubin, Léon. *Histoire de la musique dramatique en France. Le Drame lyrique.* Tours: Salmon, 1908.

Avenel, Henri. *Histoire de la presse française depuis 1789 jusqu'à nos jours.* Paris: Flammarion, 1900.

Bailbé, Joseph-Marc. *Berlioz: artiste et écrivain dans les "Mémoires."* Paris: Presses universitaires de France, 1972.

――――. *Berlioz et l'art lyrique: essai d'interprétation à l'usage de notre temps.* Berne: Lang, 1981.

――――. "Le Bourgeois et la musique au XIXe siècle." *Romantisme,* nos. 17–18 (1977): 123–36.

――――. *Jules Janin: 1804–1874, une sensibilité littéraire et artistique.* Paris: Lettres modernes, 1974.

――――. *Le Roman et la musique en France sous la monarchie de juillet.* Paris: Lettres modernes (Minard), 1969.

――――. "Le Sens de l'espace dans les textes littéraires de Berlioz." *Romantisme* 12 (1976): 35–42.

Baldensperger, Fernand. *Sensibilité musicale et romantisme.* Paris: Les Presses françaises, 1925.

Barraud, Henry. *Hector Berlioz.* Paris: Fayard, 1979.

Barricelli, Jean-Pierre. "Romantic Writers and Music: The Case of Mazzini." *Studies in Romanticism* 14 (1975): 95–117.

Bartlett, Elizabeth. "Archival Sources for the Opéra-Comique and its *Registres* at the Bibliothèque de l'Opéra." *Nineteenth-Century Music* 7 (Fall 1983): 119–29.

Barzun, Jacques. "Berlioz, a Hundred Years After." *Musical Quarterly* 56 (January 1970): 1–13.

――――. *Berlioz and the Romantic Century.* 3rd ed. 2 vols. New York: Columbia University Press, 1969.

――――. *Classic, Romantic, and Modern.* 3rd ed. Chicago: Chicago University Press, 1975.

――――. *Critical Questions. On Music and Letters. Culture and Biography 1940–1980.* Ed. and introd. Bea Friedland. Chicago: Chicago University Press, 1982.

Becker, Heinz. *Der Fall Heine-Meyerbeer.* Berlin: W. de Gruyter, 1958.

———. "Die historische Bedeutung der Grand Opéra." In *Beiträge zur Geschichte der Musikanschauung im 19. Jahrhundert.* Regensburg: Verlag Gustave Bosse, 1965, 151–59.

Becq de Fouquières, L. *L'Art de la mise en scène, essai d'esthétique théâtrale,* Paris: G. Charpentier and Co., 1884.

Bellanger, Claude et al., eds. *Histoire générale de la presse française.* Paris: Presses universitaires de France, 1969.

Bénichou, Paul. *Le Temps des prophètes: Doctrines de l'âge romantique.* Paris: Gallimard, 1977.

Besnier, Patrick. "Berlioz et Meyerbeer." *Revue de Musicologie* 63, nos. 1–2 (1977): 35–40.

Bloom, Peter A. "Berlioz and the *Prix de Rome* of 1830." *Journal of the American Musicological Society* 34 (Summer 1981): 279–97.

———. *François-Joseph Fétis and the "Revue Musicale," (1827–1835).* Ann Arbor, Mich.: University Microfilms, 1972.

———. "Friends and Admirers: Meyerbeer and Fétis." *Revue Belge de Musicologie,* 32–33 (1978–79): 174–187.

———. "Orpheus' Lyre Resurrected: A *Tableau Musical* by Berlioz." *Musical Quarterly* 61 (April 1975): 189–211.

———, ed. *Music in Paris in the 1830s: La Musique à Paris dans les années 1830.* La Vie musicale en France au xixᵉ siècle: Etudes et documents, vol. 9. New York: Pendragon Press, forthcoming.

Bloom, Peter A., and D. Kern Holoman. "Berlioz's Music for *L'Europe littéraire.*" *The Music Review* 39 (May 1978): 100–109.

Boschot, Adolphe. *Le Crépuscule d'un romantique: Hector Berlioz, 1842–1869.* Paris: Plon, 1913.

———. "Hector Berlioz, critique musicale." *Bulletin de la Classe des Beaux-Arts* (Brussels) 20 (1938): 34–42.

———. *La Jeunesse d'un romantique: Hector Berlioz 1803–1831.* Paris: Plon, 1906.

———. *Un Romantique sous Louis-Philippe: Hector Berlioz 1831–1842.* Paris: Plon, 1908.

———. *Une Vie romantique. Hector Berlioz.* Paris: Plon-Nourrit, 1919.

Bouyer, Raymond. "Critiques musicaux de jadis où de naguère." *Le Ménestrel,* August-December, 1909, January-April, 1910.

Brisson, Jules, and Félix Ribeyre, eds. *Les Grands Journaux de France.* Paris: Marlé, 1863.

Brunetière, Ferdinand. *L'Evolution des genres dans l'histoire de la littérature.* 3rd ed. Vol. 1. Paris: Hachette, 1898.

Cairns, David. "Berlioz and Criticism: Some Surviving Dodos." *Musical Times* 104 (1963): 548–51.

———. "Berlioz and Virgil: A Consideration of *Les Troyens* as a Virgilian Opera." *Proceedings of the Royal Musical Association* 95 (1969): 97–110.

Carlson, Marvin. A. *The French Stage in the Nineteenth Century.* Metuchen, New Jersey: Scarecrow Press, 1972.

Cauchie, Maurice. "The High Lights of French Opéra-Comique." *Musical Quarterly* 25 (1939): 306–12.

Charnacé, Guy de. *Musique et musiciens.* 2 vols. Paris: Pottier de Lalaine, 1873.

Chevalier, Louis. *Classes laborieuses et classes dangereuses à Paris pendant la première moitié du xixᵉ siècle.* Paris: Librairie Plon, 1958.

Clark, T. J. *The Absolute Bourgeois: Artists and Politics in France 1848–1852.* 2nd ed. Princeton, New Jersey: University of Princeton, 1982.

Claudon, Francis. "G. Meyerbeer et V. Hugo: Dramaturgie comparée." In *Regards sur l'Opéra. Du Ballet Comique de la Reine à l'Opéra de Pékin.* Publication of the University of Rouen. Paris: Presses universitaires de France, 1976, 101–11.

———. "L'idée et l'influence de la musique chez quelques romantiques français et plus particulièrement Stendhal." Diss., Université de Paris 4, 1977.

Cohen, Howard Robert. *Berlioz on the Opéra (1829–1849): A Study in Music Criticism.* Ann Arbor. Mich.: University Microfilms, 1973.

———— . "La Conservation de la tradition scénique sur la scène lyrique en France du dix-neuvième siècle: les livrets de mise-en-scène et la Bibliothèque de l'Association de la régie théâtrale." *Revue de Musicologie* 64 (1978): 254–67.

———— . "The Nineteenth-Century French Press and the Music Historian: Archival Sources and Bibliographical Resources." *Nineteenth-Century Music* 7 (Fall 1983): 136–42.

———— et al., ed. *La Critique musicale d'Hector Berlioz.* La Vie musicale en France au xixᵉ siècle, vol. 6. New York: Pendragon Press, forthcoming.

Collins, Irene. "The Government and the Newspaper Press during the Reign of Louis-Philippe." *English Historical Review* 69 (April 1954): 262–82.

———— . *The Government and the Newspaper Press in France, 1814–1888.* London: Oxford University Press, 1959.

———— , ed. *Government and Society in France, 1814–1848.* Great Britain: Edward Arnold, 1970.

Combarieu, Jules, and René Dumesnil. *Histoire de la musique.* Vol. 3. New ed. Paris: Armand Colin, 1955.

Conrad, Peter. *Romantic Opera and Literary Form.* 2nd ed. Berkeley: University of California Press, 1981.

Cooper, Jeffrey, *The Rise of Instrumental Music and Concert Series in Paris 1828–1871.* Ann Arbor, Mich.: UMI Research Press, 1983.

Cooper, Martin. "Giacomo Meyerbeer, 1791–1864." *Proceedings of the Royal Music Association,* no. 90 (April 1964): 97–129.

———— . *Opéra Comique.* London: M. Parrish, 1949.

Cordey, Jean. *La Société des concerts du Conservatoire.* Paris: Au siège de la Société, 1941.

Coudroy, Marie-Hélène. "Les Créations de *Robert le diable* et des *Huguenots* de Meyerbeer face à la critique." Diss. Conservatoire Supérieur de Musique de Paris, 1979.

———— . "La Critique parisienne face aux créations du *Prophète* et de *l'Africaine* de Meyerbeer," Doctorat du 3ème cycle, Université de Paris 4, 1982.

Crosten, William Loren. *French Grand Opera: An Art and a Business.* 1948; rpt., New York: Da Capo, 1972.

Curzon, Henri de. "Les Débuts de Berlioz dans la critique." *Guide Musical* 49 (29 November 1903): 28–31.

Dahlhaus, Carl. *Esthetics of Music.* Trans. William W. Austin. Cambridge: Cambridge University Press, 1982.

———— . *Realism in Nineteenth-Century Music.* Trans. Mary Whittall. Cambridge: Cambridge University Press, 1985.

Dandelot, Arthur. *La Société des concerts du Conservatoire de 1828 à 1897.* 2nd ed. Paris: G. Havard Fils, 1898.

Dauriac, Lionel. *La Psychologie dans l'opéra français (Auber, Rossini, Meyerbeer).* Paris: F. Alcan, 1897.

David, Jules. *Berlioz, Souvenirs intimes et personnels.* Paris: Delattre-Lenoël, 1887.

Demarquez, Suzanne. *Hector Berlioz, l'homme et son oeuvre.* Paris: Seghers, 1969.

Demogeot, Jacques. *La Critique et les critiques en France au XIXᵉ siècle.* Paris: Hachette, 1857.

Descotes, Maurice. *Le Public de théâtre et son histoire.* Paris: Presses universitaires de France, 1964.

Des Granges, Charles-Marc. *La Presse littéraire sous la Restauration, 1815–1830.* Paris: Société du Mercure de France, 1907.

Destranges, Etienne. *L'Oeuvre théâtrale de Meyerbeer, étude critique.* Paris: Fischbacher, 1893.

Devriès, Anik. "Un éditeur de musique 'à la tête ardente' Maurice Schlesinger." *Fontes Artis Musicae* 27 (July-December 1980): 125–36.

Dickinson, A. E. F. "Berlioz's Bleeding Nun." *Musical Times* 107 (July 1966): 584–88.

Dictionnaire de la langue française de Emile Littré. 7 vols. Revised edition. Paris: Gallimard/Hachette, 1961.

Didier, Béatrice. "Berlioz: conteur et écrivain." *Revue de Paris,* no. 77 (February 1970): 88–93.
————. "Hector Berlioz & l'art de la nouvelle." *Romantisme,* no. 12 (1976): 19–25.
Dieran, Bernard Van. *Down among the Dead Men.* London: Oxford University Press, 1935.
Donakowski, Conrad. *A Muse for the Masses.* Chicago: University of Chicago Press, 1972.
Dowling, John. *José Melchor Gomis: Compositor Romántico.* Madrid: Castalia, 1973.
Dresch, Joseph. *Heine à Paris d'après sa correspondance et les témoignages de ses contemporains, 1831–1856.* Paris: M. Didier, 1956.
Duckles, Vincent. "Patterns in the Historiography of 19th-Century Music." *Acta Musicologica* 42 (1970): 75–82.
Dumesnil, René. *La Musique romantique française.* Lille: Aubier, 1944.
Eckart-Bäcker, Ursula. *Frankreichs Musik zwischen Romantik und Moderne, die Zeit im Spiegel der Kritik.* Regensburg: G. Bosse Verlag, 1965.
Egbert, D. D. *Social Radicalism and the Arts.* New York: Alfred A. Knopf, 1970.
Ehrhard, Auguste. "L'Opéra sous la direction Véron (1831–1835)." *Extrait de la Revue Musicale de Lyon,* (1907): 1–49.
Elwart, Antoine. *Histoire de la Société des concerts du Conservatoire impérial de musique.* Paris: S. Castel, 1860.
Encyclopédie de la musique et dictionnaire du Conservatoire impérial de musique. Ed. Albert Lavignac and Lionel de la Laurencie. Two parts in 11 vols. Paris: C. Delagrave, 1913–1931.
Evans, David O. *Social Romanticism in France 1830–1848.* Oxford: Oxford University Press, 1951.
Faguet, Emile. "La Critique de 1820 à 1850." In vol. 7 of *Histoire de la langue et de la littérature française.* Ed. Petit de Julleville. Paris: Armand Colin, 1899, 646–700.
Fayolle, Roger. "Criticism and Theory." In *The French Romantics,* ed. D. G. Charlton, vol. 2. Cambridge: Cambridge University Press, 1984.
Festival Berlioz: Berlioz, biographie et autobiographie: Actes du colloque 1980. [Lyons]: n.p., [1981].
Fouque, Octave. *Histoire du Théâtre-Ventadour 1829–1879—Opéra-Comique, théâtre de la Renaissance.* Paris: G. Fischbacher, 1881.
————. *Les Révolutionnaires de la musique: Lesueur, Berlioz, Beethoven, Richard Wagner, la musique russe.* Paris: C. Lévy, 1882.
Fulcher, Jane F. "Music and the Communal Order: The Vision of Utopian Socialism in France." *Current Musicology,* no. 27 (1979): 27–35.
————. "Meyerbeer and the Music of Society." *Musical Quarterly* 67 (1981): 213–29.
————. "Le Socialisme utopique et la critique musicale en France sous le Second Empire." *Revue Internationale de Musique Française,* no. 14 (June 1984): 63–68.
Furst, Lilian. *Romanticism in Perspective.* 2nd rev. ed. London: Macmillan, 1979.
Gide, André. *Incidences.* Paris: Gallimard, 1924.
Girard, Henri. *Emile Deschamps—Dilettante.* Paris: Librairie Ancienne Honoré Champion, 1921.
Giraudeau, Fernand. *La Presse périodique de 1789 à 1869.* Paris: E. Dentu, 1867.
Golbeck, Fred. "Défense et illustration de Berlioz." *La Revue Musicale,* No. 297 (1977): 1–11.
Gourret, Jean. *Histoire de l'Opéra-Comique.* Paris: Les Publications universitaires, 1978.
Guex, Jules. *Le Théâtre et la société française de 1815 à 1848.* Paris: Fischbacher, 1900.
Grand Dictionnaire Encyclopédique Larousse. 5 vols. Paris, 1982–1983.
Grand Dictionnaire universel du XIXe siècle, ed. Pierre Larousse. 17 vols. Paris, 1865–18[90?].
Grand Larousse Encyclopédique. 20 vols. Paris, 1971–1976. 1 vol. supplement, 1981.
Grégoir, Edouard. G. J. *Littérature musicale: Documents historiques relatifs à l'art musical et aux artistes musiciens.* Brussels: Schott, 1876.
————. *Recherches historiques concernant les journaux de musique depuis les temps les plus reculés jusqu'à nos jours.* Antwerp: L. Legris, 1872.
Grout, Donald J. *A Short History of Opera.* 2d ed. New York: Columbia University Press, 1966.

Guérin, Eugénie de. *Journal (1834–1835)*. Paris: J. Gabalda, 1934.

Guichard, Léon. "Berlioz et Heine." *Revue de Littérature Comparée* 41 (January–March 1967): 5–23.

────── . "Liszt et la littérature française." *Revue de Musicologie*, No. 56 (1970): 1–34.

────── . *La Musique et les lettres au temps du romantisme*. Paris: Presses universitaires de France, 1955.

Guiomar, Michel. *Le Masque et le fantasme*. Paris: José Corti, 1970.

Hagan, Dorothy Veinus. *Félicien David 1810–1876: A Composer and a Cause*. Syracuse: Syracuse University Press, 1985.

────── . *French Musical Criticism between the Revolutions (1830–1848)*. Ann Arbor, Mich.: University Microfilms, 1965.

Hallays, André. "L'Esthétique de Berlioz." *Guide Musical* 49 (June 1903): 483–86.

────── . "Hector Berlioz, critique musicale." *Revue de Paris* 10 (1 April 1903): 560–95.

Hanslick, Edouard. *The Beautiful in Music*. Trans. Gustav Cohen. Ed. Morris Weitz. New York: Bobbs-Merrill, 1957.

Harazsti, Emile. "Franz Liszt—Author Despite Himself: The History of a Mystification." *Musical Quarterly* 33 (1947): 490–516.

Hatin, Eugène. *Bibliographie historique et critique de la presse périodique française ou Catalogue systématique et raisonné de tous les écrits périodiques de quelque valeur publiés ou ayant circulé en France depuis l'origine du Journal jusqu'à nos jours, avec extraits, notes historiques, critiques et morales, indications des prix . . . etc., précédé d'un Essai historique et statistique sur la naissance et les progrès de la presse périodique dans les deux mondes*. Paris: Firmin-Didot, 1866.

────── . *Histoire du journal en France*. 2d ed. Paris: Jannet, 1853.

────── . *Histoire politique et littéraire de la presse en France avec une introduction historique sur les origines du journal et la bibliographie générale des journaux depuis leur origine*. Vol. 8. Paris: Poulet-Malassis et de Broise, 1861.

Hippeau, Edmond. *Berlioz et son temps*. Paris: Ollendorff, 1890.

────── . *Berlioz intime*. Paris: E. Dentu, 1889.

Holoman, D. Kern. *The Creative Process in the Autograph Musical Documents of Hector Berlioz, c. 1818–1840*. Ann Arbor, Mich.: UMI Research Press, 1980.

────── . "The Present State of Berlioz Research." *Acta Musicologica* 47 (1975): 30–67.

Hopkinson, Cecil. *A Bibliography of the Musical and Literary Works of Hector Berlioz: 1803–1869, with Histories of the French Music Publishers Concerned*. 2d rev. ed. by Richard Macnutt. Kent: Richard Macnutt, 1980.

Hunt, H. J. *Le Socialisme et le romantisme en France*. Oxford: Oxford University Press, 1935.

Imbert, Hughes. "Hector Berlioz: Initiateur de la haute culture musicale." *Le Guide Musical*, no. 49 (29 November 1903): 8–20.

Istel, Edgar. "Act 4 of *Les Huguenots*." *Musical Quarterly* 22 (1936): 87–97.

Jensen, E. F. "Hippolyte Monpou and French Romanticism." *The Music Review* 45 (1984): 122–34.

Join-Dieterle, Catherine. "Les décors à l'Opéra de Paris." *Revue Internationale de Musique Française*, No. 4 (January 1981): 57–72.

────── . "L'Opéra et son public à l'époque romantique." *L'Oeil*, Nos. 288–289 (July-August 1979): 30–37.

────── . "*Robert le diable*: premier opéra romantique." *Romantisme*, Nos. 28–29 (1980): 147–66.

Jules Janin et son temps: Un moment du romantisme. University of Rouen, Colloque *Eureux*, June 1974. Paris: Presses universitaires de France, 1974.

Jullien, Adolphe. "La critique de Berlioz." *Revue d'Art Dramatique* 31 (August 1893): 193–206.

────── . *Hector Berlioz, sa vie et ses oeuvres*. Paris: Allison and Co., 1888.

────── . *Paris dilettante au commencement du siècle*. Paris: Firmin-Didot, 1884.

Kerman, Joseph. *Musicology*. London: Fontana paperback, 1985.

Klein, John W. "Berlioz's Personality." *Music and Letters* 50 (January 1969): 15–24.

———. "Jacques Fromental Halévy (1799–1862)." *Music Review* 23 (1962): 13–19.

Lacombe, Paul. *Bibliographie parisienne, Tableaux de moeurs (1600–1800)*. Paris: Rouquette, 1887.

Laforêt, Claude. "Hector Berlioz parmi les romantiques." *La Revue Musicale*, No. 233 (1956): 45–54.

———. *La Vie musicale au temps romantique*. Pref. by Henri Malo. Paris: J. Peyronnet, 1929.

La Laurencie, Lionel de. *Le Goût musical en France*. Paris: A. Joanin and Co., 1905.

Laloy, Louis. "Berlioz critique et écrivain, à propos de deux publications récentes." *La Revue Musicale* 3 (1903): 438–43.

Lantelme, Louis, ed. *Le Livre d'or du centenaire de Berlioz*. Paris: G. Petit, 1907.

Larousse du XXe siècle. 6 vols. Paris, 1928–1933.

L'Ecuyer Lacroix, Sylvia, ed. *Joseph d'Ortigue: Ecrits sur la musique et les musiciens de son temps (1830–1866)*. La Vie musicale en France au xixe siècle, vol. 8. New York: Pendragon Press, forthcoming.

Ledré, Charles. *La Presse à l'assaut de la monarchie: 1815–1848*. Kiosque series. Paris: Colin, 1960.

Legouvé, Ernst. *Eugène Scribe*. Paris: Didier, 1874.

Le Huray, Peter, and James Day, eds. *Music and Aesthetics in the Early Eighteenth and Nineteenth Centuries*. Cambridge: Cambridge University Press, 1981.

Lesure, François. Avant-propos. *Catalogue d'Exposition: Hector Berlioz*. Paris: Bibliothèque Nationale, 1969.

Livois, René de. *Histoire de la presse française*. 2 vols. Paris: Société française du livre, 1965.

Locke, Ralph P. "Autour de la lettre à Duveyrier: Berlioz et les Saint-Simoniens." *Revue de Musicologie* 63, no. 1–2 (1977): 55–77, and 64, no. 1 (1978): 287.

———. "Liszt's Saint-Simonian Adventure." *Nineteenth-Century Music* 4 (Spring 1981): 209–27.

———. *Music and the Saint-Simonians: The Involvement of Félicien David and Other Musicians in a Utopian Socialist Movement*. Ann Arbor, Mich.: University Microfilms, 1980.

———. *Music, Musicians, and the Saint-Simonians*. Chicago: University of Chicago Press, 1986.

———. "New Letters of Berlioz." *Nineteenth-Century Music* 1 (1977): 71–84.

Loesser, Arthur. *Men, Women and Pianos: A Social History*. Pref. by Jacques Barzun. London: Victor Gollancz, 1955.

Loewenberg, Alfred. *Annals of Opera 1597–1940*. 2d ed. rev. and corrected. 2 vols. Geneva: Societas Bibliographica, 1955.

Longyear, Rey Morgan. *Daniel-François-Esprit Auber: A Chapter in French Opéra-Comique*. Ann Arbor, Mich.: University Microfilms, 1957.

Macdonald, Hugh. *Berlioz*. London: J. M. Dent, 1982.

———. "Berlioz's Self-Borrowings." *Proceedings of the Royal Musical Association* 92 (1965): 27–44.

———. "Hector Berlioz 1969—A Centenary Assessment." *Adam* 34, nos. 331–33 (1969): 35–47.

———. "Music and Opera." In *The French Romantics*, ed. D. G. Charlton, vol. 2. Cambridge: Cambridge University Press, 1984.

———, ed. *NBE Béatrice et Bénédict*. London, Basel: Bärenreiter Kassel, 1980.

Machabey, Armand. *Traité de la critique musicale*. Paris: Richard-Masse, 1947.

Main, Alexander. "Music and the Social Conscience." *Nineteenth-Century Music* 4 (Spring 1981): 228–43.

Marix-Spire, Thérèse. "Du piano à l'action sociale: Franz Liszt et George Sand, militante socialiste." New York: *Renaissance Extract*, vol. 2 and 3 (1944–1945): 187–216.

———. *Les Romantiques et la musique. Le cas George Sand 1804–1838*. Paris: Nouvelles éditions latines, 1954.

Matoré, George. *Le Vocabulaire et la société sous Louis-Philippe*. Geneva: Droz, 1951.

Merlin, Oliver. *Quand le bel canto régnait sur le boulevard*. Paris: Fayard, 1978.

Milner, Max. *Le Diable dans la littérature française, de Cazotte à Baudelaire 1772–1861*. 2 vols. Paris: José Corti, 1960.

Mirecourt, Eugène de. *Meyerbeer*. 3rd ed. Paris: G. Havard, 1856.

Mongrédien, Jean. *Jean-François Le Sueur: Contribution à l'étude d'un demi-siècle de musique française (1780–1830)*. 2 vols. Berne: Lang, 1980.

Musical Times 110 (March 1969) [Berlioz centenary issue].

New Grove Dictionary of Music and Musicians. Ed. Stanley Sadie. 20 vols. London: Macmillan, 1980.

Newman, Ernest. *Berlioz, Romantic and Classic: Writings by Ernest Newman*. Ed. Peter Heyworth. London: Gollancz, 1972.

Niedermeyer, Louis-Alfred. *Vie d'un compositeur moderne 1802–1861: Louis Niedermeyer*. Introd. Camille Saint-Saëns. Paris: Fischbacher, 1893.

Noske, Frits. *French Song from Berlioz to Duparc*. 2d ed. Trans. Rita Benson from the French "La Mélodie française de Berlioz à Duparc: Essai de critique historique." Paris, 1954; New York: Dover, 1970.

d'Ollone, Max. *Le Théâtre lyrique et le public*. Paris: La Palatine, 1955.

Ozanam, Yves. "Recherches sur l'Académie Royale de Musique (Opéra Français) sous la seconde restauration 1815–1830." Diss. Ecole Nationale des Chartes (Paris), 1981.

Pailleron, Marie-Louise. *François Buloz et ses amis: La vie littéraire sous Louis-Philippe*. Paris: C. Lévy, 1919.

Pendle, Karin. *Eugène Scribe and the French Opera of the Nineteenth Century*. Ann Arbor, Mich.: UMI Research Press, 1979.

———. "The Transformation of a Libretto: Goethe's 'Jery und Bately'." *Music and Letters* 55 (January 1974): 77–78.

Pereire, Alfred. *Le Journal des Débats politiques et littéraires 1814–1914*. Paris: Librairie ancienne Edouard Champion, 1924.

Perris, Arnold. *Music in France During the Reign of Louis-Philippe: Art as 'A Substitute for the Heroic Experience.'* Ann Arbor, Mich.: University Microfilms, 1967.

Pierre, Constant. *Le Conservatoire national de musique et de déclamation, documents historiques et administratifs recueillis ou reconstitués*. Paris: Imprimerie nationale, 1900.

Plantinga, Leon B. *Schumann as Critic*. New Haven: Yale University Press, 1967.

Porter, Cecilia Hopkins. "The New Public and the Reordering of the Musical Establishment: The Lower Rhine Music Festivals, 1818–67." *19th-Century Music* 3 (March 1980): 211–24.

Portevin, Catherine. "Le Langage de la critique musicale." *Revue Internationale de Musique Française*, no. 17 (June 1985): 102.

Pougin, Arthur. *De la littérature musicale en France*. Paris: Alfred Ikelmer and Co., 1867.

———. "Notes sur la presse musicale en France." In *Encylopédie de la musique et dictionnaire du Conservatoire impérial de musique*. Ed. Albert Lavignac and Lionel de la Laurencie. 2d part. Vol. 6. Paris: [n.p.] 1931, 3841–59.

———. "D'Ortigue." *Dossier des correspondants: Note de M. Arthur Pougin*. Autograph MS letters, Bibliothèque de l'Opéra (Paris).

Pourtales, Guy de. *Berlioz et l'Europe romantique*. Paris: Gallimard, 1979.

Primmer, Brian. "Berlioz and a Romantic Image." *The Berlioz Society Bulletin*, no. 83 (April 1974): 4–13.

———. *The Berlioz Style*. London: Oxford University Press, 1973.

Prod'homme, Jacques Gabriel. "Bibliographie berliozienne." *La Revue Musicale*, no. 233 (1956): 97–147.

———. *Hector Berlioz (1803–1869), sa vie et ses oeuvres*. Pref. Alfred Bruneau. Paris: C. Delagrave, 1904.

_____. "Hector Berlioz jugé par Adolphe Adam." *Zeitschrift der Internationalen Musikgesellschaft*, 5th year (1903–1904): 475–82.

_____. "Nouvelles lettres de Hector Berlioz." *Rivista Musicale Italiana* 12 (1905): 339–82.

Radar, Daniel. *The Journalists and the July Revolution in France*. The Hague: Martinus Nijhoff, 1973.

Reclus, Maurice. *E. de Girardin, le créateur de la presse moderne*. Paris: Hachette, 1934.

Reeve, Katherine Kolb. "Berlioz critique ou les embarras de l'analyse." *Festival Berlioz: Berlioz, biographie et autobiographie: Actes du colloque 1980*. [Lyons]: n.p., [1981], 56–59.

_____. "A Berliozian Spoof. Three Anonymous Feuilletons of 1836." Parts 1 and 2. *Berlioz Society Bulletin* 103 (Spring 1979): 2–8; 106 (Winter 1979–80): 4–10; 111 (Spring/Summer 1981): 2–6.

_____. "Hector Berlioz." In *European Writers*. Editor-in-chief, George Stade. Vol. 6. New York: Scribner's, 1985.

_____. *The Poetics of the Orchestra in the Writings of Hector Berlioz*. Ann Arbor, Mich.: University Microfilms, 1978.

Regard, Maurice. *Gustave Planche, 1808–1857*. Paris: Nouvelles éditions latines, 1956.

Revue Musicale, no. 19 (1 Oct. 1904) [Issue devoted to Meyerbeer].

Reyer, Ernest. "La Critique musicale." In *Le Livre du centenaire du "Journal des Débats" 1789–1889*. Paris: Plon, 1889, 427–40.

_____. *Notes de musique*. Paris: Charpentier, 1875.

_____. *Quarante ans de musique*. Pref. and notes Emile Henriot. Paris: C. Lévy, 1910.

Robert, W. Wright. "Berlioz the critic." Parts 1 and 2. *Music and Letters* 7 (January 1926): 63–72, and 7 (April 1926): 133–42.

Rolland, Romain. *Musiciens d'aujourd'hui*. 19th ed. Paris: Hachette, 1949.

_____. *Les Origines du théâtre lyrique moderne*. Paris: Hachette, 1895.

Rosen, Charles. "Romantic Documents." *New York Review of Books*, 15 May 1975, 15–20.

Sablière, Françoise de la. "Quel père fut Berlioz?" *Revue de Paris*, no. 77 (February 1970): 94–103.

Samuel, Claude. "Les écrits du compositeur." In *Hector Berlioz: Collection Génies et Réalites*. Paris: Hachette, 1973, 197–209.

Shroder, M. *Icarus: The Image of the Artist in French Romanticism*. Cambridge, Mass.: Harvard University Press, 1961.

Silex [Berlioz issue.] No. 18 (December 1980), Grenoble.

Sirven, Alfred. *Journaux et journalistes*. "*Le Journal des Débats*." Paris: F. Cournol, 1865.

Smith, Patrick. *The Tenth Muse: A Historical Study of the Opera Libretto*. New York: Alfred. A. Knopf, 1970.

Strunk, Oliver. *Source Readings in Music History*. New York: Norton, 1950.

Stuart, Charles. "Did Berlioz *Really* Like Meyerbeer?" *Opera* 3 (December 1952): 719–25.

Texier, Edmond. *Histoire des journaux. Biographie des journalistes, contenant l'histoire politique, littéraire, industrielle, pittoresque et anecdotique de chaque journal publié à Paris et la biographie de ses rédacteurs*. Paris: Pagnerre, 1850.

Thibert, Marguerite. *Le Rôle social de l'art d'après les Saint-Simoniens*. Paris: M. Rivière, 1926.

Thoumin, Jean-Adrien. "Esquisse historique sur la presse musicale en France." *La Chronique Musicale* 1 (July 1873).

Tieghem, Philippe Van, with collaboration of Pierre Josserance. *Dictionnaire des littérateurs*. 3 vols. Paris: Presses universitaires de France, 1968.

Tiersot, Julien. "Berlioziana: La Nonne Sanglante." *Le Ménestrel*, 14 October 1906, 319–20, and 21 October 1906, 327–28.

_____. *Hector Berlioz et la société de son temps*. Paris: Hachette, 1904.

_____. *La Musique au temps romantique*. Paris: Alcan, 1930.

———, ed. *Lettres de musiciens écrites en français du XVe au XXe siècle.* 2 vols. Turin: Bocca, 1924.

Trésor de la langue française. Ed. Paul Imbs. 9 vols. Paris: CNRS, 1971–81.

Tsugawa, Albert. *The Idea of Criticism.* Pennsylvania State University Studies, no. 2. Pennsylvania: Pennsylvania State University, 1967.

Turner, W. J. *Berlioz: The Man and His Work.* London: 1934; New York: Vienna House, 1974.

Vapereau, Gustave. *Dictionnaire universel des contemporains.* 6th ed. Paris: Librairie Hachette, 1893.

Vyborny, Zdenek. "Paganini as Music Critic." *Musical Quarterly* 46 (October 1960): 468–81.

Walker, Alan, ed. *Franz Liszt: The Man and His Music.* London: Barrie & Jenkins, 1976.

Waters, E. N. "Sur la piste de Liszt." *Notes* 27 (1970–71): 665–70.

Weber, William. "The Muddle of the Middle Classes." *19th-Century Music* 3 (November 1979): 175–85.

———. *Music and the Middle Class: The Social Structure of Concert Life in London, Paris and Vienna between 1830–1848.* London: Croom Helm, 1975.

Weill, Georges. *La France sous la monarchie constitutionnelle (1814–1848).* Paris: Félix Alcan, 1912.

Wellek, René. *A History of Modern Criticism 1750–1950.* Vol. 3. New Haven: Yale University Press, 1965.

Werth, Kent. "Berlioz's Damnation of Faust: A Manuscript Study." Ann Arbor, Mich.: University Microfilms, 1979.

Wilcox, John. "The Beginnings of l'Art pour l'Art." *Journal of Aesthetics and Art Criticism* 11 (1953): 360–77.

Wild, Nicole. "Un demi-siècle de décors à l'Opéra de Paris, salle Le Peletier (1822–1873)." In *Regards sur l'Opéra. Du ballet comique de la Reine à l'Opéra de Pékin.* Publication of the University of Rouen. Paris: Presses universitaires de France, 1976, 11–22.

———. "La Recherche de la précision historique chez les décorateurs de l'Opéra de Paris au XIXe siècle." Report of the *Twelfth Congress of the International Musicological Society,* held at Berkeley, California, 1977, 453–63.

Wotton, Tom S. *Hector Berlioz.* London: Oxford University Press, 1935.

Index

Adam, Adolphe, 45, 91, 93, 103, 108; *Alda*, 205; *Une Bonne Fortune*, 244n.12; *Le Chalet*, 94, 198, 244n.12; *La Fille du Danube*, 175; *La Grande Dûchesse*, 206; *La Marquise*, 203; *Micheline*, 98, 205; *Les Mohicans*, 176
Adam, Antoine, 62
Agoult, Marie, Comtesse d', 34, 225n.20
L'Album, 270n.2
Ali Baba. See Carafa, Michele Enrico
Allard, M. (performer), 206
Allegri, Gregorio: *Miserere*, 190, 191
L'Angélus. See Gide, Casimir
L'An Mil. See Grisar, Albert
Artaud (critic), 178
L'Artisan, 34
L'Artiste, 14, 15, 17, 79, 82, 83, 84, 86
L'Aspirant de marine. See Labarre, Théodore
L'Athenée Musicale, 194
Auber, Daniel-François-Esprit, 91; *Actéon*, 95, 174; *Les Chaperons blancs*, 245n.19; *Le Cheval de bronze*, 96, 97, 204; *Le Domino noir*, 96, 104, 105, 213, 216; *La Fiancée*, 188; *Gustave III*, 113; *Lestocq*, 196, 244n.10, 244n.12; *La Muette de Portici*, 72, 113, 115, 118, 141, 212, 247n.46; *Le Philtre*, 72

Back, C. P. E., 20
Bach, Johann Sebastian, 141
Bailbé, Joseph-Marc, 6, 19, 21, 153
Baillot, Pierre, 5, 144, 150, 260n.44
Balzac, Honoré de, 43, 62, 137; *Gambara*, 20, 46, 223n.47; *Illusions perdues*, 11, 60, 62; *Monographie de la presse parisienne*, 60–61, 66
Barrault, Emile, 25, 31, 226n.32; *Aux artistes: Du passé et de l'avenir des beaux-arts*, 24
Bartlett, Elizabeth, 234n.1
Barzun, Jacques, 1, 51, 73
Batta, Alexandre, 211, 213, 260n.45

Batton, Désiré-Alexandre: *Le Remplaçant*, 212
Becker, Heinz, 63
Beethoven, Ludwig van, 189, 196, 202, 211; Berlioz's criticisms of, 85, 91, 160, 161; Berlioz's enthusiasm for, 42, 43, 76, 155, 164; compared with Haydn, 84, 85, 155; contemporary enthusiasm for, 16, 20, 127; impressionistic criticism of, 17, 59; performance of, at Conservatoire concerts, 137–38, 139, 140, 141, 142, 213, 214; taken as model, 146, 147; works: chamber music, 42, 144, 156, 211; *Eroica* Symphony, 138; *Fidelio*, 22, 79, 109, 200, 204; *Missa Solemnis*, 159, 161; *Pastoral* Symphony, 195, 214; Symphony No. 4, 200; *Traité de composition*, 194, 202, 231n.24
Bel canto, 118
Bellini, Vincenzo, 55, 205, 207, 208; *Norma*, 206; *Il Pirata*, 227n.44; *I Puritani*, 68, 69, 203; *La Sonnambula*, 227n.45
Bénazet, Edouard, 106, 107, 110
Benedict, Jules, 208; Fantasie on Goethe's *Faust*, 150; *Notre-Dame de Paris*, 150, 175, 198
Benefit concerts, 5, 26, 49, 150, 176, 204, 211
Bénichou, Paul, 25
Beriot, Marie Garcia de ("la Malibran"), 158, 214
Berliner Allgemeine Musikalische Zeitung, 39, 40–41, 187, 188–89
Berlioz, Hector:
—critical writings: on classicism, 42, 43, 190; on criticism, 97, 238–39nn.56,57,61; list of journals contributed to, 187; method for identifying unsigned articles in, 75–78; motivation behind his, 50–55; in relation to his music, 3, 52–53, 54, 158, 164, 234n.80; on religious music, 41–42, 189; on romanticism, 42, 43, 101, 190; on virtuosi,